PRAISE FOR

KRIS NELSCOTT

"Nelsco⁺   books
layers o   m to
remain

     Oregonian

"Nelsco   ates its
own de

     ttle Times

"Nelsco   nce
brought

     Chronicle

"(A) crii

     Tribune

"Like W   icler of
America   ng the
crime o   ping
the histc   ance."

     l finalist

PRAISE FOR
THE SMOKEY DALTON SERIES

"It's not hard to draw parallels between Nelscott's PI Smokey Dalton and Walter Mosley's Easy Rawlins, another secretive, canny black man trying to solve mysteries while circumspectly navigating the white world. But Dalton's no knock-off. (Would you label the hundreds of hard-boiled detectives who've appeared in Raymond Chandler's wake mere Marlow Xeroxes because they're white?)."

—Entertainment Weekly

"More than just offering a puzzle, this novel encourages self-examination about identity, responsibility and the consequences of choices. Smokey proves himself a man of conscience able to make tough choices. His return will be cause for celebration."

—Publisher's Weekly on *A Dangerous Road*

"A blistering rendition of the '60s racial wars marks this series as a standout as early as its second entry. You don't need to be a fan of private-eye novels to admire Smokey: You just need a conscience."

—Kirkus Reviews (starred review) on *Smoke-Filled Rooms*

"This series has all the passion and precision of Walter Mosley's early Easy Rawlins novels, but it is not derivative. In fact, Smokey just may be a more compelling character than the celebrated Easy."

—Booklist (starred review) on *Smoke-Filled Rooms*

"This is mystery fiction at its highest, most gripping level."

—Chicago Tribune on *Smoke-Filled Rooms*

The

Smokey Dalton

Series

NOVELS:

A Dangerous Road
Smoke-Filled Rooms
Thin Walls
Stone Cribs
War at Home
Days of Rage
Street Justice

SHORT STORIES:

Family Affair
Guarding Lacey

STREET JUSTICE

A SMOKEY DALTON NOVEL

KRIS NELSCOTT

wmg PUBLISHING

Street Justice

To the memory of Bill Trojan
Bill, this book would not exist without you or your generosity,
and it breaks my heart that you're not here to read it.

STREET JUSTICE

A SMOKEY DALTON NOVEL

Martin S. Gerber, Special Deputy Coroner: "Do you feel threatened by these proceedings?"

Kermit Coleman, attorney for a Black Panther Party member: "This society threatens me. I feel threatened all the time."

—Record of the Coroner's Inquest
into the deaths of Black Panthers
Fred Hampton and Mark Clark
January 6, 1970

1

A new month, a new year, a new decade. Somehow I had convinced myself that by the first Monday in January of 1970, I would feel better. Everything would be better.

Instead, the first Monday had come and gone, and I still had that jangly on-edge feeling, the feeling that I was barely holding myself together, even as the world around me was falling apart.

I opened the window in the living room of my small apartment, then stood back. No one saw me. I might have been the only person in the weekday-empty neighborhood. In cold like this, even the street kids went inside.

The thin January sunlight barely illuminated the three broken-down cars half-buried in snow. The plows, when they bothered to show up, had gone around them. None of the sidewalks on that side of the street were shoveled either. I always felt a moment of guilt about that, resolving to get my son Jimmy and his friends to shovel the walks, and then never acting on that resolution.

I wasn't acting on it now, even though some exercise would do me good. It would be better than suffering in the middle of my excessively hot apartment.

After more than a year of complaining, the landlord still hadn't fixed the heat. The radiator pumped enough warmth for the entire floor. Since I moved to Chicago, I had learned most radiators came with a hand-turned knob that allowed a little or a lot of hot water through. This radiator didn't have anything like that, and the landlord wouldn't replace it.

So I opened the windows whenever I was home, and I let in the cold winter breeze. This morning, as I drove the kids to school, a kindly but unfamiliar baritone on WVON, the R&B station, told me that today's high would be five to twelve above, but given how frosty Chicago looked, and how the wind was already blowing ever so faintly, I was beginning to think twelve was a pipe dream.

I had already pulled off the cable-knit sweater that Althea Grimshaw had made for me for Christmas and tossed it on the couch. I could grab it when I left again. I normally didn't wear sweaters like that, but I liked this one, even if I only wore it on days off. Cold days off.

Since this was Tuesday, it shouldn't have been a day off. I should have been working. I had quick, good-paying cases stacked in neglected files on my desk in the third bedroom that I used as an office. I couldn't quite bring myself to go in there.

These last few months had taken a hell of a toll on me.

My recent work had involved a lot of skeletal remains, cold cases, and survivor notifications. I had done most of the notifications, never knowing whether I would encounter someone who sobbed with relief when she heard that a loved one was really and truly dead, or someone who would scream at me to *Get out! Get out now!* Those screams were usually accompanied by some kind of flying object—whatever was at hand—and a couple of times, a shaking but loaded handgun along with a very real threat to use it.

I'd taken to wearing a concealed weapon myself and I was frightened I might get into a shootout with some grieving person. Friends of mine had been attacked at our work site last fall, so we decided that having a weapon on hand would be prudent. It still felt wrong to me.

The wrong feeling didn't stop me from wearing that weapon for weeks. I had just retired it to my safe-deposit box last month, even though I still kept my emergency gun in the glove box of my van.

Last fall's cases had given me more than enough of the past, but the present wasn't a lot better. Two important trials were taking place in the city. The Chicago Seven Conspiracy trial was in its third month, with every national news crew in the nation hanging on each word. I'd been avoiding the Federal Building for months, afraid I would see someone I knew, afraid that somehow my face would get on a national newscast and the wrong person would recognize me.

The other trial had less coverage and more meaning, even though it wasn't a trial in the *Perry Mason* sense. In the Criminal Courts building five miles away from the Conspiracy circus, the Cook County Coroner's office was conducting an inquest into the December deaths of Black Panthers Fred Hampton and Mark Clark.

I had seen the apartment where Clark and Hampton were murdered. The police hadn't sealed the building after the raid, and the Black Panthers had opened the apartment for everyone to see. Thousands of people toured it over the thirteen days that it took the police to close the apartment off.

All of us saw the very clear evidence that the police had broken in, guns blazing, and shot one hundred rounds at sleeping teenagers, claiming the kids had fired first. Two days ago, the man now in charge of the Illinois Black Panther Party, Bobby Rush, held a news conference revealing evidence that Hampton had been drugged and unable to wake up, even when the cops broke down the door.

The firefight that the cops claimed provoked their overreaction had never happened, and the inquest going on now was only in response to the community's demands that something be done. Not just the black community, either. Every social organization, every church with its heart in the right place, every activist—white or black—had called for an investigation into the police's actions. It was clear from the evidence in that apartment alone that a violent attack had happened—but the attack wasn't from the Panthers.

The police had done their best to wipe the Panthers out.

That entire event, plus the coroner's inquest, still bothered me. Coupled with the horrid cases I'd finished the day before Christmas, and it was no wonder I felt jangled.

Not to mention the constant pressure of saying *no*. Tim Minton, one of the black community's de facto coroners, had asked me to give expert witness testimony at the Panther hearing. Minton knew I had seen a lot of crime scenes and believed I could help the Panthers' case. He also knew I had toured the crime scene twice, once alone and then with the older Grimshaw children.

I couldn't agree to help Minton, and I couldn't say why. I live in Chicago under an assumed name, thanks to my friends Franklin and Althea Grimshaw. People here believe that I'm Bill Grimshaw, who has the odd nickname of Smokey. Only a few people know my real name—Smokey Dalton—and even fewer know that Jimmy isn't my biological son.

I adopted Jimmy not quite legally after I had to get him out of Memphis two years ago. He had seen Doctor Martin Luther King Jr.'s assassin, and knew that the killer wasn't James Earl Ray. I knew—and still know—that if the killers ever find out where Jimmy is, he won't make it through the day.

Jim was ten then. He would turn twelve a week from Thursday, and the Grimshaws and I had a surprise party planned for the weekend. Until he moved to Chicago, Jimmy had never had a party for his birthday, or much of a birthday at all.

In fact, his mother had abandoned him a week before his tenth birthday, something I hoped he wouldn't focus on this year like he had last year.

I couldn't quite bring myself to work on this day, but I could plan Jimmy's party. I could go to The Little Shoppe on E. 71st and get Jim a handmade black-focused birthday card, and then buy myself some lunch at one of the delis nearby. Maybe I would even pick up some fried chicken for dinner. If I stretched the shopping long enough, it would take me until school got out, and then Jim and I could rest here at home.

I'd tackle the stacked-up investigations I had to do for Bronzeville Home, Health, Life, and Burial Insurance tomorrow. Maybe by next week, I could tell Laura Hathaway that I was ready to inspect houses for Sturdy Investments again.

The very thought made me shudder. I had to get past the events of the past few months or Jimmy and I would go broke.

As I had that thought, the phone rang. In the middle of the day, I always answered "Investigations," since my company didn't really have a name. I didn't want to appropriate the Grimshaw name for my own work—it was bad enough that I used it for everything else—and I didn't want to call the business by any other name. I tell people that I do odd jobs, but everyone knows I am an unlicensed private investigator.

I used to answer with a simple "Yes?" but that caused too many initial hang-ups and callbacks. I finally gave in to some sort of convention.

Even so, it still cause some people to question. And it's a bit risky, given that lack of a license.

"Um," said a female voice on the other end. "Is this Bill Grimshaw?"

So this was someone I knew outside of work. Most people who had hired me either called me Mr. Grimshaw or Smokey. I preferred Smokey.

"Yes, it is," I said, a bit wary.

"Oh, good," she said, sounding relieved. "This is Darlene Pellman."

It took me a moment too long to place her, because she added, "You know. From the after-school program."

I smiled so that she could hear it in my voice. "Mrs. Pellman. I'm sorry. I've been so busy today."

"It's all right," she said. "It's not like we see each other all the time."

She sounded relentlessly upbeat. I remembered her now. She was the wife of one of Franklin's friends, a cheery force of nature with reddish hair that she ironed straight and then flip-curled like a white woman would. She had three boys, and she was terrified they'd be recruited by the neighborhood gangs. She had helped Franklin and I organize the after-school program, which provided more actual learning than did the public school our kids were enrolled in.

"How can I help you, Mrs. Pellman?" I asked, and hoped she wasn't bringing me a case. Like so many families involved in the after-school program, hers was hanging on financially and the older boys wanted to make money instead of learn. We'd managed to keep most of them in program so far, but it was a daily struggle against the seemingly easy money the gangs brought into the neighborhood.

She said, "I saw something in the *Defender* yesterday, and I thought immediately of you, but I thought I'd better check before I volunteered your name."

I got a lot of referrals from cases first reported in the *Chicago Defender*. It wasn't just Chicago's black newspaper. It had subscribers all over the country. I'd read the paper long before I moved to Chicago. The *Defender* was one of the many reasons I was glad I had changed my name, but I still feared that someone would mention me and the wrong person would see the paper.

"Volunteered?" I didn't like that word. It got me into a lot of trouble.

"Yes," Mrs. Pellman said quickly, and I realized she was nervous. "The Chicago Economic Development Corporation is looking for people to run the Model Cities program here, and they're asking community organizations to volunteer the names of possible candidates. I know for a fact that the pay for the top-end positions is pretty good, better than most of us get around here, and since our neighborhood is a target neighborhood—"

"Why don't you volunteer, Mrs. Pellman?" The last thing I wanted to do was work for a government agency, especially a government agency in Chicago.

"Oh, Mr. Grimshaw," she said, "I haven't worked full-time since the boys were born. Besides, I'm just a waitress. They won't look at me, a black woman who barely finished high school. But you. You clearly have an education and you have done work for that housing firm—"

"I'm sure everyone connected with the after-school program would be happy to refer you, Mrs. Pellman." I didn't want to hear how much she actually knew about me. What she'd already said made my jangled nerves worse. And I was very aware that I was saying no to her. Just like I'd said no to Tim Minton. The more active I became in this community, the more it wanted to co-opt me in ways that I couldn't do and couldn't explain.

"Mr. Grimshaw," she said, and then my phone clicked, buzzed, and I heard, of all things, traffic noise. A boy's voice cried, "Uncle Bill?" and my heart literally froze.

A professional woman's voice came over the line, loud and important. "This is the operator. Will you accept an emergency call from Keith Grimshaw? There will be a charge added to your account."

Keith? I glanced at the clock on the wall in the half-kitchen. It was twelve-thirty-five. He should be in school.

"Yes," I said. "*Yes.*"

"Uncle Bill?" Keith still sounded far away.

"I'll reverse the charges," the operator said. There was one more click, and then Keith:

"Uncle Bill, Jimmy said I had to call. It's an emergency, and they made me use a pay phone, but I don't got no money. I'm sorry. I thought the call would be free, but they said only if I called the police, and Jimmy said don't do that."

"Mrs. Pellman, I need the line," I said. "I'm sorry."

"No, I'm sorry," she said, and hung up.

I let out a small breath, not sure if I should have wasted that precious second on Mrs. Pellman, but unable not to.

"Where are you?" I asked Keith.

"The Starlite Hotel," Keith said.

I shook my head just a little, trying to figure out what he had said. Somehow I thought he would tell me he was in the school yard and Jimmy had gotten into a fight with the Blackstone Rangers again, or something worse had happened. But if that had happened, wouldn't the school have called?

The Starlite Hotel. In my mind's eye, I could see the faded neon sign, but couldn't place the hotel. I had no idea why the boys would even be at a hotel at this time of day or what they were doing there or why no one would let Keith call me. Why wasn't Jimmy calling, anyway?

"It's about a block from school," Keith said. "You know, near the Starlite Café."

Then I knew the place he was talking about. It had once been one of the premier black hotels in the 1930s, but now it had become a by-the-hour rental filled with alcoholics, drug addicts, and hookers.

"What's going on, Keith? Where's Jimmy?"

"He's upstairs." Keith sounded suspiciously close to tears. "He said I needed to call you. I was supposed to even call Miss Hathaway if I had to and tell her it was an emergency and to track you down. He said I'm supposed to tell you that Lacey's in trouble."

I nearly cursed out loud. I should have seen this coming. Now everything made sense.

"I'll be right there," I said. "You stay outside of that hotel and don't go in, you hear me? You wait for me."

Then I hung up before he could even answer. I grabbed my keys and heavy winter coat, and ran out the door, pressing just the doorknob lock as I went. I was probably inviting a robbery, but it didn't matter.

Keith's older sister Lacey was in trouble, and if I didn't get to her soon, we might never see her again.

2

I slipped on the icy stairs as I ran out of the apartment building and managed to catch the frigid iron railing before I fell. I took a deep, frightened breath, angry at myself for the slip and for so many other things. I could have prevented this. I could have saved Lacey. Instead, I believed—what? That a good upbringing would protect her?

Maybe I did believe that. Maybe I had to believe it.

I stepped off the sidewalk and into the ice-covered snow that led to the driveway alongside the building. The snow crackled beneath my feet, then slipped inside my shoes. I wasn't dressed for this weather—I had left the sweater upstairs and I was wearing loafers, for God's sake, but I couldn't waste a single second.

I fumbled with my keys as I half-walked, half-ran, my heart pounding. I'd locked the panel van, because to leave anything unlocked in this part of town was to invite theft. Still, I wished I hadn't done it now, because every second wasted was a second that Lacey—and maybe Jimmy—couldn't afford.

I knew what was happening. Jimmy had been trying to tell me for months and I hadn't really listened. I thought it his paranoia. He kept saying that Lacey would end up like his mother, and damn my idiotic brain, I kept thinking he was overreacting.

Somehow I managed to unlock the van and crawl inside. Next step: Make certain I didn't flood the engine. This van didn't like deep cold temperatures, making it a stupid vehicle to have in the middle of a Chicago winter. I kept planning to sell the damn thing, but it was useful in my work, and I couldn't quite bring myself to get rid of it, nor could I afford anything else.

It started right up, but I knew better than to shove the gearshift into reverse immediately. This stupid van had stopped dozens of times, usually whenever I was in a hurry.

I took the opportunity to lean over, open the glove box, and remove my gun. I checked to make sure the gun was loaded. I kept the safety on. Then I put the gun and an extra magazine in the pockets of my coat. Fortunately, the gun I used was designed to be concealed and not go off. I just usually chose not to do it. I hated carrying a gun this way, but I saw no choice at the moment.

I yanked the car into reverse and backed out of the driveway, fishtailing on the ice. Two winters in Chicago had made me a better winter driver, but I wasn't as good as the natives. I spent most of my adult life in Memphis where no one knew how to drive in snow and ice. I usually stayed home when the weather was bad.

Now I had to somehow drive carefully and get to the Starlite Hotel before Lacey disappeared. And I had to do it without attracting the attention of the one or two cops that occasionally came to Chicago's South Side. It would be just my luck if one of them pulled me over, to find me panicked with a loaded gun in my coat pocket.

Fortunately, I drove this route almost every day, sometimes twice in one day, and I knew it well. I knew that once I got out of the neighborhood, the streets would be plowed and salted enough so that there wouldn't be a lot of ice. I knew that at this time of the day the traffic would be minimal, and I knew how to time the traffic lights so that I could hit every single green.

I concentrated on that, and tried not to think about what could be happening to Lacey. She was thirteen going on trouble, Franklin liked to say, and he didn't know the half of it. She had developed a full-grown woman's body in the past two years, and she liked showing it off. She wore inappropriate clothes she borrowed from friends, put on too much makeup, and was boy crazy. Often, when I picked her up from school, she came out still wiping the makeup off her face and adjusting the more demure outfit she had left the house in but had stored in her locker for the day.

Jimmy had told me that she had been hanging out with the wrong people, and he said she sometimes cut class. He kept telling me that she was going to end up badly, and I didn't listen. I figured she had triggered his fears from his mother.

His mother, who had been a prostitute for Jimmy's entire life. She had gotten pregnant in high school—or maybe junior high school—and the baby's father abandoned her immediately. Her family threw her out, and she raised Jimmy's brother Joe by herself, turning tricks and trying to make ends meet.

By the time she had gotten pregnant with Jimmy, she had two or three clients per night. She had no idea who Jimmy's father was, and neither did he. She kept disappearing throughout much of his life, but his older brother took care of him until Joe got involved in gangs and drugs, and the last time Jimmy's mother disappeared, Joe was already out of the house.

Jimmy had stayed in their crummy apartment until the landlord evicted him, and then he finally had to tell me the truth about what happened. Until that point, I was just the guy who worried about this street kid and occasionally bought him meals. I tried to help him find a permanent home, but Martin's assassination ruined all of that, and brought us here.

That trauma, I had believed, made Jimmy leap to the wrong conclusions about Lacey. I had dismissed him, rationalized his opinion away, and hadn't paid attention.

I should have listened. Jimmy was one of the most intelligent kids I had ever met, and he saw things I didn't want him to see, things *I* didn't want to see. We had our last conversation about Lacey in October, of all things, and at that point, Jim had used language he learned from his mother, phrasing things in a way that made me so uncomfortable, I never pursued any of this again.

13

I turned everything over and over in my mind, and added to it the Starlite and its proximity to the school. Chicago had more than five hundred public schools and nobody cared that the schools in the Black Belt were in horrible neighborhoods. I hadn't even given the Starlite's proximity to the linked grade school and junior high school much thought, thinking the neighborhood gangs were the real problem for the kids.

After all, why would johns and pimps and small-time thieves be interested in kids?

Why, indeed.

I turned right just before I got to the school, fishtailing again. The streets were icier here and I had to pay attention or I'd make some kind of horrible mistake. The Starlite had a parking lot, but it hadn't been plowed since the last snowstorm, so I just parked kitty-corner in front of the restaurant.

Then I jumped out, slamming the van door shut but not locking it. The ice on the sidewalk here had broken in chunks. I ran across it, hearing it crack and praying that I wouldn't fall. I didn't see Keith outside. Nor did I see a pay phone anywhere close.

Then I cursed out loud. Of course I didn't see a pay phone. Places like the Starlite had pay phones on every floor, for their indigent residents to use if they needed to make a call. Keith was waiting for me inside. Or maybe he had gone to the school for help.

I could only hope he wasn't inside the Starlite. Because I had no idea what I'd do if I found some creep with his hands on Lacey.

The Starlite's glass front door was yellow with cigarette smoke and age. I couldn't see inside. I pulled my gun and yanked the door open. As I stepped inside, I flicked the safety off.

I could barely see, what with the cigarette smoke and the dim lighting. The place stank of alcohol, sweat, and semen. To my right was the registration desk, if you wanted to call it that.

I pointed my gun at the man behind it. He raised his hands, eyes wild.

I was about to demand him to let me into the room with Lacey in it when I saw movement. Beside the desk were stairs and on them were Jimmy and Keith helping Lacey down, one painful movement at a time.

Her blouse hung open, revealing the edges of a white bra. She wore a skirt so short that at first I thought it had been torn off her. The go-go boots on her feet looked like Jackson Pollack had designed them.

Then I realized that she was dripping blood.

It took all of my self-control to stop my free hand from going to my mouth. All the way here, I had thought about what could happen, but faced with the evidence—or just the beginning of the evidence—on a girl that I loved like family provoked a dozen emotions in me all at once.

My reactions would not help her right now. The only thing that would help her was to get her out of here.

I put the safety on and shoved the gun in the pocket of my coat. Then I walked toward Lacey and the boys slowly, so I didn't startle her.

I surveyed the lobby as I did so, ready to grab the gun if I needed to. But no one looked threatening. In fact, no one looked. The man behind the reception desk thumbed through receipts as if nothing unusual had happened, as if someone pulled a gun on him everyday.

Maybe someone did.

"Lacey," I said as gently as I could, as neutrally as I could.

"Some guy hurt her, Uncle Bill." Keith Grimshaw, short, not into his growth yet, spoke so loud that I was sure they heard him outside. I'd never seen this little boy—still eleven and unused to the evils in the world—so very angry. "We gotta call the cops. We gotta—"

"Not now," I said in that same calm voice. I glanced at Jimmy. The last thing we needed was for him to encourage Keith. I had to get them out of this horrible place first.

Jimmy's gaze met mine. It was level, and he seemed even calmer than I felt. But there was something adult in his face, something determined, something that I had never seen before. And then it vanished. His lower lip shook.

"I'm sorry," he said. "I didn't—"

"Jim saved me, Uncle Bill." Lacey spoke for the first time. Her voice was clear, her chin raised. "He beat the guy up and sent him away. Jim saved me."

That was why they were coming down the stairs together. Because Jimmy had somehow gotten her out of one of those upstairs rooms. I

15

didn't want to know how he had done that. Not here, anyway. I needed to get them to the door.

"Uncle Bill," Keith said, and I knew what was coming next. He was a good kid, raised right. He still believed the police could help him. More to the point, he believed they would.

I shushed him, because I had no words of comfort for any of them. Then I leaned forward and picked up Lacey. She was lighter than I expected, and I could feel the stickiness of blood against the hand cradling her thighs.

Oh, baby girl, I thought. *What the hell did he do to you?*

And then I shut that thought down.

I carried her out of that hellish hotel and into the thin, cold sunlight. Jimmy and Keith followed.

They helped me put her in the back of the van, and then they sat on either side of her, as if they still needed to defend her.

I wiped my hands on my coat so that I could grip the steering wheel, and then I drove a badly injured thirteen-year-old girl and her eleven-year-old defenders to the nearest hospital.

3

The last time I had brought a badly injured woman to this hospital, I had had Laura Hathaway with me. Laura—rich, white, connected—had managed to get the doctors to act quicker and more efficiently than I ever could have.

But, then, that woman had had an illegal abortion, which, in the doctor's eyes, made her a criminal.

Lacey had been raped.

I hoped that the fact—and her age—would make this easier.

But I still needed Jimmy and Keith with me, so no one thought I was the one who had hurt her.

Unlike the last time, I knew the way to this emergency room. I drove as quickly as I could, taking main roads only because I knew that they'd be plowed. I had to leave the care of Lacey to the boys, but I also had to let them know what we were going to do.

"When we get there," I said, "I'm going to go with Lacey. The hospital won't let you boys come into the exam rooms."

"Smoke," Jimmy said. "I ain't gonna leave—"

"It's hospital policy, Jim." I turned the van onto the road closest to the emergency entrance. The road's surface had been plowed bare. I sped up.

"It's better not to argue about that, and to get Lacey treatment as fast as we can."

"I'm okay, Uncle Bill," Lacey said. Her voice was wavery and tired. She was definitely not okay. "Just take me home."

"I'm not doing that," I said.

"Then don't tell my dad."

"Dad's got to know!" Keith still sounded too agitated for my tastes.

"No, please," Lacey said. "Please."

"I'll deal with your dad," I said to Lacey. I turned onto the narrow access road, heading quickly past the small *Emergency* sign with its red arrow. "In fact, Jim, when we get there, you need to call both Althea and Franklin. Get them here as fast as you can."

"And the cops," Keith said.

He wasn't going to let that go.

"I'll make sure we catch this bastard," I said.

"Uncle Bill." Lacey sounded tired. I wondered how much blood she was losing. "Take me home. You can tell Mom."

"We're here now," I said, and parked the van right next to the emergency entrance.

I got out, pocketed my keys, and heard them clank against the gun. There was nothing I could do about that at the moment.

Jimmy got out as well, and held the door open. Lacey had her head down, and she was shivering. Jimmy had wrapped his coat around her shoulders, and Keith had put his across her legs.

I reached in. She cringed away from me, and I hoped that was because I wasn't doing what she wanted rather than because she was afraid to be touched.

"No," she said, her voice trembling.

I ignored her. I put one foot inside the van to brace myself, then slid my arms under her and pulled her against me. Her shivering increased, and she closed her eyes. A tear slipped down one cheek, and mixed with blood I hadn't realized she had on her face. In fact, blood coated her carefully ironed hair, and the corner of her mouth was swelling.

The bastard had hit her, more than once.

The anger I'd been keeping in check rose, and I bit it back. I eased her out of the van, making soothing noises as I did.

"Uncle Bill," she said, but I didn't know if she was telling me not to carry her inside, if she was relieved I had her, or if she even knew she had spoken.

I spun and walked down the well-shoveled sidewalk to the main doors marked **EMERGENCY ENTRANCE ONLY** in solemn red. The doors had been automated since my last visit, and they opened for me. But unlike my last visit, no one greeted us.

"Need help here," I said, and a white attendant in blue scrubs peeked out of one of the nearby treatment rooms.

Then he disappeared, and I felt that anger I had bottled up rise to the surface. I was about to yell again when the attendant wheeled out a cot.

I hurried toward him, and put Lacey on it. Then I raised the bars on one side, in case she wanted to climb off. The attendant did the same on his side.

"What have we got?" he asked me.

"She was badly beaten," I said, "and, I think, raped. I don't know for certain. My son called me for help—"

"You boys?" the attendant asked Jimmy and Keith.

"Me," Jimmy said, coming up to my side, "and yeah, he was on her when I got there."

"Jim saved me," Lacey said again, ever so faintly.

The attendant looked down at her. Her skin had turned gray and her eyes were closed.

"I think she's losing a lot of blood," I said.

He nodded, then started moving the cot. Jimmy grabbed the back and after a second, so did Keith. We all pushed it toward one of the treatment rooms.

"I'm sorry, boys," he said, "I'm afraid you can't go any further. And you, sir, are you her father?"

"Her uncle," I lied.

"Then you can come with us if you want, but you might not want to see—"

"I'll come," I said as we pushed the cot inside the small treatment room. I was glad for it, rather than having her go to one of the more public treatment areas.

The boys didn't leave. I looked at both of them. "Please, make those calls."

"No," Lacey whispered, but I was going to pretend she wasn't responding to my orders to contact her dad.

"And Jim," I added, "when you've reached them, call Marvella. I need her."

Marvella Walker was my neighbor. She worked with rape victims and helped some women get safe abortions. She knew how to help women in ways that I couldn't even fathom.

"Not Laura?" Jim asked.

"Not yet," I said. I hoped not ever. I would call Laura if I ran into problems here at the hospital. Laura's connections would ensure that Lacey got the proper treatment, but at the moment, it looked like I could handle this. "If we need her, I'll call her."

"Okay," Jim said.

Two nurses had already found us. I realized the attendant had left, maybe to get more help. One nurse was examining Lacey's head to see where the wound was.

"That blood on her head," Jimmy said, "it's the guy's blood. I hit him really hard."

We all looked at Jimmy. He was coming into his growth, but he was still well under five feet tall. I hadn't really thought this through: Someone as small as Jimmy had fended off a fully grown man?

"You can't stay," the nurse said to him, and I nearly yelled at her. I stopped myself just in time. I wanted to say that we needed him, that he knew things we didn't, and then I thought of Lacey. She probably didn't even want me here, let alone her cousin and her brother.

"I'm goin'," Jimmy said.

"We don't got money for the phone," Keith said to me, peeking his head in. I reached into my pocket as Jimmy grabbed his arm.

"I got enough," Jimmy said, pulling him away. "There's a waiting room, right?"

"I'll find you," I said, and then I turned my attention to Lacey.

She was pushing the nurses away. I took her right hand. "I'm right here, Lace," I said.

"Uncle Bill," she said, but she didn't open her eyes.

20

"She's bleeding badly," I said to the nurse across from me. She was thirty-ish, with set features and sad eyes. "We'll need to do something pretty quickly."

"The boy said the blood wasn't hers."

"On her head," I said, trying not to panic. "Look at her boots."

They were smeared. The blood on them was almost black. Some of the blood on her legs was drying, though, and I hoped that was a good sign.

"How old is she?" the other nurse asked. She reached for Lacey's skirt. Lacey hunched up.

"It's okay, honey," the nurse said. "You want to move your skirt for me?"

She sounded very tender. Lacey took the edges of her skirt in her bruised hands and pulled it up just a little. Her underwear was gone. I looked away.

"That's good," the nurse said. "How old are you, honey?"

Lacey shook her head and buried her face in the pillow. The first nurse took that opportunity to investigate the back of her head. It had left bloodstains on the pillowcase.

"She's thirteen and a half," I said. "Her birthday's in June."

I didn't know why I added the half. Maybe I wanted her to be older. Maybe I wanted her better able to cope with what was ahead of her. Whatever the reason, I was surprised at the nurse's shock.

"Thirteen?" She put her hand on Lacey's forehead. "Poor baby."

Poor baby, indeed.

"Where was she attacked?" she asked.

"In a building near her school," I said, hoping that would be enough. "I guess the boys saw the man take her aside and—"

"Jim saved me," Lacey said. She moved away from the pillow, away from the gentle hands investigating her wounds. Her eyes were open, and a bit wild. "Is he still here?"

"He went to call your parents, honey," the nurse said softly.

"No," Lacey said.

The other nurse had left, and I hadn't even noticed. That told me just how shaken up I was.

She returned now, with a white doctor in tow. Fortunately, it wasn't the doctor I had encountered almost a year ago. This man was younger, with black hair just kissing his collar.

"This your daughter?" he asked me.

"Niece," I said.

"You probably don't want to be here for this. Can you just wait outside the door?"

"Uncle Bill." Lacey grabbed my hand. Her grip was tight. "Don't leave me with him, Uncle Bill."

Tears streamed from her eyes. She didn't want to be alone with a strange man, even one who might help her.

It had already begun.

"I'll stay, if you don't mind," I said to the doctor. "I'll look away."

"I have paperwork for you to fill out," the nurse said. "Just outside."

I shook my head. "Lacey needs me here."

Besides, I didn't think she would let go of my hand.

The doctor reached for her skirt. Lacey's entire body convulsed. She kicked him, and kept kicking him, silently, without screaming, her lips pressed together.

The doctor backed away, his white smock smeared with dark blood from her high-heeled boots.

"He's helping you," I said, pulling her toward me. I reached for her legs, but she pushed my arm away with her free hand.

"We can't do this like this," the doctor said to the nurses. "She's not going to calm down, and I need to examine her, stat."

Lacey had stopped kicking, but she had moved closer to me, her body on alert. She had pulled the sheet over herself, and she was glaring at the doctor. "Don't let him hurt me, Uncle Bill."

"I won't," I said. I looked at the doctor, feeling helpless.

"We're putting her under." He kept his distance, his expression calm. He didn't seem upset by her reaction at all. "Then I can examine her. Do you know her blood type?"

"No," I said, my heart clenching.

He came closer again, this time to look at her face. Her cheek was swelling, too. He reached for it, and she thrashed. She let go of my hand and turned toward him, hitting and kicking, breathing through her mouth.

The doctor didn't touch her. He'd clearly seen this before.

I reached over, and grabbed her hands. She was surprisingly strong. She kept kicking and fighting, red blood—fresh blood—dotting the white sheets on the cot.

"Lacey, honey, it's Uncle Bill. You're okay. You're okay."

She turned toward me. "Uncle Bill? Don't let him hurt me, Uncle Bill."

But I had. I had. If I had listened to Jimmy—

"I won't," I said. "We're going to help you."

She started shaking violently, but she stopped kicking.

"I'm staying with her," I said to the doctor.

He nodded grimly. "Yes," he said. "You are."

4

By the time her parents arrived, Lacey was in surgery. The doctor didn't even end up using a speculum. Once she was unconscious, he took one good look at her, and decided she needed more than he could do in that exam room.

She didn't let go of my hand even as she went under, and so I had to pry her fingers off. They were bruised and bloody. Her right forefinger was missing a nail. The other nails, carefully polished the night before in a pretty white, were ragged and broken.

Poor baby. She had put up a hell of a fight.

I stayed in that exam room after she left, filling out paperwork, signing forms giving my permission for the surgery, knowing none of it was legal, but also knowing that Franklin would arrive soon and redo everything.

The nurses didn't talk to me while they cleaned up, and I was grateful. It took all of my strength to concentrate on the forms. They floated in front of me, small type against a white background, asking for things I didn't know.

But I did sign the consent form. That was the one the nurses were the most concerned with. They needed it before Lacey went into surgery, a procedure I didn't remember from any previous time I'd been around a hospital. I seemed to recall surgery first and signatures later.

Most of the time, however, I either wasn't related to the patient or I was the patient, too ill to sign anything.

This time, I still had trouble. My shaking hand nearly wrote William T. Dalton, my real legal name. I stopped at the top of the T, leaving it off at the very last minute. I was not William T. Grimshaw, not according to my driver's license. I was William Grimshaw, no middle initial, and that was how I had signed everything for the past two years.

The fact that I nearly blew my own cover showed how shaken I truly was.

After I signed the consent form and they whisked Lacey away, I sat for a few minutes, my hand over my face. I'd seen a lot in my life, I'd lived through a lot, and none of it had hit me like this—not as an adult, anyway.

Maybe it was the last straw after the difficult year. Maybe it was Lacey's pretty face, swelling and bruised, her eyes unfocused and terrified.

Maybe it was simply the fact that I knew that little girl, that little arrogant reckless intelligent girl, would never be the same.

I blinked hard against my palm, swallowed several times, and nearly jumped out of my chair when a hand touched my shoulder.

I whirled, ready to do battle, but it was only the first nurse, the thirtyish one. She was looking at me with great compassion.

"She'll be all right, Mr. Grimshaw. Doctor Fahey is one of our best."

I shook my head, not sure I could trust my voice. I swallowed again, cleared my throat, and nearly contradicted her. But I couldn't even speak what I was thinking.

"Thank you," I said, and meant it. "Thank you for helping her."

"Young thing like that," the nurse said softly. "All that Civil Rights stuff hasn't changed everything, has it?"

It took me a moment to understand her meaning. Black women had gotten raped through most of our history in the United States, first by the men who owned them, and then by the men who thought they were uppity.

"Oh," I said, "things have changed a little. I could bring her here, and Doctor Fahey would help her, no questions asked."

The nurse smiled. I realized then that she had gotten me out of myself, made me think about something else, at least for a moment. I wasn't used to being seen so clearly, but then, I wasn't used to being this emotionally close to the edge, either.

"She will be all right, Mr. Grimshaw," the nurse said with a lot of conviction. "She's got those little boys who came to her defense, and she's got you. She's got a good family. That will help."

I almost said, *It hasn't helped so far*, but I realized that wasn't true. Bad things happened to everyone, and Lacey was in the hospital because of her family. Because of Jimmy, who had had the presence of mind to save her.

Jimmy, who was still being strong somewhere outside of the emergency area.

I couldn't rely on an eleven-year-old forever.

I thanked the nurse and finished the paperwork, feeling a little calmer. Or at least, superficially calmer. I had set the emotions to one side. I would deal with them once we knew what had happened to Lacey and how it had happened so close to the school.

I had a lot of questions, and I was going to need a lot of answers.

5

I had control of myself by the time I entered the waiting room down the hall. It was the same room I had spent hours in last spring, and it hadn't changed much. Someone had chain-smoked in there not long before I arrived, and the air was grayish yellow. Newspapers were scattered across one of the couches, and a white and pink sweater draped over the back of a chair.

But the room was empty except for Jimmy and Keith. I stepped inside and both of them launched themselves at me, wrapping their arms around me. The gun in my pocket jabbed my hip. I had to get that thing out of my coat before I did much else.

I held the boys for a long time, my hands on their small skulls. They'd been spectacular, and I had to tell them that. And then I had to find out what they knew, and why the three of them hadn't been in school on this weekday afternoon.

I let them break the hug. They had to be traumatized. I was amazed they had managed to hold on this long. They were nearly teenagers, boys who had spent the last month or two trying to prove that they were older than they were. But this had shattered that pretense, at least for them.

Finally, Jimmy pulled away. Keith followed. They both looked frail and too thin, little boys who weighed maybe eighty pounds soaking wet, little boys who might have saved a girl's life.

"How is she, Smoke?" Jimmy asked. He tugged on his shirt as he headed toward the nearest couch. The shirt was bloodstained and askew. I almost asked him where his coat was, and then I remembered: He had given it to Lacey and the nurse had bagged it, along with the rest of her clothing.

"She's in surgery," I said. "We'll know in a few hours."

"Surgery?" Keith asked.

He had a streak of dried blood on one cheek. It looked like he had wiped his hand on his face.

I touched that blood, scraping it off gently with a fingernail. "Are you boys all right?" I asked as calmly as I could. "That man didn't hurt you too, did he?"

"He didn't get near me," Keith said. "I seen him running out of the hotel. He was bleeding something fierce."

I hadn't even noticed a blood trail on the ice. That also showed how intent I had been on getting inside that hotel.

"I hit him with a screwdriver, really hard on his head," Jimmy said. "I hit him a lot, as hard as I could, and Lacey was kicking him. He couldn't grab his pants quick enough and get outta there. He was putting his pants on and running at the same time. I'da kept on him too, if he hadn't hurt Lace."

"Good job," I said, feeling stunned. Jimmy truly had saved her. "Where did you get the screwdriver?"

The question was minor, but I couldn't focus on the tougher parts of what he had to tell me; at least, not all at once.

"I brung it because me and Keith mighta had ta break into Lace's locker." His grammar had gotten bad again, like it always did in times of crisis.

"Her locker?" I didn't know how that connected to anything.

Jimmy started to answer me, when the waiting room door burst open. Franklin hurried in, bringing some outside cold with him. He was a big man, although not as big as I was, and his terror made him seem bigger.

"Where's Lacey?" he asked me.

"Didn't you stop at the desk?" I asked.

"I did, they told me she's in surgery, but I thought I'd better hear from you." He let the door bang behind him. His coat was still wrapped tightly around him. He hadn't even pulled off his gloves. His face was ruddy from the outside chill.

"She's in surgery, Franklin," I said taking his arm and moving him away from the door.

"Is she going to die?" he asked. He didn't see the boys huddled together near one of the couches.

"I doubt it," I said.

He let out a gusty sigh, as if he'd been holding his breath. "What the hell happened, Smokey? I sent my little girl to school this morning, and now she's in the hospital?"

I wasn't ready to answer that—not phrased that way. "Where's Althea?"

"On her way," he said.

"Did you fill out paperwork?" I asked. "Because I did, and you know, that's probably not good."

He blinked, frowned, and then nodded as he finally understood me. "Think they'll give me some answers?" he asked as he let himself out the waiting room door.

"He's really upset," Keith whispered. "Is he mad at us, Uncle Bill?"

Through the yellow-stained glass window, I could see Franklin almost run down the hall. He rounded a corner. I'd never seen him panic before.

I turned away. "I don't even think he saw you, Keith. He's not mad. He'll be proud of you when he figures out what happened."

"We cut school," Keith said.

"We had a good reason, Smoke," Jimmy said.

I was certain they did. I nodded. "You can tell me all about it when Franklin gets back."

Jimmy let out a small breath. Keith started to cry. He bent over and put his hands on his face, hiccupping and rocking as the tears became sobs.

Jimmy went to one side of him, and I sat on the other, putting my arms around him.

"I never...." Keith raised his head. Snot dripped from his nose, and his entire face was wet. He kept taking hitching breaths. "I mean, I'm really mean to her, Uncle Bill. I never say nothing nice. And now, Daddy said she might die."

I pulled him close. "She's not going to die," I said.

"But what if she does? I haven't said nothing nice in *forever*. I just been teasing her about her stupid clothes and that makeup and those boys. And now one of them mighta killed her."

"That weren't no boy," Jimmy said. "That was a full-grown man, and you know it, Keith. And if Smoke says she's not gonna die, she's not gonna die."

I half-smiled at him, wishing he hadn't given me that much power. I wasn't in charge of who lived or who died. I wished I was. That man who attacked Lacey would be dead right now.

I reached into the pocket of my coat. My fingers brushed coins and a guitar pick I carried as an emergency lock pick. I didn't even have a handkerchief. So I used my fingers to clean off Keith's face as best I could.

"Lacey's hurt," I said, "but she'll get through it. And so will you. You and Jim were the heroes here. You can tell us everything we need to know when your parents arrive. And if they get mad at the small stuff, I'll talk to them."

"Did you talk to the cops?" Keith asked.

I opened my mouth, about to lie to him. I could tell him that I had spoken to the cops in the emergency room. But I wasn't going to. I might need Keith's help. I was getting the glimmerings of an idea.

"Not yet." I wiped my wet hands on my already filthy coat.

Then Keith rubbed his sleeve over his nose, and his other arm over his eyes. His face was dark red.

"You gotta catch that guy," he said.

"Don't worry," Jimmy said. "Smoke will. That's what he does."

I glanced at Jimmy, who was still remarkably calm. He nodded at me, as if his sentence had been some kind of code between us, as if he expected me to run off right now and do something to the man who hurt Lacey.

"Promise?" Keith asked, his eyes still on mine.

I said, "I'll make sure he never hurts her again."

6

Franklin came back into the waiting room, Althea beside him. She wore her Sunday-best coat, and she clutched her black purse against her stomach. Her expression was fierce.

Her gaze found me and leveled me to that couch.

"What happened to my daughter, Smokey?" she asked in a voice I had never heard from her. It sounded like she blamed me. Maybe she did. I had taken Lacey to school that morning, and I had brought her to the hospital.

"I'm not certain about the sequence of events," I said.

"Don't talk around it," she snapped. "What happened?"

I swallowed, ignoring my instinct to protect the boys from the harshness of this. They'd already seen the harshness. They knew.

"The doctor will have to tell you about the injuries," I said. "I'm pretty sure she was raped—"

"She was," Jimmy said. "I seen that guy—"

I put my hand on his, silencing him.

"—and she was beaten pretty badly," I said. "The boys are the ones who found her. They saved her. They called me."

"Not me?" Althea asked, looking at Keith as if he had committed some kind of grave sin.

31

"That guy had her in a hotel, Mom," he said. "Jimmy ran upstairs and got her free and told me to call Uncle Bill."

"Why not the police?" she asked Jimmy.

Jimmy frowned at her. "Aunt Althea, the police don't come to places like that."

"Places like what?" she asked, looking at me again.

"Look," I said. "The boys haven't told me everything yet. Sit down, Althea, Franklin. Let them tell us—"

"You know where she was," Althea said to me. "You got her and brought her here."

"Yes," I said. "I did. And I'm not sure exactly what happened either. She was already hurt and the man was long gone when I got there."

"So you haven't caught him," Althea said.

"Not yet," I said.

"It's okay," Jimmy said. "I gots—"

I squeezed his hand again. I wanted to control how this conversation went. Franklin and Althea were already upset. I didn't want this to get worse.

"Raped," Franklin said, and sat heavily on the couch. "How could that happen?"

"She was wearing a really short skirt, Dad," Keith said.

"Enough," I said. "What happened is not Lacey's fault."

"Smoke, we been warning her about them guys," Jimmy said. "She shoulda listened."

"What guys?" Franklin asked, his voice calm. "Did you know about these guys, Smokey?"

They wanted to blame me. I understood that.

"No," I said. "I didn't know anything about this."

Althea still loomed over me, clutching her purse as if she were debating using it as a weapon.

"So who is 'we'?" she asked Jimmy.

"Me and Keith," Jimmy said. "Mostly me. I seen stuff like this before, with my mom."

"Jim," I said. "Enough."

"Stuff like what?" Althea asked. Her tone had changed. She knew about Jimmy's mom. She and Franklin and Laura were the only ones who did.

"Aunt Althea," Jimmy said. "It was one of them pimp hotels. He was recruiting her."

"My daughter wouldn't be stupid enough to fall for that," Franklin said.

Jimmy was shaking his head. He started to speak and I squeezed his hand a third time to silence him.

"Jim," I said, but he talked over me.

"They don't ask you to join up like the Army," he said. "They promise you stuff, and then you go with them, and they hurt you and tell you you're no good and they turn you. I seen it before, and Lace, she was yelling at the guy that he'd told her she was gonna be modeling, not be alone with him. She thought there's be other people there."

"Modeling," Franklin said numbly.

"That's one they use lots," Jimmy said. "That gets lotsa girls. The pretty ones specially. My mom, she used to slap up some of the girls and tell them not to be stupid because they was lied to, and they had to get used to—"

"*Enough*," I said as forcefully as I could. Keith was frowning at Jimmy. It wasn't just that I didn't want Keith to hear this. I didn't think Franklin or Althea needed all of the details.

"I was just tellin' 'em, Smoke." Jimmy pulled his hand away from me. "You said nice people don't know this stuff."

And they didn't. Nor did they need to know how deep their daughter had gotten into this mess.

"Where is that pimp hotel?" Franklin asked me.

"It's the Starlite," I said.

His mouth opened slightly, then closed. He shook his head once. "Right next to the school?"

"That's how come she could sneak," Jimmy said. "They do stuff like that, looking for girls. That's how they got half the girls what worked with my mom—"

"Jim*my*," I said. "I said enough."

He scooted back on the couch. He had started to do that lately when I attempted to discipline him. Or he would just walk out of the room.

Franklin didn't seem to notice. "Right next to the school," he repeated.

He cupped his head with his hands, his fingers deep in his thinning hair. Althea glared at him, then at me.

"You tell me what happened," she said.

I didn't even know where to start. Finally, I decided to concentrate on today only.

"I was on the phone. The operator broke in and asked if I would accept an emergency call from Keith Grimshaw—"

"I gave you dimes!" Jimmy said to Keith.

"The line was busy," Keith said. "I knew you wanted Uncle Bill, so I got the operator to get him."

"It was the right thing," I said, not wanting the boys to fight. We didn't need more tension here.

I looked at Althea and Franklin. I wanted them to know how fast all of this happened. "Keith told me that Lacey was in trouble and I should come to the Starlite."

"You didn't ask why they were there?" Althea asked.

"I heard trouble and Starlite and Lacey," I said. "I left immediately."

"Smoke comes busting in like Marshal Dillon," Jimmy said, "his gun out and his coat swinging—"

"Jimmy," I said.

Althea wasn't paying any attention. "I thought you said you didn't know what was going on."

"I didn't," I said, feeling like I was the twelve-year-old. "But I knew that Lacey was rebelling."

"Rebelling," Althea said.

"The makeup, the clothes," I said.

"We stopped her from doing that last year," Althea said.

"No," I said. "You just stopped her from wearing it to and from the house."

"And you *knew*?" she asked.

I had had enough. If they wanted to blame someone, they needed to blame the creep who went after their daughter.

"You knew too," I said. "And don't tell me you didn't. I wasn't the only one taking her to and from school. When she came to the van after school, she always had some leftover makeup on her face or she was adjusting her clothing. You knew, just like I did."

Althea raised her chin and narrowed her eyes, but she didn't deny it.

"And see what it caused?" Franklin asked, still looking down. "I knew it. I knew—"

"It wasn't her clothes, Franklin," I said.

"That's why they were interested in her in the first place," Franklin said. "They knew—"

"No, Dad," Keith said. "She just wanted to be pretty. She wanted to grow up to be a model or an actress or something, and you wouldn't let her."

"Those aren't professions for smart girls," Franklin said, but he sounded defeated.

"How do you know that's what she wanted?" Althea asked Keith. "She confided in you?"

"No, Mom," Keith said. "I looked at her diary last night."

"It's in code," Althea said, then flushed. Clearly she'd been trying to break in as well.

"I know the code," Keith said. "It's not a hard one."

I shifted slightly. We were finally getting somewhere, whether the Grimshaws knew it or not. "Why did you look in her diary, Keith?"

"Jimmy's been keeping an eye on her, Uncle Bill," Keith said. "He thought she was going to get into trouble."

"I *told* you," Jimmy said to me. "I told you she was going to end up like my mom."

Althea winced.

"You didn't believe me," Jimmy said.

"I was wrong," I said, but not to him. I was looking at Lacey's parents. "I thought Jimmy was overreacting. I thought Lacey was just going through normal teenage rebellion. I had no idea."

"Well, you gots to listen to me," Jimmy said. "On this stuff, I know it. I growed up with it, and I know it."

I looked away from everyone. I had to.

"So," Althea said, her voice surprisingly steady. "What did you see that we didn't?"

An adult question, one that I should have asked Jimmy long ago.

"There's been men talking to her," Jimmy said. "Not boys, neither. Not kids from school. Men."

Men. I closed my eyes just for a moment.

"Then I seen her yesterday. She was outside, smoking a cigarette, and—"

"Smoking?" Franklin asked, like that was the worst thing she could have done.

"Let him finish," Althea said softly.

"And this guy," Jimmy says, "he comes talking to her. But I—something happened in class—and when I looked again, she was gone. This guy, he was old, and that scared me, so I asked Keith if he knew who the guy was, and Keith said no, he didn't, but he could find out in her diary."

I ran a hand over my face. The ridges of the scar tissue along my cheek felt accusatory. I'd missed these signals before with friends, with clients.

And now with Lacey.

God. I had a blind spot, and it was the worst kind.

"Why didn't you talk to me?" I had told Jimmy expressly to talk with me if things got bad with Lacey.

"Because I wasn't sure of nothing. Maybe the guy was a teacher, yelling at her for smoking or something," Jimmy said. "Smoke, you always find out what's going on before you do something or tell someone, so I figured I'd do that."

I suppressed a sigh of irritation. He had tried, but he was still a boy. He hadn't known what the right choice was.

"That's why you thought you had to break into Lacey's locker," I said.

"What?" Franklin asked.

"Jimmy brought a screwdriver so that he could break into Lacey's locker if he had to," I said.

"I figured if Keith didn't get no information, the locker might have something," Jimmy said.

"He didn't need to break in, though," Keith said. "This guy'd been taking her to lunch at the Starlite Café, telling her how famous she was gonna be and how pretty she was and how everyone would think she was the best model ever."

I almost said again, *You should have called me*, but it didn't matter. They didn't. They were investigating. They thought they were doing the right thing.

"So, I figured we'd see if she went with him again, and we'd follow." Jimmy looked defiantly at me and then at Franklin. "It was my idea to skip math."

Althea let out a small laugh. She knew what the boys were worried about and how ridiculous it was.

Franklin raised his head. Apparently that got through to him, too. "If you hadn't skipped math, God knows where my daughter would be right now."

God didn't know. But I did.

"So we got our coats and stuff and went to the café," Jimmy said, "just as they was leaving. He was taking her to the hotel, and I knew. I just knew what was happening next. I seen it more than once."

Keith was frowning. Althea's expression softened. She had forgotten—or maybe she hadn't known—exactly how awful Jimmy's life had been before we came to Chicago.

"I told Keith to track down Smoke and get him here right away, and Keith did. So Keith shouldn't be in trouble." Jimmy said that last really fast.

"He's not in trouble," Althea said. "Go on."

Jimmy nodded, once. Businesslike. Adult. My heart twisted.

"They was already upstairs," he said. "That...*asshole*...he...I guess he gots a room there."

The word "asshole" sounded so wrong coming from Jimmy and yet so right. It was a sign of how very upset this made him, how angry he was, that he used that word and didn't even apologize to me or to Althea.

Maybe he hadn't even noticed. Althea certainly hadn't. And Franklin was beyond disciplining the kids for anything. He just stared at Jimmy, his eyes almost fixed, his fists clenched and resting on his knees.

"The guy at the desk, he don't care, and he wouldn't give me his extra key." Jimmy's voice shook with frustration. "So I runned up the stairs and got to the room and tried the door, thinking that you know..."

He paused then and looked at me. My breath caught. He was censoring himself.

"You know," he repeated, "that maybe the door was unlocked."

Jimmy had clearly hoped that the man had been too eager or too comfortable to lock the door. But Jimmy was thinking of his mother, who was already a prostitute when he was born. Sometimes men—sometimes *she*—didn't lock the door.

But in this instance, the door had to be locked. This man, this pimp, this procurer, this *asshole*, didn't want Lacey to get away from him quickly or anyone to get to her easily.

"But the door was locked. No deadbolt though which was good because otherwise I'da had to wait for Smokey." Jimmy glanced at me again, swallowing hard. He wasn't sure how much detail to go into. I wasn't either. I'd let him tell it.

"But," Jimmy said, "there was yelling, and Lacey was telling him she didn't want to be there, that she was supposed to be a model and then…"

Jimmy let out a small breath, and bit his lower lip.

"Then what?" Franklin asked, but the words had no force to them. It was as if he had to ask, but he didn't want to hear the answer.

I wasn't sure any of us wanted to hear the answer.

"He hit her so hard I heard it." Jimmy closed his eyes for a moment as if he were steeling himself. "That's when I knowed I couldn't wait for Smoke."

He looked at me again. I gave him an encouraging smile. He had clearly been worried I would yell at him for not waiting.

"So," he said, "I took the doorknob off."

"You what?" Althea was frowning. She didn't understand how he could do that.

"With the screwdriver. I worked real quick but real quiet. I catched the knob before it fell and got the pieces, then I pushed the door open—and I didn't think no more, Smoke. I pulled that guy off her and I hit him and I hit him and I'da kept hitting him if he didn't run away. I'da even followed him if Lace wasn't on that bed all hurt. I mighta killed him, I think, Smoke."

All of that, spoken to me, all of that filled with fear. Jimmy's eyes were red-rimmed now and he was trembling.

I pulled him against me. "You were spectacular," I said. "You *are* spectacular. You're amazing."

I wasn't going to berate him for failing to contact me. This kid did everything he could think of to save Lacey.

He pushed away from me, shaking his head. "I wasn't fast enough. He was already on her. He—you know—*ruined* her. You know. Lace'll—"

"He did not ruin her." Althea took a step closer to Jimmy. For a moment, I thought she'd hit him.

Jimmy leaned back, looking up at her, his face gray. Keith, on the other side of me, peered around my arm.

"My daughter," Althea said, shaking a fist at Jimmy, "is not ruined. She will never be ruined. She is a crime victim. That's all. Nothing more. Do you got that?"

Jimmy opened his mouth, and for one horrified moment, I thought he would argue with her. I thought all of the tension in the room would boil over in a way that all of us would regret.

Then he took a deep, steadying breath. "Yes, ma'am. Ain't nobody what knows that better than me."

And he raised his chin just slightly.

All the fight left her face. She bit her lower lip, then closed her eyes.

"This is not going to be easy," she said, more to herself than to anyone else.

"No, ma'am," Jimmy said.

"Right near the school," Franklin said again, as if the rest of the conversation hadn't happened. He looked up, his gaze meeting mine. Behind the shock, I could see anger just starting to form. "We do everything we can to keep our babies safe, and these *criminals* set up right next to the school."

"We needs to call the police," Keith said softly, in a tone that suggested he wanted to calm the entire family.

"You think they'll actually pay attention to this?" Althea asked bitterly. "They had to know what was going on in that hotel."

I wasn't going to confirm that. All of the adults—and Jimmy—knew she was right.

"But we are going to take care of this, aren't we, Smokey?" Her voice had an intensity I had never heard before.

I kept the boys close, but I looked up at her. There was no shock on her face. Unlike her husband, she hadn't retreated mentally. She knew what was happening, and she knew that the future had altered for everyone.

And she knew what she was asking me.

"No," I said to Althea. "*We* are not going to take care of this."

Her eyes flashed. "Our family—"

39

"Has done more for me than I could ever repay," I said. "Let me handle this."

"I'll help you," Franklin said.

That was just what I needed. A civilian to get in my way.

"No," I said. "You have to help your family. You let me take care of things."

"Smoke'll fix it," Jimmy said, finally sounding young again.

Young and too naïve, even for him.

"I can't fix it," I said tiredly. "But I can do what the police won't."

Althea's eyes narrowed. "See that you do," she said.

7

Althea wanted me to leave immediately, but I couldn't go until I knew how Lacey was. I also couldn't stay in that waiting room much longer. I needed to pace. I was about to step outside when my neighbor, Marvella Walker, showed up.

Marvella was tall and stunning, the kind of woman every man noticed when she walked into a room. On this afternoon, she had pulled her afro back with a red headband, revealing her majestic features. She looked like an African tribal goddess, even in her long white winter coat and bright red scarf.

She nodded an acknowledgement at me, then looked at Franklin, who hadn't gotten off that couch.

Althea stood, looking short and matronly next to Marvella even though they had to be about the same age.

"Tell me what happened," Marvella said to Althea.

I slipped out the door, unwilling to go over it all again. I leaned against the green industrial wall, wishing I smoked so that I would have something to do with my hands.

A moment later, Jimmy and Keith left the waiting room. Keith looked exhausted. Jimmy's eyes were still red-rimmed.

"We couldn't take it again," he said to me. "You gots a five? We didn't have lunch."

"Better yet," I said, "let me buy you both lunch."

"I think you gots stuff to do," Jimmy said. "Like detecting."

"It'll wait," I said.

"Well," Keith said, glancing down the hall, "one of us has to wait for the doc and he won't talk to us."

I finally got it: The boys wanted to be alone.

I grabbed my wallet and pulled out a ten. "Bring me back a cookie or something."

Jimmy was frowning at my wallet. He looked up at me, then looked over at Keith.

"I'll meet you, okay?" he asked.

Keith took the ten from me. "Okay," he said, apparently expecting one of us to protest. When we didn't, he meandered down the hall.

Jimmy watched until Keith turned a corner and disappeared.

"When you go," Jimmy said softly, "I wants to come with you. I wants to see how bad I hurt this guy."

I knew better than to protest that Jimmy couldn't handle himself. Given the right circumstances, he obviously could.

"I'm not sure I'll find him, Jim," I said.

Jimmy grinned at me. I braced myself for one of those hero-worshipping sentences, something I truly did not deserve.

Instead, he reached into the front pocket of his pants and with two fingers, pulled out a wallet.

He handed it to me.

I took it gingerly. I didn't recognize it. It was made of cheap leather and had been rubbed along the back where the coin compartment was. The brown had rubbed off in the outline of a quarter.

I looked up, not entirely understanding. Jimmy was still grinning. It wasn't his wallet. I knew what his wallet looked like. I also knew that it rarely held more than a few dollars, a note with his name on it, and a battered picture of his mother.

I slipped my fingers between the wallet's edges, letting it fall open in my palm. An Illinois driver's license, creased and battered, was half-shoved into the front plastic divider. It read *Clyde Voss*, who was born in 1940, and didn't live too far from the Starlite.

The address made me realize what I was looking at. I let out a small chuckle. "This is the guy?"

Jimmy's grin widened. He nodded.

"You got his wallet?" It must have fallen out of his pocket as he struggled with his pants. "Son of a bitch."

I pulled Jimmy close. He let me, which showed how shaken he still was.

"You're one incredible kid, you know that?" I asked.

He shrugged against me.

I was greatly impressed. He had enough presence of mind to grab the guy's wallet, even after breaking into the room, stopping the assault, and rescuing Lacey.

I had no idea what to say or how to let Jimmy know how impressed I was.

After a moment, he pulled back, just enough so that he could see my face. "So," he said. "I gets to come, right?"

I stared at the license, wondering if the address was fake. At least it was a place to start.

"Let me find him first," I said, unwilling to promise anything right now. I had set aside my own anger, but I could feel it, lurking inside me, threatening to get out.

I couldn't remember being this furious, not ever. The times I'd had to defend people I loved, I simply acted. An assailant was in front of me, and I dealt with him.

I hadn't had to deal with the crisis and then find the assailant before.

Something must've crossed my face, because Jimmy's expression got very serious.

"Whatcha gonna do to him, Smoke?"

I would have liked to think I would make a citizen's arrest. I would have liked to believe that I could give him to the police and they would take care of him, not just by imprisoning him, but by shutting down his entire operation.

But that wouldn't have even happened in Memphis, which was infinitely less corrupt than Chicago. In Chicago, the police were still trying to cover up their murder of two Black Panthers. In Chicago, more than forty blacks were killed by police last year alone.

In Chicago, blacks ducked when they saw a police car. They didn't seek one out.

Jimmy's question was a good one. What was I going to do?

When I tried to mentally answer that question, the anger waited. Dark and huge and more powerful than I was.

What was I going to do?

I was going to be exceedingly cautious, that's what I was going to do.

I was going to make sure I would not get caught.

8

The address on the driver's license took me back to the neighborhood near the school. I drove slowly, aware of my gun. I had never removed the damn thing from my pocket. I was also aware of my pounding heart.

The doctor's words ran through my head: *She was smaller than I would have expected, not completely developed. Her assailant did a lot of damage just by—um—just by—I mean, he tore her up. We did what we could but she'll be in pain for a while. We're giving her antibiotics, which should take care of everything, including VD if she caught something like that....*

And I saw the look on Franklin's face change at the word *VD*, first because he didn't understand the acronym, and then because he did.

I thought for a moment that Franklin would walk away, but he didn't. He clung to Althea, whose expression never altered. She had expected this. She had known what was coming. She would get the family through it.

But as the doctor continued, she looked at me, her flat expression instructing me. I had better do something, or she would.

Marvella stood just behind them, listening carefully. She would handle the family stuff, the woman stuff, the emotional stuff. At least tonight.

Tonight, I had to take care of everything else.

I left while Jimmy and Keith were still in the cafeteria. I didn't want Jimmy to ask again if he could go along. He had done a fantastic job, but he didn't belong at my side.

Marvella was going to take him home, and if I hadn't arrived by eleven, she promised to call Laura.

As I drove down the roads I'd sped through that afternoon, the lack of traffic surprised me. So did the darkness. It felt like I had been in that hospital half my life. Night fell early in January, but it was already six-thirty, and sensible families were home.

Most everyone else was off the streets. It had gotten colder, with just enough of a wind to make the air bitter. No one was out unless they had to be.

Like everything else in Chicago, crime went inside in the winter.

I flashed on the interior of that hotel: dark, filthy, stinky. I would never get it out of my mind, and neither would Lacey. On her bad days, she would always return to that room, to that man, pounding her with his fists, holding her down with his body—

I took a deep breath. I had to unpack my anger slowly or I would make mistakes.

The doctor said: *The next few weeks will be critical. We'll see how she heals. She might need more surgery. At the moment, we believe we've repaired the damage. If we haven't, we might have to go in again, remove things—*

Ten minutes, maybe less. That was all it had taken this bastard to change Lacey's life.

Ten minutes, plus a few weeks of wooing. Some promises. Modeling. Damn that promise. Lacey was pretty. She wanted out. She thought she could trade in on her looks. He had flattered her, coddled her, made her feel even more special.

And then he had locked her in a room, slapped her across the face, and shoved her against a filthy bed.

If we didn't handle this right, if Althea and Franklin didn't handle this right, Lacey would be broken forever. If we handled it right, she would be different. But alive. Strong. With a future.

If we handled it right.

I turned left. Streetlights had burned out here. The bastard's address was in a once-great neighborhood, about three blocks from the Starlite. About three blocks from the school where pretty little girls grew up into pretty naïve teenagers, easy prey for a bastard like this.

The building stood in the middle of the darkened block. This block didn't look that different from the block I lived on. Stately old Victorians converted into apartments. Four-plexes scattered on the once-large lawns. Buildings crammed against each other, with makeshift fire escapes, doors marring the front of once-pretty homes.

The bastard lived in a three-story building shoved between two Victorians. A six-plex, then. I hoped to hell he didn't live on the top floor. His address suggested a ground floor apartment, but I'd been surprised before.

I parked in a puddle of darkness, half a block away from the nearest working streetlight and across the street from the apartment complex. Thank God the van was filthy. The license plate was covered with snow-dirt. I'd made sure of that when I left the hospital. Nothing about this van could connect it to me.

I left my hat on the seat beside me. I didn't want to risk losing it in the wind. But I had rolled a thick scarf around my neck, and made sure I wore my expensive leather gloves.

Then I got out slowly, easing the door closed so it didn't bang. None of the buildings had exterior lights. The neighborhood was dark and dangerous, exactly what I needed.

I walked carefully around the van. The neglected block hadn't seen a plow in weeks. The snow had packed down and turned to a slick of ice that didn't have sand or salt on it, but did have ruts through a central path that cars had carved all on their own.

I picked my way across, then reached the sidewalk—or what had been a sidewalk, but what was now a trail of iced footprints deep in the frozen snow.

I didn't stop. As I approached the building, I realized the house wasn't a six-plex. It was an eight-plex at least, with basement apartments down a small flight of stairs framed by a rusted iron railing.

I went up the steps to the door buzzers. The bastard's address wasn't inside the house. His door was outside, one of the basement apartments to the side, which surprised me. I figured a thug like this would have money. Anyone who lived in a basement apartment in Chicago clearly had no money at all.

Basement apartments flooded. In bad snow storms, their doors froze shut or got blocked by accumulating snow. Basement apartments were for the losers, the near-homeless, the hopeless.

The stairs had been salted and shoveled, the area in front of the door clear of snow and ice. Bastard didn't want to get blocked in.

The door didn't have a deadbolt or a security buzzer. I had initially planned on knocking, telling the bastard that I had his wallet and maybe he wanted it back, but I decided against that.

Why warn him? A lock like this I could slip open with a slice of my guitar pick or open with the lock picks in my van.

Or hell, I could kick the whole thing in.

But that might wake the neighbors.

I decided to use the guitar pick first and see what happened. Then I might consider breaking the damn door down. Or maybe even knocking like a civilized man.

I gripped the knob loosely in my leather gloves. Moments like this justified their expense. My hands wouldn't slide off the metal, no matter how slick it was.

Then I slid the pick against the latch, and pushed ever so slightly, hoping the door wouldn't rattle.

It didn't. It eased open, and a cloud of marijuana smoke hit me. I leaned back, took a deep breath of fresh air, and then pulled the scarf over my nose and mouth. It wouldn't take out all of the smoke, but it would ease the effects.

I couldn't have my judgment or my reactions affected here. Not if I could help it.

I pulled my gun, flicked the safety off, and then stepped inside. I eased the door closed behind me. I was in a narrow entry, filled with coats and boots. Ahead of me was an equally narrow hallway. Light poured out of one room to my left. Directly in front of me, the flickering light of a television set illuminated a cluttered couch and a thin brown carpet.

I walked quietly, not that it mattered. The television was turned to one of Jimmy's favorite programs, *The Mod Squad,* and the familiar pulsing music played underneath some really bad "hip" dialogue.

There were no other doors in the narrow hallway. The gun and I peered into the lighted room. It was a galley kitchen with a tiny table on the far wall. The faint odor of rotted garbage rose from the sink, which was full of slime-coated water.

I blinked, then headed toward the television room. I passed a bathroom large enough for a shower and a toilet. There was no sink. I didn't see any other doors and certainly no windows.

Not only was this a basement apartment, but it was a studio basement apartment with only the most basic amenities. This thing was an afterthought.

I leaned against the door frame and peered into the room. Two windows covered the back wall. They were six feet above the floor, and not wide enough for an adult to get through. They provided some light and maybe a bit of fresh air on hot days. No wonder this place smelled. Nothing could refresh the air in here.

The couch was pushed against the wall. In the center of the room was an easy chair with the room's only inhabitant. The glow of a cigarette tip indicated he had inhaled. The stench told me the cigarette was marijuana.

No one else was in the apartment.

He was so engrossed in a fight between Linc and some bad guy over Julie that he didn't see me.

I flicked on the overhead light, and took two steps into the room, making certain to train the gun on him. The light was thin, but it startled him. I was prepared for it, and still blinked as my eyes adjusted.

I stopped in front of the television and turned it up. The dialogue and the music forced me to shout. "Clyde Voss?"

He sat up, the recliner moving with him. Even if he didn't answer me, I knew this was the guy. His face was black-and-blue, and several cuts covered his hairline. Jimmy had injured him badly.

"Who wants to know?" he asked, his voice barely audible over the television. He reached slowly toward the drawer in a nearby table.

"If you have a gun in there, you leave it," I said. "Or I'll shoot you where you sit."

He was tall, but not muscular. He had a blanket around his waist, and his eyes were red from the dope.

"Who are you?" he asked, and it would have sounded tough if his voice hadn't shaken.

"I'm the guy with your wallet," I said. "You dropped it when you ran away from that little girl you were raping this afternoon."

He held up his hands. "I could use it back," he said as if we were in a negotiation. We weren't.

He didn't know that yet.

"I'm sure you could," I said. "There was damn near two hundred dollars in it."

"You can keep that," he said a bit too fast.

"As what?" I asked. "Payment for the girl you brutalized?"

"Whatever you want to call it," he said. "I got some pot here. We could share."

He wasn't getting it.

"How kind of you," I said. "Did you offer that little girl some pot?"

"You know her?" he asked, finally catching a clue.

"Yeah," I said.

"Well, you know she's not going to have anything to do with me. It's over with that one. It's really not a big deal."

The music continued behind me, the pulsing beat making my heart race. "Really?" I asked. "Not a big deal."

"No, I mean, these things happen, and sometimes they don't work out. She wasn't right for us."

The "us" stopped me. "Us?"

"You know," he said. "I don't do this for fun."

Then he grinned. The grin made my finger twitch. Only my brain stopped that finger from pressing the trigger right then.

"Well," he said, "maybe I have a little fun."

The rage I'd been holding back rose. I took a deep breath, forcing myself to tamp it back.

"Do your employers know that?" I asked.

He shrugged, that idiotic grin remaining. "They don't care. They just want the girls in the right shape."

"And that is?"

"Pliable, if you know what I mean."

"Tell me," I said.

His grin faded just a bit. He swallowed visibly. "I...um...after, I give them something for the pain. Then I pass them along to the right guy."

"You carry an unconscious girl from that hotel?"

"Noo," he said, as if I were stupid. "I move her to a back room. They take care of her there. Keep her until she's ready to work."

My stomach turned slowly. Whether it was his words or the stench or both, I did not know.

"How long does that take?" I asked.

He shrugged. "Days. A week. Depends on the girl. They all come around. I get to test them later. They have experience then. They're not so tight. They don't fight either. Which is too bad. The best ones fight at first, and that makes it easier—"

My gun went off. The report echoed in the small space. Clyde Voss's face was gone, a bloody mess in its place. The room smelled of gunpowder, blood, and that ever-present marijuana. The cigarette had fallen on his blanket and was burning a hole through it.

My hand shook. Dammit. I should have kept him talking. I needed to know more.

I couldn't know more.

I couldn't have listened to him any longer.

I flicked the safety back on and slipped the gun into my pocket. Then I clicked off the overhead light, and made myself walk down the hall.

People noticed running black men. Even black people noticed running black men. Even in neighborhoods like this where no one saw anything ever. People noticed.

I tapped the scarf, glad I had it on. I made it to the door, opened it, peered out to see if neighbors were responding to the gunshot.

So far, no one had come down the stairs.

I let myself out, pushed the latch lock, and closed the door.

Then I walked up the steps to that trail of icy footprints, and retraced my steps, reminding myself with every footfall to move deliberately, as if I belonged.

No lights had come on. In fact, some lights had turned off. The windows across the street appeared empty. So far as I could tell, no one watched me.

The gun felt heavy in my coat pocket.

I thought I'd feel better. But the trembling had worked through me. And one word kept echoing in my head.

Us.

He had said *us.*

9

I drove the van out of the neighborhood as slowly as I had arrived. I didn't want to fishtail, I didn't want to squeal my tires. I did have the presence of mind to make a U-turn so that I wouldn't drive underneath the only working streetlight.

I turned left and kept driving, following a different route than I had used before I arrived. It took me a moment to realize I was heading toward the Starlite.

At the first opportunity, I pulled over. A church parking lot. Convenient. I didn't want to think about the irony.

Instead, I turned off the car and the headlights. I locked the doors, leaned my head back, and let myself shiver for a few moments. I couldn't go to the Starlite. Not alone. Not without doing building recon.

Not in this mood.

I had planned to ask Voss more questions. I wanted to find out everything he knew. Then I planned to hurt him, hurt him bad enough that he wouldn't go after kids again.

But I had thought he worked alone.

And what he said...

What he said about Lacey...

What he said…

I was shaking my head, my face warm, my scarf soggy from my breath. At least I hoped it was from my breath. I tugged the scarf down and wiped at my face.

I wasn't done. I still had some things to do before I could go home. And those things did not include a stupid vigilante attack on the Starlite, no matter how angry I was.

Jimmy needed me. An assault on the Starlite tonight, as unpredictable as I was, would probably keep me from Jimmy for the rest of his life.

Besides, I had gotten Lacey's attacker. The asshole got what he deserved. I wouldn't let myself regret killing him. Althea had wanted him stopped. So did I.

So, I would wager, did Lacey.

I could tell her with a clean conscience that he wouldn't ever hurt her again. He wouldn't ever hurt *anyone* again.

That stopped my shaking. I was getting cold. I needed to leave, but before I did, I pulled the gun out of my pocket and removed the magazine. I put it in the glove box. Then I peeled off my scarf and set it on the seat beside me. I put the gun on the scarf and folded the scarf. I removed Voss's wallet from my other pocket and used my gloves to wipe the thing off as carefully as I could. I removed the $200 and put it in my pocket.

Then I set the wallet beside the scarf.

For a moment, I debated dropping the $200 into the church's donation box inside. But someone would remember a donation that large on a night like this. They might even remember me. Plus, I didn't want to leave the gun unattended in my van.

I took a deep breath, feeling a little calmer, and turned the key in the ignition. The van's engine roared loudly. I turned on the lights, put the van in reverse, backed out of the parking space, then shifted the van into drive, left the parking lot, and turned north.

The best thing I could do was leave the neighborhood. I drove slowly, one of the few vehicles on the icy streets, and headed toward the Loop.

In rush hour, this drive could take anywhere from thirty minutes to an hour. At the moment, my van was one of the few vehicles on the street. Still, I made sure I didn't speed or make any driving errors.

I was very conscious of that gun beside me on the seat. And the wallet. I could do something about the wallet.

As I approached a dark and deserted section of Canal Street at the very edge of the South Loop, I rolled down my window. The icy air hit my face with the force of a blizzard.

With my gloved right hand, I grabbed the wallet. I shifted it to my left hand and draped my arm outside the window. Even with the gloves and thick coat, the cold bit my skin. My eyes teared up from the wind. I reached a section of neighborhood bulldozed by the city last summer, and flicked my hand, tossing the wallet on an unshoveled pile of snow. Then I brought my arm inside, rolled up the window, and kept driving as if nothing had happened.

Ahead of me, Chicago's downtown rose like a bad memory. I had worked down here when I first moved to the city, before I realized I wasn't cut out to work for someone else.

No one stood on the streets and, except for the Chicago Civic Center and the hotels on Michigan, most of the lights were off.

Good.

I took Wacker Drive and pulled into the parking lot closest to the LaSalle Street Bridge. It was the only bridge that I knew where the attendant in the bridge tender houses couldn't see all parts clearly.

I loved the LaSalle Street Bridge. It was old and elegant, with rust-colored trusses, and a protected sidewalk. The trusses interested me the most, because they were accessible. I could stand between them and remain relatively unseen from drivers passing by.

I kept the gun wrapped in the scarf, then changed my mind. I didn't want anyone to see me carrying anything onto the bridge. I unwrapped the gun, slipped it into my pocket, and silently cursed myself.

I wasn't thinking as clearly as I needed to be. My own fault, really. I had let Lacey's assault, her injuries, and her attacker get to me. I needed to reclaim a sense of — well, not calm, exactly, because calm felt beyond me. But a sense of myself, a sense of caution, a sense of the street smarts that had helped me survive for more than forty years.

I let myself out of the van, and stared for a moment at the huge bridge rising before me. This damn city and its corruption. All around me was evidence of the way Chicago worked.

I had no idea who built this bridge. I knew only that it was a year or so older than I was, and had probably been put together with a combination of the graft and greatness that were Chicago's hallmarks. The bridge was beautifully designed. And depending on how deep the graft went when the thing was built, it was either structurally perfect or structurally flawed.

The whole city was like that. If I had been a white man and Lacey had been my niece, I would have been able to call the Chicago police and let them handle this. They might not have arrested Voss. They might have scared him out of town, maybe even killed him. But they would have resolved this.

If I were a white man with the right connections. And those connections weren't necessarily the connections that seemed logical. It wouldn't matter if I had money. What I needed was clout. And right now, the clout in this city all resided with Mayor Richard J. Daley. If you didn't have South of the Yard connections or if you weren't valuable to him in some political way, then the cops might've shrugged off the news of a white girl's rape no matter what.

Until a few years ago, according to Franklin, there were a few black politicians with access to Daley and the right kind of clout. But not anymore.

It was up to us to take care of our own, just like it had been in Memphis. And in Atlanta. And anywhere else, south of the Mason-Dixon line.

The cold hadn't numbed me. In fact, it had awakened all of my senses. I kept my hands out of my pockets and walked along the well-shoveled sidewalk.

Once I started up to the bridge, the sidewalk wasn't as clean. Apparently no one expected a sane person to walk across this bridge in the winter. But I wasn't quite sane at the moment.

Besides, dozens, maybe hundreds of people had gone before me. The snow was packed and icy, not unshoveled like it had been in Voss's neighborhood, just not shoveled as often.

I had to pick my way up the slight incline.

The breeze over the Chicago River felt like the same strong wind I had gotten through my open van window. Only this time, it brought the distinctive odor of the river: damp, mildewy, and slightly foul. The Chicago River was one of the most polluted rivers in America. The city dyed the water green on St. Patrick's Day, but the joke was that the dye was unnecessary. Some days the river actually was multicolored with all of the oil slicks covering the water's surface.

I reached the top of the bridge next to the ornate white bridge-tender's house, and stood in the shelter of one of the gigantic metal trusses. I had forgotten about the streetlights. They hovered over the sidewalk at regular intervals, the bulk of their light hitting pedestrians, not the road itself.

Still, no car had gone by in the entire time I had walked up here. I doubted many would drive by as I finished my business.

I glanced at the river below. Ice had gathered near the edges, but the water still flowed freely. For some reason, this stupid river rarely froze. I thought it was the pollution, but Jimmy had learned in school that it had something to do with Lake Michigan. Maybe both explanations were correct.

If I didn't want to toss the gun, if I just wanted to drop it, I would have to go near the center of the bridge. But the metal trusses weren't as high there, and I wouldn't be able to blend in as easily.Still, there were pockets of darkness between the streetlights, and I headed toward one of those.

My heart was pounding. My mouth was dry from the cold and my eyes stung. My nose had gone numb a while ago. I walked a few yards past the bridge-tender's house. The trusses loomed to my right. To my left, an ornate chest-high railing overlooked the river. I glanced over my shoulder and saw no one on either side of me. No one in the bridge-tender's house, no one on the road, no one walking toward me.

I reached into my right pocket, grabbed the gun, and held it over the river. Then I let go.

The gun fell straight down, not pinwheeling like I expected. For a moment, I thought it would land on one of the ice flows, but it didn't. It fell between them, the splash loud in the silence of this cold Chicago night.

I leaned for just a moment longer. Problem solved. Easier than I expected, really. Even if someone saw me entering Voss's apartment, there would be no way to tie me to the man's death. There wouldn't even be any way to prove I knew him.

The wallet was gone. Jimmy was the only other person who knew I had had it. I wasn't even sure if Jimmy had looked at Voss's name, or if he remembered it.

I took a deep breath of the frigid air, felt it slide, ice-cold, through my mouth, neck, and into my lungs.

Now Jimmy and Keith were safe too. Voss could have gone after them tomorrow, searching for the little kids who had beat him up with a screwdriver, deciding to teach them a lesson. No lesson to learn, nothing to repair, nothing to fear.

Yet my heart kept pounding as if I had been in some kind of race.

Maybe I had been.

A mental race.

A race for Lacey's life.

A race for her future.

And I wasn't sure if we'd won that one yet or not.

10

I got home while *Marcus Welby, M.D.* was still on, not that anyone was watching it in my apartment, even though the TV blared. The window was open wide. We were heating the entire neighborhood and entertaining it as well.

No one was in the living room. I pushed the door closed, and locked it. I walked to the television, and started when I saw black faces. Apparently, unbelievably wise Marcus Welby was talking to a black neurosurgeon about a boy who'd been beaten in a riot. That hit too close to home. I turned the TV down, but I didn't turn it off in case someone was watching. The apartment was actually cool. I closed the window. Now that I was inside, I realized I smelled faintly of marijuana. I pulled off my coat, and looked at the bloodstains running down the front.

It was ruined. So were my pants. My shoes had a white layer of salt and water along the edges. Ruined as well.

I kicked them off and tossed them under the coat tree. The remains of a pizza sat on top of the stove, along with some Coke. It looked like no one had eaten much.

I hadn't been gone as long as I thought. I would have thought it was midnight, given how long this evening felt.

The light was on in Jimmy's room. I walked down the hall. Marvella sat in a chair beside his bed, an open book on her lap. Jimmy was asleep, his arms on top of the thick blanket he preferred during the winter.

I walked inside the room, deliberately stepping on a creaky spot in the floor. Marvella started, then put a finger to her lips. She looked exhausted.

She put a bookmark in the book, closed it, and set the book on the end table. I reached around her and turned on a nightlight that we hadn't used in months. I hated using it now, but the fact that Jimmy had fallen asleep with the lights on was a red flag for me: We might have troubled days ahead.

I didn't know why that surprised me. Given all that had happened today, troubled days were the least of my worries.

Marvella's gaze went over me, taking in the mess, and probably a lot more. She nodded toward the hallway.

We left the room. I shut off the overhead light, but peered in to make sure that didn't wake Jimmy. It didn't.

I pulled the door halfway closed.

"Why don't you change?" Marvella said. "I'll clean the kitchen and warm up the pizza."

I didn't want pizza. I didn't want anything. But I knew I had to eat.

I thanked her, and went into my room, grabbed some comfortable clothes, and took them to the bathroom. I ran the shower on scald and climbed in.

I would have to throw away my clothes, probably tonight. And my shoes. They were one of three pairs that I owned. I would need to replace them, my coat, my scarf, and my backup gun. Today had been extremely expensive.

If I hadn't wanted to work before, I certainly had to now.

I stood under the water, wishing it could burn away the day. The evening, really. That word. *Us.* I hated it.

I wasn't done, and I knew it.

I dried off, got dressed, and put my clothes in the paper bag we had as a garbage can liner in the bathroom. I closed up the bag and carried it to the front door. There I added my shoes. I slipped my hand into the pocket of my coat, removed the $200 and my guitar pick, then grabbed the coat and tossed it in the bag as well.

"You're getting rid of all of that?" Marvella asked.

I started even though I knew she was there. "Lacey bled all over it," I said. "It's just better this way."

Marvella nodded, then pulled some glasses from the cupboard.

I grabbed my keys and went downstairs in my slippers. I stepped outside into the cold, feeling it leach away the shower's warmth. I unlocked the van, and tucked the paper bag in the back. I was going throw all of that stuff away in a different part of town just as a precaution. I didn't like leaving it in the van overnight, but I didn't see much of a choice.

I hurried back to the apartment, shivering with cold.

"I didn't know you were going out," Marvella said. "I could have done that for you and taken out some of the kitchen garbage as well."

I shook my head. "I needed to do it."

She nodded, then came over to me, a highball glass in one hand. She had poured three fingers of Scotch. I resisted the urge to down it in one gulp.

"Long day," she said.

You have no idea, I thought. But I said, "How's Lacey?"

"She wasn't awake when we left. I convinced Jimmy to come home. He was getting tired." Marvella had poured herself a glass as well. She sipped it, and leaned against the couch. She had deep circles under her eyes.

"I take it Althea and Franklin stayed with her?"

"They were arguing with the hospital staff when I left," Marvella said. "The staff wanted them gone at the end of visiting hours, but Althea wanted family near Lacey when she woke up. I think Althea probably won."

"She's handling this better than I thought she would," I said.

Marvella nodded grimly. "Franklin's the problem."

I frowned at her.

She shrugged and turned her back on me. "Some pizza?"

Pizza and Scotch. The perfect capper to a horrible day. "Why not?"

She set two slices on a plate in my usual spot at the table. I hadn't realized she had visited enough to know where my usual spot was.

I sat down. My entire body ached, and if I hadn't had such a rough day, I would have thought I was coming down with the flu.

I took a sip of the Scotch. It burned as it went down my throat. I knew the Scotch couldn't actually warm me, but it sure felt like it did.

"What's the problem with Franklin?" I asked, although I had a hunch I knew.

"He thinks it's all Lacey's fault. The way she dressed, the fact that she had gone boy-crazy. The makeup. He seemed to believe that if she had just followed his instructions, she would have been fine."

"Would she?" I asked softly.

Marvella glared at me. I hadn't seen her look that fierce in almost a year. "Do you think that?"

I let out a small sigh. "Something made that creep go after Lacey instead of the other thirteen-year-old girls in that school."

"How do you know it was instead of?" Marvella asked.

The question made me freeze. I didn't know that. I didn't know it at all.

"Do you have information I don't?" I asked.

She shook her head and sat across from me. She set her glass on the table with a thunk.

"I just think it's no coincidence that this scum was working out of a hotel near the school." She swirled the glass between her palms. "He's done this before."

He's. Present tense. She had no idea what I did. She hadn't asked either. Not that I would have told her.

"How do you know that?" I asked.

She shrugged. "He knew what he was doing. It was easy for him. He had a system. People with systems perfect those systems over time. I don't know if he worked the school before, but Lacey wasn't his first victim."

His voice echoed in my head: *They just want the girls in the right shape.* They. Girls.

He added with a grin: *Maybe I have a little fun.*

"Bill?" Marvella put her hand on mine. I jumped. She frowned. "You okay?'

"Long day." I slipped my hand away from hers. Then I took the tumbler of Scotch and downed it.

Marvella watched with concern. She hadn't seen me drink like that before. I pushed the glass aside.

She got up and grabbed the bottle.

I welcomed it.

"What happens to Lacey?" I asked as I poured myself another.

Marvella made a sound that was both sad and sympathetic at the same time. "It's up to her now."

"What does that mean?" I asked.

"I've already talked to Althea. There's a group of younger women I know, survivors. They'll help her. If she lets them."

I hadn't had a drink from the new glass yet. My stomach clenched. "And if she doesn't?"

Marvella shook her head. "It's her first sexual experience, Bill. It could be—"

"It wasn't sexual," I said. "He attacked her."

Marvella gave me a withering look. "According to Jimmy, she spent time with this creep. Lunches, him treating her like gold. Telling her she's pretty, telling her she can be a model. In the end, she got hurt, but in the beginning, she thought he was her Prince Charming."

"Some fucking prince," I said, thinking of that smelly basement apartment.

"She's thirteen," Marvella said. "She has no experience with men. The first one she trusted, the first one she was probably attracted to, beat her, raped her, and might've done worse if her cousin and her brother hadn't saved her. How do you think that'll resonate?"

There was no answer to that, not one I wanted to think about anyway. I leaned my head to one side and ran my fingers over my forehead. I wasn't tired, but I was weary. Bone weary.

"She's going to need her family," Marvella said. "The group I'm taking her to will help, but she's going to need a lot of understanding. You're going to have to talk with her father."

"And say what?" I was out of my depth here.

"Tell him to use a lot of kindness. She's going to need the men in her life as much if not more than the women. Judgmental angry men won't help."

Judgmental. Angry. Could've described me at that moment.

"What are we supposed to be, Marvella?" I asked, not looking at her.

"With Lacey? Kindness itself. I don't care what you do to the animal who hurt her."

Marvella probably did care. She probably expected me to hurt the bastard, to make him stop. I doubted she expected me to kill him.

Although she did know what I did to a man who had attacked her cousin Valentina. Or maybe Marvella just thought she knew.

"You need to eat something," she said, nodding toward the pizza. "You can't just sit here and drink."

If I were alone, I could. If I didn't have Jimmy to watch over, and a wealth of obligations. Back in Memphis, on my own, in my own house, I could have spent the next three days drinking.

I tilted my head back. I hadn't let memories of Memphis slip in—not favorable memories anyway—for nearly two years.

I slid the plate toward me and grabbed a slice. The pizza was still warm. Marvella had probably heated it too much in the oven. I took a bite. Sure enough, the crust was hard and the tomato sauce had burned against it.

I didn't care. I made myself finish.

Then I picked up the Scotch and poured it back into the bottle.

"Thank you for taking care of Jimmy," I said. "I can't tell you how much I appreciate it."

She stood. She knew she was being dismissed. "He's an amazing kid."

"I know," I said.

"He tried not to have a reaction tonight, but he didn't want to go to sleep until you got home."

"I understand," I said, and I did. He was worried for me. He knew I had gone after the man who hurt Lacey, a man who had looked large and threatening to nearly twelve-year-old Jimmy.

"He'll probably check on you if he wakes up during the night," she said.

She had noticed my startled reactions. She clearly didn't want me to overreact if Jimmy startled me as well.

"I know," I said.

"It sounds like he had a hell of a childhood," she said.

I frowned at her. "He told you about it?"

"He said his mother was a prostitute. Then he got all upset that he had mentioned it. What's that about, Bill?"

I swallowed, decided half the truth was better than the whole truth. "I didn't know about Jimmy for the first seven or eight years of his life."

"Oh," she said, and she looked vaguely disappointed. As if I had slept with a prostitute. Or worse, impregnated a woman and didn't take care of her, so she had to become a prostitute.

I capped the bottle and returned it to the top shelf.

"There's more to the story, isn't there, Bill?" Marvella asked. I couldn't tell with my back to her: Was there a bit of a pleading tone in her voice?

"There always is," I said as I turned around. "You know that. There always is."

11

Marvella left shortly afterward. She wanted to help with the dishes. I told her she had done enough. I almost offered to pay her, but felt it wrong in light of our conversation.

I would go to her apartment in the morning and see how much I owed her for the pizza. Or see if I could figure out another way to compensate her for her time.

It just felt wrong on this night.

Everything felt wrong on this night.

I pulled the rest of the pizza out of the oven and shut it off. Then I put the pizza, uncovered, into the refrigerator. I got a glass of tap water and walked into the living room.

The local news was on. WLS and its stupid happy talk format did not match my mood. I stalked the television set and grabbed the dial, clicking away from Bill Frink's discussion of the upcoming Super Bowl. I went to NBC instead. I couldn't quite bear to shut off the television, and I knew I could stomach *The Tonight Show* better than I could handle the inanity on the other channels.

If I only could survive the newscasts.

Part of me worried that Voss's death would be on the local news and that I had already missed the coverage. Part of me knew that he wouldn't be found for days, maybe weeks. By then, he'd be an afterthought, and no one would connect today's incident with his killing.

I sank into the couch. WMAQ's sportscaster Johnny Morris was going on and on about the Viking's chances against the Chiefs on the weekend. Morris, who used to play for the Bears, acted as if he actually cared about this stuff. Maybe he did.

I closed my eyes, saw the flash of the gunshot, and opened them again. I swirled the water in my glass, and thought of the Scotch.

It wasn't an answer, but it felt like one.

In order to live here, I had to close my eyes to so much. The Blackstone Rangers gang operated right near that school. I had threatened them last year, and they actually took me seriously. They considered me too dangerous to take on, which made Jimmy and the Grimshaw children off limits.

I had thought that was enough.

I hadn't even looked at the Starlite. It hadn't even crossed my mind.

We drove the kids to school, walked them into the building, protected them coming and going.

I never expected them to go off on their own, like Lacey had. Even though I should have. When Jimmy warned me about her clothing, about her attitude, I thought it was inside the school itself, not in the schoolyard.

Not near that damn hotel.

How do you know it was instead of?

I had assumed. I was even assuming tonight. First, I figured that getting rid of Voss would solve most of the problem, figured he was operating alone or with a few friends out of the Starlite. Or maybe he had used the Starlite as an occasional base.

I'd been so furious, I hadn't been able to control my hand. I had shot Voss before I had asked the right questions.

Us.

Dammit.

I stood up as the familiar *Tonight Show* theme music started. I paced around the living room.

I would have to work. I needed the money, especially now. But I also needed to track this down. I had to balance it all.

And I had to figure out how to protect the kids better at school.

I understood Franklin's reaction. I wanted to take those kids and wrap them in tissue, hide them in a closet somewhere, and remove them when they were grown.

We had set up an after-school program to keep them off the streets during the workday. I was tempted to ask the after-school program's teacher, Mrs. Armitage, if she would work days as well, just teach the kids instead of sending them to school.

But there was the whole problem of accreditation, and money. It always came down to money.

And I knew, maybe better than most, if kids wanted to get into trouble, they could do it from a private program as easily as they could from a public one.

Besides, I didn't know who else was threatened. That entire school was next to the Starlite. There were the gangs, and now this threat. Or there had always been this threat.

It had just become visible to me.

I would have to talk with the principal, let him know about the problem, see if something could be done. I also needed to figure out what I could do.

I wanted that hotel gone, its sleazy clientele in jail, off the streets, away from the children.

I was going to scout the entire neighborhood and see what else lurked there.

Which was something I should have done a long time ago.

12

The phone rang, startling me out of a sound sleep. My neck ached and my left arm was asleep. Jimmy stirred against me.

We were on the couch, illuminated by static. The television was still on, but broadcasting nothing. I glanced over my shoulder at the clock in the kitchen. Five a.m. on the dot.

The phone rang again.

"Wha—?" Jimmy asked, rubbing his face.

I squinched away from him and eased him onto the couch. "Go back to sleep," I said. "I'll get this."

If the phone rang at 5 a.m., it couldn't be good.

I made my way to my office, staggering in the early morning darkness. Sleeping on the couch made my body ache.

I didn't remember Jimmy joining me, but he must have awoken in the middle of the night and come looking for me. He had clearly brought a blanket with him, because we had been covered up.

I reached the phone on my desk before whoever was on the line hung up.

"Yeah, hello," I said, not quite capable of automatic civility this early in the morning.

"I'm sorry, Smokey, I know it's early, but I waited as long as I could."

I blinked and rubbed my face before the voice clicked. It belonged to Franklin.

"Lacey?" I almost added *Is she all right?* but the answer to that question would be no, even if nothing happened overnight.

"I'm only peripherally calling about her. I couldn't sleep." He didn't sound tired. He sounded determined. "Listen, I wanted to let you know I'm driving the kids today."

I reached across the desk and turned on my desk lamp. The lighting from the window was poor in the middle of a summer afternoon. On a predawn January morning, this room was as dark as a tomb.

The pool of light revealed files I'd ignored for more than a month, and my 1969 desk blotter with December's calendar on top. The 1970 desk blotter was beneath, unopened. I truly hadn't been in this room except to grab something fast for weeks.

"It's my turn, isn't it?" I asked. I had driven the kids two days before. We switched days.

"I'm talking to the principal," Franklin said. "He needs to know about the Starlite. He needs to know how dangerous it is."

We had come to the same conclusion overnight, but now I had to ask him the same question I'd been asking myself. "What do you want him to do about it? Lock the kids inside the school?"

"One step at a time, Smokey," Franklin said, sounding like the man I used to know. "The principal has to know there's a problem before finding a solution. I figure he's going to have to deal with the school board and the zoning committee on this one. Which reminds me—"

He broke off. I heard a voice behind him, then rustling.

"Smokey, it's Althea." She sounded wide awake as well. "I just need to know: Is it safe to send my babies to school this morning?"

I had no idea how to answer that. "Um—"

"We talked about something last night," she said. "I'm worried about Keith. Do I need to be?"

"Oh." I finally understood. "Yes, it's okay to send him to school. He and Jimmy are in no danger today. No one will come after them for that beating yesterday."

"You're certain?" Althea asked.

"Yes," I said.

"And what can I tell Lacey?" She sounded so prim. Amazing how a woman could sound so prim and so fierce at the same time.

"Tell her that man won't harm her again."

"You can guarantee it?"

"I can." I was awake now, even though my eyes were still gummy.

"Thank you," Althea said, and the phone rustled as she handed it back to Franklin.

"What did you do?" he asked.

"You had something else to tell me," I said, not willing to answer his question at all.

"Oh, yes." His response showed how tired he was. Normally, I couldn't have distracted him that easily. "I was wondering if you would set up a meeting with me and Laura Hathaway."

I frowned. I hadn't expected that. Franklin and Laura knew each other, but they weren't close. Laura had helped Franklin and Althea move to the house they were currently in by lowering the rent and not charging a deposit, but she hadn't really interacted with them much since then.

"What do you want to talk with Laura about?" I asked, hoping I didn't sound as suspicious as I felt. Franklin had been up all night, angry and stewing. He might have come up with something that wouldn't be good for anyone.

"I figure with her work at Sturdy Investments, she might have some sway with the zoning commission," he said.

I let out a small laugh. "Not if her recent battles are any indication." She had been talking all winter about going to court over a zoning problem near Pullman.

"Still," Franklin said, "she can tell me about the personalities, who to talk to, maybe help me with the politics of all of this."

I frowned. Franklin was pretty savvy about Chicago politics all on his own, particularly the politics of the South Side. "Is that all you want to talk with her about?"

"No," he said, and then he paused. "Jimmy said—a while back, he said that—you know he wants to go to Yale."

71

"Yes," I said.

I had taken him to Yale over the summer while I was on a case that had brought us both to the East Coast. I had hated the snobbish attitudes of Yale. Jimmy had seen castles where I saw exclusion. He had focused with an incredible intensity on getting into Yale. He had redoubled his efforts at school ever since then, and I hadn't discouraged him in the least. If, six years from now, he still wanted to go to the Ivy League, I would do everything I could to pay for that education.

"He said that Laura Hathaway had offered to pay for his private school tuition. He also said you turned her down."

I had, but that was before the Yale discussion. It was last year, when we had first moved here. When I helped Franklin start the after-school program.

I almost corrected him, and then decided it didn't matter. I needed to hear him out.

"I've been thinking about Lacey. She can't go back to that school." And now Franklin's voice shook. "She needs a new start where no one knows what happened."

"No one knows now, Franklin," I said gently. "Just the family, and we're not going to say anything."

"I need to tell the principal," he said, and in his voice I could hear echoes of a conversation he'd had all night with Althea.

"Why don't you let me talk to him?" I said. "He'll understand—"

"No," Franklin said. "No offense, Smokey, but I have some clout in this community. He'll listen to me."

I sighed. Franklin was right. Besides, he was talking about a legal battle. He wasn't the kind of man who had stomach for the battles I fought, and I often didn't have the patience for the battles he fought.

"Okay," I said, not wanting to argue with him. "You want Laura to help you find the right school?"

"Yeah." But there was something else in his tone, something he wasn't telling me. "And maybe—do you think—she'd be willing to make a loan? Just something short term? I don't take charity."

"I know that," I said. "Do you want me to talk with her?"

"I need to do this," Franklin said. "But if you wouldn't mind feeling her out on this...?"

"I don't mind," I said. I had to talk with her anyway. I didn't want Jimmy to tell her what had happened last night before I did.

"Thank you," Franklin said.

"You want me to pick the kids up?" I asked. "You'll probably want to be at the hospital."

Franklin let out a small sigh. "I don't know what I want. Althea thinks I'm not going to help Lacey, that I'll make things worse. But god-damn it, Smokey, she's my little girl."

"I know," I said.

"And I can't fix this," he said.

"I know that too," I said. "We just have to get through it. All of us. Together."

"Easy for you to say," Franklin snapped. "You have a boy. I don't want to let my girls out of the house. Althea's making me. She says we need to have a normal day."

"The other kids—what did you tell them?" I asked.

"That some guy hurt Lacey and Jimmy and Keith stopped him. We didn't say anything else. Keith's not supposed to say much more than that. I don't know if he will. Jonathan's pretty suspicious, and pretty mad they didn't tell him."

Jonathan was Lacey's older brother.

"Yeah," I said, because I didn't know what else to add.

"I don't know how we're going to have a normal day," Franklin was saying. "I don't think we'll have a normal day ever again."

He would be surprised at how normal crept up, even after extraordinary events. But I didn't tell him that. I couldn't.

"You didn't answer me," I said gently. "Let me pick them up from school."

"Yeah, sure," he said. "You get them home safely, though."

"I will," I said. "I promise."

13

I almost picked up the phone to call Laura, then realized how early it was. Laura liked to sleep until the very last minute, and hated being awakened for any reason.

In December, we had agreed not to see each other during the week unless it was a special occasion. Laura was running a major company, and I often worked odd hours. We tried to spend at least one weekend day together, but even that was hard. Laura had a conference all this weekend, and wasn't even sure if she could get away for Jimmy's birthday party.

Which I had forgotten until now. I suspected the Grimshaws wouldn't be in a party mood this weekend. Jimmy's birthday was on the 15th, so we could postpone the party one week, and maybe not make it a surprise.

I went through my morning routine quietly so that I didn't wake Jimmy. He still had fifteen minutes to sleep and considering how restless he had clearly been the night before, I figured he needed it.

For once, I had time to make us a real breakfast. I even had eggs and bacon and bread so that the idea of a real breakfast wasn't a wish, it was something I could actually do.

Bacon was sizzling when Jimmy finally woke up. As he staggered into the kitchen, the television—which I had forgotten—sprang to life.

A familiar male voice intoned, "Good morning. This is WMAQ-TV Channel 5 NBC Television in Chicago…"

"Want me to shut it off?" Jimmy asked, rubbing his fist over his eyes.

I should have had the radio on, but we were already past the local on-the-hour news.

"No, that's all right," I said. "Let's leave it on for now."

I usually didn't watch morning television, but I wanted to see if anyone had reported finding Voss's body.

Jimmy meandered down the hall, his slippers scuffing against the floor. Like Laura, he woke up slowly. He would go through his routine relatively quickly though, especially since he knew bacon awaited him.

When WMAQ finished its sign-on, Sister Rosemary Connelly started a meditation. I almost shut the television off right there, but she was done before I could hurry across the room.

By the time the health report began, Jimmy was back, wearing a sweater Laura had given him for Christmas, new pants he had professed to hate when we bought them, and boots that the Grimshaws had given him. The clothes were much more suited toward fighting than the clothes he had worn the day before.

Which reminded me: I needed to check Jimmy's clothes for bloodstains as well. At least I could wash his. I didn't dare keep mine in case evidence of my encounter with Voss was on them.

"You got back late," Jimmy said.

"*Marcus Welby* was still on," I said.

He shrugged. "We didn't really watch nothing. Marvella wanted to talk."

I handed him a plate loaded with scrambled eggs, bacon, and toast. He grabbed a glass of already-poured orange juice and sat at the table.

"She said you told her about your mom." I hoped that didn't sound accusatory. I was about to apologize when Jimmy talked over me.

"I didn't—it was an accident, Smoke. I forgot she didn't know."

"We can't forget," I said. "And now we have one more thing to add to our lists of don't-talk-abouts. We can't talk about exactly what happened to Lacey. We're just going to tell people that she got hurt, okay?"

He hunched over his food. He had been shoveling it in, but he paused for a moment. I knew why. We had too many secrets and I hated adding another.

"Can I tell Laura?" he asked after a minute.

"I'm going to tell her," I said. "You can talk to her about it though."

"Okay." He went back to eating and not looking at me.

"But you can't talk about it with anyone else who doesn't already know. Just Keith, his parents, and Marvella. Okay?"

"And you."

"And me." I brought my plate to the table. It felt weird to have the television on, almost like we had another guest in the room.

Jimmy finally looked at me. He had an orange juice mustache, which made me smile. The smile faded when he spoke.

"I gots worried. You didn't come back. That guy, he hurt you?"

"No," I said truthfully. "He didn't lay a finger on me."

"You found him, though, right?"

"Yes," I said.

"You gonna tell me what happened?" Jimmy asked.

"No," I said.

He nodded, as if he had expected that. "But he's not gonna do nothing to nobody anymore, right?"

"He's not going to come near you or Keith or Lacey or the school ever again," I said.

"You sure?"

"Yes," I said.

He nodded. "Good," he said. "Thank you."

He sounded so adult, as if Voss had been his responsibility. I was about to say so, when the television announced that the next program would be in Living Color.

I held up a finger, then leaned back in my chair.

"Good morning, Chicagoland," one of the anchors said. I had no idea who he was. I never watched television this early. "More drama in the courtroom of Judge Julius Hoffman yesterday as Mayor Richard J. Daley testified in the Chicago Seven trial. The Chicago Teachers Union plans a strike if the city doesn't meet their demands by next Wednesday, and below zero temperatures will continue throughout the week. We'll have all this and more on *Today in Chicago*, right after these messages."

I let out a small sigh. Usually the television news liked to start out with the discovery of a dead body, even on the South Side.

"You listening for something special?" Jimmy asked. He knew me too well.

I got up and turned the television off. Then I flicked the radio on as I returned to my chair.

"For the next few days," I said, "I'll be picking you up and driving you to the after-school program."

"I thought you said the guy wasn't going to hurt us none," Jimmy said.

"He won't," I said. "I'm mostly doing this for Franklin. He'll take you to school this morning, by the way."

Jimmy used the last of his toast to sop up the bacon grease. "He's pretty upset, you know."

"We all are," I said.

Jimmy got up and put his plate in the sink. "When you got news about Lace, you'll tell me, right?"

"I promise," I said.

"Okay." He slipped out of the kitchen and headed for the bedroom.

I had half-expected him to ask for the day off school, and then I remembered what Franklin had said that morning. Jimmy had decided to become a scholar, and that required a commitment I didn't expect of a kid his age.

But then, I didn't expect a lot of things from a kid his age, things he had already done.

He was less upset than I expected as well. But chaos and turmoil were constants in his life, more than they'd been in mine, and he seemed to deal with them.

I wished I could do the same.

I finished the last of my breakfast, and listened closely to the radio news. Black stations covered the Panther inquest, even thought WMAQ didn't. But no mention of dead bodies anywhere.

I set my plate in the sink.

As soon as Jimmy left, my morning would start. And as usual, when I was on a case, it would start on the phone.

I leaned against the edge of the sink. A case. That was how I would look at this. I needed to figure out the answers to the two questions that had come up yesterday. I needed to know who the *us* was, and I needed to know if this had happened to other girls. I needed to know those answers fast.

14

When Franklin arrived, I walked Jimmy down to the car just to make sure Franklin was in good enough condition to drive the kids to school and speak to the principal. Franklin was gray from stress and lack of sleep but he looked coherent.

Mikie and Norene sat in the back, Mikie in her Girl Scout uniform and Norene wearing pink. She grinned at me through missing teeth, and waved. Keith sat between them looking protective, angry, and tired.

Jonathan seemed grim. It looked like he knew what happened as well.

"I promise," Franklin said as I leaned on his open car window. "I won't do anything stupid. I'll stay within the law."

He said that almost reverentially, not as a way of condemning me. I believed him. He was still taking night school classes to finish up a law degree that he desperately wanted. He believed it would bring more money to his family, and it probably would.

He wasn't going to jeopardize it. Althea wouldn't let him. She had probably talked to him all last night.

Of course, she had sent me to do the job her husband couldn't do. He probably hadn't even thought of it. Which was good. One of us needed to follow existing Chicago law, even if the police and city government didn't apply it in Bronzeville much.

"I'm going to stop in to see the principal just before school ends," I said. "It wouldn't hurt to hear complaints from two different parents. Besides, I'm driving the kids to the after-school program today."

"I'll make sure everyone gets there, Uncle Bill," Jonathan said fiercely.

He went to the nearby high school. He'd have to walk back to the kids' school in the cold, and he'd have to be on time.

Franklin glared, about to say something, but I spoke first.

"Tomorrow maybe," I said. "I want to find out a few things first. Let me be protective today, all right?"

Jonathan looked away.

Franklin patted me on the arm. "Thank you," he said.

Obviously he had been worried about that too.

Jimmy slid in beside Norene and pulled one of her pigtails, not hard, just a gentle tug. She stuck her tongue out at him.

My heart twisted. I was glad Franklin was driving the girls to school this morning. I wasn't certain I could have. Not and kept my temper with the principal.

"Keep me posted on Lacey, all right?" I asked quietly.

"Will do," Franklin said.

I backed away as he rolled up the window. Then I made my way to the sidewalk as they drove off.

I'd never quite felt like this before, terrified, and yet forcing myself to remain in place. I felt helpless. The kids had to go to school, and at the moment, the only school available was even more dangerous than I had realized.

I wanted those girls out of it. I wanted Jimmy out of it.

But I knew that they had to make their own way in the world eventually, and it would never be an easy path for any of us. No matter what Martin had said about kids being judged by the content of their character instead of the color of their skin, that was still a dream. Those kids had one strike against them just because of their skin color. Then they were relegated to schools in terrible neighborhoods.

If I could afford to move, I would. Laura had suggested that we list her apartment as Jimmy's home address. Schools near Lake Shore Drive were spectacular. I had thought it cheating before. I had also thought it charity.

I was rethinking those assumptions right now.

But for this week, I needed to send my brilliant adopted son to school. Not that the adoption was legal. I wasn't sure how to do that with the false names we were living under. I didn't dare use my old lawyer in Memphis, Shelby Bowler, on this, because I didn't want anyone to know where Jimmy Bailey was, let alone that he was still alive.

Jimmy had seen the man who murdered Martin, and it hadn't been James Earl Ray. I saved Jimmy from being forced into a Memphis cop car that day, a car I thought he might never get out of, and we had fled Memphis, vowing not to look back.

But I did have to take care of the legal niceties. If Jimmy was going to get into Yale, then we needed everything done properly well before that, just in case.

Maybe now was the time.

Maybe now was the time to reevaluate the way I was doing everything.

I was freezing. The car was long gone.

I turned around and went inside.

I had a lot of phone calls to make.

15

I called Laura first. I pulled the phone as close to the overheating radiator as I could, and left the window shut. I had caught a chill outside.

Laura picked up on the fifth ring. She sounded harried. When she realized it was me, she said, "I've only got a minute, Smokey."

I needed more than a minute to tell her about Lacey. "I have something important to tell you, and some questions to ask. Are you free for lunch?"

"I'm not free for anything." I could hear shuffling in the background. She was doing something else while she was talking to me. "In addition to a series of regular meetings I have to be at, I'm supposed to drop in at the Home Furnishings Show at the Merchandise Mart. There are people there I need to talk to. And then I'm supposed to meet with some professors in the University of Chicago's Center for Continuing Education. They're sponsoring that conference this weekend on urban housing and they want some of the building owners there. I'm pretty sure they're going to just smear us as slumlords, but I'm trying to keep an open mind. So, long story short, I'm not sure I have time for anything."

"It's important," I repeated.

She sighed. "Life-and-death important?"

It was last night. "Not quite that. But close, yes."

All the sound of shuffling stopped. "You heard my schedule, Smokey," she said. "I can't come down to the South Side this afternoon."

"What about your university meeting? I could find you on campus."

"They're coming here. If you and I have lunch, it'll have to be brief, and it'll have to be in the Loop. I know you've been avoiding it since the trial started, but I have no choice today."

I couldn't tell her that I'd been in the Loop the night before. Of course, the Chicago Seven trial had been closed for the day and none of those courageous national reporters had hung around.

"Do you know any place not frequented by the players in the trial?" I asked.

She gave a bitter laugh. "They spread out over the Loop like locusts. Maybe the Terminal Grill?"

I shuddered. "It's pretty rundown, Laura."

"The reporters and people you know will be in all the nice restaurants."

"How about a meal at your desk? I'll bring something good."

"That'll do," she said. "I've got 12:30 to 1:30 and I'm pretty inflexible about it."

"I'll be there," I said, and hung up. If I had to go to the Loop, then I needed to be visible for the shortest period of time. I could park nearby and head up to Laura's office, and be on the street for only a few minutes, as opposed to sitting in a restaurant, maybe attracting attention from someone I didn't even see.

Still, I didn't like going there. But I had no real choice. Both Jimmy and Franklin would talk to her as quickly as they could.

This afternoon was the only chance I had to speak to her first.

I carried the phone back to its end table, and then went into the kitchen. I poured myself some coffee. It wasn't even seven-thirty and I was already on my second cup. It was going to be a long day.

I brought the coffee into my office. I had left the desk lamp on after Franklin's call this morning. I took the old blotter and shoved it aside, then unwrapped 1970 from its cellophane.

It felt like the year was already half over and we hadn't been in it for a week. I tossed out the cellophane, then sat in the chair I had found at a yard sale. The chair, at least, felt familiar. I grabbed the coffee cup, set it on the old blotter because I didn't want to stain the new one on its first day, and dialed Sinkovich.

I had met Jack Sinkovich sixteen months ago when he was one of the undercover police officers keeping an eye on the protestors in Lincoln Park. Later that week, he beat up kids outside of Grant Park during the demonstrations at the 1968 Democratic National Convention.

Those demonstrations were at the heart of the Chicago Seven trial right now. The state claimed that the seven defendants had crossed state lines with the intent to start a riot. Sinkovich was one of a handful of cops who had been ordered by the department to attend, mostly as "protection" detail in case anything happened.

Sinkovich believed he was there so that any testimony he would be called to give would be tainted because he'd heard the entire case.

Since his behavior in Grant Park, Sinkovich had changed. That night disturbed him, and some interactions with me and, in particular, Jimmy, forced him to reconsider long-held beliefs. He defended a black family who moved into his neighborhood, prompting his wife to leave because she didn't know him anymore.

Sinkovich was one of the first people I had ever met who was actively trying to become someone else.

I had no idea if he would succeed, and that really wasn't my concern at the moment. My concern was this: Since the death of my only other contact on the force, I had to rely on Sinkovich for police department information.

Sinkovich answered the phone mid-ring. He didn't say hello. Instead, he said, "You know, Grimshaw, you're the only person who calls me before eight in the morning."

"Some day someone else will," I said, "and they'll ask you who this Grimshaw guy is."

"I'll say he's a pain in my rear end. Which, by the way, is wearing dress blues. I just put the galoshes over my most uncomfortable shoes, and I'm ready to head out the door, so unless this is important, you gotta talk to me tonight."

"I need your help, Jack," I said.

"Ain't it always the way?" he asked.

It wasn't always that way. When his wife left, I let him sleep on my couch. His friends had turned their back on him too, and the police department saw him as damaged goods.

But I wasn't going to say that right now, particularly when I was about to ask him for a favor.

"Look, it's come to my attention that the Starlite Hotel near Jimmy's school is a by-the-hour place. I was wondering who owns it and if this is a new trend or something else."

"'It's come to my attention?' You only talk fancy like that when you done something you don't want me to know." Sinkovich might've been difficult, but he wasn't dumb.

"You said you were in a hurry." I sipped my coffee. It was hot, and it started to warm me.

"I don't know nothing about the Starlite, I don't know which school is Jimmy's, and if I don't leave now, I'm gonna be late, and I don't need the hassle. You won't tell me if we're gonna partner up and as long as you don't say nothing about that, I gotta be a good boy at the station, or they'll fire my ass. I can't afford it, not with the divorce shit raining down. So, I'm outta here."

He'd been asking me to consider working with him in our own detective agency. I had been putting him off. He was afraid he would have nothing if he got fired from the force.

Still, I was going to let the "partner up" comment slide. "This is the address of Jimmy's school." I gave it to him. "Can you at least find out about the Starlite for me?"

"I'm gonna be sittin' on my ass all day listening to lawyers pretend they're fightin' for justice, and then there's that idiot judge. Yesterday, our fat slug of a mayor shows up and lies through his teeth about what he done. And we're supposed to work for the SOB! I gotta look real serious and professional and like none of this means nothing to me, and my face is starting to hurt, Bill."

"I understand," I said, wishing I could get him to stop.

"No, you don't. You wouldn't do it. You'd protest something or punch someone or something. Me, I gotta put up with it for my kid. And then you ask me to look into some hotel like I got all the time in the world—"

"It's for my kid," I said quietly.

That stopped him. Sinkovich thought the world of Jimmy.

"He get in trouble?"

"He might have," I said.

"With someone in a by-the-hour hotel?"

"Yeah," I said.

"Shit, that kid. What're you teaching him?"

"Before you judge, you need to hear the full story."

"Oh, yeah, like I got time. I don't leave now, I don't get a parking spot, and I have to use one of them cop parking signs you put on your dash which'll get me in even more hot water with the department. You say this is an emergency?"

I wouldn't put it like that, I nearly said, then stopped myself. It had been an emergency yesterday, and if Voss were still around, it might've been one today.

"It's pretty urgent," I said.

"Okay, I'll have something for you end of the day whenever the hell that is. I'll get in touch with you. Can I leave a message with the kid?"

"Only that you called. You can't tell him what it was about."

"Got it," Sinkovich said. "Pray for me and my ass. We're about to have a long day."

"Thanks, Jack," I said, but he had already hung up.

I ran a hand over my face. The fact that he hadn't heard of the Starlite meant nothing. More than three million people lived in the city of Chicago, more than 228 square miles, and the police force of ten thousand couldn't begin to know everything, even if it patrolled the South Side, which it mostly did not.

I knew all of that extremely well. I had learned all of the statistics so that I could keep myself calm when I got angry because I assumed someone should have known about some crime or another. Or some place like the Starlite.

Sinkovich would find out what he could from a desk in the precinct after his long day.

I needed to find out a few things as well. Early morning was probably the best time to do so.

I finished my coffee, shut off my desk lamp, and went to work.

16

I put on a sweater, some old pants, and a pair of thick socks. Then I grabbed a pair of tattered shoes. If I hadn't been so worried about blood spatter from yesterday, I would have kept the shoes I was going to toss out. I took an old scarf that I wore last year, and grabbed an old green parka of Franklin's that he had given me for my first winter here. The parka didn't fit well and it had lost some of its warmth, but it would do until I got a new coat of my own.

I grabbed a hat, my wallet, my pick, and my keys. Then I headed down to the van.

I slid in and looked in the back seat. The garbage bag was still there. I pulled it toward me and checked the interior. It didn't look like anyone had touched the clothes.

First, I needed to find a suitable dump site away from here. Then I had to go to the bank and get my backup gun from my safe-deposit box. After that, I would go to the Starlite for a little reconnaissance. I just wanted to see what the exterior would tell me.

I glanced at the clock on the dashboard. It was barely 8 a.m. The bank wouldn't open for an hour, and by nine, the Starlite might actually have some signs of life. I would be better off going there after I dumped the clothes.

But I didn't like going unarmed. I found that ironic, because two days ago I wouldn't have given my lack of a weapon much thought at all. Even with the Blackstone Rangers nearby, I had never felt the need to carry a gun.

I shouldn't feel the need now. I just wanted to walk the outside and see what I could learn from the exterior of the Starlite. Technically, I wouldn't need a gun for that.

And, given my mood of the last twenty-four hours, it was probably better if I didn't have one.

I took the usual route to the school. Halfway there, I made a slight detour into an alley behind two bars and a seedy restaurant. Nine garbage cans sat on top of an iced-over snowdrift. I got out, opened one of the garbage cans, and winced at the stench rising from it. Broken-down boxes, the scraped remains of plates, and empty liquor bottles filled half of the can.

I dropped the bag on top and closed the lid, resisting the urge to wipe at my nose.

Then I got back into the van and drove to the end of the alley. If anyone had seen me, they probably wouldn't remember me. And even if someone found the clothes, no one would connect them to Voss's death, or to me.

I resumed the route to school. The streets in this neighborhood were relatively empty at this time of day. I passed only a few cars.

I parked a block north of the Starlite, at the end of the block. I didn't go near the school at all. I wasn't sure what I was looking for. I didn't even know it if I saw it.

But I wanted to look at the Starlite and the rest of the block closely. I was angry that I hadn't done that before. Maybe if I had seen exactly what was here, I would have made some different choices.

Or maybe I would have taken Jimmy more seriously when he talked about Lacey.

Although I doubted that. No matter how much I tried to rewrite history in my own mind, I couldn't do it. I had screwed up. I hadn't listened. And now Lacey was paying the price.

I sighed, grabbed a stocking cap, and pulled it over my head. Then I wrapped the scarf over my mouth and nose like a good Chicagoan did in below-zero temperatures. I tugged the edges of my gloves under my sleeves, then got out of the van.

Even with those precautions, the cold seeped in. The air felt brittle, and the slightest sound echoed. There was no wind. The sun had been up less than an hour, and it still hadn't crept over some of the buildings.

Not that it would give much light when it did. At least the streetlights were off.

I had been right: This street was quiet at this time of day.

Maybe that was one of the reasons it hadn't worried me. I drove here only in the very early mornings, and sometimes in the middle of the afternoon. Streets like this didn't become fully active until dark.

I shoved my gloved hands into the pockets of the parka and walked to the sidewalk. It had been shoveled sometime in the not-so-distant past, but not well. Ice had formed over what had been a layer of slush, freezing dozens of footprints into place.

Some of those prints were child-sized, but most were men's shoes. There were some high-heel prints—the telltale triangle followed a few inches later by a tiny dot in the snow. Those clearly did not come from boots, even dressy boots.

In a neighborhood like this, without a high-class restaurant or a nightclub, those high-heel prints should have been a clue. But I wasn't sure I had ever walked on this part of the street. Not even when I had my encounter with the Blackstone Rangers months ago. All of my interactions with this neighborhood had occurred near the school.

My feet crunched on the ice. No one had sanded or salted this walk, either. The businesses at the end of this street—two bars and what appeared to be a pawn shop—had shoveled off their stoops, but little else. They looked closed. The pawn shop might have been abandoned. I couldn't tell without going up to the window, which was frosted over.

I walked toward the Starlite. It dominated the far side of the block. The hotel rose seven stories and had probably been impressive in its day. Its day was at least forty years ago. The stonework had gaps and the neon sign running down the north side of the building looked like it had been attached as an afterthought. As I got closer, I saw a lot of rust along the connecting metal.

An awning, which I had noticed the day before, hung over the entry. The awning did not have the hotel's name on it. Nor did it look like anyone ever bothered to close up the awning in a windstorm. The edges were tattered and worn.

Terra-cotta designs covered arched windows on the top floor. The windows were recessed, though, and hard to see. From the ground level, the roof looked flat, but I doubted it was. It probably had peaks that I couldn't see from below.

The school wasn't visible until I approached the awning proper. Then all I saw was the mesh fence and the wire around the top. It had always bothered me that the school looked like a prison, but I had accepted the six-foot-high fence as part of the price paid for having inner-city schools.

I had truly thought that the fence would keep the kids safe, keep most of the bad elements out, and give the school a protected space. The presence of Blackstone Rangers hadn't surprised me because they recruited their younger brothers and sisters all the time.

But the appearance of unattached male adults bothered me a lot. Even though, if I walked on the school grounds at the moment, I would be one as well. I acknowledged the irony with a half grin.

Just beyond the hotel's entry was the restaurant, the Starlite Café. In the light of day, it became clear that the café was not part of the original building. The café had been built twenty years ago as an addition. It was two stories in a 1950s supper club style butted up against the hotel, maybe in a bid to bring more money to a dying business.

The café didn't look like a supper club any longer. It looked like an eatery that had seen better days. The windows were smudged, their exteriors covered with road dirt and grime from a dozen winters. I shuddered at the thought of what their kitchen looked like.

I resisted the urge to find out. It would be easy enough to do some reconnaissance inside, at a solitary table or the counter, talking to a lonely waitress. But I'd do that when I had some real questions. Right now, I still wasn't sure what to ask.

I rounded the corner and stopped. The school stood to my left; the restaurant to my right. The hotel towered over the restaurant, looking like the separate building it was.

From here, I couldn't see inside the school. What faced me was the windowless brick side of the building pressed up against the fence. There was enough space between for snow to gather, but not enough for someone to think it important to shovel the snow away.

The restaurant had only a few windows on this side, most of them closer to the main road. It was as difficult to see the restaurant from the schoolyard as it was to see inside the school.

No wonder I hadn't thought the restaurant much of a threat.

The sidewalk on the school side was well shoveled. Early and late in the day, buses pulled up in the parking lot. There was a small break in the fence back here that the children who got bused from more remote areas walked through.

You couldn't see that from the sidewalk, either.

When Voss targeted Lacey, he had done so intentionally. And if he had gone onto school grounds like Jimmy said, he had to have gone through that small opening, which should have been locked during the day.

My fists were clenched inside my pockets. Tension made my shoulders feel like rocks. I wanted to immediately confront the principal, but I knew he was probably still reeling from the dressing-down that Franklin would have given him.

Besides, I wasn't dressed properly for a confrontation with an authority figure. I wanted the principal to respect my position, not to fear me.

I made myself take a deep breath. The frigid air went deep into my lungs, making my entire chest ache. I held my breath for a moment, feeling the air warm inside of me, and then I released it. The scarf caught most of it, making that little fog of breath almost invisible.

Calmer. I was superficially calmer.

That was all I needed.

I walked to the edge of the alley and turned to my right. The alley went behind the restaurant and the hotel. I could see all the way to the end of the block.

Someone had plowed the alley all winter long. I could see gravel underneath a sheath of clear ice. I walked carefully.

There was an empty lot to my left. Through the snow, I could see the remains of a burned building, the edges of the foundation visible. That building had burned last summer while school was out, and the *Defender* had reported some kind of gang-related cause.

The buildings beside the burned-out one were attached, like stores that shared a back. Old words had been painted above the doors, but those signs faded long ago, and it wouldn't surprise me if the buildings were abandoned.

I was getting cold, so I decided I wouldn't walk up front to check; I would simply drive by.

I knew that farther down that block, the neighborhood became residential. A lot of Jimmy's classmates lived that way and walked to school. I also knew a lot of them got harassed by the Blackstone Rangers, and some did some errands for the gang, even though none of them were older than twelve.

The back of the restaurant was fenced off, with garbage cans in their own little walled-off area, easily accessible through the alley. A dozen cans stood there, many completely full. Garbage hadn't been picked up this week, but it was due.

The kitchen door was open, and through it, I could hear the banging of pans and the chatter of voices. Someone laughed, a braying sound that grated on me. Faint music threaded with the noise.

Beyond the restaurant, the back of the hotel loomed. A small parking area, probably for employees, stood in place of grounds. But I stopped and looked up, a bit surprised at what I saw.

No fire escapes, not on this side of the building. And even if there had been, they would have done no good. The windows were boarded closed, most from the outside—including those on the upper floors. That had been done with ladders or scaffolds and a lot of deliberation.

I knew Chicago building codes backwards forwards and inside out. I knew that inspectors could be bribed, and I was certain that was what happened here, just like I knew that the hotel had been grandfathered in on zoning so that it could stand next to a school.

"Hey, you!" a man yelled.

I turned toward the voice. It was coming from the restaurant. A burly man in a suit one size too small strode out of that open kitchen door.

"Yeah," he said, when he saw me looking at him. "You. What the hell are you doing here?"

I decided to play stupid parent. "My kid said he dropped his keys back here. I was looking for them."

"Kids don't come back here," the guy said as he walked closer. He had to be cold. He wasn't wearing a coat or a hat or gloves. He had hurried out here the moment he saw me.

"Well, I'd love that to be true," I said, "but this was where my kid pointed when I dropped him off at school this morning."

"You heard him wrong," the guy said. "We chase kids out of this alley."

I looked at the ground regretfully, as if it had deliberately hidden the keys from me.

"My kid doesn't lie to me…." I said in that whiny tone that I'd heard other parents use when they were trying to convince themselves of something that they knew wasn't true.

The guy actually chuckled. I loved the sound. It meant that he believed me.

"Oh, man," he said. "You're gonna get a rude awakening some day."

I lifted my head and frowned as completely as I could, knowing he could only see my eyes and eyebrows. "What does that mean?"

"It means your kid wasn't back here. You shouldn't be either." He crossed his arms. His muscles strained the sleeves of that suit coat.

I nodded, like the frightened parent I was pretending to be. "Okay. But if you find a set of keys, will you drop them in the principal's office? I'd really appreciate it."

He glanced over at the school. "We don't go there. I find anything, I'll leave it at the front desk of the hotel in an envelope. Okay?"

He meant it. And that made me want to smile, but I restrained myself.

"Thank you," I said, and scurried out of the alley, deliberately slipping a bit on the ice so that I looked more scared than I was.

I could feel his gaze follow me. When I reached the sidewalk, I glanced over. He hadn't moved, arms still crossed, a frown on his face.

So they not only didn't want someone behind the hotel, they actively monitored the alley. I didn't like that either.

Voss's *Us* was making a lot more sense.

Something was going on here. Something worth protecting.

Something I already knew I wouldn't like.

17

I felt very uncomfortable as I walked back to the van. A parent looking for keys wouldn't have parked at the end of the block. He would have parked in the school lot and backtracked.

But I figured the burly guy was the only person who had heard my reason for being in that alley, and he had watched me until he couldn't see me any longer. I had probably reached the intersection before he went back inside.

If I were him, I would have sprinted back in. It was too cold to stand outside without a coat for longer than five minutes. Even though he had his arms crossed and had his bare hands tucked against his chest, he was probably shivering by the time I vanished from his view. He would have gone in, and then he would have to make his way through a busy kitchen and into the restaurant if he wanted to monitor my progress.

I was betting he wouldn't even go to that much effort. He had believed my goofy key story after all.

Still, I hurried around that corner, picking my way as quickly as I could across that ice-covered sidewalk. I didn't want to look like a man in a hurry, even though I was a man in a hurry.

The street was still pretty empty, and the hotel looked closed. But I wanted to put it behind me, at least for now.

I made it to the van in probably half the time it took to walk down the block. I unlocked the door, crawled inside, and turned the key in the ignition. I resisted the urge to put the blower on, knowing that it would just hit me with cold air.

But I was shivering, too.

I had been outside for forty-five minutes, which was too long in this weather.

I put the van in gear and headed out. By the time I got to the bank, it would be open. I could get my second weapon out of the safe-deposit box. Then I needed to figure out a way to get another backup gun. I hated to think of the expense, but I didn't want to explain to anyone I knew what had happened to my original weapon. I couldn't even say I was buying the gun for Franklin, because he had made it very clear to all concerned that he didn't want weapons of any kind in his house, not with the children nearby.

Children—and Jimmy in particular—were why my second gun was in the bank and why I usually kept my primary weapon locked in the glove box of the van. Hard to get to, but there if I needed it.

And I had needed it.

Thank heavens Jimmy had listened to me. Thank heavens he hadn't touched it the day before.

We might have had a very different discussion at the hospital. If things had gone as well.

It took me longer than expected at the bank. I hadn't expected lines first thing in the morning. But I went to the safe-deposit box, trying not to look nervous or suspicious, and took out my gun. It was a Colt Model 1903 Pocket Hammerless. Even though they stopped making these things about twenty years ago, Chicago was littered with them. They'd been the gun of choice for the bootleggers, gangsters, and thugs that had dominated this town thirty years ago.

They weren't cheap, though; everyone wanted a gun that could fit into the pocket and not fire accidentally. I'd been lucky to score two of them. Now I would have to find another, without seeming like I was looking for it.

I took this gun out and hefted it in my palm. Small and sleek. It looked like it had when I put it here last fall. I slipped the gun into the pocket of my parka, a move which felt strangely uncomfortable after yesterday.

Then I returned to the van and drove home. Before I got out of the van, I placed the gun in the van's glove box next to the extra magazines, where the previous gun had been.

It felt good to get the gun off my person.

I wanted to change before I saw Laura. Besides, it would take me at least forty minutes to get downtown in the middle of the morning and at least fifteen to find a place to park.

I had just peeled off the sweater when the phone rang. Busy day. I hurried into my office to answer.

"Investigations," I said, sounding as curt as I felt.

"Mr. Grimshaw?" A woman's voice that sounded vaguely familiar.

I closed my eyes. I didn't need another complication today. "Yes?"

"It's Darlene Pellman. You know, we talked yesterday about the Model Cities job?"

That seemed like three weeks ago. I made myself sound warm. "Mrs. Pellman. I'm sorry I had to get off the phone so quickly."

"Oh, that was no problem," she said. "It's actually why I called. I was concerned and then your son wasn't at the after-school program, and I wondered. Well, I figured rather than ask around, I would simply ask you."

I felt a spurt of irritation. She probably had asked around and hadn't gotten the answers she wanted.

And then I realized the thought was uncharitable. She thought we were friends. She probably *was* concerned.

"As you could probably tell, we had a family emergency," I said, not really knowing what to say to her.

"I'm sorry," she said. "I hope everything has worked out all right?"

"We don't know yet," I said. "It'll take a while for things to resolve. But the urgent part of the emergency is over."

"That's a blessing at least." She paused as if she was going to ask more and then decided against it. "I suppose you won't go after the Model City's job then?"

"It wasn't for me, Mrs. Pellman. I was going to encourage you. Did I? I don't really remember."

"You did," she said. "I spoke to my husband. He thinks that I should try."

"He's right," I said. "I will put in a good word if you need it."

"Thank you," she said. "I'll let you know when I see the application."

She sounded like she was about to hang up when I realized she was one of those people who kept track of everyone else. Such people could be useful if handled well.

"Mrs. Pellman," I said slowly, picking my words carefully. "I—um—am working on a case, and when we were starting up the after-school program, you mentioned how much you appreciated it because it kept kids out of trouble."

"I still feel that way, Mr. Grimshaw," she said primly.

"Me, too," I said, "but it got me to wondering about the trouble you were referring to. I had assumed you were talking about the gangs. Was I right?"

"Oh, that and other things." She sounded a bit relieved, as if I had hit on a topic she was used to discussing. "Some of the kids, they end up dealing drugs. And the girls get in trouble, you know, and drop out, and that's no good for anyone either. They lapse into poverty or worse, and their children grow up to become new gang members."

I wasn't going to jump on the girls immediately, particularly if Mrs. Pellman had heard gossip about Lacey. I would work my way back to that.

"I figured the drug dealing was connected to the gangs," I said.

"Mostly," Mrs. Pellman said. "Although there are a lot of other sources for drugs in this city."

"That there are," I said. "Girls getting in trouble, though, that happens in the best of schools, doesn't it?"

"I suppose," she said. "But so many, you know, find an older boy and just run off, thinking it's true love, when we both know what it is."

"I guess we do." I worked at sounding rueful. "Lots of kids go missing these days."

"They do," she said. "It's those hippies and that drug culture. They run away and think they're going to change the world. The police won't even look for teenagers any more."

"They won't?" I asked. I didn't know that. "Black children?"

"*All* children," she said. "Teenagers. I know white people who are getting very frustrated with the police over this."

I noted she didn't say "some of my white friends." I didn't doubt her story's veracity, though. It sounded true, particularly with what I'd been hearing on the local news.

"I would have thought the police would at least have searched for missing white children," I said.

"They do when the children are under twelve. But if they're teens and they have any contact with that so-called counterculture, the police want nothing to do with them. Too many runaways going off to rock concerts or San Francisco or something." She actually tut-tutted. "It's enough to drive you crazy."

It was enough to make me even tenser. Maybe I was reading something into her assumptions, but Marvella's words ran through my mind.

How do you know it was instead of?

If she had been right, if Voss had gone after other girls, then it stood to reason that some of them would go missing, like Mrs. Pellman said.

A shiver ran through me. I hoped I was making all of this up.

"Well," I said, not sure how to ask her more without making her curious about Lacey, "let me know if you need that recommendation."

"Oh, I will, Mr. Grimshaw. Thank you for that and for the suggestion."

"No problem," I said, and hung up.

I stood with my hand on the receiver for a long time, just letting the conversation replay in my mind. My reaction was pure paranoia, nothing more. She hadn't said that she personally knew anyone who had gone missing, only that it happened.

Anyone who read the news knew that.

And she had called to get gossip on yesterday's events. So she liked to spread stories, liked to make things sound more dramatic than they were.

But the back of that hotel had no fire escapes and the windows were boarded off. And Voss had said he took drugged, pliable girls to a back room where he kept them for days until the fight went out of them.

Girls who wouldn't want to go home after that.

Girls who might not feel like they could.

Surely, this sort of thing didn't happen to girls with an actual loving family, like Lacey. Surely, she would have gone home the moment she was freed from that back room.

Wouldn't she?

I honestly didn't know.

And I wasn't sure how I could find out.

18

The Loop at lunch was busier than the Loop at any other time of day. All of the downtown offices emptied between noon and two, and that included the courthouse in the Chicago Civic Center. Because Mayor Daley had testified at the Chicago Seven trial the day before and the celebrities of the so-called New Left were on this week's witness list, the national media had sent their most important reporters.

Print reporters got bored and tried to find stories outside of the normal press updates. The print reporters were the major reason I tried to stay away from the Loop for the duration of the trial.

But as more and more celebrities appeared at the trial and as those appearances showed up on national broadcasts, I had also started to worry about the TV people. The people in front of the cameras rarely did much investigating, but they always brought a team with them, and that team's job was to find the side story that the other channels didn't have.

Most of the side stories would be about the trial itself and the mostly-white protest movement that it centered around. But I didn't want to get caught on camera and have someone recognize me.

I parked near the library and walked to Sturdy's offices, my stocking cap tight around my head and my scarf pulled up against the cold. I had glanced in a mirror before leaving home and confirmed what I had hoped: No one would recognize me, especially if I kept my head down.

I clutched a greasy bag filled with the best Southern-fried chicken I'd found in Chicago along with mashed potatoes, some iffy-looking collard greens, and two pieces of chocolate cake. I needed comfort food, and hoped Laura did too.

Sturdy's offices on Randall and Dearborn were right across from the Civic Center. Eight stories of grandeur covered in grime and filth, like every other Chicago building in the winter. Laura hadn't spent a lot of time and attention on Sturdy's headquarters. Her entire focus had been on changing the nature of her father's business.

She had become chairman of the board a year ago, and she had made it her business to run the company as well. She was determined to take a corporation built on whispered mob connections, slum housing, and profiteering, and make it profitable but honest.

I applauded her efforts, but wasn't sure she would be make the company as profitable as she believed. The previous management had raked in millions on the backs of the poor, charging three times the going rate for places that hadn't seen a repair in decades.

Laura had hired me to inspect her properties one by one. I worked directly for her, even though I often told tenants I was working for Sturdy Investments. The fact that she bankrolled me took care of a lot of problems. It allowed me to work off the books on projects like that death house, which had taken most of my time since late September. Because Laura paid me directly, I would never have to answer shareholder questions about my activities. As far as Sturdy Investments was concerned, I hadn't done any work for them at all.

Some people inside the corporation knew I did odd jobs for Laura. Judith Clement, her secretary, put me through whenever I called, because Judith knew my calls were important. Others knew I had some connection to the company, but they didn't know what that connection was.

Television trucks had parked on the plaza and some local reporters were shivering in the outside chill, giving their noon update. No protestors surrounded them, although I had heard there had been a gaggle of them yesterday. It was probably too cold; besides, as far as I could tell, no one with Daley's level of fame testified today.

I turned my back on the circus and pulled open the heavy glass doors that opened into Sturdy's two-story lobby. Harried employees headed outside, wearing thick winter coats and fur-lined hats that always made me think of the movie *Doctor Zhivago*. The employees held briefcases against their sides, and their entire manner spoke of great stress.

Every time I came here during the business day, I remembered why I worked for myself. Right now, I needed the reminder. Yes, my job had been exceptionally stressful for the past six months, but it was a stress I had chosen and, more importantly, I felt like I was doing good work, instead of pushing paper around.

I loosened the scarf, revealing my face so that I didn't look like a mugger. My black skin was unusual in this part of town, and the long scar along the left side of my face probably didn't reassure anyone. A lot of people averted their eyes as I passed them.

I got into the elevator and nodded at Abe Fenton, the elderly attendant. He smiled when he saw me, a step forward for us. It had taken him months to acknowledge me.

Some of that might have been my attitude. His very presence had offended me the first time I had arrived at the office. I didn't like to think of black elevator attendants yes-sirring and no-sirring white corporate employees, like house slaves of old.

But Laura had offered Fenton the opportunity to retire with great benefits. Apparently, he had gotten angry. He thought she was dismissing him for cause. He liked his job, liked greeting people, and liking being the center of everyone's business day.

So she had given him a considerable raise, and told him he could work as long as he wanted. He told her he wanted to "die with his boots on," which she assumed meant that one day, she'd get into the elevator, and Fenton would be gone.

He shoved the lever in the ancient elevator toward the seventh floor. As the door closed and the elevator filled with the mouth-watering odor of fried chicken, he nodded at the greasy white bag.

"You get that in the Loop?" he asked.

I shook my head and smiled. "Just off Martin Luther King Boulevard."

"Now, that makes sense. Some day, they might actually get real food in this part of town, but I ain't holding my breath."

"Why do you think I brought my own?" I asked, wishing I had a little extra.

"That pretty white girl what run this place, she ain't gonna appreciate real Southern fried chicken." Over the last year, Fenton had figured out my relationship with Laura.

"I don't know," I said, "she appreciates me."

He chuckled as the door started to open. I nodded to him and stepped into the hallway. Directly in front of me, the glass doors with **STURDY INVESTMENTS, INC.** written on them in gold stood wide open.

A receptionist I didn't recognize sat behind the blond wood desk. Sturdy had gotten a lot of new employees in the past year as Laura cleaned house. She slowly learned who remained loyal to the previous management and who hadn't. She let most of the employees who preferred the previous management retire with full benefits, if they were old enough. If not, she gently asked them to leave and paid a generous severance while they looked for work. She also gave them good recommendations, which I didn't like. But she believed that would keep them quiet and not allow them to say anything bad about Sturdy.

She was probably right.

The receptionist had a pencil behind her ear. She had long black hair that flipped upward at the ends and was covered in so much hairspray that it all moved as a unit. She frowned when she realized I was about to walk past her.

"Sir, you need to check in." She was very young. She wore pale lipstick that didn't suit her and fake eyelashes that covered half of her cheeks.

"It's okay," I said. "Ms. Hathaway is expecting me."

"She didn't inform me, sir." The receptionist stood as if she could officially block me.

"You can check with Ms. Hathaway, but I'm still going back," I said, as I continued.

The receptionist almost hopped aside as I got too close to her. She tried to look stern, but her blue eyes were wide. I scared her, just like I scared most white people. She lunged for the phone, looking over her shoulder as I started down the narrow hallway that led to Laura's office.

I wondered if the poor receptionist was calling security or calling Laura. I figured I would eventually find out.

I got my answer as Judith grinned up at me from her desk outside Laura's office.

"You're mean, Mr. Grimshaw," she said, patting her brown curls. "You've scared our new receptionist, and I think you did so on purpose."

"You should've left my name up front," I said, grinning back at her.

"Not that it would have done any good," she said. "You didn't even bother to tell her who you were."

I shrugged. "You have to test the new employees every now and then."

She raised her painted eyebrows playfully. "Next time, I promise. I'll leave your name and description."

"I'm not sure that'll work," I said. "I'm sure that half of Sturdy's staff will fit my description."

"That is a problem," she said. "You blend in so well."

Then she laughed, and so did I. No one could ever accuse me of blending in, not in the Loop.

I liked Judith, and I suddenly felt guilty again for not bringing enough food. "Don't you get lunch?"

Her smile faded. "I already had lunch. I'm supposed to guard the door while you're inside, and to strictly monitor your appointment."

"Which means?"

"You have an hour and you're wasting it by flirting with me," she said.

"I never waste time when I'm flirting with you," I said. Then I nodded at the door. "Can I go in?"

She took a deep breath. "If you dare."

"That kind of day, huh?"

"The morning hasn't been pretty. I don't have high hopes for the afternoon, either."

Great. Just what I needed. Laura in a bad mood already, and then I had to tell her about Lacey.

I glanced at the door. I still loved the plaque Laura had affixed to the pale wood:

Laura Hathaway
Sturdy Investments, Inc.

For someone else qualified for an office at Sturdy, the plaque on the door gave their name and their job title. Laura had dithered about this for some time, wondering if she should include all of her job titles—from CEO to President to Chairman of the Board—and then she decided on this.

I loved it. The sign itself implied—no, it stated—that Laura Hathaway *was* Sturdy Investments.

I grabbed the knob and pushed the door open.

Laura's office was huge, with windows on three sides. She had taken the office that had once belonged to Marshall Cronk, who ran the company after her father died. Before that, her father sat in the center of this huge room.

Laura had moved the desk toward the window. She sat with her back to the Civic Center and the west side of Chicago. To her left, the windows provided a peek at the Chicago River, and the buildings going up in Daley's mad dash to redesign Chicago's downtown. To her right, she had a view of the roof of the building next door, and the decaying streets that led to the South Side.

She wasn't looking at any of that. She wasn't even looking at me.

She had pulled her long blond hair away from her face. She had woven her hair into some kind of braid and wrapped that like a bun against the back of her skull. Two strands of hair curled on either side of her face, dangling along with gold earrings. She wore more makeup than I liked, but then, she always did at work. She had colored her eyebrows black and put on heavy blue eye shadow, but left her lips pale. On her, the pale lipstick looked good.

Then, everything looked good on Laura.

After a moment, she looked up and gave me a tired smile. Not even the heavy makeup could completely hide the circles under her eyes.

"Smokey," she said, and she sounded relieved. "Let's sit at the table."

A round oak table with four heavy oak chairs around it stood to the left of the door. The table wouldn't have looked out of place in a fancy dining room, but I knew Laura used it for small meetings.

105

I grabbed a folded table runner from a drawer inside the large table. I had done this before, although it had been a long time. I put the greasy food on the fabric so that it wouldn't stain the table.

Laura stood, and I blinked in surprise. She wore a black maxi skirt that covered a pair of black boots. A matching short-waisted jacket almost hid a gold and black blouse. The jacket and the skirt were striking, though: a band of diamond fabric pieces with different patterns circled the jacket and its sleeves, and then repeated on the skirt. As she got closer, I realized that the fabric pieces weren't pieces at all, but elaborate embroidery.

The outfit looked professional, individual, and warm all at the same time. "That's new," I said.

She rolled her eyes and pulled back a chair. "You don't get to see my business attire very often. About six months ago, I decided I was tired of boxy men's jackets and unattractive skirts. The clothes for professional women are a disgrace. If I had time, I'd fund a professional women's fashion company."

She said that last as if she would never have time again.

She sat down and pulled the bag toward her. "This smells good. I forgot to eat breakfast."

Then she held up a manicured hand and grinned at me. "No lecture, Smokey."

"I wouldn't dream of it," I said. I had eaten breakfast almost seven hours ago. I was ravenous.

We opened the Styrofoam chicken container and ate directly from it. Silently, because we were both starving. I opened the large cup holding the collard greens and closed it again. They had looked iffy in the deli; they looked disgusting now.

The fried chicken, at least, was as good as I remembered.

Somewhere in the middle of it all, Laura got us coffee from the coffee pot that steamed from one of the sideboards. She had prepped for lunch as well.

We had started on dessert when I told her about Lacey.

Laura listened attentively. Her eyes filled with tears when I described the hospital, but she wiped them away with an edge of a finger so that she wouldn't smear her makeup.

"You should have called me," she said, like I knew she would.

I shook my head. "Marvella helped."

"I could have stayed with Jimmy."

"I know," I said. "But Marvella worked with the Grimshaws. She knows what they'll have to do to take care of Lacey. I wanted her there from the start. It seemed only natural that she bring Jimmy home."

"Why couldn't you?" Laura asked.

"I had some things to take care of," I said.

"More important than Jimmy?"

"At that moment," I said, and something in my face must have seemed off.

She frowned. "What did you do?"

I had prepared for this question, thinking about it during the entire drive. If I told anyone about what I had done to Voss, it would be Laura. But if someone caught me, I would put her in legal jeopardy.

"I found out a few things," I said, dodging the question as best I could while being as truthful as possible. "Apparently, Lacey isn't the only girl this happened to."

"From the school?" Laura sounded shocked.

"I don't know that," I said. "But I do know that the guy who hurt Lacey had groomed her for a while before the attack, and afterwards planned to put her to work."

"Doing what—oh." Laura blinked again, then stood up abruptly. That black outfit made her seem very wealthy and very powerful.

She walked toward her desk, stared out the window for a moment as she calmed herself, and then said, "It's a prostitution ring? And that man was trying to recruit Lacey?"

"Yes," I said. "Here's the thing, Laura. Jimmy's been telling me that for months, and I didn't understand him. I thought he was just worrying because of his past. Instead, he saw exactly what was going on, kept trying to tell me, and when I didn't listen, he took matters into his own hands."

"It sounds like he came to you," she said.

"When Lacey went into that hotel, yes," I said. "If Jimmy hadn't seen that—"

"He did. And even if he hadn't, you would have found her."

I grabbed the Styrofoam container and closed it. I couldn't look at the food anymore.

"I appreciate your faith in me," I said, "but I'm not sure I could have found her. These operations, Laura. Timing is everything. Once she left that hotel, she might have disappeared into a world I have no access to."

Laura turned around. "You're not here to tell me about Jimmy and Lacey."

"Not entirely," I said.

"What do you need?"

"Here's what I'm hoping," I said. "I'm hoping that Sturdy owns the building."

"I certainly hope we do *not*." She raised her chin slightly as she said that. She was a formidable woman, and had become more formidable in this last year.

"I do," I said, "and here's why. If you own it, Laura, you can shut it down. You can clear the entire building, turn it into something else, or tear it down."

She took a deep breath, clearly calming herself again. Then she nodded. "What's the address?"

I told her.

She leaned over and pressed the intercom on her desk. She asked Judith to check to see if Sturdy owned that property, and get that information to us before I left.

"I've updated the property lists since last fall," Laura said after she finished with Judith. "We should have everything at our fingertips."

I sighed and finished clearing the table. I put all the garbage back in the bag, and I'd throw it into the break room on my way out.

"While we're waiting," I said, "there's yet one more reason that I wanted to talk with you."

The frown creasing her forehead grew. "Okay."

"Franklin would like to see you."

"Franklin? Why?"

"I think he's going to ask you to pay for Lacey's tuition at a private school."

"I'd be happy to do that," she said. "In fact, I'd be happy to do it for all the Grimshaw children. You know I want to help Jimmy."

"I know," I said, and for once, I didn't turn her down.

She raised her eyebrows as she realized I hadn't said an automatic *no*.

"Let's just stick with Lacey at the moment," I said. "Franklin doesn't think she should go back to that school."

"I don't think any child should be in that school," Laura said fiercely. "You've had gang problems, and now this. And you know their education isn't good. I don't care about the after-school program. I know it's trying, but it's not the same as—"

"Laura," I said, feeling overwhelmed. "One step at a time."

A knock echoed. Then Judith peered in.

"It's not one of ours," she said to Laura. "And you have less than fifteen minutes."

Then, without asking, she walked over and took the garbage bag from me. "I will force you to leave, Mr. Grimshaw," she said softly.

"I know, Judith," I said, letting my smile at her hide my disappointment.

"Now what?" Laura asked as the door closed.

"Now," I said, "we go to step two."

19

And what, pray tell, is step two?" Laura rested against her desk, her hands on the surface. She looked calm, but I could tell she wasn't.

"I was wondering if you could get information for me," I said. "Well, not you, exactly, but one of your employees."

She looked at me expectantly. She didn't ask for the details. She just waited.

"I was wondering if you could find out who owns the building," I said.

"And then what will you do, Smokey?" she asked.

My heart rate rose. I was surprised, but I suppose I shouldn't have been. I was about to break one of my many personal rules. I was going to attempt to use Laura's fortune for one of my own goals.

"I was hoping you would offer them so much money for the property that they wouldn't be able to say no."

She smiled slowly. Her eyes actually twinkled. "You want me to help you with my money?"

I supposed I deserved this. We'd fought over her money so many times. Or rather, I had fought her over it.

"Yeah," I said softly.

"I would be happy to," she said. "I love problems that you can throw money at and solve."

"We're not solving everything," I said. "There's Lacey's future, and the girls who might be there, and—"

"We can move that thing away from the school, and that's a start," Laura said. "Even though you don't believe me, I do listen to you. I know that you want to help as many of the kids as possible, that sending Jimmy and the Grimshaws to a private school doesn't help the other students. I know that and I understand your hesitation. But this a solution that can help everyone."

"Yes, it can," I said.

She smiled. "This might be the high point of my day. Something I can actually do."

The intercom buzzed. "Ms. Hathaway, I'm sorry, but you have five minutes before the professors arrive."

"Lucky me," Laura muttered, and then hit the intercom. "Thanks, Judith."

"I'll head out," I said.

"Judith will call you at the end of the day with that information," Laura said, as she rounded her desk. Behind her, the windows of the Civic Center seemed even darker than usual.

I wanted to lean over and kiss her but I knew that wasn't appropriate. We had agreed that we wouldn't have any public displays of affection at Sturdy.

"Smokey?" she said as she sat down. "Is it okay for me to see Lacey?"

Laura and Lacey really didn't know each other.

"I don't know," I said. "I'll ask."

"And one other thing," Laura said. "The doctors tested her for venereal disease, right?"

"They're giving her penicillin," I said.

"Has anyone figured out how to handle it if she's pregnant?"

My cheeks warmed. I hadn't even thought of that. I doubted Franklin had, either. I didn't know if Marvella or Althea had discussed it.

"I mean, it might make a difference about the school," Laura said. "Some families send their daughters to one of those homes during a pregnancy."

I noted that she didn't even mention an abortion. But Marvella would. She knew the safe and legal places to get one, and I knew Laura did, too. Maybe she just thought it inappropriate for someone so young.

"I'll let you know," I said.

She nodded, her gaze still on mine. "I'm so sorry," she said.

"I know," I said. "Me too."

I let myself out of the office. Four white men looked up in surprise. Two wore suits, but two wore jackets and turtlenecks. The two turtle-neck men had longish hair and beards.

The professors. They would be as impressed with Laura's clothes as I had been, and wouldn't find them unusual. I tipped a mental hat to Laura. She knew her business so much better than I ever would.

"Thanks, Judith," I said, tapping the desk as I went by.

"No problem, sir," she said firmly, probably for the benefit of the professors. I headed toward reception, and tried not to let a dark mood overtake me.

I had so wanted Sturdy to own the building that I hadn't really explored the other options. Getting rid of the hotel had become more difficult, but not impossible. However, the way that real es-tate sales operated on the South Side, getting a quick sale might be impossible.

I decided not to worry about it yet. I would see what happened be-fore I made any snap judgments.

The girl in reception started when she saw me come out of the back. Then she realized who I was and tried to smile. I smiled at her, nodded, and headed for the elevator.

Refraining from snap judgments would be hard no matter what I did. I didn't want to think about a possible Lacey pregnancy, because all I would do was worry. We wouldn't know if she was pregnant until she got a doctor's test six weeks in. Six weeks would be just after Valentine's Day, an eternity from now.

I wasn't going to mention it to Franklin. I'd talk with Althea. She probably had already thought of it.

The elevator doors opened and Fenton grinned at me. "She like the chicken?"

It took me a minute to understand who "she" was and why Fenton leered ever so slightly. He thought Laura and I had shared more than a meal.

"She liked the break," I said as I stepped inside.

"Don't we all," he said, moving the lever so that the elevator doors closed. "Don't we all."

20

With the traffic in the Loop, I barely had time to make it back to the school a half an hour before classes let out. I hoped that would give me a chance to visit the principal. I didn't want to make an appointment; I wanted this to look more impromptu than it was. I wanted to make sure of a few things. I wanted to make certain that Franklin hadn't done anything rash. I also wanted to know if the principal was aware of what occurred at the hotel next door. And finally, I wanted to know what he planned to do about the problems, if anything.

I drove around the block once, just so that I could take a look at the Starlite in the middle of the day. The hotel looked unassuming, a run-down building that had once been a showplace.

The restaurant gave it all the veneer of dying old money, a swanky location that was swanky no longer.

No wonder I hadn't really noticed it. It was designed to disappear in the daytime.

The school's front door was just off the parking lot. At least twice a week, I walked the kids through the lot, up the long stairs, to those double blue doors, but I hadn't been inside in more than a year.

I parked as close as I could get, got out, walked up the stairs, and pulled one door open, surprised that no one greeted me. I thought we had set up some kind of security system with the school after the gang incidents last year. If I remembered correctly, there should always have been a teacher or an assistant near the door, making sure that someone who did not belong could not get in.

I had liked the teacher security system, because, theoretically, they would know who had graduated or been expelled and no longer belonged. That was especially important since there was a junior high attached to this grade school, and some of the kids in the junior high—the boys especially—looked particularly grown-up.

That thought made me wince. Lacey had been going to the junior high, not the grade school, and she also had looked particularly grown-up.

I went through the second set of doors, which had not been placed there for protection from outsiders but for protection against the shocking deep cold of winter. The doors blocked the frigid air from getting into the hallway. There were no heaters until a few yards inside that wide hallway, so that the school saved some money on its power bills.

The school had to save money wherever it could. It had half the operating budget it needed. The principal had allocated most of the money toward teachers, which I appreciated, but that meant the inside of the school looked more like a derelict building than a place to study.

I couldn't remember if it had looked this bad when I first enrolled Jimmy here nearly two years ago. Both he and I had been suffering from culture shock then. We had come to Chicago to escape Memphis, and this city was frighteningly different. Everything looked odd, or run-down, or dirty because we had come in April, when there was slush everywhere and the remains of the Westside fires after the riots sparked by Martin's assassination.

I had noticed the condition of the school last year, when we dealt with the gangs, but I didn't remember it being this bad. Locker doors hung off their hinges; some doors were even missing. Boards crossed others, and as I stepped inside, I shivered, realizing that the expected heat was not on at all.

No wonder Jimmy had been so happy to get sweaters for Christmas. The fury that had dissipated somewhat since last night rose again. And again, it was at myself. I was neglecting the kid I had sworn to protect, and for what reason? Stubbornness? Money? Pride?

I let out a small breath, startled that I could see it, a small white fog in the air. I clenched my fists, and then unclenched them one finger at a time. I had to be calm for this meeting, because no matter what happened, I couldn't change Jimmy's circumstance quickly.

I didn't even know what I wanted to do.

I pivoted, and headed down the narrower hallway that led to the principal's office. It was even colder here, with frost on the inside of the windows that lined the hallway's left side.

The principal's door was closed. The word "Administration" had been stenciled on wood so old that it had split at the bottom. Well, the principal wasn't keeping any of that money for himself, that much was clear.

I pushed the door open, startling the heavyset secretary behind the desk. Unlike the women in Laura's office, she wore no makeup and she didn't have her hair in the latest style. In fact, I had a hunch she hadn't changed her look in twenty years. Her hair was pulled back into a bun, and covered with straightener, which made it shine in the fluorescent lights.

"Yes?" she asked blandly. She hadn't remained startled for long.

"My name is Bill Grimshaw," I said. "I would like to see the principal."

Her expression softened. "You're related to Lacey? I was so sorry to hear what happened."

I resisted the urge to close my eyes. This was precisely what Franklin hadn't wanted; he hadn't wanted anyone to know what happened to Lacey. But I supposed, it was inevitable. If he had come to confront the principal, then the principal would tell his secretary.

"Thank you," I said.

"You do know that Franklin Grimshaw, your—"

"Cousin," I said.

"—was here this morning. He's Lacey's father." She said it as if I didn't know that. Or perhaps she was trying to point out that Franklin's appearance was more germane than mine.

"My son, Jimmy, was the one who figured out what was going on, and called for help." I kept my words deliberately vague, in case Franklin hadn't told the staff here all of the details. But I also wanted everyone to know that Jimmy had been in danger as well.

"Oh, my," the secretary said. "And he's such a sweet thing."

I was surprised that she knew Jimmy, and she saw the surprise on my face.

"He came in here last fall to find out what he needed to do to get into Yale," she said. "I thought it was very cute and a bit premature."

To my surprise, a lump rose in my throat. That damn kid. Used to doing things on his own, and getting them done. I had told him not to worry yet about Yale, so he had come here to find out what else he could do.

"May I see the principal?" I asked.

She sighed. "He's had a busy day."

"I'm sure," I said.

She leaned over and spoke into the intercom. "Bill Grimshaw is here to see you. He's James Grimshaw's father."

I couldn't hear the garbled answer, but she nodded at me.

"He says go right in."

I did. The heat was on in here, making the room stuffy. I hadn't noticed the temperature in the reception area, so it had to have been warmer than the hallway.

The principal stood over his desk, moving papers. He looked up at me, and his gaze went to the scar on my cheek. But he didn't look frightened or even worried by it. He had probably seen a lot worse down here.

He extended his hand over the desk. "Gerald Decker."

I took his hand and shook it. "Bill Grimshaw."

"Franklin was here," Decker said. "He told me what happened. I'm very sorry."

"I'm very worried," I said. "It was easy for Lacey's attacker to target her. I'm convinced he's done this before."

Decker sighed. "I called the police again this morning. I'm aware of that hotel and its clientele, and I want something done. Even though they took my name and put the complaint on file, I'm sure nothing will happen."

"Then we need to do something," I said.

"I'm open for suggestions." He finished stacking a pile of papers. He glanced at them, then back at me. "I'm sorry. I'm distracted. I was up well after midnight last night. The upcoming strike vote has me concerned."

I didn't care, at least at that moment. I had cared two days before, but a strike was the least of my concerns at the moment.

"Franklin approached you about the gang troubles we had a year ago. He told me that you had set up a plan for teachers to monitor the doors during their off hours."

Decker sighed and sat down. "I did. But in this cold, I can't have anyone sit in our hallways. It's either pay the heat or pay four teachers. I opted for teachers. That's what the teachers don't understand. We don't have the money to pay them more."

I sat, too. This man was exhausted, overworked, and given an impossible task. I didn't want to feel sympathy for him, but I did.

"Look," he said. "We're dealing with the gang problem every day, particularly in the junior high school. I've expelled half the eighth grade class. I'd love to have guards. Then kids wouldn't show up with guns or knives or brass knuckles. I have kept the heat on in those hallways, just so that teachers can report the drug deals if they see any, and they do, almost every day. Some of the teachers are scared to tell me about it, because they're afraid of retaliation."

I clutched my knees. "I didn't realize it was that bad."

He opened his hands, and shrugged. "We're in the middle of the Mighty P. Stone Nation here. Kids think it's glamorous to join, or they need money to help their parents pay rent. Or they see their siblings getting support from the gangs. It's a lot to fight, and I don't have the resources. So I've concentrated on keeping the gangs out of the grade school."

"I don't remember this from last year," I said.

"It has gotten worse in the past year. I'm sorry, Mr. Grimshaw. I thought the hotel was the least of our problems. I believed that the men stayed at the hotel and we only had to worry about drugs moving over. I had no idea they were preying on our girls. I'm not even sure what to do about it."

He looked defeated.

"My kid wants to go to Yale," I said, surprising myself. "We were visiting campus last summer, and it's become a goal for him."

Decker smiled. "I remember. Mrs. Helgenstrom sent him in here one day to talk about it."

"If he stays here, he's not going to be able to achieve that goal, is he?"

Decker's smile faded. "Not all the schools in the Chicago Public School District are equal, as you probably know. I understand that you and Franklin have started an after-school program. That's a smart move."

It was a long way to say that Jimmy had no hope of Yale if he stayed here. And Decker couldn't keep the gangs out of the junior high. Or the drugs.

Franklin was right: Lacey had to stay away.

And I had to do something—not for the school—but for Jimmy.

I nodded. "Thank you for your honesty."

I stood and was about to leave, when I remembered my other reason for coming. Decker wasn't the only one with a sleep deficit. Mine had slowed me down all day.

"If Jimmy and Keith hadn't called me," I said, "Lacey might have disappeared."

Decker moved some of the papers. He wouldn't meet my gaze. "I know."

"You know I am an investigator."

He nodded.

I continued, "I would like to see your records. How many girls around Lacey's age have gone missing in the last few years?"

He rubbed his mouth with his right hand, then leaned back. "It doesn't mean anything, you know. Girls, going missing. I hate to sound crass, but we're in gang territory. The girls get pregnant, they drop out and move in with their boyfriends. And for the past three years, a lot of them have headed to San Francisco or Madison or Ann Arbor or other hippy places, thinking that they'll find a better life."

Exactly what Mrs. Pellman had told me. I wondered if she had gotten that response from Decker.

"How many girls have you lost?" I asked.

"We didn't lose them," he said somewhat defensively.

"I mean, how many no longer attend school," I said.

"I assume you mean girls that no longer attend and we don't know why," he said.

I nodded.

He slid more papers around. "We lose about twenty a year. They hit puberty, and then they're gone."

"From the junior high," I said.

He shook his head. "From each class. In the sixth grade, we lose about two or three, but when you get to the seventh grade, we're losing at least ten out of a class of four hundred. By the eighth grade, we can lose as many as fifty."

"Fifty," I said. "Girls?"

"A fourth of the class if we're talking girls and boys. The boys drop out sooner, because they usually have to earn money for the family."

"A hundred kids stop coming to school by the eighth grade."

He shrugged, as if he didn't care. But he looked away from me, and then glanced back to meet my gaze.

"I don't know what to do, Mr. Grimshaw. Seriously. We don't have the money for extended outreach programs. We don't have the staff to search for them. We contact the parents, but often the parents aren't at the last known address. We have to give up on them and concentrate on kids like your son, the ones who want to learn. We have to hope they'll get enough out of class to continue forward."

He sounded doubtful. Hell, I was becoming doubtful.

"Let me see what you have," I said. "Girls only. Girls who have truly gone missing, where you know someone is looking for them and can't find them."

He pulled open a drawer, and gave me a folder. I opened it. It was full of hand-drawn flyers. I didn't recognize any of the names, but Jimmy might.

"Can I keep this?" I asked.

He nodded. "Maybe you can find them."

"Maybe," I said. "But I wouldn't hold my breath."

"Oh, believe me," he said. "I gave up holding my breath years ago."

21

I met the kids at the front door of the school and walked them to the van. They seemed subdued, except Norene, who couldn't be subdued if she tried. Jonathan had walked over from the nearby high school, like he did every day. He usually acted as the kids' guardian for the walk through gang territory. On this day, he had help besides me. Keith held Norene's hand, keeping her close. He looked fierce.

Jimmy stayed beside me, and he probably would have taken my hand if we weren't so close to the school.

Once they were all tucked in the van, I drove them to the after-school program. The church which gave us the rooms free of charge wasn't far away. Even in the deep cold, the kids could safely walk there.

But I didn't want to chance it on this day.

I promised them all I'd be back later to pick them up. As they filed out, I caught Jonathan's arm.

"Stay a minute," I said to him.

He glanced at the door, watching until the kids went inside. Then he turned to me.

I hadn't realized how much he had grown in the past year. He would be sixteen in the summer, and he had grown as well. His face was angular, like his father's had been when I met him in Memphis, almost twenty years ago now.

"I spoke to the principal," I said. "He told me just how dangerous this junior high is. He mentioned drug deals in the hallway. Is that true?"

Jonathan shrugged. He looked at the door of the church as if it provided answers. A few other kids straggled across the shoveled sidewalk.

"Jonathan, please," I said. "I'm trying to figure out what happened."

"Why my sister got raped?" he asked.

My cheeks flushed. I hadn't realized he knew the details.

"I figured it out," he said. "It's not hard. Everybody knows what goes on in that hotel. And you let her go there."

"I didn't know," I said.

"Yes, you did," he said. "Jimmy says he told you everything."

I nodded. "I didn't understand him. I didn't realize how big the danger was."

"You're always so concerned with other people, Uncle Bill," Jonathan snapped. "You never have time for the people you claim you care about."

The words hurt, probably because I'd been thinking the same thing. *I'm sorry* wasn't the right response. There wasn't a right response. Not on this, anyway.

"I'm making time now," I said.

"Yeah," Jonathan said. "After the crisis. You're good *after* a crisis, aren't you, Uncle Bill?"

I took a deep breath, and handed him the folder that Decker had given me. "Do you recognize any of these girls?"

"Why?" Jonathan asked without opening it. "So you can focus on someone else's kids again? Because what happened to Lacey isn't bad enough for you?"

I pivoted slightly in the driver's seat. Jonathan held the folder so tight that it bent.

"I'm actually trying to figure out who did this, and stop them, Jonathan."

"Jimmy said you already did." Jonathan still wasn't looking at me.

"I think there's an entire operation hurting girls in that hotel," I said. "I want to shut them down. I want to shut the hotel down too."

Jonathan finally turned toward me. "You can make them go away?"

"I don't know," I said. "I can try. But first I need to know the extent of this thing. That's why I want you to look at the flyers."

"Flyers," he said, flipping open the file. He stared at the top one. "What are these?"

"Girls from the school who went missing," I said.

He bit his lower lip. "Missing. You mean they were killed?"

"I don't know," I said.

"If Jim and Keith hadn't stepped in, Lacey could have *died?*"

"I don't know," I said. "I don't think so. I think she would have been put to work."

He shook his head slowly. "That doesn't make any sense, Uncle Bill. She would have come home."

"They would have moved her out of the neighborhood," I said. "Maybe even lied to her about her family, said that her family didn't want her anymore."

"We wouldn't—." He stopped himself. "Lied. Okay. I get it. This is some kind of recruiting station?"

"For lack of a better way to put it."

"Jesus." He thumbed through the flyers slowly, then started to hand me some. He would add commentary with the ones he handed me. "She moved out" or "She ain't never going home again" or "She got a boyfriend who took her north."

He gave me a dozen flyers. Then he slowed down and stared at one flyer in particular.

It was printed by some kind of printing press. The photo of a pretty girl, her head tilted, a wide smile on her delicate features, looked like a school portrait or a professional shot.

"You know her?" I asked after a minute.

He nodded. "Donna Loring. She—her brother—it was awful."

"What was?" I asked.

A small frown creased his forehead as he looked at me. "She, um, you know, to her family, she was like a thirteen-year-old Norene. Everyone loved her, and they all thought she was going to be someone. They fought to keep her in school, even when she tried to quit."

"Why would she try to quit?" I asked, not completely understanding.

"Her brother—he um—he's one of Jeff Fort's right-hand men."

I let out a small breath. Jeff Fort was the leader of the Blackstone Rangers. I'd met him more than once. He was a dangerous man, who was getting even more dangerous as time went on.

"No one wanted her near the gang," Jonathan said.

"Then she disappeared."

He nodded. He ran a hand over her image. He had known her well, then. Maybe even cared for her.

"Her brother was furious. He thought maybe someone had taken her to teach him a lesson. He tore the school up."

"When was this?"

"October of '68 maybe? Before you had the gang run-in stuff."

"That was last April."

"Yeah, before that. In the fall for sure."

"So," I said, looking at his hand, the way his fingers kept touching the edge of the photograph. "Did they ever find her?"

"No. Her brother kept looking. He probably threatened someone for the flyer or something. I mean, it looks professional. Word was around school that she was dead, but I never heard how."

I reached for the flyer. Jonathan set it beside him on the seat, out of my reach. Then he continued to go through the file.

"Do you believe she's dead?" I asked.

"There was no retaliation," Jonathan said. "So if she was dead, no one got blamed."

Which, in gang terms, was very unusual.

He continued to look at the flyers. He set several others with Donna Loring's flyer.

Then he handed me that pile. "I know nobody knew what happened to these girls. And if they figured it out, then no one told me."

He had given me almost an inch of paper. My heart twisted.

"What about those?" I nodded toward the flyers remaining in the folder.

"They're not anybody I know," he said. "Maybe Lacey...."

He let his voice trail off. He closed the file folder.

"My dad say how she is?" he asked.

"I haven't spoken to him since this morning. I was going there next," I said.

Jonathan squared his jaw as his gaze met mine. "If you hear something about these people hurting girls like Lacey, you tell me. I want to help, okay?"

"It's not my decision, Jonathan. Your father—"

"I don't give a damn about my father. I'm old enough to help you," Jonathan said. "I *should* help you. I should have helped yesterday."

I didn't want to make him that promise. I didn't dare. I couldn't be responsible for yet another of Franklin and Althea's children.

"I promise you," I said, "I'll ask for your help when I need it. Like I just did."

He pressed his lips together, as if he was trying not to be angry at me. He hadn't been talking about looking at flyers. He'd been talking about going after the criminals, like I had gone after Voss last night.

I would pretend to misunderstand him as long as I could.

"I'm gonna do something no matter what," he said.

That was what I was afraid of. "We'll do it together," I said.

"I'm gonna hold you to that," he said.

"I know," I said. "Believe me, I know."

22

After Jonathan left the van, I placed the files of the girls he believed to be truly missing in the folder. I put the ones of the girls he didn't know underneath the folder, and the ones of the girls he believed to have just dropped out on top.

Just dropped out. As if that was nothing.

I thought about Decker's revelations and Jonathan's comments as I drove to the hospital. That both of them accepted the drug dealing and the disappearances as facts of life disturbed me greatly. I suspected it only got worse in high school. Add to that the gangs, the guns, the pregnancies, and it was a wonder any kid made it out of the South Side at all.

The street lights came on as I turned the van into the hospital's visitor parking lot. These short days also affected my mood. The sunlight had been thin, the air freezing, and now it was growing dark. It seemed like it had just been dark.

At least I got to park in the visitor's lot instead of near the emergency entrance. That felt like a luxury.

Still, I knew this hospital better than I wanted to. I had been in Chicago less than two years, and I had already spent too much time in hospitals—and never because someone had gotten sick. Every single time

I had come to the hospital, it had been because someone—including me—had been a victim of violence.

I sighed and hurried through the twilight toward the main doors. I stopped in the gift shop and picked up a pink stuffed dog. It looked young for Lacey, but right now, she needed comfort, not age-appropriate material.

Then I went to the information desk, asked for Lacey's room, and was given a number on the third floor of the children's wing. Ironic that she would be there, given the nature of the violence she suffered.

I took the stairs two at a time and pushed open the swinging doors into the wing. The hospital made an attempt to make this place cheerful. Murals painted on the walls depicted balloons, clowns, and kids playing.

As I got closer to Lacey's area, I realized that each room had a famous cartoon character painted on the door. I passed Elmer Fudd and Yosemite Sam before I reached Bugs Bunny, and Lacey.

Her door was closed. I could barely see around the painted mural, but what I did see showed me Althea, sitting beside Lacey, holding her hand. I didn't see Franklin.

I slipped inside. Lacey was hooked up to an IV of some kind. Her left arm had a bandage around the bicep. I was about to ask Althea how Lacey was doing, when Lacey turned her head.

It was all I could do to suppress a gasp. The entire left side of her face was black-and-blue. Her left eye was swollen shut, and her cheek and mouth looked deformed.

She tried to smile, even though it clearly hurt. "Hi, Uncle Bill."

"Hi, Lacey," I said and sank into the chair on the other side of her bed. She had a private room. I had no idea how Franklin had arranged that, but I was glad that he did.

A radio sat on the bedside table. Some books sat on the table as well. They looked new. Flowers lined the shelf built above the radiator. A recessed window showed just how dark it had become outside.

I handed her the stuffed dog. No one had brought her stuffed animals yet. She hugged it, looking like a very little girl. A tear slipped out of her right eye, but I didn't know if that was a tear of pain, of sadness, or just residual wetness from all the medication she'd been receiving.

Her hands, holding the dog, were scraped raw, and her wrists were black-and-blue.

"Lacey's doing better," Althea said, although better than what I had no idea. "She actually ate something at lunch and is looking forward to dinner."

"The anesthetic must be leaving your system," I said. "I'm never hungry when I'm full of that stuff."

Lacey's eyes were closed. Althea looked across her at me. Althea seemed to have aged ten years since I saw her last. She shrugged, as if to say she had no real idea how her daughter was.

Lacey sighed, then opened her eyes. "I look pretty bad, huh, Uncle Bill?"

This was the girl who had gone into a hotel with a strange man in the hopes of becoming a model. Appearance was extremely important to her.

I touched the scar on my cheek. The scar, which ran from my temple to my chin, had faded. But, despite the doctor's best efforts, the scar was the first thing most people saw when they looked at me.

"You should have seen that when I was in the hospital," I said. "I looked like the mummy when I was all bandaged up. I was afraid I'd scare Jimmy."

"Nothing scares Jimmy." Lacey sounded like she believed it. "Mom says I can't see him."

"Kids aren't allowed in patient rooms," I said. "I don't know if you remember, but they tried to kick him out of the emergency room."

She smiled, then winced. "I remember."

She sighed, then petted the stuffed dog as if it were alive.

"Mom, can I talk to Uncle Bill alone?" she asked.

Althea stood. "We're not supposed to upset her," she said to me, but the fierceness wasn't there. Althea seemed to know that Lacey was already upset; all we could do was either alleviate it or make it worse.

"I'll be good," I promised her.

"I'll be in the cafeteria," she said. "Come get me when you're done."

"I will," I said.

She left, pulling the door closed behind her.

Lacey blinked and another tear rolled down her cheek. "You be honest with me, Uncle Bill. No one else will. You tell me. How bad is this?"

I leaned against the hospital bed. "I don't know your prognosis. I came up here without checking."

"That's not what I mean," she said. "My face. Is it ruined?"

"No," I said. "You were hit pretty hard, but the swelling will go down."

She nodded. "That's what Mom says too." Then she closed her eyes, took a deep breath, and seemed to steel herself. When she opened her eyes, there were no tears in them.

"I'm getting really mad when someone touches me," she said, her voice shaky. "Mom says it's the anesthetic. I did it in the emergency room with the doctor before anesthetic. I went crazy."

"It's not crazy," I said. "I've seen this before. It's a normal reaction to being attacked."

Her mouth turned down. "Does it get better?"

"Eventually," I said.

"Eventually." She repeated the word as if it were a death sentence. "Daddy won't even look at me. It's my fault, Uncle Bill."

"No," I said. "It's not."

"I *believed* him." And with that, we weren't talking about Franklin anymore. "He *lied* to me, and I *believed* him. How stupid am I?"

"You're not stupid," I said.

"I *am*. It was obvious where he was taking me. I should have thought it through. I should have known."

I sighed. Logic wouldn't work here. I touched my scar. "The day I got this," I said, "I went into the home of a man who made me uneasy. I knew he would probably try something, but he still caught me unaware. I never expected the knife, even though I should have. I thought I had taken every precaution, and he could have killed me. He nearly blinded me."

She tilted her head a little. "What did you do?"

"I got rescued, just like you did. And then I spent the next few days in my hospital bed going over every detail in my head, berating myself for being so stupid."

Another tear slide out of her good eye.

"Could I have done things differently?" I asked. "Probably. I certainly wouldn't do it the same way now. But one morning I realized that if I spent all of my time beating myself up for handling that wrong, then I was no better than he was."

She jerked her head back, as if I had touched her. "What do you mean?"

"He hurt me," I said. "He hurt me badly. And I survived. I could chose to continue to hurt myself or I could move forward. It sounds easy. It's not. It takes effort every day. And this scar, I'm aware of it whenever someone looks at my face for the first time. I could apologize for it. I never do."

"I'm scared of everybody," she said in a tiny voice.

"I know," I said.

"I don't know how to stop," she said.

"You can't order yourself to stop," I said. "You have to figure out what will make you feel safe again, and that's not something you can answer fast."

She wrapped her bruised arms around that dog. We sat silently for several minutes.

Finally, she said, "Mom says your neighbor knows people who can help me. Dad thinks it's dumb. What do you think?"

"I'm the one who decided to bring Marvella in," I said. "I think she knows how to help you, better than any of us do. She's been through this, more than once."

"She's been...attacked?"

"I don't know the details," I said. "But I know she's helped a lot of people."

Lacey let out a small breath. "I don't want to do something my dad thinks is stupid. That's how I got here."

"No," I said. "You got here because a horrible, evil man targeted you. He decided to hurt you and he did. It had nothing to do with anything you did, your relationship with your father, or defying the rules he set for you. You have to remember that."

"If I had worn the clothes my parents—"

"He still would have targeted you." I rested a hand on the railing. That was as close as I could get to touching her without scaring her. "He did this before."

"What?" she asked in a small voice.

"He's attacked other girls," I said.

Her lower lip trembled. "Who?"

"I don't know yet," I said.

"Then how do you know—?"

"I found out after I left here yesterday," I said.

She frowned, then winced, then petted the dog. "Will he do it again, then?"

"No," I said.

"How do you know?" she asked.

I wanted to tell her. If anyone deserved to know, Lacey did. But I didn't dare tell her. Not explicitly anyway.

"I made sure of it," I said.

"How?" she asked.

"You'll have to trust me, Lace," I said. "You'll never see him again."

"And the other girls?" she asked. "Has he still got them?"

"He doesn't," I said. "I'm going to find out who they are and what happened to them exactly."

"I keep thinking…he kept telling me…I was, you know, 'his.' And I was going to do what he said. Did he do that to them?"

"Probably," I said, trying to stay calm.

"You'll find them, Uncle Bill?"

"I'll do my best," I said.

She nodded. "Jimmy's gonna be just like you. He said that once, and I believe him now."

I closed my eyes for a brief second. I didn't want him to be like me. I wanted him to go to Yale and become a big shot and have a real life, not one like mine.

I opened my eyes. She wasn't looking at me. She was staring at the dog as if she didn't see it at all.

"Lacey," I said, "would you be willing to answer a few questions?"

"I don't know," she said, her voice filled with tears.

"You can say stop if you don't want to think about the question," I said.

She nodded. She continued to stare at the dog.

"How did you meet him?" I asked.

She squared her shoulders, then plucked at the blanket. "This girl I know. She introduced us."

"Is she in your class?" I asked.

Lacey shook her head. "She dropped out, you know, a year ago."

I tried to keep my voice neutral. This was important, but I didn't want to alarm Lacey.

"So how did she introduce you?" I asked.

Lacey's mouth thinned. She didn't want to tell me.

"I promise. I won't say anything to your dad. Whatever you tell your parents is up to you."

"Promise?" she whispered, still plucking the blanket.

"Promise," I said.

She nodded, her head bowed. "There's a liquor store a couple of blocks away. I go there sometimes."

I almost blurted, *You buy booze?* But I managed to stop myself just in time.

"They have a cigarette machine right near the door," she said, as if she heard my question. She couldn't see my face, and I had struggled very hard not to have a physical reaction. "Dad would have a fit if he found out that I smoke."

"I won't say anything," I said again.

She bobbed her head once. "She was there one day with…him. And I said hello, and she…" Lacey looked up at me, eyes narrowed. "Shit. I mean. Crap. I mean. I'm sorry."

She was apologizing for swearing.

"It's okay," I said. "Tell me."

"She made that little gesture, you know? That go-away gesture?" Then she raised both hands and waved them as if she were warding something off. "I thought she wanted me to go away because she didn't want me to meet her boyfriend. She always hated me, you know, thinking I was after the same boys she was."

Normally, I would have asked her if she was. But I didn't dare derail her.

"She wanted me to go away, didn't she?" Lacey asked. "Not because she hated me, but because she knew…"

Her voice trailed off, and she turned toward the window. Her shoulders shook slightly, as if she were stifling a sob. But I couldn't touch her. I didn't dare, not without her permission.

Then she took a deep breath and sat up straighter. "Anyway, he asked her if he could meet me. And I was such an idiot. I thought he was interested in me, you know, because I was pretty."

He probably had been. But I didn't tell her that. Because he hadn't been interested in her as a potential boyfriend would have been. He had been interested in her potential.

"She introduced us and then she hung back, and finally she wandered down the aisles. He talked to me, and then he said…"

"What?" I asked.

"He said I was, you know. Pretty. He asked if I liked movies, and I said I did, and he said maybe he could take me to one someday. Then Karen came back and told me to leave him alone. She looked really mad, so I left."

I made note of the name, but I wasn't going to interrogate Lacey. I was going to let her tell this her way.

"Was this a week or so ago?" I asked.

She shook her head. "Before Christmas. Then, I saw him on the 'L' during the holidays and he took me for lunch. He bought me stuff."

She twisted one hand over her injured wrist.

"He seemed really nice."

I nodded.

"He wasn't nice," she said, and brought her knees up to her chest. Then she cried out in pain and straightened them. "I—can't, Uncle Bill."

"It's okay," I said. "You don't have to say anymore."

Even though I wanted to know more. I'd have to ask later.

Lacey kept rubbing her wrist. Then she said, "Her name is Karen Frazier and I haven't seen her since. No one has. Not for, you know, a year or so. I was surprised to see her that day. You think she's okay?"

I couldn't lie to Lacey, but I didn't want to tell her what I really thought. "I don't know," I said. "I'll do my best to find out."

"God," she said, and fell back against the pillow. "I'm so stupid, Uncle Bill."

"Lace, we talked about that—"

"You remember that day you took us to that house?" She talked over me like she hadn't even heard me. "In December? When those guys, those Panthers, were killed?"

Althea and Franklin had been so mad at me. I took the older kids on a tour of the house where Fred Hampton and Mark Clark were murdered.

133

Thousands of us went through it because the police forgot to seal it off. The Black Panther Party had opened the house so everyone could see what the police had done, could see the lies.

I figured the kids had to know what kind of world we lived in. I figured they had to know the dangers of gangs and the white police, and how what you saw told you what was true when the authorities lied.

I hadn't realized that the kids were already living in the same world as Clark and Hampton. I hadn't realized that they already *knew*.

"I remember taking you there," I said softly.

"I thought that was so lame," she said. "And gross. All that blood. And it smelled."

She had walked through, eyes mostly averted, head down.

"I thought, stuff like that only happens to stupid people, people who carry guns and threaten the cops and don't get good grades and stuff."

The grades almost made me smile. It reminded me how young she was.

"I'm sorry, Uncle Bill," she said.

"For what?" I asked.

"You were trying to show us that stuff happens to everybody and I thought it was lame."

"It's all right, Lacey," I said.

"I should have *listened*," she said. "I should have."

She had started back into the recriminations.

"Lace," I said, "things happen to all of us. Jimmy and Keith, they got you out of there. They rescued you."

She nodded. "They're amazing."

"That hotel room lives here, though, right?" I tapped my forehead. "You're still in there."

She didn't move.

"We'll get you out," I said, making a promise I wasn't sure I could keep. "Me and Marvella and her friends and your family. We'll get you out."

"You'll get rid of Clyde?"

It startled me to her speak Voss's first name. "I already have," I said. That was the best I could do, the only admission I would ever make. "He's not going after anyone ever again."

"Guaranteed?" she said.

"Guaranteed," I said.

"How do I *know*?"

I almost asked, *Have I ever lied to you?* But I had. I lied to her every day. She called me *Uncle Bill*, for God's sake, when we weren't related at all.

"You know because I can't tell you any more than what I just said. If I do, then people can ask you questions and you might have knowledge that could get you in trouble."

She frowned, winced, and swallowed hard. "What does that mean?"

"Think about it, Lace. I don't want you to get into trouble because you know something for an absolute fact."

She frowned and didn't wince this time. "You're still talking about Clyde?"

"I am," I said. "He won't bother you again. That's all you know. That's all you can know. Okay?"

Her gaze tracked around the room, stopping first on the dog, then on the window, then back at me.

"Jimmy says you do secret stuff to keep people safe," she said. "Is this what he means?"

Damn that kid. Even that was too much to tell people.

"That's what he means," I said.

She relaxed suddenly. Then she pulled the dog close. "I'm gonna sleep now, I think," she said.

"I'll send your mom back," I said.

"No hurry," she said, and closed her eyes.

I wanted to tuck the blanket around her. I wanted to kiss the bruised forehead. I wanted to hug her so tight that I would never let her go.

Instead, I stood, and quietly made my way to the door.

"Uncle Bill?" she said.

I glanced over my shoulder. Her good eye was open.

"Thank you," she said.

"You're welcome," I said, and let myself out.

23

I found Althea in the cafeteria. At this time of day, the cafeteria was mostly empty, although the odors of gelatinous gravy and burned coffee hung over everything. A fat middle-aged man sat in the corner, his face in his hands. From his posture, he might have been crying. A white woman sat on the other side of the room, absently stirring a cup of coffee, a piece of chocolate cake untouched before her.

Althea clutched her own cup of coffee. A pile of newspapers spread across the table. She had pushed aside an orange tray. It was covered with empty plates. Apparently she hadn't had lunch until now.

I slipped into the chair across from her. "Okay," I said. "How is Lacey really?"

Althea's eyes lined with tears. She wiped at them angrily. "When I was sixteen, a white boy grabbed me on the beach, hit me against some rocks, and then I couldn't fight back. I didn't smile for a year, maybe more, and all I did was read. When Franklin met me, he thought I was so quiet, but before that, I was never quiet. I laughed all the time and was loud, and—dammit, Smokey. Damn."

I folded my hands. I wasn't surprised, although I wanted to be. It seemed like so many women I knew had a story like this one. The stories made me feel helpless.

She wiped at her eyes again. She wasn't looking at me.

I couldn't quite imagine a different Althea. The person she described sounded like Norene. Her youngest daughter wasn't an anomaly. She was a miniature version of her mother.

That thought made my heart literally ache.

"How is Lacey?" Althea grabbed a napkin and bent it over her forefinger. "How *is* Lacey? How do you think she is? Does she look the same to you?"

"No," I said.

Althea used the napkin to dab her eyes. "She's not. She never will be."

"At least you understand." The words hadn't sounded patronizing when I thought them. When I spoke them, they did. I wanted to take them back.

But Althea didn't seem to notice.

"Well, Franklin doesn't understand," she said, "and I'm trying to keep him from doing too much damage."

The damage had been done by Voss. But I didn't say that. I knew what Althea meant.

"Does Franklin know about you?" I asked.

She shook her head. "And you're not going to tell him either."

Other people's secrets. I was always keeping them. Sometimes it was hard to keep track of who knew what.

"Let me ask my question differently," I said softly. "Has the doctor said anything new since yesterday?"

"She's going to be able to have children," she said. "That much he's sure of. But, God, Smokey, what if she's pregnant now?"

"We'll deal with it," I said. "Whatever she chooses."

"God." She slapped her hand on the table. The dishes rattled and the white woman looked at her. The fat man didn't seem to notice. "God."

I wasn't sure if I should respond.

"I'm sending my kids back there," she said. "Every day, I'm sending them back there."

"I know," I said. "I'm not happy about it either."

She picked up a section of the newspaper in front of her and shook it at me. "This morning's *Chicago Tribune* says that eighteen thousand kids are taking an exam to get into the Catholic schools on Saturday. Eighteen *thousand*. I'll bet those are all white kids. And those kids, their parents can pay tuition. Or maybe they can't pay, and they'll get a scholarship that no one'll give to black kids."

"You don't want Lacey to go to a Catholic school right now," I said.

"That's not my point." Her voice had gone up even farther. The white woman leaned back in her chair. The fat man bowed his head, resting it on his arms.

"Where's Lacey going to go, Smokey? She's *thirteen*. She needs school, and I can't send her back there. I can't. I can barely send the other kids there, and even that…"

She let her voice trail off. She shook her head, then wiped her forehead with her right hand. Then she tossed the newspaper on top of the others.

"I've talked with Laura. She'll help," I said.

"Charity." Althea hissed out the word. "I have to take someone's charity because I can't provide for my kids. Who are going to live the same damn life I did. It won't get any better."

I had no idea what to tell her. My thoughts had gone along the same lines all day.

"I'm going to shut that hotel down," I said.

She crumpled the napkin into a ball. "And then what? Another will crop up in its place. And another. Plus we have the gangs now and the drug dealers and all that stuff on television telling the kids to tune out or drop in or whatever they say."

She set the napkin delicately on one of the plates. Her hand was shaking. "I'm so scared for her, Smokey."

"She's not going to go through this alone," I said. "She has you. She has Marvella, if you'll let her help. And I'll do what I can. I'm not good with the comforting part. But I can take care of the people who hurt her."

"People," Althea said. "You mean there was more than one?"

"He worked for someone else, Althea. It was an operation. I'm finding out who ran it. I told you this morning. I've already dealt with him."

She clutched at my hands. Her fingers dug into mine. "If you need me to do something, you just tell me. I can fire a gun."

I put one hand over hers. The last thing I wanted was an angry, bitter Althea beside me with a gun.

"You take care of your daughter," I said. "You don't think of anything else."

"I mean it," she said. "If those *people* need to be removed—"

"You'll take care of your daughter," I said. Althea wasn't exactly rational about this. She was seeing the crime through the prism of her own attack, which she clearly kept secret. "You'll trust me to do what I need to do."

"You'll tell me what happened, right? So I know?"

I ran my hand over hers, trying to calm her as best as I could. She wouldn't like what I was about to say.

"I'll tell you when I'm finished," I said. "That's all. You have a family. You have people who need you. We can't risk you."

"Jimmy needs you," she said.

He did. And I would be careful. "You'll be there if I'm not, right?"

I was gambling on a non-relative to take care of him. Either the Grimshaws or Laura. I didn't like that feeling anymore.

This crisis had gotten to all of us.

"Of course I will," Althea said. "Jimmy's like our own now."

"Good," I said.

"You're not going to let anything happen to you, are you, Smokey?"

What could I promise? That I would try? That I wouldn't do what she had just asked me to do? That I would ignore the hotel and the people who ran it?

"I'll be careful," I promised.

I just wasn't certain careful would be enough.

24

I picked up the kids from the after-school program and took them to the Grimshaw house. Franklin wasn't home yet. I wasn't sure if I was upset or relieved about that. I knew I had to talk with him, too; I just wasn't sure what to say.

Before I took Jimmy home, I made sure Jonathan would take care of his siblings and not go off on some teenage adventure. He was offended that I asked if he would watch them, but he promised me he would.

That was good enough for me. They were home, they were safe, and their parents would be back shortly.

I needed to take Jimmy home, and I needed to spend the evening with him. I couldn't do much more on the hotel right now. I wanted to wait until I heard from Laura. If she could buy the hotel and bulldoze it, that would solve one problem.

It wouldn't solve all of them.

Jimmy had moved to the front seat after I dropped off the Grimshaw children. He knew that I hated driving when he sat in the back, as if I were his chauffer. Usually we played a half-hearted game in which I had to coax him up front, but not on this day.

On this day, he sat quietly, hands folded in his lap, watching as we drove down the dark streets.

"You seen Lace?" he asked when we were nearly home.

"I did," I said. "She's better."

"Good," he said. "She coming home?"

"Soon," I said.

"Kids is already saying stupid stuff, like they knowed she was gonna get in trouble." Jimmy wasn't looking at me.

"They knew what happened?" I asked.

He shrugged. "They know some. They know me and Keith got her outta there. I think someone seen something, but I don't know who."

I turned the van onto our street. "Was this because Franklin talked to the principal?"

If so, Decker and I would have another conversation, one that wasn't so civil.

"Naw. They knowed right from the start. Uncle Franklin was in the office when kids were saying stuff. Keith wanted to punch people, but I told him that wasn't the way to do nothing. We use violence only when we gotta, right, Smoke?"

"Right," I said, not liking the "we" or the desire to fight or any of this.

I had to park half a block away. It took a little while to find a parking spot that didn't have a pile of snow from the last plow running down the side.

We got out. Jimmy was carrying a pile of books, and I put my hand on his shoulder as we walked on the unshoveled sidewalk toward the apartment complex.

Once we stepped inside, my eyes started to water. The smell of vinegar and spices and something that smelled vaguely like dirty socks filled the hallway.

"Oh, phew," Jimmy said, stuffing one mitten against his nose. "What's that?"

"Someone's cooking something," I said, although it wasn't something that we usually smelled in this building. If we smelled anything unusual, it was the African meals that Marvella tried when she thought she could impress a boyfriend or a visitor. Those usually smelled of boiled meat, which was also not one of my favorites.

"That don't smell like food," Jimmy said. "Yew."

He ran up the stairs. I walked behind him.

"It's worse up here," he said as he waited for me to unlock the door.

I had my keys out when the door opened. The waft of stink grew. It came from my apartment.

Marvella peered out. "Sorry," she said. "I figured it was easier to let him in."

Jimmy gave me a baleful look. I reached the top of the stairs.

Marvella was barefoot. She wore a thick caftan that might have been a robe. I couldn't quite tell. A multicolored scarf kept her hair off her face.

"That them?" A voice boomed from inside. Jack Sinkovich.

Jimmy gave me a look that quite clearly said, *I can't believe you invited him!*

I spread my hands and shrugged, conveying as clearly as I could that I hadn't invited him at all.

"Ask Grimshaw what's his poison," Sinkovich said. "And close the door. We don't want to gas out the neighbors."

"Too late," Jimmy said as he stepped inside. "What's that smell?"

I walked in as well. My eyes watered, but my stomach growled. Apparently something in that stench appealed to my taste buds.

Sinkovich stood near my stove, holding a wooden spoon. He was no longer wearing his dress uniform. He had on a pair of Levi's and a thick green and gold sweater that someone had crocheted for him long enough ago that it had rips in the elbows. He wore a white shirt underneath it.

"That smell," he said, "is kluskyzeekeyvasnakapoosta à la Sinkovich."

At least, that was what I thought he said. I pushed the door closed.

"What?" Jimmy asked.

"K-l-u-s-k-i-z-k-w-a—"

"I think he heard you," I said as I took off my parka. "I just don't think he understood you."

"As if *you* did," Marvella said under her breath.

"It's an old family recipe," Sinkovich said. "A favorite of mine. My mom taught me to make it when I was Jim's age. We don't do it as a side dish. We add some Polish, and then we serve it like a casserole. Comfort food. You'll like it."

I doubted it.

"Some Polish?" Jimmy asked.

Sinkovich rolled his eyes at me. "How long's this kid been in Chicago and he don't know from Polish?"

"Polish sausage," Marvella said, this time loud enough for everyone to hear.

Jimmy turned toward me, tugged off his coat, and said, "We got left-over pizza. I want that."

I wanted that too. "Don't be rude. Jack cooked for us. You should say thank you."

"Yeah, but it smells like feet," Jimmy whispered.

It took all of my self-control to suppress a smile.

Marvella didn't even try. Her eyes twinkled as she looked at me. "I found Jack sitting on the steps just outside our apartments, with two grocery bags. I let him in. He promised dinner, and I figured with the past two days, that was a good idea."

"I know you guys ain't never ate home-cooked Polish food," Sinkovich said. "Give it a shot. You don't like, you can have your pizza."

"Don't promise him that," I said as I walked into the kitchen. I grabbed a Coke out of the fridge. "He won't even try it if you say that."

"Oh, you gotta try," Sinkovich said to Jimmy. "I got a kid. I know the tricks. You gotta have at least six mouthfuls that you *swallow* before you say you don't like."

"Great," Jimmy said without enthusiasm. "Can I have a Coke too?"

"No," I said. "Milk with dinner."

"Goes better anyway," Sinkovich said. The stove's timer buzzed behind him. He opened the oven door, and a waft of scent reached me. Cardamom, cabbage, onions, and scents I didn't recognize. Yes, the smell was strong, but it was better up close.

I popped the ringtop and dumped the ring inside the can. "I thought you had to be in court today."

"Ah, hell, don't remind me," Sinkovich said. "It was so fun. And then I made phone calls for you. Even more fun. We can talk after food, okay?"

Had he come over here because he was lonely and needed friends or had he come because he didn't want to talk about what he discovered on the phone?

I couldn't tell. He had bent over the open oven door, and was struggling with something inside. After a moment, he pulled out a bubbling casserole, filled with flat noodles, sauerkraut, sliced Polish sausage, and mushrooms. I didn't recognize the sauce.

Steam rose from the entire thing. I had to admit, it all looked better than it smelled.

I got out plates and silverware. "You're staying, right, Marvella?"

"Oh," she said with a small smile at Jimmy. "I wouldn't miss it."

Jimmy sighed and flopped down at his spot. "Six bites," he said to Sinkovich.

"Big ones," Sinkovich said. He didn't even seem bothered by Jimmy's reluctance to eat the food. Sinkovich put hot pads in the middle of the table and set the casserole dish on top of them. I had napkins, courtesy of last night's pizza delivery, so I set them beside every plate.

We sat down.

"I'll serve," Sinkovich said, and proceeded to put a mound of food on all four plates.

Jimmy shook his head "I don't want—"

"I'll bet Grimshaw here don't believe in the Clean Plate Club," Sinkovich said. "I know I don't. You do me a kindness and try, and I won't say nothing if you decide cold pizza's more to your taste."

Jimmy looked at me, eyebrows raised. Then he shrugged and took a bite.

I did too. The casserole was surprisingly good. Sinkovich had cooked everything in butter so thick that it dripped off each bite. The sausage gave the meal a sharp spice, but that spice got reinforced by the sauerkraut, which crunched despite spending time soaking in butter and being baked.

"Wow," Marvella said after taking a bite. "I'm going to have to ask for the recipe."

Sinkovich shook his head. "Now you're just being polite."

"No," she said. "I'm not."

She took another bite. Jimmy took his second as well. He didn't say anything and he didn't try to chase it all down with his milk.

"I didn't expect you to be a chef," I said to Sinkovich.

"Single guy," he said. "I gotta do something to keep busy."

His wife had left him nearly a year ago now. She had taken his only child north, and had sued for full custody. After the divorce was final, she planned to remarry.

All of that broke Sinkovich's heart, but he wasn't fighting as hard as he probably should have. He felt beleaguered. His marriage was over, his job was in jeopardy, and his old friends claimed they didn't recognize him any longer.

"If you keep cooking like this," Marvella said, "you could start a second career as a restaurateur."

"Or a first one," Sinkovich said, his gaze meeting mine. "You don't know what a can of worms you opened today."

"Me?" I asked.

Jimmy looked up from his meal. The casserole mound was half gone. He liked it too, although he wasn't willing to say yet. And Sinkovich's comment might've just put him off his food.

"Simple questions ain't so simple sometimes," Sinkovich said to me.

"Is this about Lacey?" Jimmy asked.

Sinkovich nodded. "Yeah. She okay?"

"No." Jimmy actually sounded bitter. "She's still in the hospital."

I looked at Marvella. She was watching all of us. "I talked to Althea again," I said. "She needs you, even if she doesn't ask for you."

"I'll see what I can do," Marvella said.

Sinkovich was still looking at Jimmy. "I hear from Marvella here that you're some kinda hero."

Jimmy shrugged and took such a large swig of milk that it left a mustache. "I just done what Smoke woulda done."

Sinkovich gave me a sideways glance that didn't have any approval in it. "Sounds like you mighta saved her life."

Jimmy seemed alarmed. I thought he had known that, but maybe having a police officer confirm it startled him.

"God knows what would have happened if Jimmy hadn't been there," I said.

"Well, you deserve more than kluskyzeekeyvasnakapoosta à la Sinkovich for that. I got cake too, and this one I didn't make."

145

"Really?" Jimmy asked. "Cake?"

"Yeah," Sinkovich said. "Angel food, but that ain't no comment on nothing."

Marvella covered her mouth, stifling a laugh.

"You coulda said that first," Jimmy said. "I might not've been such a jerk about the pizza."

I grinned at Sinkovich. "Don't believe him. He has already forgotten that he planned on hating this meal."

"I can't pronounce it and it smells like feet. Why would anyone think it was going to be good?" Jimmy asked.

"You gotta respect logic," Sinkovich said. I wasn't sure why he was so cheerful, particularly after the day he had planned to have.

"You can tell me what you was gonna tell just Smokey," Jimmy said. "It's okay."

"Actually, it's not," I said. "This one's on me. You did the hard part. Now let me handle the investigation. That's what you're here about, right, Jack? The questions I had?"

Sinkovich nodded.

"Didn't have a lot of time because of the trial, you know. Jim, you ever wanna do a civics paper on the way trials work, you interview me. I'll tell you all about this thing. It's nuts."

"You can't change the subject," Jimmy said.

"Yes, we can," I said. "Why don't you tell us how the Grimshaws are doing. How's Keith?"

"Oh, God," Jimmy said, then he frowned at Sinkovich. "Can I do something?"

"What?" he asked.

"Can I tell you what happened so I can tell Keith I went to the police? He thinks you guys can do something about them hotels and hookers and stuff. He's just a kid. He don't know how the world works."

Sinkovich's cheeks flushed bright red. "And you do?"

"On this stuff, yeah. Smoke says I know too much. Can I tell him?" Jimmy asked. He looked at me.

"Jimmy's mother exposed him to things that no child should have seen," I said to Sinkovich.

"Ah, more of that secret stuff." Sinkovich served himself a bit more casserole and offered some to Jimmy, who, to my surprise, nodded. "I get it. And I know you're wiser than your years, kiddo. And yeah, you can tell Keith you talked to the cops. Tell him…tell him we're doing what we can, okay?"

"And what is that, exactly?" Jimmy asked.

"We investigate first, then we act," Sinkovich said.

I winced. It was that attitude, which I had also expressed countless times, that had prevented Jimmy from going to me.

"You're investigating now?" Jimmy asked.

"Yep," Sinkovich said.

"And that's what you gotta talk to Smoke about?"

"Yes," Sinkovich said.

"You guys need me, I know stuff," Jimmy said.

"Like what?" Marvella asked.

Jimmy polished off his second helping. "I dunno. Just stuff."

We all looked at him.

He shrugged. "I'm just saying, I can be pretty dang useful sometimes."

"If we ever doubted that," Sinkovich said, "you proved otherwise yesterday. Good job, kiddo."

Jimmy grinned. "Does that mean I get cake?"

"You betcha," Sinkovich said. "Then you let me and Grimshaw here talk, and you don't eavesdrop. Promise?"

Jimmy nodded. "Promise," he said.

25

C ake, conversation, and actual laughter. Sinkovich turned what I
thought would be a difficult evening into something almost pleas-
ant. If someone had ever asked me if Sinkovich could be a ray of sun-
shine on a difficult day, I would have laughed in disbelief.

But he had, and Jimmy seemed to forget just how rough the day had
been. Marvella promised to help Jimmy with the dishes so they could get
it done in time for *Medical Center*.

Normally, I would have mentioned homework. On this night, I didn't
have the heart.

Sinkovich and I went into my office and closed the door. That room
always felt particularly claustrophobic with two people in it, but it was
the only truly private room in the apartment.

I sat down behind my desk. Sinkovich sat down across from me. I
turned on the desk lamp, and bent it away from us. The overhead light
was thin, and the desk lamp helped just a little if I pointed it in the
right direction.

"So," I said, "you investigated the Starlite and there's something about
it you can't tell me on the phone."

He laughed.

"Ah, hell, Grimshaw. You don't investigate dumps like that. And besides, maybe I just wanted to see your pretty face and find out what the kid got into."

"Marvella told you about it," I said.

"She did. That kid, he's great, but he's gonna get hurt. You gotta do something about him. He's gotta learn fists mean nothing. Brains're the important thing."

"I know. I'm not happy about any of this." I didn't need a lecture from Sinkovich about Jimmy. "But let's start with the Starlite."

Sinkovich leaned back in the chair as if it was actually comfortable, and folded his hands over his stomach, hiding some of that ugly sweater. "I done a drive-by on the way back to the precinct. Lucky for you, court got out about three, so I had some time, which I ain't had a lot of lately, because of that goddamn circus."

I let him complain. I wasn't going to ask about it, because we'd have another half-hour digression.

"You ain't kidding about that dump being close. Jesus, Grimshaw, what're you thinking, letting your kid go to that school? You know that's Stones territory too, right?"

"Yes," I said tightly. "Jimmy's not the only child in that school. There are hundreds."

Sinkovich leaned his head on the back of the chair and sighed. "I know. Fucking city. I shouldn't blame you for that school. I know you're doing what you can. One reason I ain't fighting Charlene so hard on the custody is she took my kid to Minnesota and not Minneapolis, neither. To one of them smaller towns, where they don't got gangs and drugs and hookers right next to the school. My kid'll get a public school education, and it'll be a good one."

I picked up a pen and ran it between my fingers. I hadn't realized that Sinkovich had thought through the custody battle with his son. I had simply assumed that he had decided not to fight, like so many men did. I hadn't realized he wanted his child out of this part of Chicago.

It made complete sense, considering everything Sinkovich saw every day.

He said, "First thing I done when I got back to the precinct today was check the zoning for that block. It is a school zone, which means no bars close by and shit like that. But I don't know what you know about zoning in the Great City of Chicago, but lemme tell you that it's designed not to enforce the laws, but to enforce the Machine's agenda. If they don't like the Starlite, they'll use crap like zoning laws to shut it down."

I raised my eyebrows.

"You think they would shut down the Starlite?" I asked, trying not to sound hopeful.

He held up his right index finger, warning me to be quiet for a moment.

"I think if that sleaze-bag hotel was next to that fancy-pants Catholic school the mayor sends his kids to, then yeah, I think the city'd shut it down in a heartbeat. Have you looked at that damn Catholic school? It's on the edge of the Black Belt, and the neighborhood is scrubbed fucking clean."

"I hadn't looked," I said.

"Yeah, well, Catholic schools are private and the Archdiocese of Chicago keeps them up. They're all bragging about the education level and shit." Sinkovich sat up and peered at me sheepishly. "Me and my lawyer looked at them before we started on this custody thing. It'd cost an arm and a ball to send my kid to private school. I'd love to send the kid there, but even if I didn't eat and lived on the goddamn street, I couldn't afford that place."

He was serious. He had looked at every single way he could afford to send his son to a Catholic school.

"I can't afford it either," I said.

"Yeah, but you got Laura and she loves Jim. You might wanna—"

"Tell me about the Starlite." I'd been having this conversation all day, and I didn't want to continue it with Sinkovich.

He nodded, realizing I was shutting him down. He rubbed a hand over his mouth, thought, remembered where he was (although I had no idea how, since his conversation had been all over the map), and then he said, "The Starlite's a longtime operation, been handed from man to man since Prohibition. It was a Black Belt speakeasy and specialized in policy back in the day."

When I was growing up, policy had been the most popular form of gambling in the black community. It was a three-number lottery system, and the policy sheets or cards or whatever the local system used, were sold for pennies, nickels and dimes, all of which added up to a small fortune.

There were policy operations in Chicago still, but they had decreased in importance, especially since some lottery games had gone mainstream. The *Chicago Defender* was running what I considered a policy type giveaway, printing the winning numbers in every issue. Jimmy wanted to play because he was convinced he'd win the $500 prize.

So far, I hadn't let him. I didn't want him to learn how to gamble.

"So, there are policy games at the Starlite?" I asked.

"Not now," Sinkovich said. "Policy cleared out about the time Lewis got murdered."

"Who?" I asked.

"Ah, jeez," Sinkovich said. "Sometimes it seems like you know more shit about this town than I do, and then I realize you don't know nothing. Benjamin Lewis, alderman, 24th Ward—that's Lawndale, West Side, you know?"

"I know." I had been learning about local politics.

"February, 1963. He's found in his office, handcuffed to the chair and shot through the head three times. Everybody knows it was the Outfit, ain't nobody gonna do nothing about it."

"The Outfit?" I asked.

Sinkovich rolled his eyes. He had more in common with Jimmy than I realized. "You know, the Mob, the Mafia, the Syndicate, you know, like that stupid Puzo book, the whatsis…"

"*The Godfather*," I said. It was a bestseller that held no interest for me. "I didn't know the Chicago mob was called the Outfit."

All of this time with Laura, knowing her father was connected to the Chicago mob, and I had never heard the phrase "the Outfit." It actually made me wonder how many references to the organization that I had missed because I didn't know the slang.

"That's Chicago's name for it, because you know us, we always gotta have different names for the same old shit. Anyway, Lewis apparently got too big for his britches and decided after his election he'd take out the white precinct captains and install his guys—"

"Wouldn't that anger Mayor Daley?" I asked. "He *was* mayor then, right?"

"Oh, yeah, it did piss him off, and we don't none of us talk about the mayor and the Outfit, okay?"

"Not even in the privacy of my own apartment?" I asked.

"No," Sinkovich said with great force. "You want your kid repeating shit we say about that fat slug? You don't say nothing. *I* don't say nothing. It's dangerous."

I was a bit surprised at his vehemence. He was afraid of Daley. Or Daley's Machine. Or both.

"But you're saying the Outfit killed Lewis."

"It was a hit, simple as that. Ain't many groups in this town what do a hit. In addition taking out the precinct captains, this brilliant jiga— sorry, Jesus, sorry." He blushed.

He would never have caught himself in the past, nor would he have blushed. Still, the fact that he probably used such words when I wasn't around irritated me.

"You say you're sorry, and yet that filth still comes out of your mouth," I snapped.

"I *am* sorry, but you know that name is what we used to call that clown. It just snuck out from habit. I don't think like that no more. In fact, I'm talking to you like you's one of the guys. Because I don't think of you as, you know—"

"Black," I said.

"Different from me," he said at the same time. "Hand to God."

Even though I shook my head, I believed him. We'd fought about his language before. We would probably fight about it again.

"So, this Lewis," I said, prompting Sinkovich.

"Well," he said, looking relieved that we had moved on, "in addition to taking out them captains, he decides he's gonna rewrite the splits on policy and pocket most of the profits himself. *That's* why he got killed, at least that's what the rumors say, and it's a pretty good reason when you think about it. What nobody knows is who leaked the information on his changes. I don't think Daley had something to do with it because he was up for election against Adamowski, who wasn't no saint neither. Although, everybody knows nothing happens in Daley's city, especially to one of his pols, without him knowing about it."

I was trying to follow Sinkovich's point, and wrap it back to something that mattered to me.

"Whoever was managing the Starlite, then, got out of policy," I said.

"Well, not quite," Sinkovich said. "Back in the day, the Starlite was known for *escorts*, you know, the upscale girls, because it was an upscale place, and if your taste went to—forgive me—chocolate," and then he did a little bow, deciding, apparently, that he had said something offensive when it was probably the least offensive thing he'd said, "then you'd go down to the Starlite. Clientele was mostly what do you call it now? Black, right?"

"Right," I said.

"But lotsa big time white guys showed up too, because the girls were choice. After the war, the neighborhood went all to hell, and the girls went from high rent to low rent, and policy was where the money went."

"You know a lot about this for one hour's research," I said.

"Ya think?" He opened his hands in a don't-blame-me gesture. "I'll tell you why in a minute. But lemme get the history lesson out first."

I settled in my chair. "All right."

"So, Lewis dies. It's all over the news. The mayoral candidates are squealing about it, the press is eating it for lunch, everyone's talking about the corrupt mayor, and no one's looking at the policy wheels, which go right on spinning and the cash goes right into the pocket of the Outfit, like it done since the war."

"And the Starlite?" I asked.

"Well, here's where it gets interesting, least I think so. The guy what owned the Starlite, Arnold Garon, he ends up in a ditch, three shots to the head, about the same time as Lewis. Dead as the proverbial doorknob. And he ain't the only one. Lots of dead club owners around the Black Belt and the West Side, prob'ly the guys what paid Lewis for policy and looked the other way when he pocketed the cash. The Outfit can be pretty unforgiving if you don't tell them someone's screwing with them."

I felt cold. "You're saying that the Outfit, the *mob*, owns the Starlite."

"They don't own nothing, Grimshaw. That's the beauty of the whole thing. They let some guy run his own business, and then that guy pays protection or a percentage or gets his supplies from the Outfit, and that's what we call mobbed up. Sometimes they bring up a guy who's low rent, ya know? Someone trying to make his bones with the guys upstairs and if he done a good job, then he gets promoted."

Like Laura's father. He owned Sturdy Investments outright, but he had gotten his start in Chicago as a mob enforcer—at least, that was what we believed and what the evidence implied. Over the years, he became even more respectable. However, it was his goal to make Laura as respectable as possible. He kept her in the dark about all aspects of his life. She didn't find out his connection to the mob until her mother died, years later.

I was still trying to wrap my mind around the things that Sinkovich had told me. Because I really hadn't paid a lot of attention to the Chicago mob, even with its affiliation with Sturdy.

All we had been trying to do was get the mob out of Sturdy. We hadn't really—or maybe *I* hadn't really—focused on what the mob was.

"I'm confused," I said. "The mob would work with a black businessman in the Black Belt? I thought the mob was white only."

"In other cities, yeah, but imagine some white guy coming deep in the Black Belt and trying to get stuff done. He might own a building, but he couldn't run policy or handle the girls in a way that didn't arouse suspicion."

"So the mob has black members," I said.

"In Chicago, yeah, sure," Sinkovich said. "They ain't lieutenants, most of them, but if they got juice, they got connections."

I was still frowning. I hadn't realized that. It challenged a lot of my assumptions about life on the South Side.

Sinkovich could see that I was still grappling with this.

"Okay," he said. "Think it through. Chicago had a syndicate long before the Outfit, and before that, we got gangsters up the wazoo. Y'know, the Depression? Capone? There was a big Irish contingent in the Chicago Syndicate. We got Yids, we got Micks, we got Wops—"

"Now you're just doing that to piss me off, aren't you?" I snapped.

He grinned, then shrugged. "Hey, I'm your basic Polack. Whaddo I know?"

I shook my head. "Stop now, all right?"

"All right," he said. "But what I'm telling you is this: We're clannish and bigoted in this city, but we'll go to bed with whoever we need to go to bed with to make money. The Outfit is mostly I-tals and Jews, but they ain't gonna get a lot done in parts of this city with that background. So there're Irish in the mob, which is where you get your connection to the mayor. And then, here in the Black Belt, they ain't got no qualms about working with the right blacks. Rumor says they do it through Dawson."

"*William* Dawson?" I asked. "The United States Congressman?"

"One and the same," Sinkovich said. "He used to approve whatever went on down here, but after the Lewis shooting, folks was saying that Daley defanged Dawson, put some power white guys over him, and let him think he was still in charge. I don't know if that's true, but it sounds true, and in this city, what sounds true usually is."

"Okay," I said as I tried to clear my head of all the racist slurs mixed in with the strange history lesson. "You're telling me that the Outfit has an interest in the Starlite."

"I know Eddie Turner, owner of the Starlite, used to run numbers for the Outfit. I know he had a way with systems, and I suspect he got rewarded big time when Garon bit it. Turner ain't small potatoes. He shows up at all kindsa functions all over the city."

"And he's black?" I thought I would have known about black men who received city-wide attention.

"E-yup. He don't get his name in the papers much, but you see him, lurking around the edges of events, kinda like. Camera-shy. Like you."

It surprised me that Sinkovich had noticed that. Maybe I shouldn't have been surprised, since he was a cop, and a better one than I usually gave him credit for.

"Camera shy because of his mob connections?" I asked.

"You got mob connections?" Sinkovich asked, and then answered himself. "'Course you don't. Because one don't follow the other. I think there's some other reason this guy's not letting his mug get into the papers. But I ain't been curious enough to investigate."

There could be a million reasons for Turner's unwillingness to be photographed, although the main one might be exactly the same as mine: His name didn't match the name others knew him under.

"And this Eddie Turner," I said, "he *owns* the Starlite. He doesn't just run the operation."

"Oh, he runs the operation," Sinkovich said. "Not that you'd find that out from any newspaper or legal document. On paper, the Starlite hotel and its restaurant are the only businesses he owns."

"On paper," I repeated. "Meaning those are his only legitimate businesses. What else does he do?"

"Your kid stumbled into it, my friend," Sinkovich said. "It ain't just about the by-the-hour girls. It's about selling them off like so much meat."

The casserole rolled over in my stomach. I stood, unable to sit with that image, especially since my brain immediately applied it to Lacey. I walked over to the window and stood in front of it, but didn't see anything except my own reflection, a big grim man who looked vaguely defeated.

"You knew about this," I said after a moment.

Sinkovich's reflection raised its hands like I had pulled a gun. "I just found out today, Grimshaw, because you asked."

"That's a lot to find out in one hour," I said.

"That's the second time you said that. You implying something?"

"This morning, you said you didn't know anything about the Starlite," I said.

"And I *didn't*." Sinkovich moved the chair with a scrape so that he faced my back. "I'm in deep shit because I was looking into this."

His expression, reflected in the glass, looked frightened. He wasn't putting on a show for me because he didn't know I could see him.

"Someone told you all of this?" I asked.

His expression had changed as I turned around. He hadn't wanted me to see how scared he was.

"Well, some of this I did know," he said. "You know, Lewis, the death of his policy guys, shit like that. It was big news in my circles, not that it all hit the papers."

"But you didn't know about the Starlite," I said.

He shook his head.

I leaned against the big wooden filing cabinet. "They're paying protection."

"Yeah," he said.

"So they're in bed with the cops and the Outfit."

"No," he said, and sighed. "The cops don't care about some lowlife in some hotel in the Black Belt. No offense, Grimshaw."

"None taken," I said. "Although he would pay protection right? Some cop in the area is on the take."

"Not just some," Sinkovich said. "More than I like to think about. They figured I wanted in. I had to do some pretty dancing to get my so-called colleagues outta my face."

I hadn't expected him to get into trouble with one simple question. "Clarify something for me," I said. "If a bunch of cops get protection money from an operation like that, then either the powers that be are looking the other way or taking part of that cash, right?"

"There's been a lotta lookin' the other way," Sinkovich said. "The law says you can't practice prostitution within one thousand yards of a school. If you do and get caught, it raises the charge one felony grade."

I frowned. "And they let the Starlite stay in business? How much would that cost on weekly basis?"

Sinkovich sighed. "I ain't with internal affairs. I don't know that shit. I never took money from no businesses. I thought you knew that."

"I do know that," I said. He was getting testy. I didn't mean to insult him. He had done me a favor, apparently at a great personal cost. "You wouldn't be a continual guest in my home if you were that kind of man."

"If I were that kinda man," he muttered, "my kid would be going to De La Salle for fucking free."

He was right; some people were uncorruptible, even when it benefit-ted them. Maybe that was what I liked about Sinkovich. He was raised to be a bigoted hard-ass, and he had gotten disturbed by the things that attitude had brought him. He didn't like how it made him feel, and with just a little support from a man he barely knew, he changed enough to destroy much of his life.

"So," I said, "I'm not asking you this because I think you're involved. I'm asking you because you're the only person I can ask who might actu-ally have a clue. An accurate clue. Do the powers that be just look the other way or do they make money too?"

"Depends on what you call the powers that be. That fat slug of a mayor, they've been trying to bring him down on corruption charges for years. He ain't interested in money. He don't stockpile it. He wants the freakin' city to bow down to him and kiss his tiny little feet."

I smiled at the image. "I didn't really mean the mayor. I meant within the police department. If cops are on the take, then how high does it go?"

Sinkovich shrugged. "I honestly don't know. I can tell you this much, though. With businesses like the Starlite, the orders we get come from one of two places."

"The Outfit or the Machine," I said.

"Yep," he said. "One or the other or both."

"In this case, you think what?" I asked.

He bit his thumbnail like a little boy. He thought for a long moment before answering me.

"Grimshaw," he said, "I got an order to stop looking after an hour. One fucking hour. And everyone's nervous. Okay? I stopped asking questions. I got a little scared so I bought me some comfort food and decided to share. Decided that the mayor and the department and that stupid Judge Hoffman wasn't going to ruin my day. I was gonna see you and your super-duper kid and that pretty neighbor of yours, and I was gonna enjoy my night. You should too."

Loops upon loops. Sinkovich said one thing and often meant another. Or everything. He wanted me to stop asking questions, even though he knew I wouldn't.

What I did know was that I had to stop asking them of him. At least for now.

When I didn't respond, he tapped his forefinger on my desk. "I mean it. You lay off this one. The little girl's safe. Your kid's a hero. You're done now."

I nodded. "You'd think I would be."

"Jesus," he said. "Let it go."

"I can't," I said. "That hotel is right next to the school. What am I supposed to do?"

"Move your kids," he said. "Jim, them cousins of his, everybody."

"Where?" I asked.

"Hell, I don't know," Sinkovich said. "Borrow money from your rich girlfriend. It's worth saving your kid's life, right?"

I bowed my head. There were days—months, years really—where it seemed like nothing would ever go right. Ever since Martin died, it felt that way. Ever since I fled Memphis while the entire damn country burned.

Thing was, the flames hadn't made the country any better. It wasn't worse either. It was just the same, mired in the same old shit, and no matter what happened, we couldn't seem to escape it.

"Eddie Turner and his operation recruits girls out of that school," I said softly. "Those girls not even in high school yet."

"And you are not the savior of the entire world, Grimshaw," Sinkovich said in a tone I'd never heard him use before. "First thing you learn as a cop is that you can't clean up all the filth. You just gotta rejoice in the small victories."

"What victory do we have here?" I asked him. "Lacey's in the hospital, the entire family's traumatized, and in the Starlite, there's some joker who is making a boatload of money off girls just like her."

"I told you. Your kid's a hero. The girl's safe. *Those* are victories," Sinkovich said.

I shook my head.

"Jesus, Grimshaw. Think. When I solve some murder, I don't bring back the dead. I put some scumbag away, get him off the street, and maybe save some other person he'd've touched. Does it stop murder? Hell, no. It don't even stop murder on that block maybe even for that day. But it's a small victory."

"Lacey knew one of the other girls," I said. "I'll wager that the Grimshaw children know a lot of the girls who've disappeared into this 'operation' as you call it."

"And there's fucking hookers in the Bible," Sinkovich said. "Each one—each hooker from then to now—has some sob story about how she got there."

"So, if we hadn't rescued Lacey, she would have had a 'sob story'?"

Sinkovich knew he had misspoke. But he wasn't backing down, and he usually backed down when I pushed him.

He tapped his finger on the desk again. "You don't mess with the Outfit. You don't mess with the Machine. They got *protection*, Grimshaw. Good enough protection that I got warned away in less than an hour. There ain't no cavalry here, and if you go after this Turner guy, then *you'll* end up in a ditch somewhere."

He ran a hand through his thinning hair. He sighed, and gave me a set look. I realized that the fear I had seen reflected in the window was behind his eyes now.

Sinkovich was terrified.

"I thought you was smart enough to know how to pick a fight," he said. "You can't win here. You'll leave your kid without a dad, and you'll make sure that the attention comes down on the whole family. You can't do that. You can't."

I thought about the Panther house, shot up and still filled with dried blood. I thought about how I had taken Lacey there, and how she thought I was exaggerating about the way the world worked, how she thought such things didn't apply to her.

And they shouldn't have.

Then I thought about her blood-covered go-go boots, about Keith's determination to call the police, about Franklin's anger, and Althea's heartbreak.

And Jimmy, who knew it was all going to happen because he had grown up with it. I believed I had rescued him from a life like that, and maybe I still could if I did the right thing by him.

But he was one kid, among hundreds of kids, thousands of kids, all of them at risk.

I couldn't go to the city government. Parents had been fighting the city all along, trying to get better schools, trying to improve education and security and get rid of the gangs and the drugs. It never seemed to end.

No progress got made, and the fights continued, year in and year out.

"There's gotta be something we can do," I said, more to myself than to Sinkovich.

But he heard me. "Yeah, there is something we can do. We can walk away."

I hated that. I had fled here because I had to save Jimmy. I'd been running for years. And it didn't matter. The worst things still caught up to me.

To us.

"You walk away," I said. "I still have a few things to try first."

Sinkovich rocked back in his chair and ran his hand over his face. "Son of bitch, Grimshaw. You don't get this. If something happens to you, I can't take care of your kid. I can't even take care of my own. And what'll happen to the other kids, the ones you drive to school every goddamn day? What happened to that poor little girl, it's just the tip of a very nasty iceberg. Walk away, Grimshaw. Please."

He wasn't going to let go, and he wasn't going to be able to help me.

"I will walk away," I said. "I promise. After I try two things, I'll walk."

"That might be two too many," Sinkovich said.

"Yeah," I said. "But right now, I tried enough."

26

I sat on the couch as all three television stations signed off for the night. I kept one light on, a yellow legal pad on my lap, but I hadn't written anything down. I wasn't sure what there was to write.

Jimmy had gone to sleep after too many chapters of *The Hobbit*. We'd read it three times already, but he'd talked Marvella into reading it again last night, and he wanted to continue tonight. I didn't have the heart to argue with him, although I drew the line at singing the songs. It was hard enough to read them aloud, particularly when my attention really wasn't on it.

Marvella had left with Sinkovich. On the way out, he had turned to me, pointed, and said, "I mean it," as if I had had doubts about his veracity. I had nodded, thanked him for the surprisingly good casserole, and closed the door.

Then I read to Jimmy, and watched the evening news, wishing, for the first time, that I had more than one television so I could watch more than one channel at a time.

I watched WMAQ, figuring if anyone had found Voss, that channel would have the story.

So far, no news.

That was when I got the legal pad and a pen from my office, and turned on the single light. I had planned to write down all the options I was thinking about, but I couldn't for two reasons.

The first was simple: I didn't want a record of anything untoward. The second was related to that: I wasn't sure what all of my options were.

Still, Sinkovich had made an impression. Twice, I reached for the phone and started to dial Laura before hanging up. Twice, I nearly told her to stop her investigation of that building.

Finally, I had to remind myself that she was the only person who could handle the investigation into the building itself. Sturdy had mob ties. Most people had no idea she was cleaning house.

And, after my discussion with Sinkovich, I wasn't sure there was enough of a top-down organization that would care about what she was doing. Just because one lieutenant heard that Sturdy was slowly dismissing its mobbed-up members didn't mean the lieutenant would tell anyone else.

If someone thought it a threat, they would have come after Laura already, and not in the corporate ways that a handful of people had already used against her.

She would have ended up handcuffed to a chair with three gunshots to her head.

The image made me shudder. In December of '68, we had made plans so that she would survive the takeover, figuring someone would take her out then if they were going to take her out.

But I had been under the mistaken assumption that the Chicago mob didn't kill truly well-known people. Sinkovich's story about Benjamin Lewis changed my mind on that.

I got up and changed the channel as WMAQ signed off. WBBM was still on the air, and I let it talk to me for a while. I started doodling on the legal pad, trying to calm myself. For the second night in a row, I wasn't sure I would get much sleep.

I hadn't lied to Sinkovich: I hoped that Laura could buy the Starlite and shut it down. I understood that doing so would move the operation elsewhere. Operations like that didn't just vanish because they'd lost a home.

But shutting down the Starlite would accomplish at least one of my agendas. It would get the operation away from the school.

It might accomplish a second agenda as well: It might lift the veil of protection for a very short period of time.

Protection was usually tied to location, because cops worked beats, and those beats were neighborhood- and precinct-based. If the operation had to switch neighborhoods, then a whole new group of cops would have to be put on retainer. The old ones wouldn't protect and the new ones wouldn't have been enlisted yet.

Who could blame an overzealous cop trying to restore his name if he arrested someone like Turner on prostitution and human-trafficking charges? Once Turner got into the system, once the newspapers were on it, once stations like WMAQ had covered the story, then the city would have to make some kind of effort to corral this guy.

Plus, if I could get this to happen fast, then the national news would still be here, and this would be one of those stories that might be a feature to accompany the Chicago Seven trial and Black Panther trial stories. Corrupt Chicago and its seedy underbelly. National reporters liked stories like that, particularly when they were handed those stories on a silver platter.

What I found myself doing, though, was doodling the name Jonathan had given me. Donna Loring. Jonathan had said that Donna Loring was the sister of one of Jeff Fort's right-hand men.

Fort had been featured on tonight's newscast. He'd been in jail on an aggravated battery charge, and the Blackstone Rangers—or the Black P. Stone Nation, as they were calling themselves now, apparently—had raised $8,000 in less than twenty-four hours to get Fort released. Fort's $75,000 bond had been a joke.

At least that was what the slime Hanrahan had said, and for once, I agreed with him. Edward V. Hanrahan was the murderer in the form of the state's attorney who had ordered the attack on the sleeping Black Panthers a month ago. On tonight's newscast, he had stated that the speed with which the Blackstone Rangers had put up bail—so fast that Fort's attorney had gone to court to ask for more time only to find out that Fort had already been released—showed the power of the street gangs.

I'd seen that power several times already. I'd gone up against it more than once. I'd harnessed it a few times, but it had been like holding onto a tornado.

Donna Loring.

I kept underlining her name, and thinking.

I had investigating to do.

27

At some point during that very long night, I fell asleep. This time, before sleep took me completely, I managed to get off the couch, drop the legal pad in my office, and tumble into my bed. I had nightmares—Lacey screaming, bloody boots, Jimmy finding my gun in the Chicago River—and they woke me up before the alarm went off.

Or before the alarm should have gone off, since I had forgotten to set it.

I got out of bed, showered, and woke Jimmy. I had time to make him a good breakfast for the second day in a row. The lack of sleep had at least one benefit.

Franklin drove the kids to school again. For a while, he wanted to control this one thing, and I would let him. He would remain vigilant, and that was what the kids needed. Today, he wanted to handle everything, including driving them to the after-school program. I suspected he wanted to have a discussion with Mrs. Armitage. He probably wanted a second look at that neighborhood as well.

All of this freed me to take care of my own business. I made some coffee and took it into my office. I reviewed my finances, which were messier than I wanted them to be. I hadn't paid enough attention these last few months.

I did have money squirreled away in Memphis. A friend of mine rented out my house there and put the money into an account for me. But I couldn't access it without drawing attention to myself. I didn't want anyone to trace Jimmy through me.

I had initially thought of that as Jimmy's college fund. At the moment, I needed to continue thinking of it that way.

I did need to drum up as much work as I could, in addition to the work I did for Sturdy. So as 9 a.m. rolled around, I contacted Bronzeville Home, Health, Life, and Burial Insurance. I did a lot of freelance work for them in the past, although I hadn't done any for about six months.

I told them I was available again for insurance investigations, and they promised to let me know the moment they had something. They sounded happy to hear from me again, and I hoped they hadn't found someone to replace me in the interim.

I didn't want to hang out a shingle. I felt that would bring too much attention on me. And I still didn't want to partner up with Sinkovich. Too many difficulties, not just with the fact that he'd never run a business before, but also that he was a cop with a history, and people around here would remember that history.

And then there was the issue of his mouth.

Still, I wanted to make more money than I was doing, and I couldn't do it entirely alone.

Nor could I do it when I spent time on cases like the Starlite, cases that would bring no money.

Almost on cue, the phone rang. It was Laura.

"I had an interesting start to my day," she said without really saying hello. "Have you heard of Chet Klempton?"

My hand tightened on my cooling coffee mug. "No."

"He's one of the big real estate brokers in town. He knows everyone, and many of the major purchases for businesses associated with the city go through his company." She didn't sound upset. She almost sounded amused. "He wanted to know why I was interested in the Starlite Hotel."

My heart rate increased. "How did he know you were interested?"

"I figured this might happen after yesterday," she said. "I just wanted to make sure before I contacted you."

"Okay," I said, wishing I could see her face. "What's going on?"

"The owner of the hotel is Eddie Turner," she said. "He's one of the new society guys. I've seen him at all kinds of functions because he's hard to miss."

I frowned. Laura knew Eddie Turner. "Because he's black?"

"And reserved. He hangs back, doesn't schmooze like most people who've been given permission to hang out with the so-called important set. If I hadn't known better, I would have thought he was someone's muscle when I first met him."

"Why didn't you point him out to me?" I asked.

"Because," she said, and I could really hear that amusement now, "you have only been to one of those functions. Last year, when I took you to see Ella Fitzgerald. And it wasn't really Eddie's crowd. He prefers to socialize with the extremely rich."

She said all of that without any hint of irony or apology. She knew who she was, and she knew that I knew it as well.

"I can't believe he would have blended in at society gatherings," I said.

"He didn't," she said, "but no one really talked about it. That's why I thought he was muscle at first. Usually new people to the crowd try to talk to everyone. I asked about him, though, because of you."

"Me?" I rubbed the coffee mug back and forth between my palms. The liquid sloshed but didn't spill.

"I thought if he was there, and you were there, you would…"

"Fit in better," I finished. Or everyone would think we were both muscle. That was the unspoken thought.

"And that's when I was told about his shady connections," she said. "I'll be honest. I didn't believe it entirely, because people often say such things about others who are different."

I loved how she managed to hang onto part of her naiveté, no matter what had happened in her life. It was one of the things I found the most endearing about her.

"I didn't think about it again," she said, "until I assigned someone to look up the Starlite Hotel in the county records, and he came up as the owner. That confirmed everything for me, and made me believe that the rumors were true."

That would have clinched it for me as well. But she had just said something that worried me. "You had someone look this up? Was it Judith?"

"No," Laura said. "I needed her to monitor that meeting with the professors. I'm not sure I want to spend my Saturday talking about things these people profess to understand and are truly ignorant about. There's this patronizing attitude, as if they can study the ghetto from afar, without understanding its stresses and undercurrents at all, as if everything can be solved through theory. I got real impatient real fast."

"Yeah," I said, thinking not about the professors because I'd had run-ins with that type myself, but about Sinkovich and our discussion about schools.

Maybe my attitude toward Jimmy's education this past eighteen months had more in common with the professors and their understanding of the ghetto, and less to do with the reality on the ground.

That thought disturbed me more than I cared to say.

"So who did you send to find out about the Starlite?" I asked her.

She chuckled. "I sent one of Cronk's old favorites, a secretary who is supposed to retire on the first of May."

One of the people who remained from the days before Laura's father died. "You sent someone with mob connections," I said, smiling for the first time that morning.

"I did," she said. "I figured that given the nature of the business at the Starlite, I should keep my hands off as much as possible."

I let out a small sigh, and then remembered that she got a visit anyway. "So why did Klempton come to see you?"

"I found out about Turner about two hours after you left. So I had one of my mid-level people call the office Turner uses as a front to discuss a purchase of the Starlite. I made it clear that we'd spare no expense, we had plans for the area, and we'd love to look at that property."

In other words, she broke all of the rules of negotiation. She let them know she was willing to pay through the nose for the property itself.

"I was told in no uncertain terms that the property was not now and never would be available for sale," she said. "I thought the matter closed, until this morning."

"When Klempton showed up," I said.

169

"Unannounced, without going through secretaries, etc. We've known each other for years. He was a friend of Addison's—"

Addison was her ex-husband.

"—and we'd encountered each other at countless social gatherings. I couldn't tell if Chet had come to see me because he's worried about me or because someone told him to make it clear to me that I did not belong anywhere near the Starlite."

"Or both," I said, not certain how I felt about this particular old friendship. Laura probably had a lot of shady contacts that she wasn't even aware of.

"That crossed my mind too," she said. "He seemed awfully concerned. This is dangerous territory, Smokey."

She clearly wasn't just referring to the Starlite.

"I know," I said. "What did you tell him?"

She laughed. "I played the dumb blond. Addison's friends always underestimated me, and I worked that angle. I guess dumb isn't the accurate word. Naïve is better. I pretended I had no idea what was happening there and told him truthfully that I had never seen the property."

I was frowning. There was a touch of Goldie-Hawn ditziness in her voice as she told me this. I could almost hear how she had said it to Klempton, all light and clueless.

"I said that we're looking into adding a business restoring classic hotels. Unfortunately, most of the properties that have decayed are in the Black Belt and south, so we would have to do a lot of rehab work *and* PR work. Then he told me, somewhat condescendingly, that the hotel was in gang territory, and I certainly didn't want that. So I told him that I was involved in this urban planning stuff, and these kinds of businesses—rehabbing old, once-thriving communities—were the very things that counteracted urban decay."

Her cageyness was breathtaking. She was learning to use everything to her advantage, in ways I would never even consider.

"He told me that I was playing with things I didn't understand, and I shouldn't listen to academics to guide my company policy. If I wanted help managing the business, he knew some wonderful people who would look at the books and help me decide how to make *profitable* decisions, not decisions that simply sounded like a good charity project."

I let out an involuntary laugh. "He didn't say that to you."

"Oh, he did," she said. "He was so sincere, too. He really thought I was dumb enough to put the entire business at risk rehabbing old hotels in the Black Belt."

"Because of me," I said.

"Well," she said, "that was part of it. He said that he knew I'd had some unsavory influences in my life of late, and really, I should be consulting with old friends who had been in Chicago for years instead of flirting with the latest trends. He compared me to the Bernsteins."

"The who?" I asked.

"You have not been reading your *New York Times*," she said in that society voice she could put on like makeup. "Next week, the Leonard Bernsteins will be holding a fundraiser for the Panther 21 defendants. All of Society is already abuzz, and everyone is trying to score an invitation. I could wrangle one for you if you want."

"For an event in New York?" I asked.

"Yep," she said.

I was trying to wrap my mind around New York café society intermingling with the families of twenty-one Black Panther defendants who had been in prison for nearly a year without trial. I shook my head.

Sometimes the depth of her connections surprised me. I frowned, thought about it, and realized something.

"Klempton thinks you're doing this because it's chic," I said.

"Better than thinking I'm doing it to shut down a mob operation, right?" she asked.

I wished she hadn't been so blunt. Sinkovich had made me paranoid. I had no idea who was listening in, if anyone was at all.

"Yes," I said. "That is better."

I took a deep breath, trying to quell the disappointment I felt. I had truly hoped that somehow Laura would be able to buy that hotel.

"I wish I could have helped more," she said.

"Oh, you helped a lot," I said. "I just wish it had gone differently."

"Me too."

We sat in silence for a moment in our separate offices, hers with an expensive view of Chicago's downtown, and mine with its limited view of the neighboring building.

"Smokey—"

"Laura—"

We had spoken over each other.

"You first," I said.

"I called Franklin. You do know that the Catholic schools are offering testing for prospective students this weekend, right?"

"I know," I said.

"He and I are getting together tonight. I'm going to help them, with Lacey at least."

"Good," I said.

"I'm not sure Catholic school is a good idea," she said. "I'm thinking maybe the lab school at the University of Chicago. Do you know if she got good grades?"

"I don't know about the last few years," I said.

She was silent again. Then I heard her sigh. "You know my offer still stands for Jimmy."

"I know," I said. "Thank you."

I wasn't as dismissive as I've been in the past. I wasn't ready to make a full decision yet, though.

"You were going to say something," she said.

I shook my head even though she couldn't see it. "I was just going to tell you that I'll be going back to my housing inspections soon. Maybe we can step those up a bit?"

"Sure." She sounded confused. She didn't know I'd been going over my finances. "You're ready now?"

"Almost," I said. "I have a few things to wrap up."

"All right," she said. And then she added, softly, "Be careful."

"I will," I said and hung up.

I stared at the phone for a long moment. Like Sinkovich, she knew I was going to do something to the operation at the Starlite. Unlike Sinkovich, she didn't try to stop me.

I wasn't sure anyone could stop me.

I didn't even think I could stop myself.

28

After I got off the phone, I grabbed my keys and my parka. I didn't bother to zip it, though. I hurried down the stairs and stepped outside for the first time that day.

The cold hit me like a slap. A wind off the lake added a wind-chill to the three degrees above zero that WVON had reported this morning. Clouds covered the city in a thin haze. The forecasters told me that the haze would make the day warmer, but that had to be some kind of wishful thinking.

Nothing about this day could be considered warm.

I slid my way toward the van, grabbing my gloves out of the parka's pockets as I did so. After the wind hit my face, I decided I didn't want to touch the van's door handle with my bare skin.

I reached the driver's side and sank into the ice-crusted snow. Some of it leached over my shoes and started to melt against my feet. *Smart move, Dalton*, I thought. I'd been in such a hurry to grab the folder inside the van, I hadn't thought about the deadly Chicago weather.

Sometimes I truly hated this place.

I unlocked the driver's door. It squealed as it opened. I leaned inside and grabbed the folder that still rested on the bench seat. I had forgotten the folder the day before with all of the distractions.

I resisted the urge to open it here to make sure everything was inside. I wasn't dressed for the weather. I tucked the folder under my parka, slid out, shut and locked the door, and headed back inside.

Even a short trip was a trek at this time of year.

I got in, pulled off my gloves, shoes, and socks, hung up the parka, and set the folder on the kitchen table. Then I half-walked half-hopped to the bedroom for another pair of socks and some slippers.

When you looked like me, sometimes the best way to investigate was on the phone. I planned to do that after I examined the flyers more closely. Most of the questions I had to ask wouldn't receive an answer if the person I spoke to knew what I looked like.

My feet grew instantly warmer with new socks. I headed back to the kitchen, and poured myself another cup of coffee. I wrapped my ice-cold hands around the mug and started to read.

I had kept the flyers in the three piles that Jonathan had sorted for me, but I hadn't taken notes. I did remember the order I had place the piles in my folder.

The top flyers were the girls whom Jonathan had some information about. Girls who had run away from home, girls who had left with boyfriends.

I went through that pile slowly, making notes in pencil on the ones for which I could remember the exact details Jonathan had given me. Then I wrote those names on my yellow legal pad in a category I called *We Think We Know.*

Some of those descriptions had sounded vaguely like excuses, and some hit a kind of red flag for me, especially the ones who theoretically ran off with boyfriends. Someone could have described what happened to Lacey in the same way.

After a moment, I separated out the boyfriend-girls into their own pile. I crumpled up the legal paper, and started over. Four piles now.

The first: *We Think We Know.* I wrote a series of names after that.

The second: *Boyfriends.* I wrote five names after that.

I made a note above *We Think We Know,* reminding myself that some of them might have fit in the boyfriend category as well. I couldn't entirely remember.

The next pile was the one I found the most daunting. It was an inch thick. Jonathan suspected that the girls named in this pile had disappeared because of some kind of foul play.

I'd learned long ago not to dismiss rumor as an investigative tool. Jonathan believed it; he had heard stories about these girls; and some of those stories just might be true.

The pile wasn't as thick as the fourth and final pile. That one contained names and faces that Jonathan didn't know. I set it aside for the moment, and looked at the file Jonathan flagged for me.

The depth of that pile disturbed me. One reason it was so thick was that some of the flyers had been crumpled. Others had Polaroids glued on them, and some had little messages taped to them.

I made a note on another sheet of legal paper. I needed to call Decker back and find out if he pulled flyers down at any point. I hadn't asked how long they remained up or how he had gotten all of these. He had said they had been given to him, but he hadn't really clarified by whom.

I went slowly through this pile, looking at faces, looking at names. These girls all seemed impossibly young to me, all with smiles on their faces, most with too much makeup for girls who had been in junior high at the time, all trying to look older than their years.

After that, the similarities stopped. The flyers were hand-drawn or stenciled. A few were on poster board, others were mimeographed, suggesting the involvement of a library or a school. Only two were actually printed. Jonathan believed that the Loring family hadn't had enough money to pay for flyers, that Donna Loring's brother had extorted the flyers from some unwilling business. He was probably right. Which meant that the second flyer was also of a girl with ties to the Blackstone Rangers.

I set those two aside. I would start with them.

Then I listed the names under my third category: *Definitely missing.*

The fourth category, *Unknown*, broke my heart. I didn't write the names down. There were too many. I set them aside for now. If the others led me in the wrong direction, then I would turn to these.

I had to get up and move around. I couldn't sit with this. Decker had told me that girls just disappeared, *kids* just disappeared, and he couldn't do anything about it. He didn't have the resources to do more than call the parents, and what I firmly believed he did not say was that if the parents didn't pick up after the first one or two contacts, then they didn't receive another call.

These kids literally slipped through a crack or were forced into one, like Lacey nearly had been, and no one did a thing about it.

And you are not the savior of the entire world, Grimshaw, Sinkovich had said to me, and he was right. But how did anyone look at these stacks of flyers and not realize that something had to change?

These flyers ranged over years. I didn't look to see if the fourth pile was filled with students who had disappeared before Jonathan's time, but I would have bet that it was.

Decker said twenty or so students *per class* per year. That was hundreds of students over time, kids whose parents didn't have the resources to find them, kids who didn't want to be found, kids who dropped out, and kids who were the victims of some kind of crime, like Lacey.

I put my hand on the flyers. These were the kids someone cared enough about to search for. How many of those who had disappeared had tried as hard as they could and finally gave up—whatever giving up meant. It might have meant joining a gang or leaving the neighborhood. Or it might have meant truly giving up.

I ran a hand through my hair, grabbed my coffee mug, and realized I hadn't sipped any of the coffee. It was cold now, but I downed it.

Jimmy would have been one of the kids who just vanished. If he hadn't talked to me in Memphis, if I hadn't been watching him, who knew what would have happened to him? His mother ran off two years ago this week, and Jimmy hadn't told anyone. His brother had already moved out, and joined a gang.

Jimmy had still been struggling, still tried to feed himself, still tried to go to school.

Then the landlord evicted him. How did the average ten-year-old kid survive on the streets of Memphis in the winter? How did any kid? Jimmy wasn't average, and the circumstances nearly destroyed him.

I leaned against the counter.

It would take months, maybe years, to find out what happened to all these girls. And even if I worked on it full time, I wouldn't find all of them. Not counting the new girls who disappeared.

Sinkovich told me I had to rejoice in the small victories. He would probably think that Voss's death was a small victory, that Lacey's rescue was a small victory.

I would consider shutting down the Starlite a small victory.

No, I would consider it a tiny victory.

I poured myself another cup of coffee. It steamed. I opened the lid on the percolator. The bottom was beginning to look like sludge. Apparently I'd left the burner on too high.

I moved the percolator to the sink. I would deal with that in a moment.

I grabbed the legal pad and headed back to my office. I hadn't expected to get there this early, but I needed a few answers.

I turned on the gooseneck lamp, and sat down at my desk. In the group of index cards that Laura laughingly called my Rolodex, I had the school's number. I dialed it.

Mrs. Helgenstrom answered. I recognized her voice. I identified myself, exchanged a few pleasantries, then asked for Principal Decker.

She hesitated. Then I realized I might get better answers from her.

"If he's busy," I said, "can you answer some questions for me?"

"I can try," she said, and I didn't think I was making up the relief in her voice. She hadn't wanted to disturb him. She had probably received instructions to bar the Grimshaw family from talking to Decker.

He probably felt there was only so much pressure he could take.

"Principal Decker gave me a folder filled with flyers of missing girls," and as I said that, I realized something that had been bothering me, something I had forgotten to ask him from the beginning. "Does he separate out missing children flyers by gender?"

"I do," Mrs. Helgenstrom said quietly. There was something in her voice, a firmness, an anger maybe, that seemed out of place for the professional woman I had talked with yesterday.

"You gather the flyers," I said, thinking aloud. "And you give them to Principal Decker."

"I do," she said. "He doesn't like them cluttering up the board."

I had been right: I heard anger. Restrained, soft-spoken fury.

"The board?" I asked.

"When you come in? There's an announcement board? We put school flyers there, and the community is allowed to use it for approved things. I approved the flyers that you have."

"But Principal Decker doesn't like them," I said, mostly to encourage her to continue.

"We have a compromise. They stay on the board for a week. Or they're supposed to anyway. I'm in charge of taking them down."

I got the message. She only took them down when the principal noticed.

"And then you give him the flyers," I said. "By gender."

"He thinks all the boys join the gangs, so I put the girls on his desk. I keep the boys out here."

I wished I could see her. I wished I had thought to ask this the day before.

"Do you think all the boys join the gangs?"

"No," she said, and this time she spoke with such force that it almost felt like she was shouting. She must have heard herself, because she added, quieter this time, "No, I don't. I think a lot of them get hurt or die and no one notices. I like your boy, Mr. Grimshaw. He's wonderful. He's ambitious. And some of the boys who disappear, they're just like him."

That chill I had gotten from the van returned. Her words echoed my thoughts from earlier—and I didn't like it.

"What do you think Principal Decker can do?" I asked.

"Now you sound just like him. What can he do? Pay attention, maybe."

"You pay attention," I said, again to encourage her.

"Of course I do. I'm the one who calls the families. I'm the one who notifies the police. I'm the only one who notices, and…." Her voice trailed off.

She didn't finish the sentence. She had no idea what anyone could do. She was doing what she could, and hoping someone else, someone with real authority, would step up.

"I'm not sure what to do about this either, Mrs. Helgenstrom," I said, speaking to her unspoken concern. "But I'm going to see what I can find out."

"Really?"

"Yes," I said. "I do odd jobs like this, and it seems to me that we need to look closer at what's going on here."

"Yes, we do," she said. "We really do."

She sounded relieved, maybe not that I was going to do anything, but that I would at least look at the situation. I had a hunch no one had done so before.

"If I stop by," I said, "can I bring the folder and go over the names with you?"

"The folder?" Her voice had gone frosty again. "He gave *you* the folder?" She clearly didn't like that.

"He did when I asked him if other girls had gone missing." I almost added that he clearly wanted to do something about it, but I wasn't sure if that was true. He might simply have wanted the problem out of his hands. "These aren't all of the girls who dropped out in the last few years, is it?"

"No," she said. "Most never have anyone search for them."

And she would know, based on her phone calls and her own follow-ups. No one would have searched for Jimmy, if I hadn't been watching out for him.

"I'm not sure if I can help you much," she continued, and it took me a moment to realize she was answering my earlier question. "What I know about most of those girls is on the flyer. I don't think sitting here, going over it would help us."

I caught the implication. It might get her in trouble.

"Principal Decker believes in helping kids who help themselves, doesn't he?" I asked, wanting her to know that I understood her.

"Oh, I'm not even sure he believes that," she said. "I think he's putting in his time now, and I don't blame him. He has a nearly impossible job."

And hers was worse, as the go-between between him and the students, and him and the parents.

"He is going to a meeting tomorrow with other district principals and the school board to talk about the strike vote," she said. "He'll be gone from eleven through lunch."

I nodded, then remembered she couldn't see me. "If I have something to confirm, I'll check in then," I said.

"Thank you," she said.

I was about to hang up when I heard her speak again. I thought she said my name. I brought the receiver back up to my ear. "Yes?"

"The fact that you're doing this," she said very quietly. "There's a special place in Heaven for people like you."

I almost laughed out loud. There was no place in Heaven for a man like me. But I appreciated the sentiment.

I thanked her and hung up. I almost left the legal pad here and started to make the rest of my calls, but I wasn't done.

I needed to get a few facts straight first.

29

By the time I returned to the kitchen, my coffee had cooled enough to drink. I took a sip and winced. It tasted burned. But I was too lazy to clean out the percolator and make myself a new cup. I had more important things to do.

I sat down at the table, and looked at the two printed black-and-white flyers. I picked up Donna Loring's flyer first.

It was definitely professionally done. The heading—*Missing!*—ran like a banner across the top, followed by *If You Have Seen This Girl, Call The Number Below!*

The phone number, at the bottom of the page, had a South Side exchange. Next to the final digit were the words *Day or Night!*

The flyer had two photographs of Donna. On the upper left, what appeared to be a school photograph. It showed a very pretty girl with straight-combed hair, a blouse with something I'd heard Lacey mockingly describe as a Peter Pan collar, and a plaid jumper over it all. She had a tentative smile, as if whoever took the picture made her nervous.

The second photo, on the lower right, was a candid shot. Donna was laughing, her head tilted back just a little, her mouth open in an infectious grin, her eyes bright. She looked older here, but when I inspected closely, I realized the difference was the careful application of makeup. Her skin, which had a young teenager's blotchiness in the first photo, had the smoothness that good liquid foundation created. Her hair was still smooth, but it didn't look contrived. She wore hoop earrings, eye shadow, and lipstick, although I couldn't see the color on any of it. Her shirt was short-sleeved and was unbuttoned far enough to show too much cleavage for a girl her age.

Next to the school photo were these facts:

Donna Elizabeth Loring
Born October 1, 1955
Brown hair (naturally kinky)
Chocolate brown eyes
Distinctive mole on her left wrist
Straight-A student
Good friend, great sister, beloved daughter
Help us find her!

A different paragraph ran below the school photograph (to the left of the candid shot):

Donna Loring disappeared from school on Tuesday, October 29, 1968. She was last seen on the school grounds at noon by several teachers, but she did not show up to her afternoon classes. Some reports state she was talking to a tall adult male just before she vanished. Any and all information welcome. Confidentiality maintained, if need be. Please call!

The placement of the photos, the design, all convinced me that the flyer wasn't just professional printed; it had been professionally designed as well. "Confidentiality maintained" was not a term that the average family would use. That was something a member of law enforcement or someone who had been in trouble with the law would add.

There was also a hint that whoever designed the flyer thought she was dead. They added an identifying mark, something that coroners used to help ID an unrecognizable body.

182

Jonathan had read this, and then he had run his hand over the flyer. I had thought that perhaps he was closer to Donna Loring than he let on, but now I wasn't so certain. What happened to her had happened to Lacey, only Lacey had Jimmy and Keith to defend her.

Jonathan wasn't dumb; he had realized just then how lucky his sister had been.

The second printed flyer looked very similar to Donna Loring's. It had the same heading, and had two photographs, spaced apart for balance. A phone number at the bottom, asking for calls day or night, and two informational paragraphs.

The missing girl was named Wanda Nason. She was thinner than Donna had been and she actually looked a bit scared in her school photograph. She wore a white blouse with a gigantic flower pin on one shoulder, her straightened hair pulled back on the same side with a barrette.

The candid shot showed a girl who didn't seem to smile easily. Her head dipped away from the camera, as if she didn't want to be photographed, and her right hand was up, fingers splayed, as if she tried to block the camera. She wore a light-colored blouse, but I couldn't tell if it was white, and a beaded necklace with a large cross on the end. I couldn't tell if the necklace doubled as a rosary.

The paragraphs were similar to those on the Donna Loring flyer in structure and terminology.

The first paragraph read:

Mary Wanda Nason
Born December 11, 1955
Brown hair
Dark brown eyes
Small scar on her lower lip
Beloved only child of MaryAnn Nason
Help us find her!

The second paragraph chilled me in its similarity to the paragraph about Donna's disappearance, and in what almost happened to Lacey:

Wanda Nason disappeared from school on Tuesday, March 18, 1969. She was last seen in her morning classes, but she did not show up to her afternoon classes. Any and all information welcome. Confidentiality maintained, if need be. Please call!

I pulled out the other flyers in that pile. Most identified the date of disappearance. Some mentioned that the girl had been in or around the school. Only a few had the day of the week—and they all had the same day:

Tuesday.

That was not a coincidence.

I turned the page on my legal pad and wrote down the dates of the disappearances. At least one per month, sometimes more, every month of the school year for 1968 and 1969. And now, 1970.

I got up and hurried toward my office. I grabbed 1969's blotter from under a pile of papers and carried it back to the kitchen table.

I didn't even sit down. I set the blotter next to the legal pad and compared.

Every single date was a Tuesday. In some months, girls disappeared every week. In others, only one girl disappeared.

But I knew that meant nothing. For all I knew, a girl had gone missing every single Tuesday, but only some girls were missed by family and friends, so their disappearances were noticed quickly.

I tapped the blotter, and cursed, both at it and at myself. If I hadn't killed Voss, I would be able to get some answers.

Of course, if I hadn't killed Voss, then he would have warned the people at the Starlite that I was onto them. He would have connected me to Lacey, and through that connection, probably found Jimmy and Keith.

I didn't really regret killing the man. It had been the right decision, even if my finger had moved faster on the trigger than my brain would have liked. I just wish I had asked him a few more questions before he died.

Because it was absolutely clear now that the operation at the Starlite used the school as a recruiting site. The fact that it only happened once a week perplexed me a little. Did the handlers—like Voss—go elsewhere during the week?

That didn't jibe with Jimmy and Keith's observations of Lacey and Voss. He had worked on her for a while, but brought her in on Tuesday.

So maybe other places had other days of the week, or maybe the operation could only handle one new girl at a time. After all, it would be a bit work-intensive to break a girl and hold her hostage, even a young girl.

Then I rubbed my fingers over my forehead. My back cracked in protest. Which was just fine with me. Because I didn't want my thoughts to continue along this line.

When I thought too deeply about what could happen, all I saw was Lacey, and then I got furious.

I rapped my knuckles on the table, trying to do something with the anger. Fury did me no good. I needed to remain calm.

I walked around the living room, forcing myself to focus on the facts. That was all I could do.

Fact: the Starlite ran a by-the-hour operation that either trained hookers or it fueled some kind of human trafficking operation, sending young girls elsewhere. (I voted for sending the girls elsewhere, since these girls were not seen again.) There would be no real payoff in intentionally killing the girls, so I had a hunch that, for a while at least, most of them lived past the date of their disappearance.

Fact: The girls were all thirteen at the time of their abduction. Lacey had been the oldest, five months from her fourteenth birthday, followed by Wanda, at nine months from her birthday. Donna was the youngest. She had just turned thirteen. But she had cleavage and didn't mind showing it off, judging from that candid photograph. Wanda didn't seem to have as much, although her demeanor might have made her seem older. Lacey had been risqué and flirty and trying hard to look older than her age.

I personally thought no one could take her for an adult, and I was beginning to think that didn't matter. There were men in the market for younger girls, although I had always thought they wanted unspoiled girls. Voss's actions had proven that this operation wasn't looking for girls like that.

Fact: The girls all appear to have been targeted. Had Lacey come to Voss's attention because she had spoken to Karen Frazier? Or had Voss found her some other way?

Figuring out how Voss found the girls might not be that important now that he was dead, but it might also be part of the pattern, a pattern that suggested more than one man's system. Because…

Fact: The girls disappeared on a Tuesday, and from what I could tell, only one girl at a time vanished. That spoke to an organization ready to take in a new candidate at a certain time and in a certain place.

It also suggested some cunning. If three or four or five girls vanished every Tuesday, even Decker would have noticed and done something about it. One girl per week out of an economically and educationally challenged school might have been expected, particularly if a good portion of those girls did not have a parent who looked out for them and who would contact the school when the girl did not come home.

I wondered: If I dug deeper into each girl's background, would I find a pattern of skipping class, of smoking outside of school, of being tardy or vanishing from school for weeks at a time?

I ripped out another piece of paper. I had questions for Lacey, even though I didn't exactly know how to ask them. I needed her to be honest with me about her contacts with some of the girls on my lists, and I also needed to know how much (or little) she attended school.

If she did skip classes, why had no one called Althea? Lacey had the benefit of an active, involved, stay-at-home mom, something very rare in the Black Belt, not because of culture, but because of economics.

If Lacey had skipped class and no one had noticed or contacted Althea, then we had a greater problem here. Then this particular school was easy pickings for predators like Voss.

I stopped for a moment, set down the pen, and took a deep breath. Then I grabbed the percolator. I needed to do something else for a moment.

I needed to think.

Lists of lost girls were more than I could handle on my own, particularly given my financial situation. I wouldn't get paid for this job. Even if I wanted to get paid, I didn't know who to ask. It felt tacky to charge the distraught parents, particularly if the girl had been missing for a long period of time.

In my entire career, I had never been the kind of investigator who preyed on other people's pain. I wasn't about to start doing that now.

But all of this had come to my attention, and I did want to find out what happened. I could work these cases slowly and figure out what happened to the girls.

Of course, if I went after the organization itself, even in a small way, I might find out a great deal more.

I poured out some of the coffee and dumped the grounds into the garbage under the sink. Then I carefully scoured the percolator, careful not to use any soap at all. I probably scrubbed harder than I needed to, but the physical action felt good.

I finished, dried off the percolator, and set it down. I had planned to make another cup of coffee, but I didn't want one.

Instead, I went back to the table.

To the list of questions I made for Lacey, I added one more. I needed to find out what I could about Karen Frazier. Friends, family, anything that might help me figure out exactly what was going on.

I moved that page aside and went back to my fact page.

When Lacey told me about Karen Frazier, she said that her first encounter with Voss had happened before Christmas. Then she had seen him over the holidays. Had she meant *between* the holidays? Or before school let out?

He took her out to lunch then, and had bought her "stuff," whatever that meant. I needed to find that out as well. I added that to my Lacey list.

By the time school started for the semester, he was taking her out for lunch regularly. She had waited for him the day before, so they had clearly set that up.

Had he taken her into the Starlite's restaurant to parade her in front of someone as possible merchandise? Or had he done that earlier?

I leaned back.

The Starlite. It was the center of this particular operation. The restaurant, that hotel room where Jimmy had rescued Lacey, the hookers, the fact that no one wanted to sell the building.

Was the operation only recruiting through that particular school? There were no other junior highs nearby, but the high school that Jonathan went to was only a few blocks away.

I sighed, not liking how my brain worked.

I placed my hand on the flyers. I didn't need to find more victims, at least, not yet. I had enough, and they probably had enough points of intersection to give me a clear picture of what was happening. More victims would distract me.

I needed to focus on the missing junior high school girls, the Starlite, and the operation there.

With that in mind, I slid the two professionally done flyers in front of me. I didn't see any information about where the printing and design had been done. But I did notice something I had missed before.

The contact phone number at the bottom of both flyers was the same. Not only had Wanda Nason's family used the same printer, whoever had contacted the print shop had a phone number that united both girls.

In what way, I couldn't tell.

But it was one more mystery to solve on the way to figuring this all out.

30

I took my legal pad and the two professional flyers into my office. I sat down at the desk and slid the phone toward me. Then I grabbed the fat Chicago phone book off the floor. I opened it to the pages for the police department and stared.

I knew a lot about police procedure, but every city was different. Each city had different traditions and behaviors, unspoken rules and the code that the officers abided by. I didn't know as much about Chicago's as I did Memphis's. Part of that came from the fact that I had an outside-the-law relationship with the Chicago Police, whereas in Memphis, I was a licensed private detective who occasionally had to do things with city officials, whether I wanted to or not.

In Memphis, I had dozens of people to contact or I knew the right department. Until now, I had let Truman Johnson or Jack Sinkovich do most of the work with the Chicago Police.

Sinkovich had gotten into trouble in less than an hour by asking about the Starlite Hotel. Laura had a visitor warning her away less than twenty-four hours after she put out her first feelers. If someone wanted to look into the connection between Sinkovich and Laura, that someone would find that the only point of intersection was me, which none of us wanted.

Besides, I knew better than to go to the local precinct. The information I needed was not about the hotel per se, but about two missing girls. Girls who would be noticed in the white areas of town, but they wouldn't be noticed in black neighborhoods.

That was where I would start.

I decided that the West Side precincts were the best place to start. They were far enough away that most South Side parents, families, and friends wouldn't regularly go into those areas. Plus, after the Panther raid, the most people considered the West Side much more dangerous than the South Side.

I started with the precinct farthest west, but still inside the neighborhood.

A bored dispatch answered the phone.

"Hello," I said in my best Tennessee accent. "My name is Detective Eustace Fittle of the Nashville Police Department. I would like to speak to someone in your precinct regarding a young woman named Donna Loring."

"Just one moment, Detective Fittle," the dispatch said and put me on hold.

I knew better than to get excited about this; I was probably being transferred to the precinct's information officer.

"Detective Fittle?" The voice that greeted me was deep and rich. "I'm Officer Sal DePalma. How may I help you?"

"Officer DePalma, I have here in custody one Mark Jones." I spoke slowly, conversationally, like so many of whites in Tennessee did. I made certain that I sounded unconcerned and unconvinced. "He says he has some information on the kidnapping of a Donna Loring of Chicago and he is willing to trade that information for reduced charges. He says she's a colored girl who was taken from her school in 1968."

"Did he say what school?" DePalma did not sound that interested.

"He did not. He said it was quite a coup because she has a brother who is associated with someone named…" I paused here for effect. "…Jeff Fort. Does that mean anything to you?"

DePalma grunted. It was a sound of surprise. "Actually, it does, detective. Jeff Fort is the leader of one of our largest gangs. He does not operate in our neighborhood, and I'm not familiar with the kidnapping of Miss Loring. You probably want one of the South Side precincts. Let me get you those numbers."

"Before you do," I said, "let me add that Jones claims that Miss Loring was taken from her neighborhood so that Mr. Fort's people could not track her. That is why she has not been found."

"Did he say if she was alive?"

"Unfortunately, he did not. He was quite cagey about the information. He asked through his lawyer that we check on the kidnapping of Miss Loring first, and then he would give us the information we need. This is a fairly high-profile case, or I would not even be talking to you. We believe that in addition to Miss Loring, Mr. Jones has information on one of our other suspects, and we are using this Loring angle as a way to check this young man's veracity. Am I being clear here?"

DePalma chuckled. I had just told him that I didn't care about Jones's case, and I wasn't sure I wanted to deal with my made-up criminal. Because my made-up case was high profile, however, I had also just told DePalma that I could get in trouble with higher-ups if I didn't do the obligatory research.

"Give me your number, and I'll call you right back," DePalma said.

"I would love to," I said, "but it would be better for all concerned if I just remained on the phone. If you cannot find any information or need to point me elsewhere in a few minutes, well, that's just fine and dandy with me."

His chuckle went deeper. "I'm putting you on hold. This should only take a minute."

He vanished, and that blank, flat sound that marked being on hold replaced the faint precinct noise behind him.

I clicked my pen while I waited. My stomach was twisted. I had to play this carefully or he would call the Nashville Police and ask for Eustace Fittle. If DePalma did that relatively quickly, he might send out some kind of alert to the other precincts that someone posing as a Nashville Police officer was trying to get information on Donna Loring.

I had had one phone investigation go awry like that when I was still in Memphis. I had called a precinct in Los Angeles, and had done something so obviously wrong that when I called a nearby precinct, I had already been made. I'd had to try something else to finish that investigation.

"Detective Fittle?" DePalma had returned. "How do you spell your last name?"

That twisting in my stomach had grown worse. "F-i-t-t-l-e. My family has been in these parts for more than 150 years. We lost a goodly portion of the Fittles in the War for Southern Independence."

"The...what?" DePalma asked, and then before I could answer, said, "Oh. The Civil War."

"We think of it as uncivil here," I said.

"I suppose you do." He no longer sounded amused. More perplexed, as if I were some kind of species of human he did not understand.

I wanted to tell him I had never understood that particular species of human, either, but I couldn't.

"Unfortunately for you," he said, "Jeff Fort just got out on bail last night or we could have checked with him about his lieutenants or at least, put you in touch with the Cook County jail and they could have worked with him for you. I did check with one of our gang experts, and he said that Fort does have a lieutenant named Raymond Loring. He has a long sheet. I don't see anything about a sister, though. At least the name checks out."

"That it does," I said. "I thank you, and I'll take those phone numbers now, if you don't mind."

"Sure," he said. "But before I give them to you, I need to warn you. If there is a sister and if she was kidnapped in fall or winter of 1968, she was probably taken by the Black Panthers. You know we've had some Panther troubles here. They were bitter rivals of the Black P. Stone Nation, which is Jeff Fort's gang."

"They *were*, not they *are*?" I asked. "Have they joined forces?"

"No one is joining forces with Chicago's Panthers," he said. "Aren't you familiar with what happened to their leader in December?"

"Oh," I said, dragging out the word. "That is the Hampstead boy, right? I hear you gentlemen handled him the way that he should've been handled. A little Southern justice Northern style."

"Hampton, yes," he said. "Sometimes the best justice is the kind that saves the taxpayer money."

"It surely is," I said. "You think this Jones is a Black Panther?"

"It's possible," DePalma said. "If he is from Chicago—"

"He says he is," I deliberately interrupted.

"Then he might also be a Vice Lord. They're rivals of the Stones, but they're not as powerful or connected as the Black Panthers. Be careful, if he is with those thugs, all right?"

"I most certainly will. Thank you for that information. And do thank your gang expert," I said. "I had no idea that this could go that dangerous so quickly. I will inform my chief and the chief prosecutor. We might not want to negotiate with a man like this."

"Or," DePalma said, "you might want to find out everything he knows. If there's anything useful to us here, please contact me."

"You can count on me. I thank you," I said. Then I wrote down the phone numbers he gave me, and hung up.

I stared at them for a moment. Dangerous? The Panthers? I knew that the media liked to portray them that way. I considered that the problem all black men had when they carried guns. When they carried guns and pointed out that they had guns, they automatically scared white people.

I hadn't liked the Panthers, although Hampton had impressed me each time I'd met him, but they did call themselves the Black Panther Party For Self-Defense. And so far as I could tell, they never initiated an action. They defended themselves when they had to.

Not that they had had a chance on December 4th. That shoot-out had been cold-blooded murder, and I might have been talking to one of the members of the assassination squad. Or maybe, talking to him via DePalma, who probably hadn't had a high enough rank to go on that particular mission.

Raymond Loring, Jeff Fort's right-hand man. That was a start.

I could either call the numbers that De Palma gave me as Eustace Fittle or I could continue my trolling for information.

I decided to try a different tack. I contacted the next precinct, not too far from first one I had called.

When the dispatch answered, I said, "I need to talk to someone in Vice."

I got patched through to a Detective Stan Birns. It only took a moment.

He answered with a curt, "Stan Birns. What can I do you for?"

"This is Detective Michael Larew," I said, making sure my vowels had flattened. I pitched my voice higher than it usually was. "I'm calling from Gary, Indiana. Last night, two of our officers picked up a strung-out young woman who says her name is Donna Loring. She says she's from Chicago, and she's telling quite a story. She claims she's been kidnapped and taken across state lines. Because she is so strung out, I am disinclined to believe her. She's dressed like a hooker. She smells like a hooker. I believe she's saying these things so that we do not arrest her. But my captain wants me to contact Chicago PD to see if she has an arrest record there."

"How did you end up calling this precinct?" Detective Birns asked. "You should contact headquarters and request something from the department of records."

"I have," I said. "They tell me it will take a week or more to get the paperwork I need if indeed she has any records with the Chicago Police. I then asked for the numbers of precincts in your colored neighborhoods, hoping that someone there might remember a girl with this name. She's very thin, about 5'4", and has one of those kinky hairdos the colored girls like so much now. She says she has family in Chicago, a brother who is associated with some stones? She actually wanted me to contact him, as if I would do that. I don't know if that makes any sense to you...."

"It rings a bell, actually," Detective Birns said. "I'll call you right back."

"How about I call you?" I said. "That way the charges are not on you. I don't know about your district, but ours is getting quite rigid about long-distance telephone charges."

"All right," he said, and he sounded distracted. He was thinking of something. "Give me about fifteen minutes."

I promised that I would call back shortly. Then I hung up and wondered if I dare call another station. I decided to wait.

I got up, made myself that cup of coffee I had skipped, and by the time it was poured, my fifteen minutes were up. I called him back in twenty, just so that I wouldn't seem to eager.

"Found the file I was looking for," he said, without preamble. "I don't think your girl is Loring, but the story she tells is pretty curious."

"What were you looking for?" I asked.

"We pulled up a body in November, dumped in on West Madison. We have a lot of burned-out properties there from the riots in '68."

"At the Democratic Convention?" I asked.

"Naw," he said. "The niggers went nuts when King got shot, burned half their neighborhoods, which I guess you gotta expect."

A wave of anger flowed through me. I had to take a deep breath, mentally reminding myself this was why I used the phone. He automatically assumed I was white, and automatically assumed I agreed with him.

If I tried to agree with him, my voice would betray me. So I said, "You found her in a burned-out building?"

"Naw," he said. "A lot of 'em were just bulldozed. Empty fields that the mayor wants someone to invest in but with the gangs and the Panthers and the crime, smart money is staying away."

"Yeah," I said. "I guess it would."

"So she was in one of them burned-out lots. She'd been dumped."

"And she's—?"

"Donna Loring," he said.

"You know that for sure?" I asked.

"Oh, yeah," he said. "We didn't say nothing about it though. Her brother's big in the Stones, and they're at war with the Panthers. We were afraid something would get set off. But the brother more or less ID'd her anyway."

"What does that mean?" I asked.

"We all knew her as La Donna, which one of the guys said in Italian meant 'the lady' and we thought it was funny because it was kinda true. She acted like hooking was beneath her. She didn't call guys, she didn't go up to cars unless she had to, she didn't do nothing, never smiled, never looked at anyone. If you wanted to pay for a strung-out warm body, you got it with her."

I shuddered. Hadn't Jonathan said everyone loved her? He compared her to Norene, always happy, always effervescent.

"Wasn't even worth my time to arrest," he said. "Just a skinny piece of meat."

A series of thoughts went through my mind. Wouldn't someone like Donna have been an opportunity for Vice? If she was clearly unhappy in the life, then she would have been a prime target for helping the cops go after the pimps or the organization that she worked for.

Then I realized what he meant, exactly. He worked Vice, because he got what he considered benefits.

"Never took her in, never made her promises?" I asked, trying to sound like a comrade.

"No point," he said. "Usually it's tit for tat if you know what I mean. And there wasn't tit there, let alone tat."

He confirmed what I thought. I swallowed coffee-tasting bile.

"But you said her brother identified her," I said.

"Oh, yeah. When we found her. We had to figure out what to do about her—Potter's Field, send her home, you know. And one of my guys remembered some flyer the brother's lieutenants were putting up about a year before. We actually got one in the file. She had some mark on her wrist…"

I could hear papers fluttering.

"Yeah, here it is. 'Distinctive mole on her left wrist.' And she had one. Big as a bruise, ugly thing."

"Flyer," I repeated. "You had a flyer?"

"She disappeared. The brother wanted her back. We figured the Panthers or the Vice Lords or someone took her for a few days, made him upset. Then he got her back and she was damaged goods, so he put her to work."

"You know that for a fact?" I asked.

My tone might have been off, because he snapped, "Well, yeah, of course. You know your neighborhoods too. Girls like this, they work for gangs, bringing in money. She got broke in somewhere, then got sent home, and they put her to work."

"I thought you said she was in a new neighborhood." I hoped he had said something like that, because I needed to confront him on this. I needed to confront him on something.

"Stones are South Side, this is West Side, we figured they were just making inroads to piss off the Panthers."

"Who had kidnapped her in the first place," I said.

"What's it matter?" he said, his voice going up. "She was just a hooker."

She was someone's sister, someone's daughter. *Good friend, great sister, beloved daughter.* Hadn't he seen that on the flyer as well?

"What did she die of?" I asked.

"Who the hell knows?" he said. "What they always die of. The life killed her."

That much was probably true. "You didn't do an autopsy."

"Dunno about you, but if your superiors are breathing down your neck to save phone costs, then they really don't like it when you order an autopsy on a dead hooker." He sounded angry now.

"I was just wondering, considering what my girl was telling me. It sounds like there was something strange going on."

"Yeah," he said. "Sounds like your girl's trying to get out of whatever lockup you got her in, thinking you might know some of the Chicago stuff because Gary's almost a suburb, right?"

I had a hunch those were fighting words to someone from Gary. "Look," I said, letting a low level of the fury I felt at him into my voice, "you've been helpful, and I know I was taking quite a bit of your time. If we find out something about this girl or your dead hooker, you want me to let you know?"

"Naw," he said. "Hookers die. Gangs fight. The monkeys burn their neighborhoods. And we let them. If they kill each other off, things get better in the Great City of Chicago."

I hung up. I couldn't do anything else. Let him think I was pissed about the Gary comment. I simply couldn't deal with that level of in-humanity.

Was this what Sinkovich was talking about when he said that cops learned to take small victories? They ignored girls like Donna Loring, girls taken just a few miles from their homes, destroyed, and then put to work. Their deaths weren't even worth an investigation? They weren't pretty enough to arrest. Hell, Birns didn't even think he should contact her family when they first figured out who she was.

Maybe she could have been saved. Maybe she would still be alive now, and maybe she would be on the road to some kind of recovery.

Then I shook my head. I could almost hear Sinkovich. *You think a girl like that, with her brother, coulda gone home and become a citizen?*

197

Birns's right. She'd just keep hooking. Can't save them all, Grimshaw, and sometimes you gotta cut your losses.

I knew for a fact that the Blackstone Rangers had brokered a truce with the Panthers by the time her body had been dumped. She'd been dumped on West Madison, which put her body right near the house where Hampton died. Or maybe on the same road.

Would the Stones have retaliated against the Panthers?

I wouldn't have put it past them.

The cops seemed to believe in Panther involvement. But no one had told Conlisk or any of the higher level members of the department. Because if they truly believed that Donna Loring had been killed by Panthers, they would have leaked that information to the Stones and hoped that the Stones took out the Panthers.

The cops had tried several times to do it themselves last year, and succeeded only when they raided that house in December.

People on the West Side only knew her as La Donna, not as Donna Loring. The fact that she ended up there, on the low end of the hooker ladder, meant either she hadn't worked out or the operation was more low-end than Sinkovich thought.

Although it would make sense that the operation had prostitutes of all levels, from the high-end ones to the streetwalkers who barely knew their own names.

I thought of Jonathon's fingers, tracing that image of her face.

I thought of her infectious smile.

I stood up. I had one of the links I wanted. A direct line from the school to the hotel to a dead prostitute on Chicago's West Side.

I wasn't sure what to do with it all yet, but I would figure it out.

I always did.

31

I was too sick to my stomach to eat lunch. I went back into the kitchen and poured out my coffee, leaving the mug on the counter. Then I shut off the burner beneath the percolator and moved the percolator to another part of the stove.

I cleaned off the kitchen table, making certain I kept my piles in order, and slowly carried those piles to the office. I didn't want Jimmy to come home and see all of those missing faces.

I took the list of questions I had written up for Lacey and tucked it into my shirt pocket. Then I put on one of the few good pairs of shoes I had left, covered them with galoshes, and grabbed the parka.

I needed to see Lacey, not just to get my questions answered. I needed to see my small victory, just to remind myself that she was safe.

I locked the apartment door and paused for just a moment in front of Marvella's. I didn't hear any sound inside. I had yet another favor to ask her and no time to do it. I had no idea where she had gone off to, but I would find her eventually.

I hurried down the stairs and out into the cold, zipping the parka as I went. It felt colder than it had a few hours ago, and I wasn't certain how that was possible. The entire street had a breathless quality, as if it had been frozen under glass.

I unlocked the van and got in, wishing, as I had all winter, that I lived in a neighborhood where I could leave the van running while it heated up. Instead, I had to sit on the cold seat, looking at my breath, while the van coughed its way into some kind of life.

I checked the glove box for the gun, saw that it was still there, and closed the box. The van's chugging smoothed as it warmed, and my face slowly stopped stinging.

I put the van into gear and headed to the hospital.

I probably should have called first on the off-chance that Lacey had gone home. She struck me as too ill to leave quickly, but I wasn't a doctor, and I could never quite figure out how they made these decisions.

The hospital looked grim in the pale winter sunlight. Some of the trees along the edge of the parking lot were covered in a layer of ice. I hadn't noticed anything like that in my neighborhood, but then there weren't many trees there. All it would take was a short ice storm or some ice fog, and everything would get coated.

I got out, put my head down, and headed to the hospital's front door. A blast of hot air as I entered made me realize that the van's interior had never heated up all the way. I walked past the information desk to the children's wing, deciding to take the stairs to both warm up and to burn off some of that anger that had arisen in my talk with Detective Birns.

I had to realize over and over again that the bigotry I heard out of Sinkovich's mouth was nothing compared to the filth he had to listen to all day long.

Lacey was still in her room. Someone had brought her a beautiful pink-and-white crocheted bed jacket. The colors accented her lovely brown skin and her black hair, but it also accented just how battered she was. Some of the puffiness in her face had receded, although her left eye was now nearly swollen closed. The worst bruise on her face was starting to turn yellow, making her seem jaundiced.

She was alone. She started when she saw me at the door, then smiled and gestured me inside.

The smile warmed me, and I smiled back.

"Where's your mom?" I asked.

"They think I might be able to go home tonight, and so she's getting my room ready." She sounded a bit stronger than she had the day before.

The stuffed dog I had given her rested on the far side of the bed. I suddenly felt awkward, as if I should have brought her something else for this visit. I hadn't been thinking in terms of healing or nurturing. I'd spent the last two days thinking about vengeance, which wasn't at all the same thing.

"When will you find out for sure?" I asked.

"The doctor's supposed to be here at four," she said. "If he says I can go, I can go."

"You happy about that?" I asked.

She nodded, but didn't look at me. I wasn't sure how to take that reaction.

"Do you mind if I sit?" I asked.

She shook her head and gave me another of those tentative smiles. I was beginning to love them.

I sat down in a nearby chair with an inadequate leather cushion, at least for someone my size. I eased out of the parka and let it rest behind me, protecting me from the chair's badly designed metal back. Then I scooted the chair close enough that I could touch Lacey if she wanted me to.

"I have some more questions," I said. "Is it all right if I ask them?"

She tugged on the collar of her bed jacket as if it rubbed against her neck. "You didn't get him after all?"

She misunderstood the reason I wanted to talk to her. She thought I was still searching for Voss, even though I had told her the last time that I was not.

"It's all right," I said. "He's not going to bother you. I promise. Like I said yesterday, he'll never bother you again. But it looks like he might have hurt some other girls, and I'd like to find them if I can."

I hadn't planned that approach but it sounded right. I hoped Lacey wouldn't ask too many questions. I knew that underneath her brave front, she was scared to death, and I didn't want to make the fear worse.

"I guess it's okay," she said in a tone that told me she'd rather I didn't ask.

"It's probably good your mom's not here," I said. "I want you to be as honest with me as you can, even if you broke some rules, okay? I promise, I won't tell your parents."

She looked at me then, good eye wide. Her eyelids fluttered. I could feel her nerves. "Okay."

"All right." I took the paper out of my shirt pocket. She watched my every move as if she expected me to jump across the hospital bed's railing and grab her.

If I knew how to make that reaction go away, I would do it first.

"I wrote these down so I wouldn't forget," I said. "Some might not seem important, but they all are. I'm finding pieces of information and I need to put them together."

She punched up the pillows behind her, slid back, and took a deep breath. "Okay," she said again.

I held the paper tightly but didn't look at it. I wanted to maintain eye contact with Lacey as long as I could.

"You had said to me that you saw Voss with Karen Frazier before the holidays. Then you saw him during the holidays, and he took you out and bought you stuff."

She nodded, her fingers toying with the holes in the crochet.

"When you saw him with Karen Frazier, was that before school let out for the year?"

She nodded, but didn't look up at me.

"How long after, then, before you saw him again?"

She shrugged a shoulder.

"Lace," I said gently, "I wouldn't ask if it weren't important."

"I thought you weren't going to ask about him. I thought he's not going to bother us. This sounds like you're still looking for him."

She was a very smart kid, and I couldn't hide a lot from her. I didn't want to tell her how big I thought this organization was. I wanted her to regain her confidence and go back to living her life.

I wasn't sure I could ask all the questions and keep her in the dark about the nature of the organization itself.

"I'm not looking for him. I found him. He's no longer going to hurt anyone."

She raised her chin, took another deep breath, and nodded. Maybe this time my reassurance would go in.

"My investigation has moved away from him specifically to finding out what, exactly, happened to some of the other girls who knew him."

"You think he hurt them too?"

I knew he had. But I wasn't going to say that. "I think he might have. And as you know, events like this are hard with family around you. Some of the other girls don't have your kind of support."

A tear worked its way out of her bad eye.

"If I can find out what his system was," I said, "then maybe I can establish a timeline, and check on some of the other girls."

"What other girls?" she asked. "Karen?"

"I don't know," I said. "No one has said anything about her, except you. Does she have family who would look for her?"

Lacey frowned, then shook her head once. "I think her mom ran off. Her dad—I don't know. I didn't like her, so I didn't pay a lot of attention."

Then her face flooded with color. It made her bruises stand out.

"I didn't mean that. I mean, if she's hurt—"

"We don't know if she's hurt or just fine. I'm just writing down names right now of girls who were seen with him," I said.

Lacey bit her lower lip, then winced. "Okay. I don't know a lot about her."

"That's all right," I said. "You might not know a lot about any of the girls I'm going to ask you about. It's okay."

She nodded, then smoothed one hand over her hair, as if calming herself.

"Did you see Karen in school after she was with Voss?"

Lacey shook her head. "She skipped a lot though. I never looked for her. I don't remember seeing her."

That was probably as good as we'd get. I would work my way back around to the skipping.

"So," I said, "how long between the day you met Voss and him running into you outside of school?"

Her frown deepened. She leaned back against the pillow, her hands finally calm. "I met him after you took us to that house. But I'm not sure exactly when after."

I took them to the Panther death house on December 7. School ended for the semester on December 19.

"So you met him the week before school let out for Christmas vaca-
tion," I said.

She nodded.

"Do you remember the day of the week?" I asked.

She shook her head. Her lips were pressed together, almost as if talking about this was as bad as having it happen all over again.

"And then you saw him…?"

"I was Christmas shopping with some of my friends," she said.
"Down on 71st. We took the 'L.'"

"Was he on the 'L'?" I asked.

"I don't know," she said. "I didn't see him. We were having a good
time. Giggling, and stuff. We…"

Her voice trailed off, almost as though the idea of having fun was too
much for her.

"He saw you and bought you things," I said.

"He came into that bookstore Daddy likes so much."

"The Claiborne Bookstore?" I asked.

"Yeah," she said. "I was trying to find something for Daddy, and then
Clyde showed up and asked me if I was a big reader."

"And you said?"

"I was doing Christmas shopping. He didn't ask who it was for. I
didn't tell him." That color in her cheeks grew darker. "I didn't want to
think about Daddy just then."

"So you didn't mention your father," I said.

"I didn't say anything about my family and stuff. I…" She closed her
eyes, then shook her head. "I wanted Clyde to think I was older."

She opened her eyes and looked down.

I thought about offering words of comfort, then figured it would
be more comforting for her if I got through this list of questions
quickly.

"Did he take you out that day?" I asked.

"No," she said. "I was with my friends."

"Did he meet them?" I asked.

"No!" she said. And then she faced me. "He didn't go after any of them, did he?"

"I don't know who you were with," I said. "Were they all in school this week?"

"Yes," she said.

"Then he didn't go after any of them."

She let out a gasp of relief and leaned back on the pillows.

"You were the only one in the bookstore?" I asked.

"Yeah," she said. "I told him I was with friends and he said that was cool. He asked me if I could meet him on that Monday at that deli, you know. The Golden Skillet. He'd help me finish shopping. I said that was really nice."

I kept myself perfectly rigid. I hated thinking about this. But I made myself focus. The Golden Skillet was on 71st, just like the bookstore was. They weren't far from each other.

"Did you go?"

"Me and Lillibeth," Lacey said. "I brought her along. He seemed kinda mad about that, but he bought us lunch. Then he gave me a present and told me not to open it until later."

Lacey had tried to be smart. She had done her very best.

"I know Lillibeth is okay," she said, angling herself so that she could see me better. "I know she is. She was here. She wanted to know what happened, and Mom answered her. Mom says I got hurt real bad and we aren't going to talk about it. But Lillibeth is my best friend."

And suddenly we were in waters that were extremely unfamiliar to me. "I think you get to decide who to tell," I said. "But if you're worried about it, talk to Marvella. She's been here too, right?"

"This morning, with Mom. They're talking about some stupid group I should join."

"It's for healing," I said.

"It sounds like dumb grown-up stuff," she said.

I smiled. I could almost hear myself say the same thing at her age. "Yeah, it probably does. But dumb grown-up stuff has a point when grown-up bad things happen to you."

She picked up the dog and squeezed it. In her pink and white jacket, clutching the stuffed animal, she looked nothing like the pretty young woman who had accidentally lured an asshole.

"Are we done?" she asked.

"Not quite," I said. "Just a few more questions."

Actually, most of them, but I didn't tell her that.

"What did you do with the present?" I asked.

She gave me a perfect sideways teenage look, filled with annoyance and exasperation. "I opened it. It was a nightgown, like one Mom has. It was really pretty, but I couldn't keep it. Daddy would've had conniptions. So I put it in the church basket."

For the clothing drive. The nightgown was gone now. I probably didn't need to see it. It had to have been lingerie. That told me more than enough about it—and would have told Lacey, too, had she been old enough to understand.

"What did Lillibeth think about him?" I asked.

"She said he was creepy. She said all old guys are creepy and they shouldn't talk to little girls. I'm not a little girl, Uncle Bill."

Lillibeth sounded like a sensible girl. I wished that Lacey had listened to her. But clearly, Lacey had heard the "little girl" comment as a criticism, which allowed her to ignore her friend's sound advice.

"I know," I said. "Did you see Voss again during the holidays?"

"No," Lacey said. "But there was a note in the present. It said I should meet him at noon on Monday so he could take me to lunch."

"And you went."

"Yeah," she said, her voice thick with tears.

"It's all right, Lace," I said. "He was nice to you. It's hard to say no to people who are nice to you."

"I thought, you know, I owed him. Because he gave me a present and I didn't give him anything."

I almost winced. That asshole had known how to manipulate little girls. Bastard.

"On Monday, did you apologize to him for not giving him something?" I asked.

She swallowed hard. It looked like she was swallowing back more tears. "He said it was okay. My company…was…enough."

I had to look away just for a moment. I didn't want Lacey to see the fury that crossed my face.

But I couldn't keep quiet anymore. "He was a manipulative bastard, Lace. He was using lines he'd practiced before."

"Really?" she asked, her voice small.

"Really," I said. "He'd tested them. He knew what worked."

"So I'm dumb?"

"No," I said. "This is called a con. It's something that people do, like putting on a show, and it's designed to trick you. I've fallen for cons."

"You have, Uncle Bill?" She sounded incredulous, as if I couldn't fall for anything.

"A lot when I was in the military," I said. "I wasn't happy, and I wanted to believe what people told me."

"Yeah," she said with obvious recognition. I wondered what was so bad about Franklin and Althea's house. I hadn't seen anything. Or maybe this was just what happened with teenagers. I hadn't been the easiest kid to live with when I was a teenager. Sullen, unhappy, angry. I got out as soon as I could too—and my adoptive parents had been wonderful.

"So," I said, "give me a picture of this con. What did you talk about on Monday at lunch?"

She squared her shoulders. Somehow calling what happened to her a con had given her strength she hadn't had before.

"He wanted to know stuff. How old I was, stuff about my family, how my grades were. He said I was really pretty, and I could model for his company, but I couldn't tell my folks until I had the job."

She didn't say that last as if it bothered her, and it should have. I had heard both Franklin and Althea warn their kids that anyone who told them to do something that they couldn't confess to their folks was a bad person.

I had to ask her about that in a nonjudgmental way. It took me a moment to find the right words. "Did that bother you?"

"Kinda," she said. "But I'd already told him I was in trouble for how I dressed, so I told myself I thought he was talking about that. We'd get the modeling thing done, I'd have a real job, and then Daddy would have to say yes."

"You told Voss you were in trouble with your father?" I asked.

She nodded.

"What did you say, exactly?" I asked.

She ran her hand over the stuffed dog. "I said Daddy was really mad at me, and I didn't talk to him much anymore. I tried to stay away from him as much as possible. I made him sound worse than he is, Uncle Bill. I don't know how to tell him that."

"You don't have to," I said.

She gave me a different sideways glance, this one more eloquent than the one before. This one both thanked me for saying that and disbelieved my words at the same time.

"I actually thought about how to answer that question," she said, and I could hear the regret. She'd been going over this part in her mind. This was where she blamed herself. "If I'd said that Daddy watches me like a hawk, I figured Clyde wouldn't have anything to do with me. I figured he'd walk away, and he was so nice to me, Uncle Bill. I mean, he seemed nice. I mean, he seemed interested."

She made his interest sound unusual. His niceness too. Had we stopped being nice to her? Stopped paying attention to her? Stopped being interested?

For the past year, Lacey had been getting the wrong kind of attention in the family. Dressing badly, asking to go to events that didn't allow kids her age, mouthing off to her parents.

I hadn't known her before she slipped into puberty. Had she been more like Mikie? The kind of girl who had been so good that no one noticed her?

"Is that wrong, Uncle Bill?" Lacey asked.

I wasn't sure what she was referring to. "That he paid attention to you?" I asked, and censored the rest of the sentence which was, *when the rest of us didn't?* "No, it's not wrong. People pay attention for good and bad reasons."

"Why did he come after me?" she asked.

"That's what I'm trying to figure out," I said.

She focused on me for the first time in that conversation. "You mean, I caused it?"

"No. What I think, what I believe, is that he went after girls he got introduced to. He'd see how pretty they were, and decide if he wanted to go after them."

God help me, I lied. I couldn't let anything I learned make Lacey blame herself any more than she already was.

She pulled her bed jacket tighter, stretching some of the crochet work. "I only introduced him to Lillibeth. I didn't tell him about anyone else, not even the friends I went shopping with."

"Good," I said, stuck now with my lie. It might help me move to my next group of questions. "And the first time you saw him was with Karen Frazier."

She frowned. "I think so. I keep thinking maybe I saw him a couple of other times, though. I just didn't pay attention."

"With other girls?" I asked.

"I think, maybe, you know, before you and Daddy set up that whole after-school thing. I think maybe I saw him when I was waiting for someone to pick us up or for the bus. Maybe the bus."

She sounded a lot more sure of herself than the "maybes" implied. She had seen him.

"Was he with other girls?"

"Probably," she said.

"We set up the after-school 'thing' as you call it last April. So you saw him in the fall before that?"

"I think so," she said. "I wasn't paying a lot of attention. He was just some guy then."

"And he was interested in girls who were older," I said.

"Not my friends," she said. And there was that certainty. She had seen him.

"Did you know Donna Loring or Wanda Nason?" I asked.

"I knew Donna," she said. "She was *funny*. She'd make jokes after school and on the bus, and stuff. But Jonathan made me stay away from her. Her brother is in the Stones."

"How did Jonathan know that?" I asked.

"Everybody knew that," Lacey said. "She used to talk about how stupid the gang kids were and how they didn't know the best thing to do was go to school and get a scholarship and become someone. She was gonna do that."

Lacey's frown grew.

"She's one of the girls, right? One of the girls who was with Clyde?"

"You tell me," I said.

"She talked to everybody," Lacey said. "I don't know if I saw her talking to him, but he probably listened to her. She always stood around after school while we were waiting for the bus. She was so pretty."

Then Lacey swallowed.

"Tell me she's okay," she said.

"I don't know," I lied. "When did you last see her?"

Lacey shrugged. "She went away. I thought she got one of those Catholic school scholarships or something. You can test for that in the eighth grade and she was going to. She was going to do better than all of us forever and ever, that's what she said."

"And you believed her," I said.

"Oh, yeah," Lacey said. "You would have, too. She was great."

Son of a bitch. Voss had picked his victims well. He targeted unhappy girls with ambition, girls who already knew their circumstances were challenging, and he promised he'd get them out of the neighborhood.

Judging from what little I knew about Donna Loring's last days, he had gotten her out of the neighborhood. He just hadn't told her he was sending her somewhere worse.

"I didn't know someone named Wanda, though. Was she one of the girls he met?"

"I'm not sure," I said. "Who else did you see him with?"

"That I remember?" Lacey said. "Just Karen."

"When you saw Voss with Karen, Lace, was that during the school day?"

Lacey gave me a narrow look. "What do you mean?"

"Were you skipping? I promise I won't tell your parents if you were."

"I don't remember," she said.

"Lace, please."

She sighed. "School's so easy, Uncle Bill. I get straight As."

210

"Without going to class," I said.

"I go," she said. "Just not every day. Why? I mean, there's nothing to do, and most of the stuff is in books. I take the tests. I do better than almost anybody else. So I don't always go to class. Sometimes we stand outside and smoke and talk."

"You and your friends," I said. "And girls like Donna Loring?"

"We're the big kids now," she said.

"You took their smoking spot," I said.

"They went to high school. They don't use it anymore."

I nodded. That was the missing piece.

"Thank you for being honest."

She tightened her hug around that dog. "Is that where he saw us first?"

"I have no idea," I said. "But let's see if we can figure that out. I have a list of names here that I got from the school, girls who stopped coming to school. There's a bunch of reasons kids drop out, and I don't expect you to know why. But if you know the girls, would you tell me? I'll just read them—"

"No." Althea was at the door. I wondered how long she'd been there. It couldn't have been very long or Lacey wouldn't have admitted to the smoking or the skipping.

Lacey looked terrified.

"We're not talking about this anymore, William," Althea said to me in a tone that she reserved for her misbehaving children. "You've done what you can. The man is no longer out there. We're moving forward."

"Althea," I said.

"My daughter is going to concentrate on healing. She's not going to think about other girls or what's happening at that school. She's going to get better, and you're not going to drag her back there."

My breath caught. Althea had been the one who wanted me to solve this. I didn't say that, though. I didn't want to contradict her in front of Lacey.

"I'm not taking her back to the school," I said.

"I don't mean physically," Althea said. "I mean mentally. We need to get her to focus on life now, not what happened then. None of this is her fault, and she's not going to pick over it like a new scab, all right?"

I opened my mouth, then closed it. But Althea must have seen what was on my face anyway.

"I asked you to make sure this man would not harm my daughter again. You have reassured both of us that he will not. We believe you. Case closed."

Lacey had paled, her bruises standing out in sharp relief.

I couldn't say anything, not about the school, not about the other girls. I didn't dare, because on some level, Althea was right: Lacey didn't need to think about what might be out there. She knew. And she didn't need to imagine more bad things happening to other girls.

"I wanted to help him, Mom," Lacey said. "He says there might be other girls."

"There might be," Althea said to me, not to Lacey. "That's not my concern. My concern is *my* daughter. We're going to take care of her and our family. Franklin is already lining up ways to take care of our children so that they don't have to face anything like this again. You might be advised to do the same, Smokey."

"I am," I said, knowing she was referring to Franklin's upcoming talk with Laura.

"We are not going to tilt at windmills," Althea said. "We are not going to bring any more attention on this family. Is that clear?"

It was. She had a hunch how deep this went, and she didn't want any part of it.

Which was smart.

"But the other girls…?" Lacey asked. She was looking at me.

I smiled at her as reassuringly as I could. "I don't know if you heard Jimmy talk about the police officer we know. Now that I've talked to you, I can give him all of this information. He'll make sure the police will do everything they can to help anyone who had a run-in with that man."

"Promise?" Lacey asked.

"I promise," I said, lying again. Son of a bitch.

I grabbed my parka and put it on.

"Will you need help getting her home?" I asked.

"If she's going, and no, thank you." Althea came farther into the room and put a hand on my arm. "I'm sorry, Smokey. I know how much you've done for us in the last few days. I don't mean to yell."

"You're not yelling." I bussed her cheek. "You're right."

She leaned her head against my shoulder for just a moment. Then she straightened.

"When God put us on this earth," she said, "he made sure that we always moved forward. I try to keep that in mind by not dwelling on what's behind."

I wished it were that easy. My gaze met Lacey's. She looked down. I bet she wished it were easy too.

32

After I left the hospital, I realized I had forgotten to ask if I should pick up the kids. Franklin had said he would do it, and I had to trust that he was going to. Otherwise Althea would have told me.

It looked like they had divided up family duties. Althea kept Franklin from her daughter as much as possible by taking care of the hospital matters. It prevented Franklin from saying the wrong things while Lacey was healing.

I hoped I hadn't said the wrong things either.

Before I got into my van, I stuck my gloved hands into my pockets and walked toward the hospital's charity shop. It was across the parking lot, near a diner that the hospital recommended for families.

The diner looked like a way station on the way to hell. The charity shop didn't look much better.

It was stand-alone river-brick building that looked like someone had hastily assembled it in the 1930s and hadn't done anything to it since. The windows had condensation on the inside, but that hadn't stopped an employee from putting items on display near it. Those items were visibly faded, even through the grime.

I pushed the door open and winced at the stench of mildew and cigarettes. I stepped into what felt like a sauna. I appeared to be the only customer.

In fact, I appeared to be the only person alive in the entire place. No one greeted me. A cup of coffee, a film floating on its surface, sat next to the ancient cash register. The fluorescent lights hummed and one of them flickered. I took a deep breath, and regretted it.

I yelled a tentative hello. When I got no answer, I walked over to a rack of men's coats. Most of them were too small for me. They were all tattered and priced higher than they should have been, even in a store that donated most of its proceeds to the hospital's charity fund. The information about the donations was displayed prominently on printed signs hanging on the dingy white walls.

I found one coat shoved underneath several others in a pile behind the rack. It was black and it was wool. I pulled it out. The scent of mothballs came with it.

I shook it out, and dust rose. Then I held it up. It was a greatcoat of uncertain lineage. It was long enough for me, and wide enough on the shoulders. The shoulders held the memory of some kind of military bars that had clearly been removed. The buttons were brass and covered with an insignia that I didn't recognize, a crown and some kind of bird. The crown made me realize that the coat's origin was not American.

The interior was satin. I slipped it on, and instantly gained ten pounds. I had never worn such a heavy coat. But its pockets were deep, and it would keep me warm.

That was what I needed. I didn't plan to keep this coat for long.

Someone had put a $20 price on it with masking tape. I did not want to spend that kind of money on this. I slipped the coat over my arm and looked around the back.

A stout woman sat at a desk covered in magazines and papers. She was smoking a cigarette and talking on the phone.

I waved at her, then pointed at the coat. "I'd like to buy this," I mouthed.

She put her hand over the receiver and said in a cigarette-ruined voice, "Leave the money on the counter."

"The coat's a little pricey," I said aloud.

"Then don't take it," she said. "See what I care."

I let out a small sigh and walked back to the counter, pulling a twenty out as I walked. I didn't have a lot of cash. I had forgotten to get some at the bank when I picked up the gun.

I lifted the coffee cup, set the twenty down, and put the cup over it. Then I carried the coat out of the shop.

The coat brought the odor of the shop with it. Because I couldn't wash wool, I would have to live with that smell as long as I had the coat. I didn't plan on having it dry-cleaned.

I opened the back of the van and put the coat on some cardboard I'd left after I transported open cans of paint. Maybe some of the paint chips would flake off on it and decrease the smell. Maybe Jimmy and I would suddenly come into millions of dollars as well.

I shook my head. Too bad about the odor. If the coat had smelled better, I would have put it aside as my good coat and worn the parka for the next few days. I really wasn't fond of the green.

I closed the back door, then got into the van and drove back home. I needed to talk to Marvella before I did anything else.

For the first time in more than a year, I felt very alone. I hadn't realized how much I relied on the Grimshaws. If I needed someone to watch Jimmy for a few hours, I called Althea. She complained about it sometimes, but she always kept him at their house, always fed him, and sometimes let him sleep over. He used to wear Keith's clothes to school on those days, but now their growth patterns differed, I had dropped off a few changes of clothing for Jimmy.

Before this incident, Althea offered to loan me some of the clothes Jonathan had grown out of, as if Jimmy were one of her own. We both knew he would be in his next set of clothes for only a year or maybe even a few months. He had started into that painful growth spurt so many boys went through, and it would be costly.

I gripped the steering wheel tighter as I turned the van into my neighborhood. That twenty had been painful. Maybe I should listen to Althea and just give up on this. I did need to focus on bringing in money. This last week had proven that to me.

But I kept thinking of Donna Loring and how vibrant she had sounded, back at the school. How she had lost everything long before she died.

The same thing could have happened to Lacey.

The same thing was happening to other girls right now.

I had to prevent even more from getting taken from that school. Even though Voss was gone, his legacy would live on, and Eddie Turner, or whoever ran his operation, would just find someone to take his place.

And, I could hear Sinkovich say, if I got that hotel shut down, the operation would simply move to a different neighborhood and more girls would get lost.

I was fighting a war that I couldn't win alone.

But I could win a few battles, and maybe cause enough pain to make the operation too costly to continue in the Black Belt.

I needed to find a way to get rid of the hotel and discredit Eddie Turner, not just with the society set, but with the Outfit as well.

And then I needed to make it seem impossible for the Outfit to try this again on the South Side.

I pulled into my usual parking spot and sat for a moment. The neighborhood was quiet, like it usually was in the early afternoon. No cars on the slick street, no one on the sidewalks. Some window curtains were open in some of the buildings, but no one had lights on, and lights were necessary on days like today. There wasn't enough sun to penetrate the interior gloom.

I shut off the van.

My biggest problem was a lack of backup. Not just with Jimmy, but also to take care of that hotel and Eddie Turner. I couldn't do it alone, which would have been my preference. Sinkovich couldn't help me; he'd already done as much as he could. Malcolm Reyner, who had helped me for most of last year, had been drafted and shipped off to Vietnam.

I pulled out the keys and let myself out of the van.

I couldn't use Franklin or Jonathan. Even if they had experience in matters like this, they would be too emotionally involved. Hell, I was too emotionally involved. I did my best to remain calm, although my trigger finger hadn't.

I let myself out of the van, grabbed the coat from the back, and headed into the apartment. I needed muscle, and I didn't have any. I had no one to rely on, no one to even ask.

I could go to Tim Minton, I supposed. He knew a lot of people. But I didn't want him to ask questions, use my name, and associate me in any way with that hotel.

He finished that death house alone. He was as broken up about it all as I was. But he couldn't help me here. He never was a fighter. He still had injuries from last fall. His cheekbone hadn't quite healed properly, although the doctors had been able to save his eye.

I didn't ever want to put him in a situation where he faced violence again.

The inside of the apartment building was hot. Something had changed with the radiator system, and probably not for the good, at least in my apartment.

I took the stairs two at a time and knocked on Marvella's door. This time, she answered it.

"Bill?" she said.

"I have a couple of questions for you," I said.

"Yes, I can watch Jim tonight," she said, "if you tell me how Lacey is."

"They still haven't called you?" I asked.

"Don't worry about it." She stepped back and let me into her apartment. It smelled of her sandalwood perfume. "I'll contact Althea if I have to. She won't be able to say no to me. Right now, though, I think they're just worried about healing."

Marvella's apartment had the same layout as mine, but that was the only similarity. She had a matching sofa and loveseat set, covered with blankets made in some tribal region in Africa. Beautiful wood sculptures of black faces sat on mahogany tables. The sculptures looked like Marvella herself, even though they weren't. They just emphasized how strikingly beautiful she was.

A bay window overlooked the back yard. A window seat covered with brown, red, and orange pillows looked a bit mussed up. An overturned book half-hid among the spider plants trailing from the window to the floor, as if Marvella had set the book down when she had come to answer the door.

"Lacey might get out tonight," I said.

"All right," Marvella said. "I'll call tomorrow."

She wandered into the spotless half-kitchen and opened the fridge. "You want anything to drink?"

I shook my head. "I can't stay long."

"So what are your questions?" she asked.

"That organization you want Lacey to go to, is it affiliated with anything?" I asked.

Marvella shook her head. "We're rather informal. Like some of the other groups I belong to."

One of those groups helped women find safe abortions. Even though abortions were illegal in the state of Illinois, the women knew of providers who would do the work well. Too many abortion providers here and in the other states where it was illegal accidentally killed many of the women who had gone to them for help.

A year ago, Marvella had told me about her involvement with that group and swore me to secrecy. I hadn't told anyone.

"Are any of the women involved...tough-minded?" I asked.

"What are you asking, Bill?" Marvella said as she pulled out a kitchen chair. She swept a hand toward it, inviting me to sit down.

I remained standing. "I don't know yet. I'm trying to figure out a few things."

"Tough-minded, yes," she said. "They've gone into terrible places to help injured women. But able to fight? I doubt it."

"Okay," I said. I had had a half-hearted idea that an army of women might not be a bad thing. But it didn't sound like Marvella's army was a fighting force. It was the medical unit that came in after the battle was over.

She hadn't sat down either. She was watching me, her head tilted to one side.

"This is going to sound strange," I said, "but do you think some makeup would cover this?"

I tapped the scar on my cheek.

She grinned. "Feeling vain, Bill?"

I couldn't quite bring myself to grin in return. "It makes me too recognizable."

"Unlike your build and general manner?" she asked, this time seriously.

"There are a lot of big men in this world," I said, "but not a lot associated with that school who also have a scar on the left side of their face."

"Why are you worried about identifying marks?" she asked.

I raised my eyebrows.

She sighed with obvious exasperation, pushed the kitchen chair in, and started down the narrow hallway.

I followed her.

She flicked on the bathroom light. It smelled even more like sandalwood in here, and like Marvella herself. The last time I had seen this room, it had been a mess with towels in the tub, and a bloody handprint on the sink as Marvella had tried to save her cousin's life.

Now, the room was so pristine I would have been afraid to use it for its intended purpose. A brown and orange shower curtain hid the shower. A matching rug, toilet seat cover, and a whatever-you-call-it on the back of the toilet made the room feel both decorative and claustrophobic. A basket of magazines propped the door open.

Marvella turned on the light over the mirror, then pulled out a makeup mirror. She opened an apron that covered the area under the sink and removed bottles of makeup.

She held them against my skin one at a time, then finally chose one.

"First, I'm going to use a little concealer and then I'm going to put on some foundation. I'm looking for a match, otherwise you'll have to wear some all over your face."

"That's not going to happen," I said. "Won't the concealer be enough?"

She rolled her eyes at me as if I should know better. I didn't even know what concealer was, so how would I know about it? If it was called concealer, it should conceal right?

"You'll have to sit down," she said, nodding at the commode.

"I'm not going to hurt anything?" I asked, worried about that seat cover.

"They're built for people who are much bigger than you," she said, obviously misunderstanding.

I sat.

She tilted my head up. "Now close your eye."

I closed both of them. I felt her fingers, feather-light on my skin. She touched that scar gently as if it still hurt. Laura had touched it like that when she first saw it as well. It had been redder then, angrier.

Something cool touched my temple. It had a flat smell that reminded me of ChapStick. It felt like ChapStick, too, gooey and dry at the same time. She slid it all the way down the scar, then rubbed her finger over it.

"Almost," she said, although I think she was speaking more to me than to herself.

"Can I see it?"

"Sure."

I opened my eyes. She tilted the makeup mirror downward. The magnifying mirror showed my skin down to the pores. The scar had vanished along the top part, but along the cheek it had simply faded.

"That's why I thought concealer wouldn't be enough and I was right," she said, pushing the mirror away. "Now close your eyes again."

I did and felt her forefinger raise my chin. Then the slightly perfumed scent of makeup reached me. I heard liquid slosh, then something wet coated the left side of my face. Marvella used a fingertip to trace the scar again. It felt like some kind of pasty gel covered my skin.

"Eh," she said. "We need a real light. Come on."

"I can open my eyes?" I asked.

"Yes," she said, and her voice came from the hall.

I stood, then stopped and peered in the bathroom mirror. That was my old face, the one I had lost last year. I hadn't realized how much I had missed it.

"Come on," she said again, this time from the living room.

I followed her in there. She had every light in the room on and she was standing by the bay window. In her hand, she held a compact.

"Come here," she said, beckoning with her right hand.

I walked over. She was staring at me critically, as if I were a half-finished version of one of her sculptures and she was the sculptor.

"Crouch a little, would you?" she asked.

I did. She grabbed my chin, and tilted my head, first toward the artificial light, and then toward the window.

"I think it works," she said. "Take a look."

221

She snapped open the compact and handed it to me. It felt tiny in my hand. I held it up as I had seen all of the women in my life do, feeling extremely ridiculous.

But the scar was gone, and the only way I could tell that there was makeup on my face was that pulling feeling of something drying against my skin, and the slight smell of perfume.

"Do you have any without perfume?" I asked.

She laughed. "No. Smoke a cigarette, pour some alcohol on yourself. No one will notice."

Except me. The sensation of it all made me hold my head awkwardly.

She said, "I'm going to show you how to do this without me, all right? It's pretty simple. And I will buy more of the concealer and the foundation so that you won't have to."

I smiled at her. It felt like the makeup cracked, even though, as I looked in the mirror, there was no way to tell the difference.

"Thanks," I said.

"Don't mention it," she said. "You'll now know how to be a secret master of disguise."

"You're making fun," I said.

"I'm not, actually," she said. "And you're lucky that our skin tones are similar. This could have taken all afternoon."

I didn't have all afternoon, so I was glad that it hadn't. "Will you watch for Jimmy?"

"I'll wait at your place if you don't mind," she said. "About, what? Five?"

"Yeah, starting then. I might be back by then."

"And if you're not?"

"Tell him I'm still working on the case he opened for Lacey. He'll understand."

I hoped.

Marvella looked like she did, too. She eased the compact out of my hand, and closed it with a snap.

"Don't get hurt, Bill," she said. "Makeup can't hide everything."

"I know," I said. But on this day, it was going to hide more than enough.

33

I put the makeup in my bedroom and left my parka on the bed, so that its presence in the apartment wouldn't worry Jimmy. Then I grabbed some cash from my emergency kit in the closet. I left a ten on the table with a note in case Marvella wanted to order pizza again.

I took an old fedora that Franklin had left behind when he moved and placed it on my head. I wrapped a scarf around my neck, and put on the greatcoat.

Between the weight of the coat and the makeup on my cheek, I felt like a different person. I didn't need to worry about the perfume smell; the stench of the coat more than covered it. I grabbed two pairs of gloves, shoving one pair into the coat's pockets and carrying the other pair.

Then I hurried out of the apartment.

Even though the sun wouldn't set for another hour or more, the sky had turned twilight gray. The wind had died down, which was a good thing, since I doubted this hat would stay on my head in anything stronger. Still, I kept one hand on the hat and used the other to unlock the van.

I needed to turn on the lights to see more than half a block ahead. A car turned onto the street as I pulled out. The driver startled, the car fishtailed, and narrowly missed me. If I remembered, I would buy a bag of road salt on the weekend, and salt a few of the icy patches. It was getting dangerous just to drive, and I doubted the city road crews would come down here any time soon.

I left the heater and the radio off. I didn't have far to drive, and I didn't want to warm up too much before I got there. Besides, I needed to concentrate. I had several ideas of what I might do to that hotel, but I had no idea if any of them would work.

I had to check the place out first.

I parked a block farther north than I parked the previous morning. The van was now two blocks from the school, and not on the route that Franklin usually took to the after-school program. I had worried just a little that he would drive past me, see the coat and fedora, and wonder who was in my van.

But I didn't pass him on the road. After I parked, I leaned over and removed the gun from the glove box, making certain that the gun's safety was on. Then I shoved it in my pocket. It would be even less visible in this coat than it had been in the parka, which was good.

I got out, locked the van, checked the back gate, and headed down the sidewalk to the hotel.

In the short time it had taken me to drive, the sky had gone from twilight gray to near dark. The streetlights hadn't come on yet, if the streetlights in this part of the neighborhood even worked. I shoved my hands in my pockets, one fist bumping the gun, and kept my head bowed, turned away from the street. I tried to look like a man down on his luck, and after the last few months I'd had, it wasn't that hard.

When I reached the hotel, I gave the entrance a long glance, as if I was tempted to go in. Then I walked just a few yards farther, went up the shoveled sidewalk, and let myself into the restaurant.

It smelled like fifty years of boiled meat and burned toast. A coffee smell tried to override everything, but it couldn't, anymore than the gray haze of cigarette smoke could change the stench of this place.

A counter ran the entire length of the back wall. Once upon a time, that counter had been a bar, and still looked like you could belly up to it and order some kind of hard liquor. But behind the counter, where the liquor used to be, the owners had opened up the wall to create a pass-through to the kitchen. Food sizzled back there, and someone laughed.

A man in a tattered gray coat sat at the counter, nursing a cup of coffee. Several sugar packets sat beside it, along with a handful of ripped cracker wrappers. I wanted to slip him some cash so he could get a real meal, but I didn't dare.

Along the windows were booths. They were made of a dark red vinyl which had probably looked classy when they had been put in. Several tables cluttered up the floor space, making it almost impossible to exit the building quickly. The tables were either set up for another meal or had the remains of a meal on top of them.

Two of the booths had customers, elderly couples who didn't seem to have anything to say to each other. The only meal I could clearly see was some kind of gravy-covered meat, with mashed potatoes and carrots so orange they looked fake.

I didn't want to take a seat at the counter; I would have my back to the room, even though I could see into the kitchen.

Instead, I took the booth farthest from the door. The booth actually had two windows, one for the row heading off toward the back door, and one for the row I had to walk down to get there. I sat with my back to the school, but noted that even if I turned slightly sideways, I could see what was happening in the school yard.

A stained menu had been propped between the condiments and napkin holder. The menu offered breakfast, lunch, and dinner, and proudly claimed that the Starlite Restaurant provided twenty-four hour service.

I bet it did.

A plump waitress with tight gray curls slipping out of her hairnet came over. She was wearing a black uniform that had probably fit ten years before but now it was too short and too tight. I wasn't sure how she could breathe.

"Coffee?" she asked as if my answer really didn't concern her. I half-expected her to walk away before I replied.

"Yeah," I said. "What's good?"

To my surprise, she chuckled. "Well, you never been here before, have ya?"

"No, ma'am," I said.

"Nothing's good, but some things are edible. Stay away from the soup at this time of day, and don't even think about a salad. I'd have a burger and make sure they cook the hell out of it."

I tipped my hat back so I could see her more clearly. She looked as tired as I felt. "They don't mind that you talk like that."

"*They* don't give a damn about the restaurant," she said. "*They* make their money in the hotel. There's a bar in there, if you want some alcohol, and that's what you'll get. *Some* alcohol. And a whole lot of water, whether you want it or not."

Then she walked away. A man in his mid-thirties let himself in, and reached behind the cash register, pulling out a packet of cigarettes. He held it up to her, and she shook her head as if she didn't like it but couldn't control it.

He walked past her to a door that clearly led into the hotel. The door opened, letting in a bit of conversation—or was that music?—and then eased shut.

She had poured my coffee, and brought a tiny tin pot filled with cream. I opened the pot's lid, and sniffed. The cream had curdled. I set it aside.

If I ordered something, I would have to eat it, and I wasn't sure my stomach was up for that.

When she walked past a second time, I handed her the pot with the cream. "It's gone south," I said. "And I'm dying of hunger. What do you have that you can guarantee won't kill me."

She grinned, and it took years off her face. "The sweets are good. They're baked fresh every morning. Don't use the butter, though."

I chuckled. "You trust the sweets, but not the rest of the food."

She picked up the pot of cream. "We don't make the sweets. The bakery down the block does. We don't have a lot left by this time of day, although if you come in later tonight, we'll get whatever they have leftover."

"That's a lot of sweets," I said.

Her smile faded. "We have a lot of sweet tooths in this joint."

Then she carried the cream away before she could take my order. Sweet tooths. Heroin addicts in particular binged on sweets; they couldn't get enough.

226

I felt sad. I picked up the spoon and inspected it for grime. When it came out clean, I used it to stir my coffee. Then I took off the fedora and set it on the booth beside me.

Through the half-moon window in the door leading into the hotel, I could only see shapes. Conversations, banging pots, and laughter continued to come from the kitchen. This place felt like a dingy old restaurant that had once seen better days. The clientele had the look of people who came here because they didn't know any place better, and the waitress had a good solid feel to her.

If I had come in here without knowing about the hotel next door, if the hotel hadn't existed at all in fact, I would have thought this place like a hundred restaurants in the Greater Chicago area. Good enough to withstand the changes to a once-nice neighborhood, but not good enough to attract any new clientele.

"So? Which sweets?" She was back with her notepad in hand.

"Donut sounds good. Whatever you have left. And some dry toast."

"No dry toast," she said. "Donut it is."

I had no idea how even the toast could be bad, but I wasn't going to ask. I wished I had a way to see more of the place without walking around. But I didn't know what that would be.

So I stood up and went to the counter. She was opening the donut case. Three crullers and two chocolate remained. She saw me, and moved her hand over the top of all of them, in a silent question.

"The chocolate," I said. "And where's your men's room?"

"Through that door," she said, tilting her head toward the door into the hotel. "Make sure you wash your hands when you're done."

I couldn't tell if she was still joking with me or if that was an actual warning. I suspected it was both.

"Thanks," I said, and walked through the door. It was a swinging door, which I hadn't expected. I expected something that locked. It appeared to have once led into the kitchen. So the redesign had somehow moved the bar into the hotel, or added the wall here, or something. I didn't have a chance to look closely at the architecture.

Instead, I pushed the door open, and stepped into a haze of cigarette smoke. The Supremes blared from some overhead speakers.

The lobby was bigger than I remembered. Of course, when I had been here two days ago, I had been focused on the registration desk, which was all the way across the room, and the stairs off to the side.

Now I saw that the lobby had three distinct sections, the bar to my left, a general area near the front door, and then the registration section. The bathrooms were behind the bar, illuminated by a red and white sign. I ignored them for a moment, and walked deeper inside.

Now the stench of sweat, cum, and spilled alcohol reached me, bringing me back to the other morning. The carpet stuck to my shoes, and the wallpaper to my right was peeling off. The tables in the bar all carried glass ashtrays, most of which hadn't been emptied in a while, and a matching glass bowl filled with peanuts.

The bar itself was still a little attractive in the dim light. The red upholstered barrel chairs had been built to last. Brass buttons lined the sides, holding the red leather in place. The bar was made of a deep reddish wood, and had been coated with some kind of laminate, making it shine even in the bad light. A mirror behind the bar reflected oddly, which made me think that it wasn't just a mirror, but a one-way window that someone could watch the entire area without actually entering the lobby.

A single bartender sliced lemons while keeping an eye on me. He was as big as I was, which had to be deliberate, since the white shirt and red vest that he wore over black trousers fit perfectly.

I gave him a deliberately nervous grin, and headed toward the men's room. I would come back in here later if I could.

The men's room smelled of piss. The grimy counter had a pile of roach clips in one of those glass bowls used for bar snacks. Matchbooks with the name of the Starlite written in white script on a black background lined up in their own container.

I used the urinal, because I had a hunch the mirror in here was one-way glass as well and I wanted to look like I needed the room. Then I washed my hands, checking my reflection as I did so. The makeup hadn't flaked or peeled, and in this light, it looked like I had never been scarred. Good to know. Marvella was right: I had another disguise tool in my arsenal.

I looked at the cloth roll towel dispenser and wondered if that rotating cloth had ever been cleaned. I shook my hands to air dry them, figure that even if someone was watching me, they would see that action for the critique it was.

Not that it mattered. Like the waitress had said. No one here cared about the restaurant or the bar or anything except what happened upstairs.

And that included me.

I stepped out. The bartender had his back to me. Apparently he figured I was just another customer, and not one who interested him.

I went back into the restaurant to find my chocolate donut waiting for me, and a new cup of coffee steaming.

I wiped my hands on a napkin and forced myself to take a bite of the donut. It was good and fresh as promised.

One of the elderly couples had left. It was now full dark outside, and as I looked sideways toward the school, it seemed abandoned despite the teachers' cars still in the parking lot.

The waitress came by with a pot of coffee and topped off my cup even though I didn't need it.

"That bar doesn't look so bad," I said. "How come it's not part of the restaurant? You'd think it would be."

"They built a wall about five years back. They needed more room in the lobby, and they took it out of the restaurant." She didn't sound as if she approved.

"I take it you've worked here a long time?"

"Yeah," she said. "Fifteen years now. They pay me more than they should, which is good, because the tips suck."

"That's what happens when there are too many regulars and not enough new customers," I said.

"You worked restaurants?" She actually seemed interested.

"I used to own one," I lied. "A long time ago."

She nodded. "Things change, don't they? Even when they stay the same."

"This looks like it was a classy joint fifteen years ago."

"Not classy," she said. "But nice. The right kind of people, if you know what I mean. New owner came in about six, seven years ago now, and it's been...well. I should get out. I really should."

229

"Why don't you?" I asked.

"Not sure I can," she said, then bit her lower lip. She'd said too much.

"I get that. I should've shut my restaurant down when it was clear it wasn't working. I didn't. Lost my shirt." I plucked my coat. "Maybe everything but my shirt."

She chuckled, clearly relieved that I had misunderstood her. But I hadn't. She was afraid to leave this place. She held too many secrets.

I sipped my coffee. "You just starting your shift?"

"Got about an hour. It's a ten-hour day today. The lunch girl didn't show."

"Don't you hate that?" I asked.

She shrugged. "I'm not sure. I make more this way. But I sure get tired these days."

"Yeah," I said, then leaned back. An hour. I could meet her when she got off, see if she would talk to me some more. It was a risk, and I had no idea how much cleanup she had to do.

She topped my coffee again. She didn't want to leave any more than I wanted her to.

"I take it with a new owner, the restaurant's not for sale."

She frowned just a little. "I heard rumors someone was interested in the hotel. Was that you?"

"Hell, no," I said. "Restaurants are hard enough. I couldn't imagine trying a hotel too."

"This kind is easier," she said, then took the coffee pot back to its station. A different man pushed open the door from the hotel. He looked around, glowered at me, and then walked out the front door.

I didn't like that the whole place knew about Laura's offer. That seemed strange. Or maybe the offer had been strange.

I finished the donut, then drank the coffee slowly, but the waitress didn't return. She had disappeared into the back.

I picked up my hat and slid out of the booth, but no one seemed to notice that I was leaving. So I reached into my wallet and removed a five. I waved it at the kitchen window as I walked by.

She came out of the back, her face flushed.

"I figured you got off early," I said.

"No such luck," she said.

I handed her the five. She took it to the cash register. I waved my upraised hand at her. "No need."

"I thought you didn't have a pot to piss in," she said.

"I thought no one tipped you," I said.

She smiled. "That's why you got no money."

"Truer than you know." I knew if I walked back into the hotel, I'd lose any chance of talking to her again. She would figure I was one of the johns, and I wasn't worth her time.

So I nodded a goodbye and walked out the front door into the cold.

Night had settled early. The cold had acquired a brittle edge. I bowed my head as if I were lighting cigarette. Then I walked toward the front door of the hotel.

I looked back at the restaurant to see if anyone was watching. So far as I could tell, no one was. I pushed open those glass doors again, like I had done two days before.

The interior looked different after dark, a little less seedy, a little more alive. A couple of men sat in the barrel chairs now, cigarettes dangling from their fingers. I didn't recognize the guy behind the reception counter. He didn't look up. He wasn't interested in me at all.

The staircase had a formal railing that curled toward a corridor which led to the back area. A long mirror placed at eye level ran the length of the wall between the bar and the corridor. I was now convinced that all of the mirrors, which covered walls into the back area, had one-way glass.

I let my gaze pass over that, then rest on two of the women sitting suggestively on the couch under the mirror. They were older than Lacey, thinner, and they wore leather miniskirts and thigh-high boots. Instead of shirts, they wore tube tops that barely covered their breasts. The women had to be cold; the lobby was warmer than outside, but not *that* warm. I wanted to walk over to them and wrap blankets around them.

I didn't find them attractive at all. Just sad, cold, and clearly underfed.

I gave them a nervous smile, then glanced at the bar. The bartender was watching the two patrons who sat in those barrel chairs. One of the men waved one of the girls over.

The other girl watched as her companion went over to him.

I headed toward the couch, but at the last minute, I went down the corridor. As I suspected, a bank of elevators covered that wall, just far enough back that a false back could have been built behind those mirrors. There was not a mirror anywhere near the elevators. I pressed the call button. One of the elevators opened immediately, and I got in.

It smelled of spilled beer. The door closed quickly. I had several choices. I could go to any floor. I picked the top, but the button wouldn't stay pressed. Nor would it press for the next floor. There was a keyhole beneath that button, which meant the access to those floors was restricted.

So I hit the next button for the fifth floor, and that button stayed pressed. The elevator trembled its way up, and I wondered if the thing had been repaired in recent memory. The last thing I needed was to get stuck in an elevator in the Starlite Hotel.

The elevator opened into a corridor on the fifth floor. The smell was actually better here—less cigarette smoke, no beer smell, and no stench of sweat or sex. The doors near me were closed. Jimmy was right: The locks were flimsy. I could have broken a door down with a kick. He just didn't have the strength yet.

I winced at the thought. I didn't ever want Jimmy to need that kind of strength. I wanted him to survive by his prodigious brain, not by his street sense and his muscles.

Maybe Jimmy's heroism, more than the attack on Lacey, was the bigger impetus for my search for another school for him. I didn't want Jimmy anywhere near the life he'd been born to, and this damn hotel was way too close, both in proximity and in lifestyle.

I looked for mirrors and saw none, not even the anti-shoplifting mirrors that some hotel security people used to keep track of who was on a floor. A few doors were cracked open, probably so someone would know they were usable. I pushed them all the way, saw rooms with just a bed and a chair and not much else. The beds in the empty rooms had been made, if you called pulling a once-white chenille bedspread over the messed-up sheets "made."

One, at the end of the hall, was spotless, and the bed actually had crisp military lines. Clearly this room didn't get used often.

The window had iron bars over it on the outside, but through them, the alley was visible. I slipped out, saw a sign for the fire escape, and tried to open that door. It was locked.

I started back down the hall when a girl came out of one of the rooms wearing a white satin dressing gown over a black lace bra and matching panties. She had on white heels so high that she was almost standing on the point of her toes.

She started when she saw me. "Who brought you up here?"

"I got sent up for Gwen...?" I said, grabbing the first name that came to mind.

She frowned. "Gwen? We don't have no Gwen."

"They said fifth floor, last room...?" I made myself sound tentative. I kept my head down.

"Shit. I don't know everybody who works here. But this is a break floor unless we're so busy that we need it. You got to go to three."

"Thanks," I said. Then I raised my eyebrows at her and hoped she would think I was being timid. "But I'm already here, if you want to..."

"I," she said with a flourish, brandishing a key, "am the lucky girl who gets to go upstairs tonight. You gotta hope there'll be some blow and a lot of booze, because Eddie—" And then she shuddered. "Believe me, I'd rather stay here."

"I can pay," I said, as if that would make a difference.

"Not enough, Big Boy. Once a girl gets the key, she's stuck with Eddie until he gets tired of her. And no telling what will make him tired."

She grinned at me, but there was no humor in it. Just some terrified bravado. I couldn't even tell how old she was.

"I'd invite you into the elevator, but I'm going up and you're going down. So find the stairs, and be careful. You see anyone in the corridors, you tell them you're looking for your girl on the third floor and you got off in the wrong place, okay? They don't take too kindly to explorers around here."

She pushed past me, leaving a wave of Chanel and beer in her wake. She'd started drinking before she got upstairs, maybe for a bit of Dutch courage.

So Eddie had the top floor, or at least part of it. I headed for the stairs, but stopped the moment the elevator door closed. I looked in the other open rooms, and didn't see anything different. Then I went down one flight.

The fourth floor had no mirrors, more closed doors, and a carpet so worn that those heels the girl had worn could have easily torn through it. I tried one locked door, and a deep man's voice yelled, "Fuck off!"

I moved away. I had no backup here. I really didn't want to get caught.

No fire escape markings at all and no open doors. The window in the hallway had been boarded shut.

I went down to the third floor. These doors were all closed except a door toward the back that was missing the doorknob. This had to be the room where Voss assaulted Lacey. I stared in there for a moment. The bed had been stripped, and the mattress propped against the wall. Another mattress covered the floor. It looked someone was turning this room into storage.

"Help you?" A female voice.

I turned, and a light-skinned woman stood behind me. She too wore a white satin robe over black lace bra and panties, but she didn't wear heels. In fact, her feet were bare.

"I thought I was supposed to come here," I said, nervously.

"Ah, hell," she said. "The new guy at the desk is a major screw-up. Come with me."

She took my hand and pulled me with her toward the other end of the hall. "I suppose he didn't tell you the rules, did he? No all-nighters, no matter how much you pay. Twenty dollars gets you the standard stuff. Weirdo crap costs fifty, and if you like it rough, go downstairs and talk to Ramon. He'll take direct you to a different house. It's more expensive, but you're paying to break the goods. You gotta remember that. If you hurt anyone here, you'll get hurt worse. In fact, you'll get hurt so bad you won't be able to walk for a week. We clear?"

She said all that in a flat voice as if she had it all memorized and said it several times a day, which she probably did.

My head spun at the way anyone could be calm about what she said. I knew it was all in a night's work for her, but still. Break the goods? As if the women were nothing but commodities?

Which, of course, was all that they were.

I had to make sure that my shock and sadness didn't show on my face. I was actually grateful for the makeup. The caked feeling on my cheek reminded me to keep my expression neutral.

We had reached the middle of the corridor. She was leading me toward an open door in the back.

I finally came up with a question that I could ask and still sound like a john, albeit a new one. "What's weirdo stuff?"

"Oh, for God's sake." She shook her head and didn't even turn around. She kept pulling me toward the room. "If you want to stick it somewhere unusual or you want to wear costumes or you want to mess with anything except breasts and pussy, then you're crossing into weirdo territory. Got that?"

"I suppose," I said.

"Good." She entered the last room down the hall. It looked like all the others, a single bed with a chenille spread that she immediately tossed to the floor, messed-up sheets that didn't even try to hide the fact someone else had been there already, one chair, a nightstand with one lamp on it, and a blocked-off window.

I pushed the door closed. "Is, um, talking weirdo stuff?"

"You got twenty bucks?" she asked, extending her hand.

I reached into my back pocket and removed my wallet, trying to make my hand shake just a little. I had two more twenties. I hoped she wouldn't consider conversation a fifty-dollar charge.

I pulled out one of the twenties and handed it to her. She put it in the drawer on the end table.

"You can talk, you can scream, you can sing the national anthem," she said, "as long as you're only doing the standard stuff at the same time. Some guys are just naturally loud and we deal with that. Hell, I'll scream if you need me to. No one cares. It's not a big deal."

Screaming was not a big deal. Got that. My stomach turned.

She sat down and patted the bed.

I was not going to sit next to her. I pulled off my hat, but I kept my coat on. Then I reached for the chair and sat in it slowly, nervously, like a man who was extremely unsure of himself. I placed my hat on my knee, and kept my hand on the felt crown, my thumb and little finger in the two dents.

I hoped the message was clear: I was going to bolt if I got any more uncomfortable. "I, um, actually meant, you know, a conversation. Nothing else."

"Oh, God," she said, and flopped back on the bed, legs spread. Her pubic hair crept out of the underwear, probably on purpose. "Seriously? You're one of them? Believe me, I don't have nothing interesting to say. I get five guys, usually, except on the weekends. There's five, I try to wash off between and that's it. I'd rather just do it than talk about it, okay?"

I had never been in this situation before, either intentionally or accidentally. I had talked to prostitutes; I used to talk to Jimmy's mother to try to get her to take care of her son. But never about her life.

My cheeks had actually grown warm, and it wasn't just because the room was stuffy.

"I, um, don't care about that. The details about other men don't do anything for me. I just want to have someone talk to me, okay? No one does."

She raised up on her elbows. "Why not? You're not bad looking. You're quiet. People should talk to you."

I shook my head. "I don't...it's hard to explain."

Because I had no idea how to lie about this. It was beyond my expertise.

"Believe me," she said, "I've heard it all. Mother issues? Shy? You don't seem shy. How many girls have just tried pulling down your pants and seeing what happens?"

I tightened my grip on my hat. "I'm a vet."

She frowned. "Vietnam? You're too old."

"Korea," I said, and finally, the right lie presented itself. "I can't...you don't want...I don't let anyone..."

"What'd they shoot it off?" she asked, looking at my crotch.

I shook my head. "Just, it's not pretty."

"Ah, hon," she said, "it's never pretty. They're all different. I can take it."

"I can't," I said quietly.

She sighed. "Shit. If I'd known you were a talker, I'd've given you to one of the new girls."

"New girls?" I asked.

"There's always new girls and they're always scared and the talkers usually calm 'em right down. Talkers bore me. Same old, same old. Lonely, misunderstood, not that I'm trying to be insensitive."

Even though she was, probably deliberately so. She hated being in here with me.

But I moved the hat nervously to the other knee. I'd paid her. I wanted to get some information out of her. "How about *you* talk?"

"I told you. Five guys, except on weekends—"

"No," I said. "I really don't care about those details. I just want to hear a voice. You know. Just talking."

"About what?" she said. "I don't got education like you. I don't watch much TV. I don't got opinions."

She probably wasn't allowed to have opinions. I clamped down on my thoughts and focused on keeping the conversation on track. Information. As much as I could get without tipping her off. "Just...tell me about the hotel."

"The hotel?" She sat all the way up and wrapped her robe around herself. I felt myself relax slightly. I really didn't want to see every part of her. I didn't find her attractive. I found her sad. "Why do you want to know about the hotel?"

I shrugged. "I don't want to know about the other men, and I can't ask you about your...the guy you work for. And you live here, right?"

"I work here," she said coldly. "This is a working hotel. Only the new girls live here. And Eddie. He's got some palace upstairs."

"Eddie?"

"The owner," she said, "and I'm not supposed to talk about him, so forget I said anything. I don't live here. You can't come here in the middle of the night and get something. Remember, I said, no all-nighters. Last call, last customer. Then we actually get out of here and get some fucking sleep."

"Last call?" I asked. "That seems awful early. You'd think there'd be a lot of business after the regular bars close."

"Last call for nightclubs is 4," she said, as if I was stupid. "And we're not allowed to take big jobs after that. By that, I mean, something that's expensive, not, you know, guys built like you, without the...injury."

The deliberate crudeness actually bothered me. I was more of a prude than I realized.

"They just bus you outta here, huh?" I asked. Just before they bussed in the kids next door. I knew that couldn't be a coincidence.

237

Her eyes narrowed. "What do you care? We don't sleep here. You don't need more than that. And you don't even need that. Jesus. That's enough business talk. Why don't you pull down those pants and let me see if the damage is too much—"

"No," I said. "And I can't think of anything else to talk about. I could ask for a happy memory or something, but that doesn't seem right. Those things are personal. And this isn't about personal, at least for you, right?"

"This is weirdo shit." She stood up and turned her back on me. She rapped her knuckles against the end table, but the sound wasn't loud. I hoped it wasn't some kind of signal. "I should've asked for fifty."

"You can give me my twenty back," I said.

"Hell, no," she said. "You been in here too long for that."

I swallowed. "I don't want you to get hurt. That's what they'll do, right? If you spend time with me and I don't pay you?"

She whirled. The robe flared around her calves. "You gave me money. I'm not giving it back."

I held up both my hands as if she had pulled a gun on me. I kept my hat in my left hand. "Okay. I didn't mean to offend you."

"You're not offending me. You're weird, and I don't like weird."

"You said you can't talk about that Eddie guy and you don't want to talk about the hotel, and you don't live here, and so just tell me something. Do you eat in the restaurant? What do you like for breakfast? Do you—"

"Coffee. I don't eat much else, okay. I don't need to." Her nostrils flared.

"How come the new girls get to sleep here and you don't?" I asked.

Her lips thinned. "They're not working yet," she said. "They're learning, and Jesus. That's enough. I don't got to tell you nothing. You a cop?"

There it was. I'd been afraid of that question all along.

"No," I said. "I told you. I'm a vet. I just ask questions because I can't do anything else."

"You see action?"

I nodded. "I don't like to talk about it."

"Now you know how it feels." She studied me for a moment, her arms wrapped around her torso. "It's been long enough. You can get out now."

"But we just got started—"

"We're done with that. Fifty or nothing."

I figured I had asked her everything I could without making her even more suspicious. I stood slowly, eased my hat onto my head, and said, "Thank you for talking to me. Can you at least tell me your name?"

"Not my real one," she said drily. "So I can make up something if that makes you feel better."

"What do they call you here?"

"I ain't tell you," she said, "because I don't want you to ask for me again. Next time, you tell them at the desk or the girl you see in the lobby that you're a talker. They'll know what that means. Some girls like it. I don't. Now get out."

I nodded, and let myself out, leaving the door open. She slammed it behind me, and cursed loudly, apparently so that I could hear.

If I tried that again, and she and the other girl compared notes, I would get banned from this place. I wasn't sure how much I needed to return, so I slouched and shuffled toward the stairs.

I felt dirty, even though I hadn't touched her.

I made my way down the stairs. No one looked at me as I reached the lobby. The bar was full. Men sat in the barrel chairs, and girls sat on their laps. Other girls lounged on the couches in the middle of the room.

Laughter now covered some peppy Motown song that I couldn't quite identify. I did some quick math as I scanned the room.

Twenty dollars an encounter, not counting drinks, "weirdo shit," or something that went longer than planned. At least thirty girls were waiting or working the men in the bar. Six hundred dollars for this hour, and it wasn't even full on night yet.

Six hundred dollars. That was as much as I made in a month.

No wonder they didn't want to sell this place. No wonder they didn't want to close. They were making much more than six hundred dollars an hour and they did business for at least twelve hours per day.

That was over $7,000 per day, from just what I could see in the lobby, not counting what was going on in the rooms upstairs. Or the restaurant. Or the bar.

No one spoke to me as I made my way out. No one leered at me and asked me if I had a good time. The girls didn't even give me a second glance, since they figured I had gotten what I had come here for.

239

I had, but not in the way I expected.

I let myself out and took a few steps north so that the protective darkness of the street enveloped me. The cold cleared my lungs, not that it mattered.

I kept my head bowed, and walked to the van, making sure no one followed me because it was time to go home.

34

The clock in the van told me it was only six o'clock by the time I got home, but I didn't believe it until I walked inside and saw the national news still playing on my television set. My apartment smelled of fried chicken. My mouth watered.

I stank of mothballs, cigarettes, and all kinds of foul things. I peeled off the coat and dumped it outside the door. If someone wanted to steal the damn thing, fine. I needed it, but I didn't need it enough to keep it in my apartment.

Marvella peered at me from the stove. Something boiled in front of her, and she held a cooking spoon. "Thought you were going to be gone longer."

"Felt like I was," I said.

"Hey, Smoke!" Jimmy popped his head over the back of the couch. "What'd you do to your face?"

I touched the makeup. It flaked into my palm. "It's just...stuff," I said.

Marvella grinned. She realized that I couldn't tell Jimmy I was wearing makeup.

"Marvella's making fried chicken," Jimmy said. "I gots half my home-work done already."

"'Got,'" I corrected half-heartedly.

"Gots," he said, and bounced back onto the couch. As I walked past it, I realized he had his thumb in the middle of an open book. He wasn't really watching the news; he was reading.

"I need a shower," I said to Marvella, and kept going to the back.

I could feel my mood, dark and angry, like a gigantic cloud moving through the apartment. I had no idea how I would hide it from the two of them. There was only so much I could do.

I turned on the shower, then for the second time this week, I bagged my clothes. This time, I wouldn't throw them away. I just didn't want to smell them, and I didn't have time to do laundry right now.

I climbed in the scalding water and let it run, my head tilted back. That hotel was big, and I was facing an impossible task, especially alone.

The bathroom door opened, and then the shower curtain slide back.

"Hey!" I said, turning toward the wall.

Jimmy chuckled. "Just me. Marvella says you'll need this."

He handed me a white jar. Cold cream. Of course. How many women had I watched remove their makeup with this stuff?

"Can you take the lid off?" I asked.

"She says you gots to be—*got* to be careful with it. She'll buy you your own later. So just dip your fingers in, okay?"

I stepped out of the water a bit, dipped my fingers in the chill gooey liquid, and smeared it on my cheek. Jimmy watched me, then laughed.

"I'm gonna pretend I don't know what you done," he said, and slid the shower curtain closed.

I presumed he meant the makeup, but I felt vaguely guilty anyway. What I'd done was something I'd never done before; I paid for time with a woman, and even though I hadn't touched her, I still felt odd about it.

I leaned out of the shower again, grabbed a washcloth, and scrubbed the makeup off my face. The washcloth turned brown, and I had to hold it under the water to get the makeup off the cloth. Then I washed myself, and stood in the steaming hot water until it became lukewarm. I hoped no one else needed a shower in the next hour or two, because I had just used all the hot water, the first time I had done that since I moved into this building.

I got out, and as I dried off, I realized I hadn't grabbed a change of clothes. I stepped out of the shower and saw my robe hanging on the back of the door.

I smiled, my mood lightening a little. Jimmy really was a good kid.

I put the robe on and walked to my bedroom, still feeling somewhat naked with Marvella down the hall. Things that wouldn't bother me had Laura been here disturbed me greatly with Marvella around.

I put on a T-shirt and that ugly but warm sweater that Althea had given me, and another pair of pants, socks, and my slippers. I didn't want to go out again on this night if I could help it, even though I probably should have refereed Laura's meeting with Franklin.

But I didn't want to. They were adults. They could come to some kind of conclusion on their own.

Besides, I had planning to do.

By the time I got back to the kitchen, Marvella had the chicken draining on some paper towels. Cooking-oil-soaked paper towels were already crumpled in the sink.

Freshly baked biscuits sat on a cooling rack that didn't belong to me. And Marvella had a big bowl in her arms. She was stirring its contents with that wooden spoon.

"Don't yell at me," she said. "I don't have vegetables. This is what I could do on short notice."

"Yell at you?" I asked. "This is fantastic."

She smiled, and set the mashed potatoes on the table. Then she cut half a stick of butter and plopped it in the middle of the potatoes.

"No gravy either," she said. "The biscuits took it out of me."

"Smells great." Jimmy went to the refrigerator and poured himself a glass of milk. "You should let her cook every night, Smoke."

I gave Marvella a sideways look.

"I only cook on special occasions, pal," she said to Jimmy.

"Why's this a special occasion?" He set his milk on the table, then climbed into his chair.

"It's not now. I thought it would be just you and me, but Bill crashed our party."

Jimmy gave me an appraising look. I half-expected him to tell me to leave, but his gaze was very serious.

"It's good Smoke's home," he said. "I been worried."

I didn't need to hear that either. Not right now. I almost grabbed one of the last beers out of the fridge, then thought the better of it. I needed a clear head for the next few days.

I grabbed one of Jimmy's Cokes instead.

"Hey!" he said as I set it on the table.

"You haven't been worried enough to share," I said, smiling at him.

He made a face. "I have too been worried. But you're here now."

"I am," I said.

Marvella set the plate of fried chicken on the table, and gave us each a biscuit. The biscuits steamed. Before she sat down, she went over and turned off the television.

"Hey!" Jimmy said for the second time. "You said I could watch."

"Not during dinner," she said. "We have things to discuss."

And we did. Jimmy's homework. The Chicago Seven Trial, which was in the news today for not having much news. The Panther Trial. Lacey going home.

Jimmy finished first, of course, and asked if he could be excused.

"Only if you go finish your homework," I said.

"'Kay." He set his plate beside the sink, then grabbed that book and flopped on the couch. I almost told him to go to his room, but Marvella had promised him television.

"When we're done here," I said softly to her, "may I discuss something with you?"

"We can talk about it now," she said.

I shook my head, and glanced toward Jimmy. He was sprawled on his stomach, his feet crossed at the ankles and swinging in the air.

"No, you can't," Jim said, getting my point before Marvella did. "Because 'little pitchers have big ears.'"

I raised my eyebrows at her, and smiled just a little. She laughed. "Sure. In my apartment. Your office is too small."

I almost protested, but we would be across the hall. And I really didn't want Jimmy to hear any of this conversation.

Marvella and I finished dinner. There was some chicken left over, and she didn't want it. I wrapped it and put it in the fridge, along with six biscuits. Marvella took the remaining three to her apartment. She was going to put on coffee.

I rinsed the dishes and stacked them. I would do them when I got back.

"No TV until you're done," I said to Jimmy as I got ready to leave. "I'll be right across the hall."

"I'm not a baby," he said.

I knew that. I even knew better than to tell him where I would be. But I was feeling incredibly overprotective at the moment.

I took my keys, and locked Jimmy in. Then I knocked on Marvella's door.

It took her a minute to open it. She had changed into an orange and brown caftan, and put a beaded orange headband on to keep her hair out of her eyes.

"Come on in," she said.

The apartment's familiar sandalwood scent mixed with coffee. She had already set two coffee cups on the table, along with some chocolate chip cookies. An extra plate of cookies sat to one side, with Saran Wrap covering it.

She saw me looking at it as I sat down. "I figured you could take some to Jimmy."

"You're being awfully kind," I said.

"I'm making a mental note," she said. "I figure you'll have to repay me at some point."

Her tone was light, but serious. She meant it. I made note as well. I would repay her as soon as I could.

"What couldn't Jimmy hear?" Marvella poured our coffees. "He's already pretty deep in this."

"Not this deep," I said. "I was wondering you know of anyone who rehabilitates prostitutes. There's dozens of women there. Maybe Helping Hands could take them in...?"

Helping Hands was a charity Laura had funded and Marvella helped run. It found employment and housing for the homeless families that I came across while inspecting Sturdy's buildings. At least, that was how it started. It also helped others that some of the founders deemed appropriate.

"No." Marvella stood beside me, still holding the coffee pot.

I was startled at her response. "That was quick. I'm sure some of the women we've helped have been prostitutes."

"They have been," Marvella said, "and they're the toughest cases. They're also usually addicts who don't want to go to rehab. A couple of them have brought men to the temporary housing we've put them in. They've caused a lot of complaints in the neighborhoods. The staff asked that we try not to bring in working prostitutes anymore."

"Is that fair?" I asked. "These women had to make a living when they were homeless—"

"Yeah, they did." She took the coffee pot back to the stove. "The problem is that they only know one way to do to earn money. Then they get sick or they take drugs to cover up how they feel, and the whole cycle starts all over again."

"So, you know of no way to help prostitutes?" I wasn't sure I believed it, yet it sounded true. Could experience take someone so far from "normal" life that they couldn't be rehabilitated? Part of me refused to believe that. "In other words, these women are just stuck."

"They have to choose to get out on their own. They can't just quit the life because some guy comes in and breaks up a brothel." Marvella sat down. "The women that try to get out on their own have a tough enough time. One financial problem, and they want to solve it the easy way rather than hunt for a job or come back to us for more training or ask for help. They have no self-esteem, and that makes them almost impossible to work with."

"All of the women I've brought you have no self-esteem," I said. "They're homeless, squatting in a place not their own, usually running from abusive men—"

"They got out," Marvella said. "That takes self-esteem. It's usually buried, but it's there. Prostitutes, hell, they have nothing left."

"And we should accept that," I said.

Her eyes narrowed. "If you can find someone to help them, more power to you. You asked me if we could help them. I said no."

I picked up my coffee cup, just to give myself something to hide behind. Marvella usually had answers on these women's issues. She knew how to solve things. She knew people who had found solutions if she couldn't solve it herself.

I'd never heard her be so negative before.

"You're saying I should just let them go," I said.

She took a sip from her own cup. We were two neighbors, discussing prostitutes over coffee. It felt strange.

"I don't know what else you can do," Marvella said.

I set my cup down. "But what about the kids?"

"Kids?" she asked.

"I found out that there are other girls at the hotel. They're called new girls, and I'm pretty sure that's where Lacey would have been if Jimmy and Keith hadn't saved her."

Marvella set her cup down so hard I thought she would break the saucer. "Girls?" she repeated. "Like Lacey?"

I nodded.

"Roaming free?" Marvella asked.

"I don't think so," I said. "I can't get to them. I think they're in the process of having the self-esteem beaten out of them."

Marvella winced.

"But I have an idea about how to rescue them," I said. "The question is what happens after I get them out."

She picked up her spoon and tapped its edge against the table. I wasn't sure she knew she was doing it.

"What do you mean what happens after they get out?" she asked. "You take them to their families."

I shook my head. "I suspect most of the families are nothing like the Grimshaws. And the Grimshaws are having enough trouble dealing with the attack on Lacey. I'm not sure they would know how to handle it if she'd been imprisoned too."

I wasn't sure I would have known how to handle it either.

Marvella set the spoon down. She leaned back in her chair. "Maybe we treat them the way that we're going to treat Lacey. Like an assault victim, not like a prostitute."

That made sense to me. And I had to ask: "Wouldn't that make sense for the women who'd been working as prostitutes? Aren't they victims?"

Marvella's eyes narrowed. "One problem at a time. How do you plan to get the girls out?"

"I don't know exactly," I said. "I'm working alone here. I have some ideas, but it'll be hard since it's just me."

She ran a fingertip around the rim of the cup. It made a ringing sound. "You can't do this by yourself. If those girls truly have been imprisoned and assaulted, it won't matter if it's you or you and an army, they won't be easy to get out of that building."

"You'd think they'd want to escape," I said.

"They'll be too afraid," she said. "Besides, you're a man. They won't know if they can trust you."

I flashed on Lacey, kicking the doctor. And she had been attacked only the once.

"So what do I do?" I asked.

"I might know some women who can help," Marvella said.

"You said the women you know can't fight," I said.

"I said I didn't know if they could fight." She spoke clearly. She almost sounded irritated. "I know they can convince abused girls to leave a room."

I shook my head. "I am not taking any women in there."

Marvella smiled at me. "We're tougher than you think, Mr. Grimshaw."

"It's too dangerous," I said. "What if they catch you? Jesus, Marvella, the people who run that place know how to hurt women and make it last."

"I know," she said quietly. "The women I would bring with me all know."

"You can't defend yourselves and I can't defend you," I said. "I'll have enough trouble—"

"We can defend ourselves, or at least some of my friends can. The rest of us will rely on them and we'll get those girls out. I'm sensing you don't even know how many girls are trapped in that hotel."

I let out a breath. She caught me there.

"No," I said, "I don't."

"So you're going to go in there, all James Bond, and get a dozen scared and battered young girls out of a hotel under the noses of their captors, without help, and without scaring any of the girls?"

248

"When you put it like that, it sounds stupid and impossible." I ran a hand across my forehead. Saying things out loud did that some times.

"By yourself, yes," she said. "But there are quiet times, right? Times when there are no clients?"

"Yeah," I said. "That's when I plan to go in."

"Chances are they won't have a lot of security, and what security they have won't be expecting it. We'll get the girls into vans, and we'll get them away. We're probably going to have to take them to the hospital and get them some treatment. Helping Hands can pay for that."

I didn't say anything. I hated the idea of a gang of women going into a brothel. "You're going to go all Carrie Nation on me, aren't you?" I asked, thinking of the famous turn-of-the-century reformer who went into bars with axes and attacked men.

"For a bright guy, you have a truly limited imagination," she said. "A few of the women I know teach women how to shoot at a gun range outside of the city. And most of us know how to hit guys. We all know how to scream. They won't expect a group of us, and we'll have you."

"I thought you said I can't be around the girls or they won't leave," I said. "Male, remember?"

She smiled. "You can guard us. You can make sure we get the girls out. Then you can do whatever you were going to do."

Sometimes I disliked how clearly she saw me. She knew that rescuing the girls wasn't my only priority.

"I want to meet these women," I said. "I am not committing to this until I know who they are and what they can do."

"You mean, unless you believe they can do what they say," Marvella said, and she sounded disappointed in me.

"That too," I said.

"Most of them aren't going to want to meet you. They're not fond of men." Her gaze met mine.

"Well," I said, "they're going to have to deal with me sooner or later. And I get to decide if they're coming along."

Marvella's lips thinned.

"It's my mission," I said, and as I said it, I realized that "mission" was the right word. I felt like I was on a mission, a crusade even.

"Yes, but you need help. Have you asked Jack?"

It took me a minute to realize she meant Sinkovich. She was calling him Jack now? When had that happened?

"I'm not going to," I said. "He's a cop."

"He won't tell anyone," she said.

"That's not my concern. He could lose his job over this."

She stared at me. "Shouldn't that be his choice?"

"Look, Marvella, this is not some kind of game. Eddie Turner has ties to the mob, and hotel makes more money each night than you or I see in years. We're doing something—I'm going to do something—that could have major repercussions. I'm not asking Franklin or Jonathan to come with me. I'm not putting anyone in danger who can't afford the danger. And that includes your friends and Jack Sinkovich."

"My friends as you call them already put themselves in danger, always to help other women. Usually they run clinics—" and by that Marvella meant abortion clinics, *illegal* clinics, which I already knew about because of an incident last year "—and sometimes they rescue women in bad circumstances, usually from an abusive spouse. This is a bad circumstance."

"Times one thousand," I said. "This isn't one abusive spouse. These are criminals."

"I know," Marvella said. "That's why you can't go in alone."

I stood up and walked to that bay window. Lights from apartments across the alley flickered. People were having dinner, watching television, thinking about their jobs or their kids or whatever it was that normal people thought of at night.

They weren't talking about raiding a hotel filled with injured girls and prostitutes next to a school.

I sighed. "Let me think about it."

"If you're going to think," Marvella said, "think about all of it. Consider what happens if you decide you're not the one to take this on."

"Meaning what?" I could see part of her reflection in the glass. She appeared as streaks of brown and orange with an indefinable face.

"Meaning that should be an option. Not doing this should absolutely be an option."

I nodded. It might have to be.

"In the meantime, I'll see who's willing to help," she said.

"Don't tell anyone where I'm going or what I'm planning."

"I'll tell them in general terms." She got up from the table. The brown and gold blur that the glass reflected moved up and into the kitchen.

"I'm not taking in amateurs," I said, realizing that with that sentence, Marvella would know that I wasn't abandoning this mission.

"Well, the professionals don't seem willing to do anything," she said. "It seems to me that amateurs are all you have left."

Almost all, I thought. I had one other idea. It was a long shot—these were all long shots—but it just might work.

"Tomorrow," I said, "at four o'clock. Pick a location. I'll meet with whoever shows up."

"Tomorrow?" Marvella asked. "You're doing this tomorrow?"

"I'm not waiting, Marvella." I turned around. She was leaning on the counter, holding her coffee cup in both hands. "The situation on the ground could change in a heartbeat."

"All right then," she said. "I'll see what I can arrange. I'll have a meeting location for you in the morning."

"Thank you," I said, and headed toward the door.

"One more thing, Bill," she said. "You'll need someone to watch Jimmy."

"You're not going with me," I said.

"If my friends are going, I'm going," she said. "Get someone for Jimmy."

I nodded, but didn't promise anything. I hadn't yet agreed to work with these women.

I wasn't sure I ever would.

35

Jimmy was still up, watching Petula Clark sing a duet with Dean Martin on *The Dean Martin Show*. It didn't seem like the kind of show Jim would happily watch.

I walked around the couch, expecting to find him sound asleep. Instead, he was still on his stomach, engrossed in whatever book he had been reading since dinner.

I smiled. Jimmy had come a long way.

I shut off the television.

"Hey!" he said.

"Hey yourself," I said. "Did you finish everything?"

"No, I still have this." He waved the book at me. I still couldn't see the title. "And I like the noise."

I also noticed that since he was preoccupied, his grammar was better. It made me wonder if he had been using bad grammar as much to annoy me instead of as an example of his ignorance.

I decided not to point it out.

He got up, book in hand, and turned the TV back on. Now, Martin was joking with Gale Gordon. Jimmy made a face, but didn't change the channel. He went back to the couch and the book.

First, I did the dishes, making enough noise to mostly drown out the inanity on the television. I hated hearing Marvella echo my thoughts on the difficulties of what I wanted to do.

I also didn't want to bring innocents into this. I had already ruled out Franklin and Jonathan without even telling them. I certainly wasn't going to bring in "tough" women if I could help it.

Although Marvella's comment about the girls being unwilling to come with me resonated.

The dishes took less time than I expected. I glanced over Jimmy's shoulder, saw that he had about ten pages left, and went into my office. I grabbed a legal pad and brought it back to the kitchen table.

While Jimmy and Dean Martin finished up, I diagrammed the interior of that hotel, as best I could remember it. Then I leaned back and stared at my drawing.

That was a lot of real estate. More than I could cover alone. I needed to clear the place out and then check to make sure it was empty. Those one-way mirrors bothered me, and so did the boarded-up windows.

I would have to be very careful.

I realized that the television show had ended and late night news had started. I listened for a moment, heard nothing about a body, and felt some of the tension leave me.

Then I stood and looked at the couch. Jimmy was sound asleep on top of the closed book.

I went into his room, pulled down the covers on his bed, and turned on the night light. I left the door open, came out, and got him. I debated putting him in his pajamas, but that seemed redundant. I supposed smart—or at least attentive—parents would have had him change when they realized he was going to take longer than usual on his homework.

He was making little snoring sounds. I crouched, and picked him up, careful not to wake him. He was getting heavy. There would soon come a time when I wouldn't be able to do this. But for the moment, he was still a kid. I cradled him close as I carried him to bed.

I took off his shoes, and put his pajamas on the chair next to the bed. I covered him up, and pulled the door closed.

That was the other problem I would have on this mission. If some of those girls were in as bad of shape as Lacey had been, they wouldn't be able to walk out. They would need someone to carry them. A group of women couldn't do that. And Marvella seemed to believe these girls would be afraid of men.

I sighed.

I went back to the kitchen, and froze as Floyd Kalber's voice informed me that police had discovered a body on Chicago's South Side. I glanced at the clock on the kitchen wall. It was ten after ten, which meant that this was not a main story.

I wasn't sure if I should have been grateful or not.

"Police identified the victim as Clyde Voss," Kalber intoned. "He was found shot to death in his apartment...."

I walked to the back of the couch so that I could see Kalber. His hair looked sprayed on and his suit, some kind of plaid, seemed to vibrate on the black-and-white screen. He stared through the television as if he could actually see me.

"...Voss, a convicted drug dealer released last year on parole, was under a blanket, surrounded by drug paraphernalia. The building's manager discovered the body while investigating a complaint about the victim's blaring television. A police spokesman said that such noise was not uncommon in Voss's apartment. The neighbors say it took two days to get up the nerve to complain. Voss had threatened many of them at gunpoint when they had complained before, so they were willing to put up with the sound."

I swallowed hard, my hand gripping the top of the couch.

"Police have no leads, but neighbors believe Voss's death was the result of a drug deal gone bad. In other news, police in Rogers Park..."

I let out the breath I had been holding. No leads. A drug deal gone bad. No one had even tied Voss to the Starlite Hotel.

I glanced at my front door almost involuntarily. If the police didn't contact me in the next few days, they wouldn't contact me at all. Police didn't work hard on drug-related homicides, especially those that occurred on the South Side.

But I couldn't be complacent. I had to remain wary. Someone at the hospital might have heard Lacey talk; someone might have figured out that I went after Voss.

I had to be prepared for questions, and I had to remain calm if anyone spoke to me.

I shut off the television, trying to identify my mood. It took a moment.

I was relieved, relieved that Voss's body wasn't waiting out there to be discovered at the exact right moment. Relieved the police had tied him to drugs, not the Starlite. Relieved that, at least according to this report, no one really cared about him.

Someone probably had once. Just like an entire family cared about Donna Loring, even though she slipped deep into a life that Marvella said no one could escape from.

Maybe that had happened with Voss as well.

It didn't matter to me. I had met the man he had become, not the boy he had been. And the man he had become had tried to destroy someone I loved.

Just like the Starlite was doing every day.

I returned to my diagram.

It would take planning and a little bit of help, but I could get that hotel away from the school.

And I could do it in one very long night.

I just had to be as willing to destroy the Starlite as I had been to get rid of Voss.

I had crossed lines there. I needed to cross lines again.

I needed the right kind of help.

And I knew just where to get it.

36

I took the kids to school the following morning. After I dropped them off, I circled the block, getting one last long look at the Starlite. It seemed quiet and almost harmless in the chilly sunlight. Through the cloudy windows of the Starlite café, I could see elderly couples somehow braving the filth for their morning breakfast.

I saw very few cars in the alley, and those that I could see belonged to other houses. Only two cars in the street. The ice on the windshields told me the cars had been there all night, if not longer. And they were parked nearly a block away from the Starlite, so I had no idea if they were even connected to the hotel.

I drove back home in contemplative silence. I felt calmer than I had the last few days. I had spent a few hours after I put Jim to bed examining and re-examining my plan. I saw a lot of flaws, but I had reduced the luck factor to almost nothing.

I could get rid of that hotel, and do it quickly.

Franklin was going to pick up the kids and take them to the after-school classes. We had touched base just briefly this morning, enough for me to realize his talk with Laura had gone well, at least in his opinion. He wouldn't discuss Lacey, telling me I needed to talk with Althea. But on the way to school, Keith said that Lacey's screams had awakened the household twice last night.

"Daddy kills the monsters in my room," Norene said quite seriously. "I dunno why he can't kill them in hers."

That's my job, I thought, but didn't say. As I tried to think of some kind of comforting response, Mikie answered her. "Mom says it's just from the hospital. She'll get better. There's no monsters to kill."

Jim looked at me in the rearview mirror, and I wouldn't meet his gaze. I remained silent the whole way to the school, letting the kids talk.

While I thought.

And worried.

Back at the apartment, I grabbed those flyers and pulled out the two professionally produced ones. It was still early, but I figured that was better.

I sat on the couch and dialed the phone number at the bottom of Donna Loring's flyer.

"What the hell, man?" a sleepy voice said.

"I have information on Donna Loring," I said.

"What?" A rustle, followed by a cough. I had woken the owner of the voice up and now he was forcing himself into full wakefulness.

"This is the number, right?" I asked. "I found it on the bottom of a flyer."

"This is it, yeah, what do you know?"

"There's a lot," I said. "I'd like to tell you in person."

"Tell me over the phone."

My stomach clenched. I was going to control this. "There's a bakery about two blocks away from her junior high. I'll be in there in twenty minutes, and I'll buy you a cup of coffee."

"I don't need no damn coffee," the voice said. "You talk to me now."

I hung up. Then I got up, grabbed my keys, parka, and wallet, and let myself out of the apartment.

I had used the gangs to my own purposes before. It had been scary and uncomfortable. It had also been an extreme situation.

Like this was.

Before I left the driveway, I checked my gun to make sure it was loaded, and then I put it in my pocket. I needed a better system, if I was going to carry a gun around.

Not that I wanted to, or even planned to.

I drove back toward the school and the Starlite, stopping on a side street two blocks south. I left my hat and scarf in the van and walked the half block to the bakery.

It was a cheerful place, but it had a wary feel. Daylight businesses worked best in gang territory, especially businesses that did most of their business in the morning.

And this bakery looked like so many others across the city. Men in business suits stood in line as they waited for a middle-aged woman wearing a long dress coat handpick the three dozen donuts she was trying to purchase.

The bakery smelled of fresh bread, cinnamon, and coffee. I joined the line, but didn't have to wait very long. A young woman joined the man behind the counter, and she took care of the single orders.

Theoretically, yesterday, I had had a donut that originated here, so today I ordered a cinnamon roll and a large coffee. I paid for a second coffee, and told the woman that someone would be joining me a few minutes. I asked her if she minded bringing the coffee when he arrived.

She smiled, and it made her seem both older and prettier at the same time. She didn't mind.

I left a good tip.

I put my roll and coffee on the only remaining table near the wall. I sat with my back to that wall, facing both the door and the plate glass window, filled with this morning's fresh pastries.

Then I focused on the cinnamon roll.

It was still warm and gooey, the frosting sweet and thick. I piled butter on top of it, and watched it melt. The bakery was warmer than I had expected. I hung my parka on the back of the chair, but made sure, with a single touch of the hand, that my gun was still easily accessible.

A dozen people had entered and left in the time it took me to get my roll and my coffee. I tried not to look too anxious as I watched the door. I was worried that I would miss my contact.

I shouldn't have worried. I recognized him when he was half a block away.

Four young men walked down the sidewalk, coming from the south. They wore different heavy coats, and black pants. Two wore ankle boots, which had to do them no good in this cold, and the red tams that were the group's hallmark. The older two wore combat boots, and no tams.

As they got close, the man behind the counter opened the cash register, grabbed some bills, and disappeared into the back, leaving the girl up front. The moment he did that, two customers left the line. The man waiting for his coffee looked over his shoulder. A woman, sitting opposite me in one of the other tables, stood, grabbed her purse and coat, and headed toward the door, only to stop as the four gang members gathered outside.

A man near me swore. The young woman stood nervously behind the counter. The system for dealing with the Black P. Stone Nation should not have surprised me, but it did. It made me wonder how much this place paid for protection, not just to the Blackstone Rangers, but to the police as well.

The woman slipped her coat on and tried to vanish as she waited, head down, for the four gang members to stop blocking the door.

I pushed the half-eaten cinnamon roll aside and leaned back.

After a moment, all four came in. Three of them pushed past the woman and took her table, cleaning it off daintily as if they worked in the bakery.

She slipped out the door as they moved past her.

The other gang member, one of the men without a tam, scanned the room, his gaze finally alighting on mine. He raised his eyebrows in a silent question.

I nodded, then kicked the chair across from me back with my foot.

He grinned, grabbed it, and said, "Me and my boys—"

"I'm only talking to you," I said.

His voice hadn't been the one on the phone. Someone had relayed the message to him.

"I don't talk without my main men," he said.

"Then we don't talk." I looked over at the young woman behind the counter. She was staring at me in both fear and wonder. I raised my hand and beckoned with my fingers, reminding her about the coffee. She already thought I was an asshole because I was associating with these guys. Might as well complete the picture.

After a moment's reflection, he sat down. He was too thin, and his eyes were red-rimmed. His nose was caked, and either he or his clothes or both hadn't been washed in a while.

I was glad I had finished with the cinnamon roll, because there was no eating around him.

"You got information on Donna," he said.

"You're not the person who answered the phone this morning," I said.

"I'm her brother," he snapped.

This guy was one of Jeff Fort's lieutenants? He looked too strung out to be someone the head of a gang as big as the Blackstone Rangers would trust. Maybe he had been one of Jeff Fort's main men a year or two ago, but now, he was just another junkie, one who was getting lost in the product he'd been selling.

My heart sank. I had been hoping for a young tough man like the ones I had met a year ago.

He spoke into my silence. "You said you have news about her. You do something to her?"

"No," I said, and then clammed up as the young woman came over with a paper cup filled with coffee, a small pot of cream, and five sugar packets. Apparently, she knew Loring enough to know how he took his coffee.

He took it with enough sugar to make me wonder if heroin was his poison of choice.

She set everything down, then glanced at me. Keeping her face out of Loring's view, she mouthed, *Friend? Really?*

I ignored her, and she walked away. The line that had existed five minutes ago was gone. Most everyone who had been in the bakery was either gone or sitting silently at the tables, waiting for this meeting to end.

"It's too quiet," he said. "Let's go to my place, talk this through."

"No," I said.

"You sure as hell say no a lot," he said.

I shrugged. "My information, my terms."

He studied me for a moment, clearly surprised I wasn't frightened of him like everyone else in the place seemed to be.

Then he grinned. Slowly. "You're the guy with the scar! You're a legend, man. You got a flock of kids, and you'll break a guy's balls if he gets near them. Literally."

So the Blackstone Rangers had an organizational memory. That surprised me. I was not surprised that the guy I had used as an example had ruptured something. Apparently that incident had done exactly what I hoped: It had kept the gangs away from the Grimshaw kids.

Too bad it hadn't kept other predators away as well.

"So," Loring said, "you got news about Donna, you say. Which means you want something in trade."

I had wanted something. I wanted the gang to join me, under my orders, inside the Starlite. But Loring here had that easy doped-up laziness that came from too much drug use, and his men didn't look a lot better. One tried to watch me, but one of the others had fallen asleep with his head on the table.

The Mighty P. Stone Nation didn't seem so mighty all of the sudden.

"No trade," I said. "I just stumbled on something while I was looking for something else."

"*Looking?*" he asked.

"I do odd jobs. I was finishing one of those," I said.

He stirred the coffee with his dirt-encrusted little finger. The scalding temperature didn't seem to bother him.

"So who's got Donna?" he asked.

"No one," I said. "Not anymore."

That caught him. He frowned at me. "What're you saying?"

"I was at a West Side precinct, looking for a missing girl, and the cops there told me about a girl they saw on the street a lot." It didn't matter who Loring was, I couldn't quite bear to tell him his sister had become a hooker, although from the irritation that flashed across his face, it looked like he figured out my meaning clearly enough. "They called her La Donna, the lady, and they found her last fall."

"Found her how?" His voice had grown chilly. The two awake Stones focused on me. One put a hand on his side. Gun under his coat.

"Someone had killed her," I said. "Beat her to death."

261

Loring was shaking his head. "That's not possible. She wouldn'ta been on the street. We made sure she had a *home*."

"I don't think she had a choice," I said. "I found a man who'd been kidnapping girls and then…sending them to work."

"She wouldn't have. She would have come home."

"He might have told her you didn't want her anymore. One of the girls I found," I said as carefully as I could, "said that this man had broken her."

"Who?" he asked, and he was starting to get jittery. "Who is this son of a bitch?"

I had planned to tell him about Eddie Turner. I'd planned to mention the Starlite. But this young man and his friends were in no condition to do anything. I doubted they even had Jeff Fort's ear. And if they did, I couldn't trust them. If drugs had infiltrated the Stones in this way, then they were completely unreliable on job like the one I had planned. They would have no discipline, and they wouldn't listen to me.

Innocents would die, and I couldn't have that.

"His name is Clyde Voss," I said truthfully. "He chats up girls after school, and eventually takes them somewhere, rapes them, and imprisons them for days, maybe weeks. Then he puts them to work."

Loring knocked his coffee off the table. Brown liquid spattered across the floor. He kicked his chair over, pounded a fist on the table beside us.

The young lieutenant who had put his hand on his gun pulled it out of his belt. Idiot. That was a good way to shoot something off.

The girl behind the counter had run into the back. A couple of the other customers dove under their tables.

I remained in my seat, watching these jerks tip over tables and kick aside chairs.

Finally, they stopped. Loring pushed his face under mine, his index finger half an inch from my nose. "You'd better not be making up any of this."

"I'm not," I said.

"Someone shoulda told me Donna's dead," he said.

"It was on the West Side. That's not your territory, right?"

"Still," he said.

"I'm sure you have someone who can check out the police reports," I said.

He kept his face close to mine. His teeth were rotting and his skin was turning yellow, either from jaundice or hepatitis.

Then he let his hand drop. He braced himself on the table. "Why the hell would anyone hurt Donna?" he asked more to himself than to me. He raised his head. "What're you gonna do about this?"

"I told you," I said. "That's what I'm gonna do."

If the organizational memory went real deep, he would know—or someone in the Stones would know—that I had told them something important before, something that had gotten rid of a mutual enemy.

"You want us to take care of Voss?" he said softly, as if no one had heard our conversation, even though the entire bakery had.

"I want you to do what you do," I said.

"Who'd he take of yours?"

"My family's all right," I lied.

"You don't need no girl rescued?" Loring asked.

"Not anymore," I said.

He barked out a laugh. "You're something, old man. Does anyone stand up to you?"

"Not if they're smart," I said, keeping up the bravado. It was the only way to deal with these guys.

"Jesus," he said, and stood all the way up, swaying a little. "This don't check out, we'll have us a little talk."

"It'll check out," I said.

The other Stone, the one without the gun, shoved the one who had fallen asleep. He snorted, then sat up, looking like a little boy awakened in the middle of the night.

Loring snapped his fingers, and the others fell in line around him. He said nothing to me. He nodded at them, and together, they walked out of the bakery.

I waited until they had disappeared down the block. Then I stood up, and began putting the tables back into place.

"You've done enough." The man behind the counter had come out of the back room.

"I didn't expect them to do this," I said. "I would have picked another place if I thought they'd trash your bakery. I'm sorry."

"Sure," he said. He clearly didn't believe me. "You don't have to do this."

"I'm going to." I put the tables back, set the napkin holders on top, checked for damage. The girl had given Loring a paper cup and the pitcher that held the milk was plastic. Loring had broken nothing with his fit of temper, for which I was relieved. I would have paid for the damage, if there had been any.

I couldn't have done anything less.

The man carried a mop and bucket around the counter. "What the hell are you doing with those guys?"

"I could ask you the same thing," I said. "They've obviously been here before."

"Of course they've been here," he said. "About five years ago, they decided they owned the neighborhood. What the hell are we supposed to do about it?"

His hands were shaking. His cheeks were flushed.

"The bakery's been here a long time," I said.

"My dad built this place. I grew up working here." He dry-mopped the coffee first, then dipped the mop head into the bucket and squeezed out the coffee with his bare hands. "I keep praying for these assholes to go away, but I'm afraid worse assholes will join show up in their place."

"Yeah," I said softly. "I used to think they were the worst part of the neighborhood."

"They're not?" He looked at me in surprise.

"Everything changes, and not always for the best." I put a five next to my half-eaten cinnamon roll. "Again, I'm sorry."

"Just don't come back, okay?"

It was a promise I could keep. "Okay," I said, and let myself out.

37

I drove home, feeling more frustrated than I had when I left. I had actually been counting on Loring's anger. I had wanted to use it to manipulate him and some of his friends into helping me.

I would probably have to abandon my plans after all. It broke my heart. With Laura's help, I could get Jimmy and the Grimshaw kids away from Starlite Hotel, but their friends and their friends' friends were stuck.

Dozens of girls had already disappeared into that place, and so many more would go as well.

And as everyone pointed out to me, day after day, I couldn't go up against the mob or their police protectors all by myself. I had already narrowed my focus to that damn hotel.

Now I had to narrow it further, to the kids I loved.

That was what made these messes in the first place. Everyone ignored the neighborhood or thought action was too hard or too risky.

But, I had to admit to myself as I parked the van in its usual spot, in this case, action was both hard and risky and not something the average person could do.

Hell, it was looking like it wasn't something I could do either.

I pulled the parka close and hurried inside. Theoretically it had gotten warmer—at least that was what the radio told me on the drive back—but "warmer" was a relative term. The cold in this city was nightmarish, the kind that could kill you in less than an hour.

I had lived in Boston: I should have known about this kind of cold when I brought Jimmy to Chicago. I just hadn't thought it through.

And now we were entrenched.

I walked up the stairs to my apartment, feeling twenty times older than I had when I left. Marvella had taped an envelope to my door.

I unlocked the door before carefully peeling off the tape and taking the envelope inside. Then I shut the door with my foot, opened the envelope's flap, and pulled out a slip of paper.

> Had to move the meet to 3. I hope you
> can still make it. We'll be at the ballroom at
> the Wabash YMCA (3763). Be there until
> at least 3:30. Thanks!
>
> M.

Her note managed to provoke a reluctant smile out of me, although had anyone been in the apartment, they probably would have considered my expression a grimace. I didn't need the address. I'd investigated the Wabash Avenue YMCA when Franklin and I were looking for a site for the after-school program.

The Y wanted to control our classes, and I didn't blame them. They wanted to make sure we didn't let gang kids inside. Besides, there was a membership fee. That, plus the money we were paying our teacher, made the Y unaffordable for us. The church gave us its basement for free.

And then, abruptly, the Y canceled its programs at the end of the year. Lately, there'd been talk of shutting the Wabash Y down. Apparently, the much bigger, more modern Washington Park Y had taken most of its members.

I glanced at the kitchen clock. I had more than enough time to get to the Y. In fact, I had time to have a leisurely lunch before I left. I hung up my parka and paced the apartment.

I would go to the Y. Marvella had gone to the trouble of getting these women there. But I wouldn't do anything else. My plans were pipe dreams. Maybe later, when I had people who could actually help me, maybe then we could solve the problem of the Starlite Hotel.

I had just wanted to move quickly. I wanted this hotel off the street, away from the school, away from easy pickings. I would tell Decker, of course, and get parents to monitor, but it wouldn't be enough.

By waiting, I was dooming at least half a dozen girls to life inside that hellhole and a fate similar to Donna Loring's.

I took out a couple of pieces of fried chicken and ate them cold, along with one of the biscuits Marvella had made. I organized a few things, and made some calls to line up next week's work. I would have to figure out how I could call Memphis as well and get the information I needed on my savings account back there.

I dithered until 2:30, then grabbed the parka and started out the door. At the last minute, I went back into my apartment, grabbed the folder with the flyers, and shoved my drawings inside. Maybe the women would have some ideas on what we could do down the road.

I was out of ideas. What I did know was that I needed backup. Malcolm was gone, and Sinkovich couldn't help without losing his job. I had no idea how to bring someone else into my little operation.

Maybe I couldn't. Maybe I would just have to do jobs for Sturdy and for Bronzeville Home, Health, Life, and Burial Insurance. Safe jobs.

As if that had worked. I'd been working for Laura when I discovered that damn house last fall. It had nearly cost two good men their lives.

I hurried down the stairs and back to the van. The drive to the Y took less time than I expected. The traffic was light. Finding a parking place near the Y was hard, however. The plows had pushed snow up against the curb in gigantic mounds, so there was no street parking. I spent ten minutes circling until I finally decided to park in a liquor store's lot two blocks away.

I hated walking in this cold. I shoved my hands in my parka's pockets and realized I hadn't removed the gun. I debated going back to the van and putting the gun inside the glove box, then decided the neighborhood was too dicey for that. Someone could have been watching. One tire iron to my passenger-side window, and some kid would have easy access to a gun.

The Y dominated this part of South Wabash. The five-story red-brick building towered above its neighbors, and look like nothing short of a nuclear bomb could knock it down.

A nuclear bomb and neglect. As I got close, I noted that some bricks were missing and the white concrete first level had turned brown with age and dirt. The red doors, which seemed so cheerful just last spring, had soap across their windows.

This place was obviously going to shut down. The only question was when.

I pushed the doors opened and stepped inside. The building smelled dusty and abandoned, even though a man sat behind the sign-in desk. He was reading the *Defender*. He lowered it and peered at me warily.

"You're meeting them?" he asked.

I didn't have to ask who "them" was. "Yeah," I said. "Ballroom, right?"

"It's your funeral," he said, and shook the *Defender* back into position. It covered his face, as if he didn't want to see what was about to happen to me.

The first floor of the Y showed decades of use. Elevators hugged one wall, but the stairs were more dramatic because they were original to the building. It had been built at least fifty years ago, and had that solid permanent sense that most public buildings from the time had. Signs mentioning the second floor areas were falling off the wall, and another sign, older, maybe from the 1930s, mentioned guest rooms upstairs.

Like so many Ys, this one doubled as a hotel, a home for the nearly homeless. I wondered what would happen to them if this building closed for good.

The ballroom was a remnant from a better time. This Y had been one of Chicago's major Negro hotels. Booker T. Washington had stayed here. This place provided everything for displaced Southerners who had come to Chicago for work during the Great Migration. There had been job training courses, famous dining rooms, and of course, that ballroom.

Franklin had told me a lot of the history last year, when he had been trying to convince me (and himself) to use the Y for the after-school classes. Once we had looked at the fee structure and the rundown condition of the Y, we had looked elsewhere.

Besides, at the time, this neighborhood seemed worse to me than the neighborhood around the school.

I pushed open the doors to the ballroom. Dust rose around me. Someone had turned on the chandeliers, but they hadn't been cleaned in a long time. The light was as thin as the sunlight had been all week.

Still, the William Edouard Scott mural caught me, just like it always did. The thing covered one entire wall, which made it at least thirty feet long and about nine feet high. I'd thought it was a WPA project because its strong figures clearly had a 1930s look to them, but Franklin said he'd heard that the YMCA had hired Scott on their own.

The mural was beautiful. It hadn't been kept up, though, so parts were faded or two dark. Still, the message always took my breath away. The mural was titled *Body, Mind, and Spirit,* and it had several distinct sections, all of them pertaining to the Y—kids in athletic clothes, young men singing, a nurse helping an elderly man stand.

The very center took the "Christian" in the Young Men's Christian Association seriously, by placing the Y's old symbol in the middle of some clouds, illuminated by sunlight, just like those church basement portraits of Jesus, surrounded by his flock.

My eye always went to the sunlit symbol first, and then wandered to parts of the mural so dark and dirty that it was almost impossible to see the illustrations. The last time I was alone in this room, I'd spent half an hour studying the mural and felt like I still hadn't seen it all.

"Impressive, huh?" a woman said beside me.

I looked next to me, then down. A short, square woman stood beside me. She wore overalls with a turtleneck underneath.

"It's falling apart," I said. "I think that's a shame."

"It's old and out of date," another woman said. She was sitting at a table, her legs crossed in front of her. She was gaunt, her hair cropped so short that she was nearly bald. "All the women are in helping roles."

"What women there are," Marvella said. She had been standing toward the back, in the gloom that the chandeliers didn't penetrate.

269

I turned. Someone had set up a dozen tables, but only three had people sitting at them. *Women* sitting at them.

Marvella wore a white angora sweater over black pants. Somehow she managed keep the sweater fibers off those pants, which was a trick not many women could pull off. Around her neck, she wore a long necklace made up of wooden mismatched black and orange beads.

"Come and join us, Bill," she said, sweeping a hand toward the tables.

Somehow I felt like I was auditioning for a job, rather than talking to them about helping me.

My eyes were slowly adjusting to the dimness. There were ten women at the tables. Marvella and the short woman beside me made twelve.

I sat down on a metal folding chair that one of the woman pushed at me. It creaked under my weight.

The women pulled their chairs closer, looking at me like they'd never seen a man before. I set the folder on the table.

"I think I've wasted your time," I said to them. "I went over everything this morning, and what I want to do is just not possible—"

"What is this?" The gaunt woman took the folder and opened it. I started to snatch it back, but Marvella, who was just inside my line of sight, shook her head.

I reminded myself that the folder held nothing proprietary, not even the diagram of the Starlite Hotel.

Two other women leaned in as the gaunt woman turned the pages.

An older woman, her hair graying, her face lined, said, "Marvella already told us about your niece, and she told us about the girls they have imprisoned in that hotel."

"I don't know how many are there," I said.

"Well, you can't give up on them," the woman snapped at me, as if it were my fault that they had been taken in the first place.

"Everyone I've contacted for help can't help me for some reason, and I can't do this alone," I said.

"You haven't asked us yet," the short woman said.

I gave Marvella a sideways glance. "I had hoped to have you ladies—"

And someone snorted at that word. I ignored her.

"—get the girls out while a group of us made sure the men who were there didn't interfere."

"A group of you *men*," corrected a woman I couldn't quite see in the dimness. "And the men aren't going to help, are they?"

I sighed, disliking her tone. "Honestly, the men I know can't help. And the people I usually rely on aren't available."

I didn't want to tell these women any more details than that.

The gaunt woman slapped her hand on the back of the folder, then closed it and slid it across the table. The women on the other side opened it and started through it.

"You can't abandon this idea," the gaunt woman said. "There's a hundred girls in that folder, all from the school."

"Spread over years," I said.

"That doesn't matter," the gaunt woman said. "We can find them."

I looked at her. Her black eyes glinted in the half light. Her face was long. I would have thought her a teenage boy who had just started into his growth if I hadn't known I was meeting only women.

"I already found one of them on the flyers. She'd been working as a prostitute for two years, and she was beaten to death last fall." I said that in as flat a tone as I could manage. "They found her in a vacant lot off West Madison. I expect we're going to hear the same story about a lot of the girls in that folder."

"So that's reason to give up?" The short woman leaned into toward me. "The girls imprisoned in that hotel, that's their fate, right? They're going to end up in a ditch somewhere, and no one's going to care, and everyone's going to say there's nothing we can do."

I gave Marvella a helpless glance. She smiled at me, and her smile told me that I was on my own.

I stood up. "I'm not taking a bunch of women into a whorehouse run by the Chicago mob. No offense, ladies, but I need people who can fight—"

My leg went out from underneath me, and I fell, landing so hard on the wooden floor that I grunted. Pain jilted up my tailbone.

A woman half my height and maybe a third my weight stood over me, her hands on her hips. "We can handle ourselves."

I had to unclench my teeth. I felt that blow through my entire body. She was good, and I was impressed, just not as impressed as she wanted me to be.

"Maybe you can handle yourself," I said, pleased that I didn't sound breathless. "When you have time to think about the attack and there's an element of surprise."

"There's always an element of surprise," she said. "Especially with sexist assholes like you."

"Kim," Marvella said in a warning tone.

"Oh, don't get all high and mighty on me, Marvella," Kim said. "He's not taking us in because of our gender, not because of our abilities."

"I don't know what your abilities are," I said as I stood up. My body ached from the hard landing. I brushed off my pants.

"I had six brothers," said the gaunt woman. "I know how to fight."

"You don't know how to fight a man who runs security for the mob," I said. "Those men have fought hand-to-hand all their lives."

"And," she added, as if I hadn't spoken, "I can shoot better than all of them."

That was just what I needed. A group of armed, angry, trigger-happy women heading into the Starlite with me.

I was shaking my head before I realized it. "I'm glad you want to help. But this isn't the way. I'm thinking I'll have to wait until I can get a team together, and yes, I mean men, and I'll bring you in to get the girls out."

"How long will that take?" I recognized that voice too. Paulette Shipley stood up. She had been sitting in one of the chairs in the back. She was Marvella's sister. They shared height, build, and those amazing cheekbones. The last time I had seen her, she had been pregnant. She was no longer and didn't seem to be carrying any baby weight either.

"It'll take me a couple months, maybe," I said.

"A couple months?" asked the gaunt woman. "More girls will disappear. More will die. Can you live with that?"

I shoved my hands in my pockets, bumping against the gun. I couldn't live with it, but I saw no other choice.

"I'm going to talk to the school's principal on Monday, and I'll see what I can do through the school board," I said. "We'll try to bide time. Maybe we can go through the system—"

272

"You already tried going through the system, Bill," Marvella snapped, "and you know that hotel is bought and paid for with the complicity of a lot of city officials. Don't lie to these women."

"It's just the tip of the iceberg," I said. "Getting rid of this hotel is just a Band-Aid on top of a gushing stomach wound."

I sounded like Sinkovich. I sounded like every bastard who looked the other way because the problem was too big.

The older woman stood up. She was almost as tall as I was. She wore a man's business suit, and it made her look fine. She walked over to me, and everyone watched.

She slipped her arm through mine. "Tell you what, Mr. Grimshaw," she said in a honey voice. "Why don't you sit down and tell us how this would have worked if you had found some men to help you. We'll figure out if there are modifications we can make or if we have some friends who might be able to be your backup."

I almost missed the look she gave the gaunt woman, which was a look of shut-up-and-let-me-deal-with-this-idiot. She was humoring me.

But she also had a point.

"All right," I said, letting her lead me to the table. "I'll tell you what I wanted to do."

38

I grabbed the hotel diagram and spread it on the table. It took several sheets because I had drawn each floor separately so that I could see how many stairs I would have to run, how much ground I would have to cover.

"The prostitutes do not spend the night in the hotel," I said. "No john can pay for an entire night. Apparently the mob has different hotels for different purposes. This isn't a high-end hotel, but it's not the bottom either."

I almost told the women that there were other, specialty hotels, and then I decided that the less they knew the better. Besides, I didn't want to go into detail if I could at all avoid it.

"The entire hotel is empty of clients and prostitutes by 5 a.m. By seven-fifteen, the first buses arrive in the back of the school. That's a two-hour window. I planned to use the first hour, and have the second hour as my cushion."

The women had gathered around me. They were leaning over the diagrams too, blocking what little light there was.

I hesitated for just a moment: I was going to confess to planning a major crime here. However, if I could believe Marvella, these women were committing crimes themselves, mostly by providing illegal abortions. But Marvella had implied that they had done other things as well, things that would make them as unwilling to report me as I was to report them.

"First," I said, "I would cut the phone lines."

"You know how to do that?" the short woman asked.

"You'd get them all?" the woman named Kim asked at the same time.

"Yes," I said to both of them. "I wouldn't want any security in the hotel to call for backup, and I doubt they would be on the phone at that hour."

"If there are no prostitutes in the hotel," Paulette said, "why would there be security?"

"You forget the imprisoned girls," I said. "Plus the man in the penthouse. Apparently he lives there."

"You mean Eddie Turner," the older woman said.

My gaze met hers across the table. Her eyes narrowed. "Yes, I know him," she said. "I always thought he was a snake, but he has half of Bronzeville buffaloed. You're after him."

"He owns the hotel," I said.

"And he lives above all of that sin," another woman said.

I hated that word. I looked at her, but she didn't look at me. Her head was bowed. She was studying the diagrams.

"He knows what's going on inside," I said. "He profits from it."

"Including girls like Lacey," Marvella said softly.

"Yeah," I said. "I'm sure he knows exactly how those girls get brought into the life."

I had switched to the euphemism midway through, and the gaunt woman shook her head just a little. She knew what I meant. I suspected they all did.

"There will be security for Eddie," I said, "and I think the girls are locked in. I wanted to go into the hotel, yell *Police Raid!*, and then we would all split up. You ladies would go with someone to the sixth floor and get those girls out. Another group of men would start searching the hotel, rousting people out of the rooms, if, indeed, they were in rooms. Another small group would make sure the restaurant was empty."

"Where would you be?" the short woman asked me.

"He'd be going after Turner, wouldn't you?" Kim asked me.

"Yeah," I said. "I'd deal with Turner. He also has favorites that he tends to keep for the night. I'd make sure there were no girls inside."

"You'd take care of him," Kim said.

I didn't answer that.

"And then what?" she asked.

"I'd make sure you were all out," I said. "And then I would burn down the hotel."

Gasps all around me.

"Bill," Marvella said. "You're not serious."

"I'm perfectly serious," I said. "If we did all of that and left the building alone, they'd just set up with better security two nights later. The police would be looking for us, and so would the mob, and the operation would start all over again. Girls would get taken from the school, and nothing would have changed."

They were all staring at me. No one was looking at the diagrams.

"But with hotel burned to the ground, they wouldn't rebuild next to the school. That would be too expensive. The operation would be down too long, not to mention all the money to contractors and zoning officials and bribing all sorts of city government types. Plus there are Federal government employees on the South Side these days trying to see how Model Cities money gets spent, so they might see something untoward, and report it. They're harder to bribe than Chicago officials."

No one smiled. I half-thought that would get a grin or two. I think they were all still shocked that I wanted to burn down the hotel.

"The police would know it was arson," Paulette said. The cousin of a cop, she knew how police methods worked. So did Marvella.

"They would know anyway," I said. "We would have conducted a fake police raid, remember? Someone would have seen us. The girls would certainly know that we had gotten them out, and a few might be angry about it."

"They wouldn't," the short woman said.

"Sure, they would," the older woman said. "Sometimes people can get co-opted fast. You know that."

"What were you going to use to burn it down?" the gaunt woman asked. "Gasoline?"

"Too dangerous," I said. "I'd lose control of the fire. I was going to do something really simple. I was going to go through the hotel room by room. After I made sure no one was hiding in the room, I'd light two books of matches. I'd leave one under the curtains, and the other on the bed. Not every fire would catch, but enough would. The hotel would smolder. No one would return right away. Even if someone saw the smoke by seven thirty or so, and the hotel didn't burn down all the way, the damage to the interior would be too much for them to rebuild. The mob would move to a different location."

"Maybe only a block or two away," Paulette said.

"Maybe," I said. "But at least they can't watch the school girls stand outside and gossip every day. At least they can't spy on their targets and figure out how to wheedle their way into the girls' lives. It would be harder to compromise girls from the school. And that's all I was trying to do. I wanted to save the ones who could be saved, and get that damn hotel out of the neighborhood."

They stared at me. My heart started pounding and my mouth was dry. Had I trusted the wrong people? Not even Marvella said anything.

Finally, the older woman stuck out her hand. "I'm Beatrice."

I took it. "Bill."

"Bill, I think we can do this with you."

I shook my head. "I told you, I don't have enough people."

She grinned at me. She had to be in her fifties, maybe more. She had laugh lines around her eyes.

"You have plenty of people," she said. "You just don't have enough men to make you comfortable."

My cheeks grew warm.

"As I see it," she said, before I could defend myself, "your plan requires a lot of stealth, a lot of room-searching, and very little muscle. If you run into security, then you do something, but first you try to chase them all out of the hotel."

"By telling them it's a police raid." I tried to keep my tone level. I didn't want her to think I was patronizing her, although part of me felt like I was patronizing her. "They're not going to believe a police force filled with women."

"They don't have to," Beatrice said. "Because you send in someone—me, for example—to warn them there's a police raid coming."

I shook my head. "They wouldn't believe a woman like you would want to warn them."

Her grin widened. "Then you warn them. Marvella's told us you already made some deal with the gangs to protect your kids. The people in the hotel would trust you to tell them the truth. You get them out, and you'll still be someone they trust, because they won't know you were the one to torch the hotel."

The word "torch" sounded odd coming from her.

"You run through the entire place, yelling it's a raid, then we go in. We split into the same groups you were talking about, and most of us get the girls out—"

"And what will you do if there are guards upstairs?"

"We can take care of them," the gaunt woman said. "My name is Sam, by the way. I'd be happy to hurt one of those goons."

"They won't expect it," Kim said, "any more than you did."

"No," I said. "It's still not enough. Most of you will be getting the girls out, and that hotel has a lot of rooms."

"We know a few other women," Paulette said. "People we can trust."

"You shouldn't go at all, Paulette," I said. "You have a family."

"So do you, William," she said. "Who'll take care of that little boy if something happens to you?"

"And something will," I said. "We don't have the right team for this."

"I figure we need about twenty people," Beatrice said. "I can get us that. Many of the women are good shots. Several of us are strong enough to carry the girls out if we have to. We can do this."

I let out sigh. "I know it sounds like a grand adventure, but it's not. Let's ignore the fact that we're breaking and entering, we're taking girls off the premises without permission. Let's think about this: that place has police protection. If we get arrested, we'll all get charged with arson. It's a felony. And they'll bring other charges as well. And that's if we survive this."

"Your plan is good," Beatrice said. "If we're going to rescue the girls, we do it your way."

"We could kill someone," I said. "Accidentally. We might miss someone. They might be hiding. There's a lot that can go wrong."

"It's a risk," Kim said. "We take risks all the time. I don't see much choice here."

"Me, either," Sam said.

"What we need," Paulette said, "is a backup. If something goes wrong, we need a way to get a signal to everyone to vacate the hotel. Even if we only manage to get a few girls out, that's a start. Then maybe we can go to the *Defender* or something and put the story out there."

"It won't matter if the story's in the *Defender*," I said. "The city doesn't care about the South Side. It'll be a rumor, and it won't stop the hotel."

"But we'd save some girls," Paulette said. "Even in the worst-case scenario, we'd save some and maybe get some outraged parents to put the right kind of pressure on the school board."

"It's that kind of naiveté that would hurt this mission," I said. "I'm sorry, Paulette, but it just doesn't work that way."

"Well, I don't like your other solution. If we wait until spring and it gets light earlier and it's not cold and they might change their habits and they might take more girls, and suddenly we've missed an opportunity to do something. I don't like missed opportunities, Bill. I've learned that if we wait, things get worse."

Paulette was referring to the loss of her cousin's family. She had seen police corruption up close and she knew how damaging it could all be.

"We have lawyers," Sam said.

"We have *good* lawyers," Kim said.

"You do too, Bill," Marvella said. "Your girlfriend can afford an entire army of lawyers. If we're careful, they're not going to be able to prove anything except that we went in to rescue the girls. Since you don't want to use an accelerant, they can't even prove arson or that we put the matches on the beds."

"I would do that," I said.

"We need a team. And there are too many rooms to search in that hour-long window without a group of us doing it. We can do this, Bill. The only thing that's preventing us is your chauvinism."

I frowned. I wasn't a chauvinist. I respected women. I had encouraged Laura to take over her father's business. I worked for her, for heaven's sake.

"I keep telling you," Marvella said into my silence. "Women are a lot tougher than you think."

Beatrice kept watching me. She could tell that I was unmoved by those arguments. So she shrugged.

"It's pretty simple, Bill," she said. "We have your diagrams. We know your plan. We're going to do it, with or without you. I think you might be helpful. After all, you've been in the hotel and we haven't. But we can do it alone. We've done worse, just not on as big a scale."

"What does that mean?" I asked.

She leaned back and crossed her arms. "Our acquaintance is short. I'm not going to tell you everything we've done, just like I'm sure you don't want to tell me everything you've done."

Touché, I thought, but didn't say. She won the argument right there.

"We go in, it's my plan," I said. "I'm in charge."

"Of course you are." She said it with a straight face. She didn't sound patronizing, but I had the sense she was. What was it my adopted mother used to say? *It's a wise woman who lets her husband believe he's in charge.*

I had a feeling I had just been subjected to the same treatment.

"If we go tonight," Beatrice said, "we don't have to worry about school. No one will be there that early on a Saturday morning, even if there are Saturday activities."

"But the customers will stay later at the hotel," I said.

"Not that much later," said a young woman who hadn't spoken until now. "The girls and the security will want to close down for the night. They won't care if it's Friday or Monday. They want out."

She sounded like she knew what she was talking about. I frowned at her. Her gaze held mine, then skittered away.

"It's personal for some of us," she said softly.

"It's personal for all of us," I said, and with that, I knew I had given in.

39

I called Laura from a pay phone at the Y.

"I'm sorry to ask you this, but I have no one else," I said, crowding against the scratched wood wall. The men's locker room door was behind me, and this narrow hallway smelled of decades-old sweat. "Can you pick Jimmy up from the after-school program and keep him for the weekend?"

"Why?" That one question crystallized her voice, as if she hadn't been paying attention before and she was now.

"Lacey just got home yesterday, and Marvella's busy tonight. I really need someone to watch him."

"You're not going to tell me why," she said.

My breath caught. She was going to say no. I was sending these women into that hotel unsupervised all because I couldn't find someone to keep an eye on my kid.

"Are you protecting me, Smokey? Because I'm a big girl. I can handle what you're going to tell me."

I let out that breath. "Laura, listen, if something happens to me, will you make certain that Jimmy's cared for? I can't ask the Grimshaws, and he's got no one else—"

"What the hell, Smokey?" she snapped. "What's going on?"

"I should have asked that a long time ago," I said, "and I'm just realizing it now. Can you, until I figure out something formal?"

"Yes," she said. "Yes, of course."

"And can you watch him *at your place* this weekend?"

She made a small sound, a release of air maybe or an exasperated grunt. "I take it you've all postponed the party."

Party? I blinked. Something fell in the men's locker room, echoing throughout. I didn't even jump. Party. And then it clicked. We were going to have a surprise birthday party for Jimmy. I had given it a moment's thought back on Tuesday, and forgotten it. Althea hadn't mentioned it, either.

"The Grimshaws can't host anything this weekend. We'll have it next week. It's closer to his birthday anyway," I said.

"Well," Laura said, sounding all businesslike. "I'd set aside time for that, and I had been on the fence about going to this stupid conference anyway. I've been very worried that I was there to play either the stupid woman or the villain. I'll have Judith cancel me out of that, and Jimmy and I will have a great weekend trying not to worry about you."

She sounded flip, even though we both knew she wasn't. Her words made me feel guilty. I rested my head on three different phone numbers scratched into the wood.

"I'm sorry, Laura," I said.

"You've got to stop doing this, Smokey," she said.

She didn't even know what I was doing. And she didn't seem to mind when I was doing something similar for Sturdy. Not that I'd ever told her everything that I had done, even for her company.

"Thank you for taking care of him," I said.

"I'll make sure he's fine, no matter what happens," she said.

"Thank you," I said, and hung up.

I didn't move for a long moment, my entire body frozen in place. I was committed now, and while I wasn't going to do it exactly the way I wanted to, it would get done.

I stood up. A clock above the front desk said I'd been here less than an hour. I could go home and get some sleep. I would need that to be sharp—if I could sleep at all, which I doubted.

I also needed to do just a little extra planning, so that I would feel comfortable.

I left the Y, nodding at the man at the desk as I went out. The cold air hit me like an open palm. The Y's interior had been a lot hotter than I had realized, and just a bit humid. I sneezed, clearing the dust and mold out of my lungs, then walked to the van, head down.

I didn't plan to stop near the Starlite. I didn't plan to do anything except drive by. It took longer to get there than it had earlier. The streets were congested with Friday traffic, people leaving the first week of work in the New Year as early as they possibly could. For people who didn't like their jobs, work seemed especially hard at the holidays.

Ironically, I usually liked mine. The freedom. The hours that I could choose. Doing things my way.

I was truly doing things my way here. I wasn't even getting paid. Which was good, because if I got paid for tonight's job, I would be no better than some of the men who worked security for the mob.

I smiled a little bit. It was a tiny, irrelevant distinction. What I was going to do, with the help of some very determined women, was completely against the law.

Not that the law was working here.

I passed one school bus as I reached the Starlite. A few teachers' cars were backing out of the parking lot.

The Starlite's kitchen door stood open, and steam poured out like it had the day before. No one parked in the alley, but the alley would be a death trap in the middle of the night. Sounds there would alert the neighboring houses, and maybe bring in the cops.

I drove around the block so that I would pass the Starlite on the right side of the street. As I approached, I saw Loring and his gang of three hunching their way inside.

My stomach clenched. I didn't want them at the Starlite. I hadn't told them about it, but apparently, it didn't take a lot of brains to figure out where Donna Loring had gotten her introduction to the life.

Or maybe these guys occasionally used the place. I had no idea, and I didn't want to know. Just watching them walk a little unsteadily on the ice made me realize that I had been right not to count on them for anything.

I turned the van around and headed home, feeling calmer than I had in days.

40

We met at the Y at four in the morning. The street was deserted. One streetlight fritzed as it tried to decide whether it would burn out or not. The ice-covered streets reflected ambient light from the city itself, making the neighborhood seem a little brighter than it should have been.

Still, we were just past the new moon, and the sky was as dark as it could get. The air was frigid, but there was no wind and there were no clouds.

I arrived at the same time that two other vans did. One was a VW microbus, painted black and almost invisible. The other was a panel van like mine, only with a logo running along the side. Two pickups were already parked in front of the Y, along with several sedate sedans.

I should have brought Marvella with me, but I didn't think of it.

I wore my smelly greatcoat and some gloves I didn't care about. I also wore old shoes that I knew I could get rid of. In fact, everything I wore would get thrown away.

The Y's front doors were locked. I knocked on the glass, and someone pushed the door open from the inside. A dozen people milled around the main area. They were all wearing black—black pants, black ski hats, black coats, and black gloves. Most looked like teenage boys unless you actually peered at them.

Sam, the gaunt woman, towered over most of the others. I recognized both Marvella and Paulette from their shapes. No one would ever mistake them for teenage boys.

The area smelled like coffee, and someone had actually bought donuts, laying them out on a table near the front desk which was shut down. A rope cord ran across the stairs, and the lights were out everywhere but this front area.

It made the Y seem creepy and nearly abandoned.

No one talked. Someone knocked on the main door. One of the women headed toward it and in those small movements, I recognized Beatrice. She had looked like one of the teenagers to me until she pushed the door open.

Jack Sinkovich hurried inside, head bent against the cold.

"I didn't invite you," I said to him, wondering how the hell he even knew about this. I didn't want him to shut us down. I wanted him out.

"I know and you shoulda," Sinkovich said. "Marvella told me."

She had pushed her way through the group. She looked thinner and older in her all-black costume. Her gaze met mine.

"You were going to pull off a police raid, so I figured you needed actual police," she said.

"Jack has a family and a job. He could lose both doing this."

"You have a family and a job too," she said.

I turned to him. It wasn't her decision; it was his. "You can't do this. Think about your kid."

"I did," he said. "Then I thought about yours. Mine's in Mini-fuck-ing-sota. Yours is right here, and he ain't got nobody. At least, my wife has mine, and she'll do right by him if something happens to me. Your kid needs you, so that means you need me."

"No," I said.

"You don't get a vote," he said. "I'm going. Marvella told me your little plan and it's pretty good except for the blinds."

"The what?" I asked.

"See?" he said moving his way toward the donuts. "I figured you didn't know."

He grabbed a donut and a small Styrofoam cup filled with coffee. He took a sip, winced, and set the coffee down.

"Is this the group?" he asked Marvella.

"Yes." Paulette was the one who answered. Five more women flanked her. I hadn't seen them when I arrived. A quick count told me that twenty people filled this room.

"Okay, gather up," Sinkovich said.

Someone muttered in the back. The question ran through the women like a game of telephone: *Who put him in charge?*

"I put him in charge," Marvella snapped. "Bill's good, but Jack knows some things that the rest of us do not. He will take care of us here. You can trust him."

"He's a cop," one of the women said.

"For my sins," Sinkovich said. "Without me, you don't know how to do this right. You listen up or this'll get messy."

They quieted down. I crossed my arms. I couldn't get rid of him now. And, truth be told, I needed him. Just his presence was enough to reassure me.

"Bill here, he cased the joint, but he don't know a few things that the cops do. There's one-way mirrors all over the place in that lower level of the hotel. They're called blinds. Like deer blinds, you know?"

They probably didn't know. Women from Chicago's South Side probably weren't hunters, at least in the traditional Midwestern sense.

But I had no idea how Sinkovich knew about the blinds. I certainly hadn't. I knew that the one-way windows had a purpose, but I figured it was security. The word "blind" implied something else.

"Them blinds, they're money to this place," Sinkovich said. "Lotsa money. There're cameras in there. Usually no one's in the blinds in the early mornings, unless there is a police raid. Then the blinds get filled up."

He stopped, waved his donut, then set it down.

"I gotta back up. These blinds, they're there to photograph anyone who might not want the wife or the girlfriend or the boss or the mayor to know they're frequenting this place, you know what I mean?"

"Blackmail?" one of the women asked.

"You betcha," Sinkovich said. "Lotsa money in blackmail. And when there's a raid or lemme say when there *used* to be a raid, a designated group of guys would go into the blinds and they wouldn't defend at all. They'd take pictures. So Idiot Rookie Officer Yahoo gets a bug up his ass to shut down the Starlite, thinks it'll get him a promotion inside the ranks, and instead, he either gets his butt busted or he gets compromised, offered a lotta cash to never do it again or gets his kid threatened or gets fired for cause."

Sinkovich looked at me, just to reinforce his words. He hadn't turned me down because he hadn't wanted to do the job. Initially, he'd been afraid to do the job.

I wondered what changed his mind.

"And, no," Sinkovich said, "this did not happen to me. This will be my first trip into this particular little hellhole. But I read some of the files, and talked to some of the guys when my buddy Bill here first asked me about the place, and I gotta tell you, the ruthlessness that these guys go at this stuff makes your blood cold."

The women shifted, clearly uncomfortable. I was glad I hadn't taken a donut. My stomach was in knots.

"So, here's the thing. We gotta go in organized, and neutralize them blinds right off, which I'm sure Bill was gonna do."

"I was," I said. "I saw the mirrors, and I knew that someone was watching behind them. But I thought they were security only."

"Oh, they are," Sinkovich said. "Just not the kind you'd expect. I see some of you ladies got ski masks. I suggest you use them. Those what don't got them, you keep your heads down. You don't want no one to get a picture of your face. They got regular cameras in there and they got Polaroids, and you don't want some jerkwad, pardon my French, to take your Polaroid, and escape out the back with it before we get to him. Because he's gonna take that Polaroid to his bosses, and they're gonna find someone what knows you and can identify you and they're gonna make you pay."

My stomach twisted. I hadn't realized that.

Sinkovich turned toward me. "They probably already got a Polaroid or two of you, but Marvella tells me you prettied up your face some, so they ain't gonna go after you, not for this."

I nodded.

"So, ladies," Sinkovich said, "here's your moment. This's not a game. It's gonna be rough and someone's gonna get hurt. Might even be you. If we're not careful, it'll be after the fact. So if you're gonna leave, you do it now, before we get there. Ain't no one gonna think bad thoughts if you walk out that door this instant."

The women stood very still. I moved out of the way of the door so that anyone who wanted to leave could leave.

No one did.

They didn't even look at each other. They didn't even try to measure each other's willingness to go in. They seemed ready to go.

Sinkovich took a bite of his donut. He watched them while he chewed and swallowed. Then he ran the back of his hand over his mouth, just like Jimmy would have.

"Really?" Sinkovich said. "You're all committed to this little mission, even though it could cost you big time?"

"We're committed," one of the women said.

"Although," another woman said. She stepped forward. I saw that it was Kim, the woman who had kicked my leg out from underneath me. "I got one request."

"Just one?" Sinkovich asked.

She nodded. "Stop calling us ladies. It's insulting."

He glanced sideways at me, as if to say, *Broads. What can you do with 'em?*

"Well," he said after a moment, "I'd promise ya I wasn't gonna do that, but I'd break my promise prob'ly in ten minutes. I ain't gonna think about the right way to refer to you *people* when we're on this raid, and you can't think about it neither. Marvella tells me some of you ain't fond of men, and I'm sure most of you ain't fond of cops, and then there's the whole white/black thing that Bill here keeps schooling me on. I'm just a walking bundle of stuff you hate to be around, which is why I got the experience of going into places like this and you don't. So you're gonna listen to me, and I'm gonna get you and them poor teenage girls out alive. And then you can teach me how to talk all you damn well please, okay?"

Sam grinned and turned her head away. Marvella bit her lower lip. A couple of women smiled. But Kim's eyes narrowed and she crossed her arms. Beatrice put her hand on Kim's shoulder.

"He's right," she said softly. "Later."

"I don't like this," Kim said.

"Then you can go home," Sinkovich said. "Ain't none of you gonna offend no one if you go home. Because if you leave now, what we know is this: You ain't committed to the task. And this task is probably the hardest thing you're gonna do. It's dangerous and we gotta move fast, and ain't none of us got time to take care of one of you what gets the heebie-jeebies, got that?"

I closed my eyes on "heebie-jeebies." That man had an ability to zero in on the most offensive terms possible.

"Okay?"

"Okay," Beatrice said, with amusement in her voice.

"Okay." Sinkovich shoved the last of the donut in his mouth, and had to chew with his mouth half-open. He gestured for everyone to come near.

They moved forward slowly, some looking at Marvella as if she were the one who had lost her mind.

"I don't know you girls from Adam," Sinkovich started, then made a small irritated noise. "I mean ladies—fuck!—*people*, oh, pardon my French—you see? I can't think about this crap right now." He took a deep breath and started again. "I don't know you *people* from Adam, so I gotta trust you on something. I need four groups. I need the restaurant group. I need the group that's going to the sixth floor and getting those kids out. I need a group to start on floor five and clear out the entire place, and I need muscle to go with me and Bill."

"We don't need any help," I said.

"The hell we don't," he said. "We're going in like a bulldozer, you and me. We're clearing blinds, we're clearing bathrooms, we're clearing the entire first fucking floor, and we're taking out whoever's in our way."

"I thought Bill was going to go in saying a raid was coming," Paulette said.

"And, missy, I told you, them blinds are for raids. They'd fucking fill up with security guys who would be so damn happy that you warned them cops were on the way. Wrong-o. This is why you need me. I got a badge. I got plain clothes, and you ladies, no offense, look like young men in your little black outfits. That's a good thing. They're gonna think half of you are rookies on your first assignment. That's even better."

"I don't want them to think at all," I said.

"Which is why, first thing we do, you and me, is trash out them blinds and smash the cameras."

"The first thing we do is cut the phone lines," I said.

He rolled his eyes at me. "The first thing we do *inside* is smash out the blinds. And we need some backup, good backup."

"Do you want someone who can handle a gun or is good in a fight?" Marvella asked.

"Yes," Sinkovich said.

My turn to roll my eyes. "If someone here is good at both, like Sam said she was, that's what we need."

"I'll go with you," she said to me.

"How many people do you need on your team?" Beatrice asked Sinkovich.

He looked at me and shrugged. "We just need two, right? Because we're gonna be moving fast."

"Two's good," I said. Then I stepped forward. "Before we go any farther with this, though, I'm going to be very clear. You get to empty the floors, but I'll be following. And I'll be the one with the matches. No one else. I want the rest of you out of the hotel as soon as the girls are rescued. No arguing."

I looked at Sinkovich.

"And that includes you, Jack. I want you out."

"I ain't leaving you, Bill."

"You are," I said. "Because I'm going to take this from a rescue mission to a felony and you need deniability. All of you do. You honestly say that you had no idea what I did in those rooms if I did anything at all. Do you got that?"

Heads nodded. All except Sinkovich.

"Jack?" I asked.

"I don't like it none, Bill," he said.

"Well, I don't like you being here either," I said. "But I'm going to put up with it, as long as you agree to that."

He sighed. "Jesus, you're a hard-assed son of a bitch."

"Yes, I am," I said. "And this is my operation. I don't want any of you to forget it."

41

We took four vehicles to the Starlite, all of the vans and one pickup truck. I drove my van. Sinkovich rode with me. I already informed him that he would leave with someone else. He didn't agree or disagree. He just looked out the window as if I hadn't spoken at all.

The women divided themselves between the vans and the truck. We agreed that the other panel van would park directly in front of the hotel. The sign on the panel van was for coffee and supplies, the kind of coffee most often used by restaurants. Apparently, the van had belonged to some traveling salesman, and the car dealership where one of the women worked as a secretary had repossessed it.

I almost protested its presence, figuring it could be traced back to her, and then I decided not to worry about it. There were dozens of these vans all over the Midwest. There would be no proof that this particular van had been involved in this particular operation, unless someone took down the license plate number. That would take a bit of work, because I checked: The license plates were covered with slush and muck from the Chicago winter. Just like mine were. Only I covered my plates with dirt deliberately.

I hadn't even noticed what the logo said until someone pointed it out to me. It was hard to read in the dark, and we really didn't have to worry about what people could see in the daylight. We had to be done before sun-up, or this plan wouldn't work at all. The sun didn't come up until seven fifteen or so. If we weren't long gone by then, something would have gone horribly wrong.

I parked in the school lot. I wore a ski cap and thin gloves. In one pocket of the greatcoat was my gun and extra magazines, and in the other, a whole mess of tools, including wire cutters and a small flashlight. I held those now.

I hurried across the street, keeping my head down. The streetlight above the entrance to the school parking lot was too bright for my taste. Sinkovich had offered to come with me, but I wouldn't let him, figuring two of us would be more conspicuous than one.

But I needed to work fast, and I had to make sure I cut the telephone wires. I hadn't seen a phone in any of the rooms. There was probably one wired into the penthouse, and I wouldn't worry about that. It had probably been spliced from one of the downstairs lines. That was the only way it made sense, since I knew no one wanted those girls on the sixth floor to have access to a phone.

I figured there had to be at least two boxes, maybe three. One would be for the restaurant and two for the hotel, maximum, in case the hotel did want phones in all the rooms.

But a hotel this old probably had its own internal system and one large line coming into the hotel. An internal switchboard would route calls to outside lines; that way the hotel could charge for each call made.

I was counting on that. I was also counting on the fact that the switchboard was no longer in use. The phones inside the hotel probably had buttons that would access the various lines. I would wager most of those buttons on the phones themselves weren't even active.

I started searching at the end of the hotel farthest from the school, and used my flashlight, going up and down the exterior wall on the first story. I was looking for both the electrical box and the phone box. I didn't want to cut the electricity. That would definitely clue someone into our little operation.

Cutting the phones first was dicey enough. I had to start with the phones I figured got the least amount of use at this time of day. That was why I was cutting the restaurant last.

The metal phone box was in the exact center of the hotel's back wall, near a much larger metal box. That large box had to be the electrical lines. Someone had kindly shoveled a path to both boxes. They were locked. I had expected that. I had brought my burglar's tools, something I hadn't used in months.

Before I hauled them out, though, I peeled off the glove on my right hand and felt for the ridge between the two pieces of metal. The metal was so cold that my finger hurt. But there was a slight space, which I figured might have happened.

After surviving decades in the heat of Chicago summers and the deep cold of Chicago winters, this metal had to be fatigued. If I was lucky, I would be able to break the box open with just a little force.

I took out a screwdriver and wedged it into the opening. Then I tugged.

For a moment, I thought the metal wouldn't give. Then it broke open with a squeal that sounded like a child screaming.

My heart pounded. I shut off the flashlight for just a moment, then looked around very slowly, trying to see if anyone else heard the sound.

No lights had gone on in the buildings across the alley. No one opened a window above me. No one shouted.

I took a deep breath, and regretted it. The frigid air dug into my lungs as if I had swallowed a bucket of ice.

I turned the flashlight back on and stared at the cables. They were loose. Rather than guessing which one went to the phone company and which one went inside the hotel, I cut everything. I took a chunk out of the middle of all of the lines, and dropped those pieces into the snow.

Then I put my gloves back on and wiped away everything my finger had touched. I doubted anyone would come here and take prints off this box—I doubted the box would survive our plans—but I had to be careful, just in case.

Then I slid the wire cutters back into my pocket and shut off the flashlight, letting my eyes adjust. I slowly walked back to the alley.

When I reached it, I took out the flashlight again, and scanned the rest of the hotel's back wall. I saw no other boxes.

Which only left the restaurant.

That would be harder. People were awake, sipping coffee, taking out garbage, cooking on that filthy grill. I had to make sure I stayed out of sight.

My feet had already become blocks of ice. I worried as I scanned. Logically, the restaurant's phone and electrical boxes would be on the back wall, but it looked like the kitchen entrance got a lot of use. I didn't want to open that gate, go between the trash cans, and try to cut the phone lines right next to that kitchen door.

It would all depend on when the restaurant's boxes got wired in, and whether or not the company service people cooperated with the owners of the restaurant. I'd seen boxes in this city that were wired all the way around the building, as far from the street lines as possible. Usually it had been done that way at the request of a landlord or building owner who wanted a quick and dirty way to shut off utilities to get rid of a recalcitrant client inside.

My flashlight found both boxes, nearly hidden by a gigantic snow drift. The drift piled up against the fence holding the trash cans, but the boxes were on the alley side.

No one had shoveled a way to them, but meter readers had stomped their own path over the winter, and it hadn't snowed since the last reading.

I walked in someone else's iced-over footprints, and fortunately, whoever he was had bigger feet than I did. Even though the ice crunched beneath my boots, the sound wasn't gunshot-loud. It only seemed loud to me.

The box was closer to the kitchen door than I wanted it to be. I could hear banging pots, and conversation. The smell of bacon drifted toward me. My stomach growled until I realized that what I smelled was burned bacon. Someone had probably just tossed it out.

Strangely, this box wasn't locked. I opened it easily. I didn't even have to remove my glove. Then I cut the lines, tossed bits of them into the snow, and closed the box again.

I shoved the wire cutters into my all-purpose coat, then picked my way out, stepping in the ice my boots had already broken.

I reached the alley in no time. I bowed my head just enough that I could still see what was ahead of me and on either side, but not enough to look like a guy in a hurry. More like some poor schlub on his way to work, walking to a car he'd parked too far away.

Sinkovich stood near the school's fence. Even though he wasn't in uniform, he looked like a cop. His posture, his air of wary watchfulness, his do-not-fuck-with-me attitude, all screamed that he was official, that he was in charge.

When he saw me, he beckoned behind him. The coffee van drove carefully out of the school parking lot and moved to its spot directly in front of the hotel. When the driver saw the rest of us on the sidewalk, she would give the word to her team. They were the ones who would hurry up the stairs.

I waited for Sinkovich on the sidewalk across the street. As the remaining women joined him, he crossed the street like a cop leading a parade. Faces were hard to see in the dim light, and I hoped everyone remembered to keep their heads down as we went under the working streetlight on the corner.

They reached me quickly, and we marched up the rest of the block, me and Sinkovich in the lead. As we rounded the corner, I thought I saw movement in one of the windows across the street. But as I stared at it, I realized that I was probably seeing our reflections as we scurried under that streetlight.

The coffee van blocked the entrance to the hotel. As we approached, the doors opened. I ignored the women and headed straight for the hotel. I pulled open the glass double doors just like I had two days ago, with more strength than I needed.

As per our agreement, I went in first. The guy behind the desk gave me a bleary look, then opened his mouth in surprise. He was the same guy who had been on duty, if that was what you wanted to call it, the day Lacey got hurt.

I reached across the desk, grabbed him by the back of the shirt, and slammed his face into the riser that separated him and me. Then I dragged him over the desk.

He was smaller than he looked, thin and wiry, not that it did him any good. I tossed him on the ground, and held him in place as Sam tied his hands behind his back with the rope the women had brought. They had brought a lot of rope, all cut into good tying length, probably more than we needed.

Then she shoved a scarf in his mouth and tied it tight.

I pulled him upright. His forehead was bruised and bleeding, his eyes frightened. Sinkovich waved a badge in front of his face.

"Police raid, you fucking son of a bitch," he whispered.

Then Sinkovich headed behind the desk and stuck out his hand. "Wire cutters," he said to me.

I handed him mine as the women spread out around us, going to their various stations. They crept up the stairs, ski masks on, heads down, moving more quietly than I ever believed possible.

The restaurant crew broke left and headed through the bar. They looked as wiry as the desk clerk, and a whole hell of a lot tougher.

I told myself it was because of the black they wore. But they moved like a unit.

I tried not to worry about them.

Something clattered beside me. Sinkovich tossed what looked like a doorbell on top of the desk.

"Knew they had to have one of these," he said.

A warning bell that let the upper floors know something was going on. It probably was a doorbell with extra long wires.

He handed me the wire cutters back as Sam finished tying the clerk's legs. We'd free him as we were leaving, but not before. Sinkovich and I figured he was probably the only guy who had the phone number to the mob, and if he had it, there was a possibility that he had it memorized.

Kim had gone behind the desk, removed a pile of matches, and handed them to me. Then she ripped down papers that contained phone numbers. She started to shove them in her pocket, but Sinkovich took them.

He raised his eyebrows at me, and I understood. He was protecting dirty cops. Or maybe he was keeping them for his own blackmail possibilities.

He shoved the papers in the pocket of his coat, then nodded toward the mirrored wall next to the stairs. He and I went to the wall first. He mimed shattering the glass, but I shook my head. Too loud.

We went down the hallway, saw an unmarked door in the right place, and I tested it. Unlocked. It opened into a small room with a couple of chairs and a table. The room stank of old cigarette smoke. Both ashtrays were full.

We both looked toward the wall. The entire front area opened before us. The clerk was struggling against his ropes. Neither Kim or Sam were visible.

On the counter underneath the one way window were two Polaroid cameras and two high-end cameras with telephoto lenses. Sinkovich knocked the Polaroids off the shelf and stomped on them. I thought those cameras were damn near indestructible, but Sinkovich proved me wrong.

I grabbed film canisters lining the counter. Sinkovich pulled a plastic sandwich bag out of his pocket and held the bag open for me. I dropped the film inside.

I turned.

"What about the cameras?" Sam asked softly.

She meant the ones with the telephoto lenses. Those things *were* indestructible. I hoped the heat of the fire would destroy anything inside them. As I was about to reply, Kim grabbed one off the shelf and expertly opened the back. She removed batteries and tossed them to the ground. She also exposed the film, then shut the back.

"Just in case," she said as she did the same to the other camera.

I nodded, feeling a slight weight lift off me. I wouldn't have done this nearly thoroughly enough.

Now, if we only got out of here.

We left the first blind mostly intact. The second was behind the bar. I opened the door and discovered no one manned that one, either. This room had two windows, the one overlooking the bar, and the one that showed the men's bathroom. The one for the men's room was smaller, but the Polaroid cameras rested on the shelf beneath it.

I suspected the blackmailers who ran these rooms got some of their most candid shots here, showing men in authority who couldn't quite wait to get upstairs to take advantage of the women around them.

This time, Sam stomped on the Polaroid cameras. Her face was bleak as she did so. She had to stomp twice before destroying them, but she finished as Kim finished disabling the other cameras.

I left first, checking out the rest of the downstairs. I grabbed an entire box of matchbooks from behind the bar. Sam extended her hand so I could give some to her, but I didn't.

She frowned at me.

Before we went upstairs, I glanced through the swinging door into the restaurant. It looked recently abandoned. Coffee pots still steamed on their burners and half-eaten breakfasts sat on tables.

In the back, something smashed.

Sinkovich grabbed my arm. "Not our job," he said softly.

I nodded. I knew that, but that didn't stop me from wanting to help. I backed away from the door and headed to the stairs. I finally pulled my gun. Sinkovich had his as well.

I could hear voices echoing down the stairs. Female voices, soft but sharp, issuing orders. When we reached the second floor, Sam looked at the elevator, silently asking if that would be better for us.

I didn't want to get out of a box on the seventh floor, only to have Turner's muscle waiting for us. It would be a kill zone.

Only I couldn't tell her that.

I glanced down the hall. All the doors were half open, as if someone had already searched them. I realized then that the hotel staff had probably done so to make sure no girl got left behind. My teams were starting on the fifth floor and working their way down.

Except, of course, for the most important team, trying to free the girls on six.

We crept up another flight. Sinkovich and I checked the floor, looking for our people, and seeing nothing. This one looked as abandoned as the second floor.

Then we went to four. Nothing there either.

On five, closed doors, and women working their way in teams of two down the hallway.

"Empty so far," one of the women said softly. She was wearing a ski mask. All I could see were her mouth and eyes, making her seem eerily anonymous.

I nodded, mouthed "Thank you," and went up to the important floor.

Crying, banging, shouting. There was no way the group on seven could ignore this noise. The question was, would they believe it part of every day living in this hellhole or something strange?

For the first time, I realized that there was a subtle side effect to having women rescue these girls. There were no male voices, so the cries probably did sound routine.

Marvella stood at the top of the stairs. Paulette had a gun trained on the elevators. She looked like she knew how to use it.

They were not wearing ski masks.

"Progress?" I asked.

"Only eight rooms with girls inside," she said. "And Jesus, Bill, they're in bad shape."

"Get them out," I said. "Worry about their condition later."

She nodded. "We got four out already. But it's taking a bit to get the rest."

"You two," I said to Kim and Sam. "Help them."

"But—"

"Jack and I are doing this last part alone," I said.

"You need us," Sam said. "You have no idea how many—"

"Stop fucking arguing and follow orders," Sinkovich growled. "God-damn civilians."

He started up the stairs. I caught his arm.

"You're probably not going to want to go, either," I said.

"Too late," he said. "I'm already committed."

I had to hurry to get ahead of him. The calm I had felt earlier had dissipated.

So far, it had been easier than I thought. And that was a very bad sign.

42

I reached the top of the stairs first. A row of doors went off to my left. But to my right, a single door, and only one elevator where on the previous floors there had been two. One of those elevators opened into the penthouse itself.

I didn't see a soul. Apparently the cries below had sounded normal.

I walked to the penthouse door, reaching for my burglar kit, when Sinkovich shoved me aside. He held the master key ring in his right hand.

He gave me a grin and mouthed, "Experience," and stuck the key in the deadbolt.

At that moment, a chorus of screams rose from the floor below, followed by five gunshots.

"Son of a bitch," he said, and pulled the key out. "Go check it out."

"No," I said. "You do it. Let me handle this."

He glared at me. "You need someone at your back."

"You already got it. Come back up when you're done."

He cursed under his breath, but didn't move. The door opened. We both trained our guns on it.

A bleary-eyed guard came out, hair tussled, suit messed up as if he had fallen asleep in it.

I grabbed him and pulled him out before he could shout a warning inside. Sinkovich punched him in the face, knocked him to the ground, and cuffed him in what looked like a single move.

"Baxter, what the hell's going on?" That voice came from inside the penthouse and had to belong to Turner. "Phone's dead."

"Yeah." I pushed my way inside, gun close enough to my body that it couldn't be knocked out of my hand, far enough away that I could use if I need to. "I cut the line."

There was chair near the door, with a blanket crumpled on the floor beside it. Apparently, Baxter had deliberately fallen asleep on the job.

The room stank of beer and sex and rotting food. A food tray from below sat on a table, the remnants of a meal still scattered everywhere. I didn't see a girl, not yet anyway.

Sinkovich was right behind me.

Turner came out of the bedroom, completely naked, holding a double-barrel shotgun. "Get the fuck out of here," he said. "Or I will use this."

"Guys who threaten don't actually shoot," Sinkovich said softly to me, but we both moved away from each other just in case.

"Put it down," Sinkovich said. "I'm a cop. You shoot me, you live in hell the rest of your life."

"I don't know you," Turner said, still holding that shotgun. His right hand was shaking. "I know half the cops on the South Side. They'll have your badge."

"Let 'em try," Sinkovich said.

Behind us, another gunshot echoed and it was close. Turner looked past us. I angled my body just enough to keep an eye on him and see the door.

A man came through it, waving a gun. He wore the same coat he'd had on yesterday morning. Same coat, same pants, same boots.

"Get out of here, Loring," I snapped.

"You fucking cop, what the hell have you been doing to the girls here?" He pointed his gun at Sinkovich. "You and him."

And then he waved his gun at Turner.

The blast from Turner's shotgun damn near deafened me. Loring flew backwards out the door, and I turned toward Turner, who was already aiming at Sinkovich.

I pulled the trigger.

Turner didn't move. For a moment, I thought I'd missed. Then he staggered backwards, crumpled to his knees, and dropped the shotgun.

Both Sinkovich and I moved, terrified that the shotgun would go off when it landed.

It didn't.

The room stank of gunpowder and blood. Sinkovich moved forward as Turner fell on his back, his eyes opened.

Sinkovich didn't go near the body, but peered into the room. Some sound was making its way into my consciousness. It took me a moment to realize it was a woman, sobbing.

"Looks clear," Sinkovich said. He kicked Turner. The man didn't respond. Then Sinkovich kicked the shotgun out of Turner's reach, and went inside the room. I moved a little to the right, toward the bathroom. The door was open, and baggies sat on the counter. Mostly marijuana, but also some multicolored pills, probably LSD.

Otherwise the bathroom was empty.

I made my way to the bedroom. Sinkovich had his gun trained on the woman I'd seen going upstairs when I cased the hotel. She had tugged on the black underwear and the white robe, but not the bra. She was kneeling on the bed, her hands over her mouth, and she was crying, although she was trying not to.

"Come on," I said. "We're getting you out of here."

She shook her head.

"We're getting you out now, unless you'd like someone to shoot you...?" Sinkovich. Always the charmer.

She stood, her legs wobbling. She was on something.

"Anyone else here?" I asked.

She shook her head. I couldn't tell if that was a shock response or an answer.

"How many guards were here?" I asked.

"Baxter," she said.

"That's it?"

"Didn't need anybody else." She slurred her words.

Sinkovich put his arm around her, and pushed her forward. She stopped when she got to Turner's body.

"He's dead?" she asked.

"Probably not," Sinkovich lied. "Get out so we can help him."

She looked at Sinkovich and for a moment, I wondered if she would grab his gun. Then she stepped daintily past him, careful not to get her bare feet in the blood.

"You got clothes downstairs?" I asked. The mention of downstairs made me realize it was eerily quiet below us.

"I dunno," she said.

Sinkovich cursed, grabbed a pair of high heels off the floor, and then a man's coat. He wrapped her in it and handed her the shoes.

She looked at them like she didn't know what to do with them.

"Put them on," he said. "We're going outside."

She glanced at me. I couldn't tell if she recognized me or not.

Then she walked to the couch, sat on its arm, and slipped the heels over her feet. She tottered toward me. I kept the gun on her, and so did Sinkovich.

We headed toward the door. She looked at Loring as if he could hurt her, but he was dead too, his entire torso gone. Sinkovich put a hand behind her back and propelled her forward. She tripped on Loring's arm, then caught herself on the door jamb.

"Keep moving," I said in the most commanding voice I could manage.

She stepped into the hallway, her heels leaving little prints in the blood. Sinkovich placed his feet around the blood, then he shook his head slightly.

"Oh, Jesus," the woman said. I couldn't see her, but I heard her, puking.

Sinkovich dipped out of my view. As I made my way around Loring, I saw what finally got to her. Baxter, on his back, the top of his head gone. That gunshot we heard just before Loring came into the suite marked the end of Baxter.

Sinkovich was removing his handcuffs from Baxter. The woman wiped her hand over her mouth, then puked again.

Sinkovich put his cuffs on his belt, then grabbed her and yanked her upright. "You don't got time for that," he snapped. "You wanna end up dead too?"

She teared up. I looked down the stairs. I hated the silence. I had no idea what it meant.

"Me first," I said.

"No," Sinkovich said, but by the time he finished the word, I was nearly to the stairs. I went down them as quietly as I could, peering ahead. I saw one person, dressed in black, hovering near the steps. I also saw legs prone.

My heart pounded.

I reached the landing, looked down, saw Marvella who whirled at me, pointed a gun in my direction.

"It's me," I said, putting my hands up anyway.

"Oh, thank God," she said, her tone watery. She leaned against the railing. I doubted she would do that if she were feeling threatened, but I couldn't entirely predict.

Behind her, two of the gang members I'd seen the morning before. They were sprawled on the floor near the elevator. The elevator door kept trying to close, but it couldn't. The third gang member was lying across the entrance, as dead as the other two.

They had gotten caught in that killing box that had had me worried. Only they hadn't gotten off any shots at all. Only Loring seemed to make it past, and he hadn't gone after the women. He had run up the stairs to us.

"I thought maybe he killed you," Marvella said.

"I'm hard to kill," I said.

There seemed to be no one else on the floor. The women who had guarded the doors were gone. There were footprints in blood, pointing down the stairs.

"Ohjesusohjesusohjesus." The woman from upstairs, peering over the railing at the bodies.

"Keep going," Sinkovich said.

"I can't," she said, and her feet twisted.

"Can you get her downstairs, Marvella?" Sinkovich asked. He used a different tone with her. Respectful, but commanding.

"I think so," she said.

"Where's everyone else?" I asked as Marvella made her way to the woman.

"They were willing to go after they heard the shots," Marvella said. "We had to carry most of them, but we did it. Or rather, the 'ladies' did."

She looked at Sinkovich, and to his credit, he grinned. He knew she needed that, even though it wasn't funny.

"Good job," he said.

"No one else waited?" I asked.

"I was waiting to see who came down," Marvella said. "I was gonna duck into a room if it was Turner. If he was alone, I'da shot him. And then I would've burned this place down."

"With us in it?" Sinkovich asked.

"I'd've started upstairs," she aid. "If you were still alive, I'd've gotten you out."

I believed her. She would have gotten help and the women would have figured out a way to get us out of here.

"Who shot the Stones?" I asked.

"Paulette. Sam. The Stones came up the elevator, but that other one, he was on the stairs. I heard him run past as they were firing."

Sinkovich looked at me. "I didn't expect gangs."

"Me either," I said, and decided to leave it at that.

The woman's teeth were chattering. She was leaning on the railing and looking as if she might puke again.

"Can you get her out of here, Marvella?" I asked again.

"Yeah," she said.

She put her arm around the woman, and led her to the next staircase.

"What's your name, honey?" she asked in a soothing voice.

I didn't hear the answer.

"You need to get out too, Jack," I said.

"No fucking way," he said. "We're finishing this."

"It's—"

"Oh, don't give me the legal crap. We're past it." He extended his hand. "I need matches."

I gave him half a box of matchbooks.

He flipped one matchbook open with his thumb. "Okay, Grimshaw," he said. "Let's finish this thing."

43

It took longer than I expected. The two of us worked out a system. One would check the room, looking under the bed, behind the shower curtain, in the closet, and then the other would start the curtains on fire, light the matchbook, and toss it on the bed.

We started on the seventh floor, in the rooms we hadn't investigated before we went into the penthouse. Those rooms looked like they hadn't been touched in years.

We avoided the penthouse entirely without even discussing it. I think we both believed that it would vanish with the hotel. Or maybe that the story the penthouse suite told would give a different impression of the events of the morning.

Either way, we didn't start a fire there. Instead, we worked our way down, floor by floor.

We worked fast, except in the first few rooms we went into on the sixth floor. Those were the rooms where the girls had been held. We both stopped at the filth, the stench, the conditions. Sinkovich kicked a long chain that I recognized from history books about my own people. And I shivered, regretting that I had simply shot the son of a bitch upstairs. I should have castrated him first.

We wanted to trust that the women had gone through every room, that the place was clear. But neither Sinkovich nor I were built for trust. We moved faster the lower we went, because the smell of smoke trailed us. We knew if we weren't careful, we could become victims of the fire we set.

When we reached the second floor, Sinkovich saw flames on the far wall. He hit me on the shoulder.

"We gotta get out," he said.

"No more burning," I said, "but we have to check the rooms."

He nodded and went left while I went right. We ran through the remaining rooms, yelling for people to get out, get out, but no one answered. The hotel was empty except for the two of us.

When we reached the main floor, we saw the desk clerk. He was still tied up, but he'd been shot multiple times. I figured Loring killed him, but I didn't know. The level of overkill suggested something personal, something I didn't want to completely understand.

Sinkovich and I both ran through the restaurant, which looked no different than it had when we first looked at it. The kitchen was empty, but the griddle smoked.

Sinkovich gestured at a vat of cooking oil, but I shook my head. Let the fire work its way down.

We needed to get out.

We went out the kitchen door and stepped into thin morning sunlight. The operation had taken a lot longer than we planned. I took a deep breath, then turned around.

The entire upper story of the hotel was engulfed in flames. The whole place had been a tinderbox just waiting to ignite.

"I hope we got everyone," Sinkovich said.

"Me, too," I said.

Then without consulting each other, we hurried to the corner. No cars went by. The ice was slick beneath our feet.

The coffee van was gone, just like it was supposed to be, on its way to a hospital where Marvella had already set up some of the staff to handle the incoming patients.

Sinkovich put a hand on my shoulder. "Damn women. Didn't expect it of them," he said.

I hadn't either.

We walked across the street to the school parking lot. My van was the only remaining vehicle. Marvella must have gotten the woman out. I hoped she figured out a place to take her.

"We gotta dump these clothes," Sinkovich said. "They probably smell like smoke."

I nodded. I swung the van out of the lot, and headed back to my place.

"The kid's gonna ask about the smell, ain't he?" Sinkovich asked.

"He's with Laura," I said.

"Good," Sinkovich said. "Then he ain't gonna see me having a beer at eight in the goddamn morning."

As if that was the thing to worry about. We had caused the death of seven people, and burned down a hotel, and Sinkovich was worried about drinking a beer before noon?

I grinned at him. He shrugged. He looked awful. His face was smeared with soot. He had blood along one sleeve.

"You still got matches in your pocket?" I asked.

"Shit," he said, and rolled down his window. Freezing air blasted us. It felt good, especially against my smoke-encrusted lungs.

He tossed matches out the window like breadcrumbs.

"You could've asked me if anyone was behind us," I said.

"I looked before I dumped. Whadda ya think, I'm dumb? Now, gimme yours."

I freed one hand from the wheel and emptied the matchbooks out of my pockets. This time, I saw him glance behind us, and then he dumped them. It looked like a matchbook truck had lost control and spilled its load all over the street behind us.

"Isn't that a driving hazard?" I asked.

"Shit, the ice in this parta town is a driving hazard," he said. "That's just free matches for the smokers of the world."

I looked at him.

He shrugged and opened his hands like a man expecting to get in trouble. "What? It is."

"Thank you," I said. "You were right. I couldn't have done this without you."

He caught my tone. It was serious. "Them women were something else too. They're gonna be messed up when they realize what went down."

"I don't know," I said. "They were a lot tougher than both you and I expected."

"I ain't calling them ladies no more," he said. "Not that I know what to call them. Because really, they're broads, in the best sense of the word."

I smiled for a second time. "You're not going to tell them that either, are you?"

"Hell, I ain't talking to women again until someone approves my vocabulary. Seems from the time I met my wife to now, everything in dealing with the female sex has changed."

I nodded. I drove us to my apartment. I would bag our clothes and toss them out. Sinkovich was smaller than me, but he could wear my clothes home.

Maybe by the time we were done, Marvella would come back. Maybe by then, she would have news on the girls.

We didn't dare show up at any of the hospitals.

We had to pretend this hadn't happened at all.

I could do that. And I now believed that Sinkovich could.

When we reached the apartment, I would join him in his early morning beer. We deserved it.

We got rid of the damn hotel. We got rid of Turner. We had cleaned up the neighborhood, just a bit.

And we had come out of it alive.

That was more than I expected.

It was a small victory, but it was a victory all the same.

44

One week later, I stood in the back room of a restaurant in Hyde Park. The room was filled with birthday balloons. A cake half the size of a wedding cake stood on a pedestal in the middle of a long serving table. Already-cut pieces of a marble sheet cake sat on paper plates. Round tables covered in paper cloths filled the room, and in the center of each, a small centerpiece made out of Matchbox cars surrounded pitchers filled with Kool-Aid.

Laura had rented the place and planned this whole thing the moment she realized that I had no idea how to do it, and Althea was too overwhelmed with Lacey to give a party any thought. Laura, of course, had given it too much thought, but the kids didn't seem to know that.

Jimmy and his friends sat on the floor on the far side of the room, playing some kind of game that I didn't understand. Laura and Althea were running it. It involved a lot of shouting and laughing and prizes. Althea had already warned me that when this party was over, I would receive a sugared-up kid who was so jittery he wouldn't know what to do with himself, and my job would be to take him home and calm him down.

I stood near the door, with Franklin, watching. Lacey had walked around the room twice, inspecting the doors and windows. She had peered at the cake several times as well, and actually looked interested in it. She didn't look at the presents, piled obscenely in the corner.

She knew that the hotel had burned down. I had a hunch she suspected who had done it. She claimed it made her feel better, but I doubted it. She claimed a lot of things, and did nothing. She had spent the week at home, recuperating. On Monday, she would start at the Laboratory School attached to the University of Chicago.

Laura had pulled some strings to get Lacey in during the already-started winter term but, she insisted, Lacey's grades had done the rest. Now Laura was talking about setting up a scholarship program for deserving South Side students. She had also agreed to fund the other Grimshaw children into the private school of their parents' choice, but the problem was that no school was taking students at this time of year.

Jonathan had taken the Catholic School exam without telling anyone he planned to do it. He had, in fact, left for it about the time Sinkovich and I were driving to my apartment. Jonathan's score was high, but the Catholics only wanted him to go to the school in the Black Belt, and that school had a waiting list as long as my arm.

We would work on a campaign for all of the children in our little family for the fall term. I felt better about sending them to the school at the moment.

The neighborhood still reeked of smoke. The Starlite Hotel remained as a burned-out shell. Part of the hotel's roof had fallen on the restaurant and burned it down as well.

The police called the burning of the hotel arson, but they blamed the Stones. The body of the desk clerk had been found in the rubble still intact, with all of the bullet wounds to his body. The other bodies were as yet unidentified, but a police spokesperson claimed that at least one of them had to be Turner.

No one found or interviewed the woman Marvella had taken out of the hotel. Marvella had taken her to a different hospital from the girls we had rescued. The story Marvella had given hospital staff was that she found the woman wandering a few blocks from the school in her night-clothes, clearly high on something.

She never got arrested and no one seemed to know she existed. Marvella promised me that she would get help, just like the girls would.

Eight girls got rescued from that hellhole. Three had intact families. The other five would get help from Marvella's group or Helping Hands. And, Marvella told me, my folder was in the custody of the women. I had accidentally left it at the Y the day we planned the operation. Some of the women took it, and would try to find the girls who had disappeared.

I offered to help. She turned me down.

"I wasn't kidding when I told you they don't like men," she said. "Better to let them do it."

For once, I agreed. I had to get back to paying work. But more than that, I finally felt comfortable with giving away some of my workload. Those women taught me something. They taught me that help sometimes came from the most unexpected places, and I needed to be open to that.

I looked across the room at Jimmy, who had started all of this. He seemed no worse for the wear. If he knew how much danger I had been in, he didn't show it.

In fact, he'd had more trouble with official birthday celebrations for Martin. Every school in Bronzeville had had some kind of remembrance. Several let any kid who wanted to go to the special church services held that Thursday morning.

Jimmy had asked me if he could stay home. I let him. Thursday was also his birthday, an irony I'd noted the year before, but one I had ignored. This time, I decided he deserved something special. I let him sleep in, and then we went to the Field Museum, which was probably a better learning experience than anything he would have gotten that day in school.

Gradually, the on-edge feeling I'd had eased. I did ask Sinkovich to follow up on the girls, just to make sure no one reported any of them as prostitutes or as victims of a possible fire. No one did. The police seemed clueless about what happened at the Starlite, and I hoped it would stay that way.

More laughter erupted from the far side of the room. Lacey looked over, longing on her face. I walked toward her, making sure she could see me so she wouldn't think I snuck up on her.

"Why don't you join them?" I asked.

She shook her head. "That's for kids."

"Laughing's for everyone," I said.

"Then you join them," she snapped.

"I will if you will," I said.

She gave me a sideways look. "You're just taking care of me."

"Of course I am," I said. "But I'm also taking care of me. Everyone's going to stop laughing if I go over there by myself and join that circle. I need you as cover."

She looked at them, and then up at me, as if she were assessing me. Then she took my hand, and led me over to the group.

We sat down together. The kids, mostly little boys, looked at us like we didn't belong. But after a moment, we'd been clued as to the rules of the game, and Lacey was letting out the occasional reluctant chuckle.

Laura smiled at me. She maneuvered the game so that I would not win, which was just fine with me. I decided I would go home with my son, just as sugar-high and just as relaxed.

I'd never been to a real birthday party, either.

I wasn't all that good at normal life. I used to think I wouldn't like it. But as the damaged teenage girl next to me smiled and touched my arm, I realized that I liked a lot of it.

I especially liked how much other people enjoyed it.

And I would do everything in my power to make sure that they could continue to enjoy it, every single day.

Acknowledgements

As always, these books come together due to a variety of people, many of whom gave me research and technical help when I couldn't find an answer on my own. (All mistakes here are mine, though, not theirs.) I want to thank my husband, Dean Wesley Smith, for answering questions, brainstorming, and challenging me when I thought something sounded cool. Lee Allred for finding solutions that fit my already-established specifications. The Driftwood Library staff in Lincoln City, Oregon, who helped with the research. The Facebook friends who answered all of the really obscure questions I couldn't find the answers to on the Internet. (It's so nice not to have to guess!), and most of all, thanks to the fans who have kept Smokey alive in their hearts while he and I searched for a new publishing home.

About the Author

Kris Nelscott is an open pen name used by *USA Today* bestselling author Kristine Kathryn Rusch.

The first Smokey Dalton novel, *A Dangerous Road*, won the Herodotus Award for Best Historical Mystery and was short-listed for the Edgar Award for Best Novel; the second, *Smoke-Filled Rooms,* was a PNBA Book Award finalist; and the third, *Thin Walls*, was one of the *Chicago Tribune's* best mysteries of the year. *Kirkus* chose *Days of Rage* as one of the top ten mysteries of the year and it was also nominated for a Shamus award for The Best Private Eye Hardcover Novel of the Year.

Entertainment Weekly says her equals are Walter Mosley and Raymond Chandler. *Booklist* calls the Smokey Dalton books "a high-class crime series" and *Salon* says "Kris Nelscott can lay claim to the strongest series of detective novels now being written by an American author."

For more information about Kris Nelscott, or author Kristine Kathryn Rusch's other works, please go to KristineKathrynRusch.com.

The

Smokey Dalton

Series

NOVELS:

A Dangerous Road
Smoke-Filled Rooms
Thin Walls
Stone Cribs
War at Home
Days of Rage
Street Justice

SHORT STORIES:

Family Affair
Guarding Lacey

CPSIA information can be obtained
at www.ICGtesting.com
Printed in the USA
LVOW12s1631071216

516244LV00003B/770/P